The DEAD LETTER

The DEAD LETTER

by Finley Martin

The Acorn Press
Charlottetown
2015

The Dead Letter © 2015 by Finley Martin

P.O. Box 22024
Charlottetown, Prince Edward Island
C1A 9J2
acornpresscanada.com

Printed and Bound in Canada
Substantive edit by Jane Ledwell
Copy edit by Laurie Brinklow
Design by Matt Reid

Library and Archives Canada Cataloguing in Publication

Martin, Finley, author
    The dead letter / Finley Martin.

Issued in print and electronic formats.
ISBN 978-1-927502-35-8 (pbk.).--ISBN 978-1-927502-36-5 (epub)

    I. Title.

PS8626.A76954D43 2015   C813'.6   C2015-900887-5
                                             C2015-900888-3

Canada Canada Council
for the Arts

Conseil des Arts
du Canada

The publisher acknowledges the support of the Government of Canada through the Canada Book Fund of the Department of Canadian Heritage, the Canada Council for the Arts Block Grant Program and the support of the Province of Prince Edward Island.

To my mother, Anna R. (Hamzik)
Martin, for the self-sacrifice, perseverance,
and guidance she modeled in her life as a
working widow with children.

1.

"All right, I'm having an affair. So what? You don't own me."

Simone Villier hooked her thumbs under her waistband and rotated her hips slowly back and forth as she adjusted her skirt. She evoked an uncommon sensuality, and she was aware of its effects—carnal glances from men, and the confused mix of disapproval and guilty envy from women.

Constable Jamie MacFarlane's fingers gripped the web belt that held his service pistol, handcuffs, night light, and radio, and listened in disbelief. Like many other men around Charlottetown, Jamie MacFarlane had been drawn to her, but his advances had had greater success, and they had engaged in a fiery and tumultuous romance for eight months.

Now it was over. And, tonight, her alluring moves, which once had thrilled him, felt hollow, taunting, and cruel.

"Who is it?" he asked.

"I'm not going to tell you who it is. It's none of your business."

Simone looked away. His jealousy pleased her. Then, to fill the silence, she straightened a few items on her office desk and hoped that Jamie would stomp off into the night and be done with it, but he didn't. He remained. He said nothing. The silence was uncomfortable. She ignored him and stared out the second-floor window of her office into the darkness of the harbour and focused on the beads of light that framed the skyline of the city of Charlottetown.

Then Jamie's hand slammed the top of the desk, and his voice snapped like a bullet.

"I want to know! Who is it?"

"Screw you!"

He grabbed her shoulders and shook her. Her eyes widened in surprise, then narrowed with anger, and she pulled away and circled behind her desk. Jamie didn't follow.

"Then why! Tell me that," he demanded.

"What difference does it make?" she asked, her tone quieter now. Tired, but not conciliatory. "We're over. Finished. It was a laugh for a while. A few great times even. Now it's done."

"It's not over…not 'til I say it is."

"You sound like a spoiled kid. Grow up." Simone grabbed her jacket and strode toward the door, but Jamie blocked her way.

"You're not leaving until I get an answer. Why?"

"You want to know why? Okay. Here the story. You were cute, but not cute enough. Is that reason enough? You were charming, but it wore so thin I could see right through you. Is that enough? No? How 'bout you work all the time! You're not fun anymore…and haven't been for a long time. Is that enough? Plenty enough for me, anyway."

"You're just a fucking tramp!"

"And what are you? You think that cop uniform makes you some big shot? You're not. You're nobody! A big mouth with pocket change."

"Slut!"

"Loser! Oh…and here's another reason! I'm pregnant…and before that idea starts rollin' around your empty head, it's not yours."

The muscles in MacFarlane's jaw flexed.

"How long?"

"Three months or so."

"You've been bangin' him…and me…for the last three months. Who is he?"

Simone laughed.

"Oh, it's been a lot longer than that. And you don't need to know. It's none of your business."

"Who is he?" he shouted. "Do I know him?" He grabbed Simone and shook her hard until her head snapped back and forth like a broken toy and her face blanched. "Who is he? Who is he?"

She struggled in his grip like a frightened dog, squirmed and writhed. Her strength and tenacity surprised him. His hands slipped as the point of her shoe caught him sharply on the shin. Simone broke away. Her right hand swiped painfully across his eye. As she took a step back, his one hand rose to his eye, and his other dropped onto the top of the desk. It fell on a heavy metal three-hole punch. With an emerging hatred, he swung the club-like machine above his head and struck, down and diagonally, across her skull. The bone sounded with a sharp crack, and Simone fell to the floor.

She remained motionless but for her eyes, which were closing slowly, like those of a cat drifting into sleep.

MacFarlane felt for a pulse. There was none. He walked to the door and flicked off the light. He started to leave, but the sudden darkness swept over him like a wave. It smothered his panic and dampened his anger. It also woke him to the realization that Simone was dead, that he had killed her, and that the murder weapon was still frozen in his hand.

He lingered a few more minutes in the dark until his heart slowed and his thinking cleared, and the only sound that filled his ears was the clack clack clack of a cheap wall clock beating away at the minutes.

By the time he flicked the light switch back on, he knew what he had to do. He wiped his fingerprints from the doorknobs and switches and desk. He cleaned his prints from the three-hole punch and dropped it near her body. Simone's purse lay on the desk. He dumped the contents and took her wallet and cell phone. He yanked a gold necklace from her neck and slipped a sapphire ring from her finger. He stuffed all of it into a pocket of his uniform, crept into the stillness of the hallway, and descended the fire stairs to a side street exit.

Someone will have to pay for Simone's killing, he thought.

2.

The office was stuffy, the radiator pumped heat relentlessly, and the thermostat was tamper-proof. So Carolyn Jollimore sometimes left the door open when she worked evenings. That evening she couldn't help but hear a man and woman arguing on the floor below her. Sounds carried far in a nearly empty building late at night, but she could only make out a few words. *Slut* was one of the kinder epithets that reached her ears. That word offended her, but the cadence of the quarrel disturbed her even more. It sounded hateful—like two people stabbing each other with words—and, at the same time, it sounded almost operatic—a powerful baritone punctuating a warbling protest. All of it was distasteful, and she wished she could shut her ears to the whole vulgar affair.

Quarrels belong on the stage or in a film, thought Carolyn, *not in one's own living-room...or workplace.* Carolyn wanted to put the matter out of her ears, but the drama one floor below called to mind another struggle, one that centred on her mother, now in the grip of dementia.

Carolyn's mother had suffered with the illness for the last three years. Its onset had been almost imperceptible at first. Some words just slipped away: the name of a cousin...*but I scarcely knew the child*; the year she married... *Ah! But it was so long ago*; or where she had left a shopping list...*you must have thrown it in the trash, dear.* In the beginning, Carolyn and her sister Edna accepted such lapses as the muddlings of a too-busy mind. A diagnosis followed. A home care worker was called to join the household, first one and then another... *Why is that woman in my house? Who is she? I don't know her. Make her go away.* Carolyn and Edna divided the rest of the day and night duty between themselves... *Where's Edna? Why does she hate me?* Then darker, more frightening, more confusing days... *Where is my... you know... Where is my...thing? You know, Carolyn, you know...where is it?... Help me, Carolyn... Why won't you help me?*

Carolyn wished she could help her, but she couldn't. Carolyn wished she could escape, but she couldn't do that either. Most times, a stolen hour of solitude on an empty beach replenished Carolyn's spirit. Sometimes, it couldn't—like early this year when she wove a path between ice floes grounded along a March shoreline and, day after day, watched the progress of a cold sun etch the frozen surfaces and carve deep holes into places where memories once lived.

Carolyn gathered some papers together and placed them in a file. It was midnight. Her shift was over, and she made her way down the stairs. The lovers' quarrel had ended several hours before, but, as she passed that second-floor office, she noticed a light still burning behind the frosted glass door, the door ajar, and no hint of life within. Carolyn frowned disapprovingly. *Such shoddy work habits in young people these days*, she thought, and continued down the stairs and into the light of a waning moon.

3.

Sunday, 7 October 2001

Chief of Police Bruce Quigley and Sergeant Ryan Schaeffer of the Stratford Police Department stood in the doorway of Tidewater's second-floor office and stared at the corpse of Simone Villier, still undisturbed in the position it had fallen two nights before. A weekend janitor had found the body and called police. There had been no need for paramedics. The blood she had spilled had hardened, and the grimness of rigor mortis had taken hold and then passed.

Schaeffer received the call. Quigley met him at the scene.

"It's Jamie's girl," he said. "Simone."

"I can see that," said Quigley.

"How do you want to do this?"

"Process the scene. Work the neighbourhood. See what shakes out."

"The department's first murder," Schaeffer mused.

"Yeah, and on a Thanksgiving weekend when any witnesses would have gone off to Grandma's for roast turkey and pumpkin pie."

"Who do you want to process the crime scene? We could get the unit from Charlottetown police."

"No...call the RCMP. We'll look like the poor cousins if we go to City for help. If we tap the Mounties, it'll look like City isn't up to the job. Politics. You know. But we'll handle the investigation ourselves. We close it...we get the blue ribbon."

"What about him?" No one else was in the room, but Quigley knew who Schaeffer meant.

"Check him out...informal interviews...on the quiet, nothing public for now."

"What are you thinking?"

"I'm thinking that some things never change. Odds are it's either a boyfriend or a husband, and it's either money or hate. So follow the bread crumbs. Prove me wrong. Please. I'd hate like hell to think that one of our own would kill somebody."

"It'd be hard on the department."

"No, it'd be the end of the department."

Quigley felt the shadows of the vultures circling overhead. Four years before, a cadre of town councillors had unsuccessfully opposed a plan to give Stratford its own police department. *Start-up costs would be perilously high*, they said. *The town couldn't afford to pay police salaries*, they said, and they had been right. The following year property tax rates rose to meet the shortfall.

It was just recently, however, that scars of that struggle had begun to heal. A scandal now, though, would energize the old naysayers. They would muster public support, and memory of the fledgling Stratford police force would slip away, leaving only a quaint footnote in town history.

Sergeant Schaeffer didn't call ahead. He drove north of town along the Hillsborough River and into some older, less-structured subdivisions. MacFarlane's place was on the river side of the road. It had been built as a cottage twenty years before, but a new addition and some renovations had converted it into a small, comfortable, attractive house.

Schaeffer knocked and rang the bell. He waited and then knocked again, louder. MacFarlane opened the door and motioned him in.

MacFarlane was six-foot-four. A solid, muscular build made him look even taller. He wore loose grey sweatpants and a faded green T-shirt. He hadn't shaved. Schaeffer noticed his puffy eyes and suspected that he hadn't slept either. He caught a sour smell of liquor on his Sunday-afternoon breath.

"Sorry for your loss, Jamie."

"Thank you... I take it you have some questions."

"Sorry for that too, but...," said Schaeffer.

"I know... I've been expecting you...or somebody."

Schaeffer took out his notebook, settled into an armchair across from MacFarlane, and asked him to account for his activities on Friday night.

"You know I was on duty," said MacFarlane as if to remind him. Schaeffer nodded.

And MacFarlane went on to describe his shift. Two officers had been on duty overnight. Docherty had manned the office, while MacFarlane patrolled in an unmarked car. At eight o'clock he had written a report on a fender-bender in front of the liquor store. After that he had responded to a noise complaint in an apartment on Pondside Court. Then he cruised the community park for underage drinkers. After Docherty had received complaints of two cars being broken into, MacFarlane spotted three juveniles scurrying through backyards. He lost them, but they resurfaced an hour later near the fire hall. He questioned them—the Curry brothers and a Lowell Matheson—but there was no legal reason to detain them and, after that, he returned to the station. The rest of the evening was quiet, he said.

"Were you at her office that evening?"

"No."

"Did you talk to her...by phone...text...?"

"No...not Friday. I slept most of Saturday. Saturday night I called her cell, but it was turned off. When I couldn't get hold of her this morning, I called her mother. She hadn't heard from her either. We both worried...but there wasn't much we could do. Then Bernadette, her mother, phoned just after noon. She told me Simone was dead. She was angry. She thought I knew, but I didn't...not until she told me."

"Does she have enemies? Anybody bothering her? Strange behaviour?"

"No, nothing."

"Did you kill Simone?"

The bluntness of the question stunned MacFarlane. His lips parted, but no words spilled out. He swallowed the dryness in his mouth. Then he said, "No... I could never do anything like that," and he turned his head away and stared at an empty wall.

Schaeffer was about to ask MacFarlane how he and Simone were getting along the last week or so, but he never got the chance. Jamie, still staring at the empty wall, said, "We were expecting a child...did you know that?...a child."

Jamie's voice had a detached quality to it.

Schaeffer sensed that he had lost him. He asked nothing more, and nothing more was offered. So Schaeffer saw himself out and closed the door behind him. MacFarlane continued to stare at the blank wall until long after the sound of Schaeffer's car faded away. Then he reached into his pocket, drew out Simone's cell phone, and scrolled through the chronicle of her secret love affair—her saved text messages—just as he had done several times already.

4.

Chief Quigley stared through the glass wall of his office toward his officers working the case in the station's meeting room. He wasn't watching them. He didn't see them. Instead, his eyes fixed on the hazy space beyond them where questions hovered without answers and leads dead-ended without resolution and the paths left for his men to investigate dwindled.

Schaeffer knocked and entered. Chief Quigley welcomed the interruption from his preoccupation. "What?" he asked, as if he had been rudely taken from something important.

"The Crime Scene Unit sent their report."

"...and..."

"Looks like a robbery gone bad. No usable prints on the murder weapon but hers. It was either wiped or the killer wore gloves. Other prints on the door, door frame, and light switch matched others who had business in the office. Some jewellery had been taken. A ring... and a necklace that was ripped off. It left a mark on her throat. Wallet, cell phone gone."

"I'm surprised our search didn't turn up the wallet and cell phone. Most of the local village idiots would figure to dump any link to the crime."

"Probably tossed 'em in the river."

"What about the jewellery?"

"Mother described the ring. She'd bought it for her graduation. MacFarlane bought her the necklace, she said."

"Put out a description to the pawnshops, jewellers, and second-hand stores...anyone who buys scrap gold or silver. Have somebody check online trading sites, local flea markets et cetera." Quigley turned back toward his blank wall again.

"Something else," said Schaeffer.

"What?"

"MacFarlane wants to work."

"No." Quigley slowly leaned back in the chair and folded his hands across his stomach. Then he popped forward again. "I thought you said he was a mess."

"He was when I interviewed him, but he showed up for his shift this morning. He was sober, looked squared away, positive attitude. I sent him home anyway. He seemed anxious to help. And we could use some help."

"He's too close to the case. Anything from the Coroner?"

"Just a preliminary report. Cause of death: blunt force trauma to left section of frontal bone."

"What else have the boys come up with? Anything?"

"Nothing came out of our interviews of co-workers, at least those that could be reached over the holiday. We canvassed a two-block radius of the crime, door-to-door, and turned up a short list of people in the area that evening. Some local kids...a few itinerants camping under the Hillsborough Bridge. We still have to track them down. We're also looking at cab companies, pharmacies, and pizza joints— any business that might have made deliveries in Stratford."

"Any complaints?"

"The boys were happy to get overtime. They'll work until you send them home. On the other hand, I stopped over at Town Hall earlier. I brought Jill a coffee, and she told me that a few jokers on the Council are grumbling about where the money for all our overtime is going to come from. Delaney and Fitzpatrick are the most vocal..."

"They want to turn the investigation over to the Mounties."

"Peale, Jameson, and Carmody are backing us so far. The rest are not committing."

"They don't have the balls to commit to anything. They couldn't commit to a free lap dance."

Schaeffer, nodded, laughed, and headed for the door. He stopped there and turned around.

"Something else while I remember it. Constable MacKay. He's leaving. He's a reservist, and he's been called up for a military police unit deploying to Afghanistan."

"When's he leaving?"

"He's due in Winnipeg in two weeks, but he wants off the end of this week to get his personal affairs in order."

"Shit!"

"That's about it, Chief." Sergeant Schaeffer stepped out the door of Quigley's office.

"Wait a minute!" Schaeffer stopped short, and Quigley fell into a long, thoughtful pause. Then he said, "Let's do this. Bring MacFarlane in tomorrow. Put him on the phone, housekeeping stuff, filing, whatever, and see how he performs. If he's a hundred per cent okay, then he can do some leg work, but under no circumstances does he get access to the case file, evidence, or information on where we're going with the case. If he wants to contribute, he can do so on the sidelines next to the water boy. Understood?"

"Gotcha."

Island residents old enough to remember the Korean War would have called it a "glorious day." The sky was a clear, deep, lively blue. Maple trees, poplar, apple, and willow quivered in a light wind, and their leaves glowed like tongues of flame in a brush fire. Roofs, cornices, chimneys, and power lines etched a startling profile against the sky, and each breath of air energized the body like water from a mountain spring. It was a day to make people feel alive and vigorous, even Jamie MacFarlane.

MacFarlane hadn't returned home after Schaeffer told him to take a couple more days off. Instead he drove around the all-too-familiar streets of Stratford with no particular purpose in mind and with no twinges of conscience. In fact, it was a perfect day to forget things and to escape, and it was not until his aimless driving took him past the building where he killed Simone that the thought of her flooded back like a shameful act in a squalid dream.

He wished that he hadn't killed her, but she had brought it on herself, he concluded. She had betrayed him. She had berated him. She had laughed at him. She had stripped him of his pride. Then she had enraged him. She should have known better. She should have known that no man would put up with such abuse. He hit her, yes. Too hard, certainly. An error in judgment, of course. Perhaps even a weakness in character.

In spite of all that, he thought it foolish to dwell on past mistakes. That would change nothing and, although he was confident that things would work themselves out, the incident with Simone did make his life more complicated than he would have liked. There were loose ends, things that needed tending, wrongs that wanted righting.

Toward those goals, MacFarlane drove across the Hillsborough Bridge into Charlottetown. He stopped at a public phone booth in a shopping plaza and dialled a number.

"This is Constable Jamie MacFarlane. I have some information that involves my former girlfriend, the affair you had with her, and evidence that suggests that you may have killed her."

There was a long period of dead air on the other end of the phone line.

"Are you still there?" asked MacFarlane.

"I... I'm afraid I don't know what you're talking about."

"That's unfortunate. Since I hadn't had the chance to process the evidence yet, I thought we could discuss it privately...unofficially... seeing as how it might affect your marriage and other areas of your life...but if you're not interested, then I'm sorry to have bothered you..."

"Wait! Don't hang up. I'll meet with you...but...someplace public."

"Olde Dublin Pub. Charlottetown. Tonight at seven. The bar is quiet then. I won't be in uniform. I'm not looking to embarrass...or hurt anyone. I hope we can work something out."

5.

Friday, 12 October 2001

Davidia Christian emerged from the photocopy room where her interview had taken place. Her face was flushed, and she chirped excitedly.

"He's so cute," she said, grabbing Carolyn Jollimore's wrist. Then Davidia leaned in close to her ear, squeezed her wrist tightly, and whispered loudly, "and he's not married either."

Davidia giggled and gave Carolyn a playful shove toward the door. "You're next...and last," she added.

It was four o'clock. Carolyn had just arrived for her shift as fellow workers were gearing up to end their workday. She had not been back to the office since Thanksgiving. Over the holiday, her mother had taken a turn for the worse, and the home-care worker could no longer cope and had quit. Carolyn had filled in until she and Edna had found a replacement. The new caregiver was older and more experienced, and, to their immense relief, she possessed a storehouse of patience.

Carolyn stepped into the little room and took the only vacant chair. It was across from the investigating officer, Constable Sam Best. A tiny plastic table, provided by the office manager, separated them.

Davidia was right, thought Carolyn. *He is handsome.* Best glanced up from his notebook, looked directly into her eyes, and smiled. Carolyn felt an involuntary blush redden her cheeks. She smiled back at him, certain that her attempt at smiling produced only a foolish, self-conscious, ineffectual smirk.

"I'm Constable Best," he said, "and I just have a few questions, if you don't mind."

He smiled again.

Carolyn felt another hot flush. She felt suddenly girlish. Her face reddened even more, and a surge of mortification swept it along.

The knock on the door to the makeshift interview room was a welcome distraction. The door opened. Constable Jamie MacFarlane poked his head through.

"Sergeant wants you back at the station when you're through here, Sam."

"But it's the end of my shift. Got plans."

"A meeting. He wants everyone there."

Best nodded.

Carolyn felt hairs bristle on the back of her neck and blood drain the blush from her cheeks.

Carolyn's terror grew as her head slowly turned toward the door behind her. It was the same voice Carolyn had heard one floor below her on the night of the murder. There was no doubt in her mind. It was a deep voice. It was rich and clear. Robust. It had strength and control. It was a voice she could never mistake. It was a voice she wished she had never heard.

MacFarlane acknowledged Best's response, smiled apologetically toward Carolyn, and closed the door behind him.

"Miss Jollimore..." said Constable Best. The now-closed door had gripped Carolyn's attention. Her eyes were transfixed.

"Miss Jollimore..." he said again. Carolyn slowly turned toward him. "Do you mind if I ask you some questions?"

"I...uh...yes... I mean no."

He smiled again. This time it was more forced. He had tired of feigning interest. The same questions, the same answers from each of the twenty-two women who worked in that office. It had been tedious and a waste of time. Now a staff meeting to look forward to. Best drew a deep breath, refocused, and began again.

"No need to be nervous. Your full name?"

Terror welled up, and once again she forced it down.

"Carolyn Jollimore." For a moment it sounded like the name of some person she scarcely knew.

"Did you know Simone Villier?"

"No."

"Were you working on Friday, October 5?"

"Yes."

"What time did you leave the building?"

Carolyn stumbled over a handful of inaudible words. Best looked up quizzically.

"Six o'clock," she said.

"What time did you begin work?"

"Four."

"Four?"

"Yes, I work different hours from the rest."

"You only worked two hours?"

"Yes. I received a call from my sister. An urgent one. Our mother was ill. She has Alzheimer's. I had to go home. I've been out a week. I just returned to work today," she said. She had stressed "urgent one" and "had to go home." Now she regretted it. It made her sound like a child making desperate excuses, and she feared that he would see through her pretence and know that she was lying.

"Did you observe anyone in the building when you left?"

"No."

"To your knowledge would anyone else be working in the building then?"

"No."

"Did you notice anyone outside when you left the building? Anyone?"

"No. No one."

"Very good. That's all we need. Your help is appreciated. One more thing before I go. You said you left the building at what time? Seven?"

"No, six. Six o'clock." Her voice sounded stronger, more confident.

"Thanks for your cooperation, Miss Jollimore."

Carolyn got up, went out to her desk, and sat down. Davidia bounced over. She was excited.

"Isn't he gorgeous? I'd squeeze him to pieces if I had the chance... and Bert wasn't around to catch me."

"I'm feeling faint."

"That's just how I felt when I left...faint...and a touch giddy, too."

"I'm going home. I came back too soon."

"Oh dear."

The meeting at Stratford police station lasted half an hour, but even that was a mind-numbing duration for Sam Best, a young constable cultivating plans to bed the waitress at a local diner. It was the end of his shift. It was the beginning of the weekend. He was growing impatient. He was anxious to get out of there, but he tried not to show it. So he only half-listened to Sergeant Schaeffer drone on and on about progress in the Villier murder, evidence, day-end oral reports, new lines of questioning, and confidentiality. He thought Schaeffer's spiel would never end. He looked around the room. Everyone was there except MacFarlane, whom they'd tucked into a patrol car for evening shifts—Sam Best's former shift. At least that had worked to Best's advantage. It injected new vigour into his social life.

Constable Best's thoughts drifted to the blonde ringlets of the waitress. His fingers caressed the file folder of interviews he had conducted that afternoon. His imagination slid from the ringlets of hair toward the warm cleavage of her breasts.

"That's about it," said Sergeant Schaeffer. His voice was raised, declarative, and final. His voice interrupted Best's sensual reverie. Best shoved the folder toward a corner of his desk, grabbed his jacket, and hurried out the door.

It was long after midnight when Constable MacFarlane finished his shift and returned to the near-empty headquarters building. The stack of interviews had remained on the corner of Best's desk. MacFarlane thumbed through the folder until he reached Carolyn Jollimore's statement.

6.

Saturday, 13 October 2001

It was serendipitous.

John J. Dawson, also known as "J.J. Jumble" or "Johnny Jughead" or "Cracker Jack," was on a rampage again, this time at the local supermarket. He had filled his cart with flats of pea soup and cases of Pepsi, proceeded through the checkout line, and flustered a young cashier by scribbling an indecipherable message on a scrap of paper and offering it as some sort of IOU or cheque. Then he left.

A security guard caught up with him just outside the automatic glass doors of the store. Dawson had lost control of his top-heavy cart. It tipped over and spilled dozens of cans and glass bottles across both lanes of parking lot traffic. Car horns blared in frustration at the impasse, and Dawson answered by throwing soup cans at the impatient drivers and hitting their cars instead. The guard tried to restrain him, but Dawson struggled away and pelted the guard with other cans and a barrage of unintelligible but seemingly profane words. Police arrived. MacFarlane was the responding officer. Dawson struck MacFarlane with two cans, the first on the chest and a second on his lip, before he subdued Dawson and took him into custody.

MacFarlane frisked Dawson for weapons and, as he did so, he slipped Simone Villier's wallet into one of Dawson's coat pockets. He slipped the sapphire ring into another. Both had been cleaned of prints and had lain in MacFarlane's uniform jacket pocket, waiting for the right person and the right time.

MacFarlane drove to the station for booking, but Sergeant Schaeffer ordered Dawson taken to the Queen Elizabeth Hospital psych ward for examination. While there, hospital nursing staff found the wallet. Police were called. His clothing and personal items were bagged for a forensic team. The ring was discovered later, having slipped through a hole and fallen into a recess in the lining.

MacFarlane was pleased with his own judgment. In fact, it was intoxicating.

7.

Monday, 15 October–Friday, 19 October 2001

If Timothy Townshend hadn't jumped from his grandfather's barn loft and missed the hay bales he aimed for, he wouldn't have broken his leg and landed in the paediatric ward of the QEH. And, if Timothy hadn't been there in the hospital, then his father, Tommy Townshend, wouldn't have overheard the nurse's gossip about the "murderer" in Unit 9. But Timmy did jump. He did break a leg and go to hospital and, as a result, his father was there to catch the biggest scoop of his career as reporter for *The Guardian* newspaper.

Townshend broke the story the morning after Dawson's arrest, even before his arraignment on charges of first-degree murder. Townshend followed up the next day with a feature story documenting Dawson's history of bizarre behaviour, assaults, drug and alcohol addiction, and panhandling. He portrayed Dawson as an unpredictable and danger-ous criminal whose capture was a relief for every young woman on PEI. But Townshend hit the journalistic trifecta when, in a weekend story, he portrayed Constable Jamie MacFarlane as a tireless hero leading the investigation into his "fiancée's" murder. He shaped it as a story of two devoted lovers whose dreams were shattered by tragedy. In his rather fanciful version, "Cracker Jack" Dawson murdered the beautiful young Simone Villier in a manic rage. Her boyfriend, Jamie MacFarlane, heartbroken and with a dogged determination, tracked down and captured the madman. Townshend's feature story brought not only a kind of closure for a jittery public but added a note of poetic justice as well.

MacFarlane, on the other hand, wanted no part of the publicity and desired no recognition for any role in the capture or arrest. Chief Quigley thought otherwise, however. He encouraged Townshend's inclination to play up the role of his Stratford police force in seeking justice for an innocent victim, and he strong-armed MacFarlane into accepting—however willingly or however silently—whatever com-mendations or praise the press, or anyone else, wished to heap upon him. In spite of the Chief's efforts, though, MacFarlane did his best to duck the limelight and play down his role in the investigation, but Tommy Townshend interpreted MacFarlane's reluctance to accept accolades as natural proof of an admirable humility.

The vision of a police officer's diligence and modesty in the face of great praise registered deeply with many readers, and it vaulted Mac-Farlane even higher in the public's estimation. The human interest value of the story caught the attention of the wire services. The story was reprinted in *The Globe and Mail* and even earned a spot on CTV and CNN headline news.

MacFarlane slowly warmed to his new celebrity, but he didn't pursue it. He realized it was short-term, but it couldn't hurt his career, he thought, and it was a welcome distraction from any reconsideration of him as the killer. His life could go on now, just as he had envisioned it would, and maybe even a little better.

One thing still bothered him, though. Sam Best's last interviewee at White Cross. Something about her didn't feel right. The woman had been nervous. That was understandable. Even Best, none too sharp at the best of times, had noted that she seemed too nervous. It made him wonder if she were holding something back. If she knew anything, she would have to have been in the building or nearby, but she claimed she had an emergency and had gone home early.

All of that could be a lie, he thought. To find out, he could request her work schedule for that week. That would tell him. However, if he went in that direction, it could backfire and turn suspicion toward him. After all, a suspect had already been charged, and public opinion had already convicted Dawson. People might think it peculiar if he began to poke around.

Then MacFarlane smiled to himself. *There is another way to find out,* he thought. Constable MacFarlane grabbed his cap and called out to Sergeant Schaeffer as he passed his office.

"I'm heading over to Town Hall. Some personal business. Back in half an hour."

"Any more than an hour, and it'll be time lost," he warned. "Just so ya know."

"You're a tough guy, Schaeffer. Keep it up, and some day you might make sergeant."

"And you're a funny guy, MacFarlane. Keep that up, and you could replace that cop with the Village People."

Stratford Town Hall was a large structure that held not only municipal offices, but also a library, a sports centre, a rental space for public service groups, and administration offices for the local school board. Sixteen video surveillance cameras monitored the interior and exterior of the building. Security personnel watched the monitors only during special events. Otherwise, images were simply recorded automatically in digital memory and stored for thirty days.

The monitors were located in a basement communications room. The door was locked, but the maintenance supervisor opened the room for MacFarlane, who said he needed to look at old footage that may have recorded some vandalism. The maintenance engineer showed him how to access a particular time and date. Then he left MacFarlane on his own.

First, MacFarlane watched the live, real-time feed of camera seven. Camera seven panned back and forth across the large parking lot in front of the building. In doing so, it also captured part of the town beyond it—part of the supermarket, the bridge, and Hillsborough Bay. It also caught the back of the office building in which Simone had worked. Trees and houses blocked sight of the lower floors. Simone's office was not visible, but a view of the third floor, where Carolyn's company had offices, could be made out, though it was too distant to reveal details. MacFarlane pulled up a recent historical day recording of the same building, froze the pan, and enlarged that image until it disintegrated in grey pixels. That convinced him that no evidence of his presence at the time of the murder could exist.

Then MacFarlane changed the time and date settings to the time of the murder—10:00 p.m. on Friday, 5 October. By that time, darkness had obscured the entire building. Not even its outline was visible, but a small point of light lit a third-floor room and shone clearly against the night skyline. He continued to review the recording. The light wasn't turned off until midnight. Carolyn Jollimore had been working in her office at the very moment he was killing Simone, and she didn't leave until her shift had finished.

So far Carolyn had avoided calling the police. That in itself was a miracle, but why had she waited? Had she feared for her safety? Was it possible she didn't want to get involved? Had the arrest of Dawson made her doubt her own judgment? Or was she too stunned by the truth to act? Like a deer caught in a car's headlights.

Perhaps nothing would come of it, but that didn't matter. Jamie couldn't take that chance. Whatever the deterrent that kept her from informing police, it could vanish in an instant. In the final analysis, she was a loose end. She needed fixing. And she needed fixing soon. Very soon.

8.

Eleven Years Later
October 2012

"Soon."

Anne Brown pinched the phone between her ear and her shoulder and continued to shuffle papers into a case file while talking with her daughter, Jacqui. The clock on the wall of her office showed four-thirty.

"What does that mean?" asked Jacqui.

"What do you mean, *what does that mean?*" Anne's tone of voice didn't change, except for a hint of crispness to her diction and a more deliberate pace to her delivery. She knew that another exasperating conversation with her daughter was about to begin, but she had become almost immune to such conversations.

"Soon. What does 'soon' mean?"

"What kind of question is that? *Soon* is a basic concept. That's why they put it in a single syllable like *ball, tree*, or *hat*."

"...but are you coming right away or in x-number of minutes? Leaving immediately or stopping off somewhere first? You're really not being clear, Mom. Besides that, we've already waited an hour."

"Hold on now. You called me not more than fifteen minutes ago, and who's *we*?"

"Rada...and me. She stayed after school for...some extra help. She needs a ride, too."

"Who?"

"I'll explain later. We're still waiting, Mom, and this dialectic doesn't shorten the time."

In frustration, Anne made a growling noise over the phone.

Where does "dialectic" come from, she wondered, *and what kind of sixteen-year-old uses a word like that?*

"...and I love you too, Mom. Bye."

"Bye, Jacqui. See ya *soon*."

"Mom," she protested, but it was too late. Her mother had already hung up.

Anne Brown put the case file into the cabinet and closed the drawer with a brassy clank. She grabbed her jacket and headed out the door. Then she stopped and rushed back to the dictionary on her desk.

Dialectic—another of those twenty-five-cent words she had learned at university and then parked in a lonesome corner of memory after she returned to the real world—*the art or practice of examining opinions or ideas logically.*

It took ten minutes for Anne to drive from her downtown Victoria Row office to the west side suburb and Central High School where the girls were waiting.

"That was quick," said Jacqui. She got into the back seat with Rada.

"As *soon* as I could," said Anne. She looked into the rear-view mirror. The amusement in Jacqui's eyes matched the twinkle in her own, and she smiled.

Anne pulled away from the student pick-up lane and turned onto the main road. She looked back again through the rear-view mirror at the two girls laughing in the back seat. *Jacqui is almost grown up now*, she thought regretfully. Sixteen years old. Just starting high school. Jacqui was as tall as her mother, but that wasn't saying much, and she was filling out. She had a heavier bone structure. She was strong and athletic, less delicate, more like her father. A natural colour reddened her cheeks, her eyes were mischievous, and a youthful self-confidence shone from her as if innocence somehow would gird her against the ways of a deceitful world.

"Where to?" she asked.

"Langley Court," said Jacqui. "Mom, this is Radmila Kikovic. Everyone calls her Rada. She's my friend," she added with a giggle.

"Radmila. What a pretty name. Where are you from, Rada?"

"Croatia," she said. Her voice was soft and mellow. "My parents immigrated twelve years ago. First to Italy, later to Canada..."

Anne flinched. A ripple of silent uneasiness followed. A picture of her husband, a journalist, flashed into her mind. He had been killed in Croatia seventeen years before.

"...just after the war," the girl added.

"Her father's an engineer. They lived in Quebec and moved here last summer," said Jacqui.

Anne glanced into the rear-view mirror again. Both girls were attractive. Jacqui had boundless energy, green eyes, and light brown hair that brightened to copper when sunlight struck it. Rada had a quieter prettiness. Her skin was smooth and pearl-like. Her eyes were powerful, and her hair was long, black, and silky.

As the car pulled into Langley Court, Rada pulled a long black scarf from her coat pocket and wrapped her head carefully in the hijab. Then she thanked Anne, clutched her books, and waved goodbye. Rada's mother watched from a window.

9.

Anne's feet padded along the Victoria Park boardwalk following the curve of Hillsborough Bay. No other sound broke the stillness. No breeze rustled the trees. No bird chirped songs. No squirrel chattered peckishly. It was dawn. It was a colourless and vapid dawn, and on this particular morning dawn had turned cheap and unseemly. Even the air was cloying, and it clung to Anne's skin like a moist web. She shuddered.

Ordinarily, Anne's two-mile jogs through the park would be invigorating experiences, but today's run left her with an unsettled mind. She was glad when the run ended. All she really wanted now was to step into a shower and wash away that untoward feeling.

Jacqui was up by the time Anne had towelled off and dressed. They had breakfast together. Anne offered to drive Jacqui to school on her way to the office, but Jacqui had already planned to walk with Rada.

It took less than five minutes to drive from home to her office in the small downtown core of Charlottetown. The office was in a string of nineteenth-century brick buildings across from the Confederation Centre of the Arts and the provincial legislature. Anne's office was in a second floor walk-up on Victoria Row, a restored cobblestone street, fitted with period lamp posts and refaced brick fronts to please a trendy crowd visiting the artsy shops, boutiques, and restaurants that had set up on the ground floor there.

Anne unlocked her office door. The bold black letters that emblazoned the frosted glass panel read *Darby Investigations and Security.*

Two rooms made up the business suite of her detective agency. The first contained a receptionist's desk, an empty magazine rack, several straight chairs, and a wooden cabinet. The inner room was spacious and more comfortable. A large old mahogany desk stood near the windows. A sofa, two comfortable stuffed chairs, and a coffee machine nestled along one wall. The other side of the room held several metal filing cabinets and a bookcase and, next to them, nearer the desk, stood an enormous antique Wells Fargo safe. Bill Darby, Anne's uncle, had stored his small arsenal of firearms in that safe, along with other useful pieces of equipment, ammunition, sensitive documents, and special files.

Remembrances of Bill Darby hung along the walls. Among them were a framed commendation for bravery from when he pulled two teens from the Rideau Canal after they had lost control of their car; a picture of him receiving a decoration from the Lieutenant Governor of Ontario for a fire rescue; and a group photo of his police academy graduation class. Anne had packed away a few other treasures, but she couldn't bring herself to remove any more. After all, it had been his detective agency, his retirement project, and it was his name on the door for ten years before she came down from Ottawa to join him.

In the five years that followed her move, Anne worked as his recep-tionist, accountant, researcher, and sometime investigator. Just over a year had passed since a sudden, massive heart attack had killed her uncle. He had willed Anne his small estate. His detective agency was part of that bequest. It was worth nothing on paper but, having no other job prospects, she tried to make it work and, so far, she had been able to make a decent living for herself and her daughter Jacqui.

Anne pulled back the blinds and looked out over the Confederation Centre of the Arts across the street. The sun was bright now; a warm morning breeze seemed to stir the city below, and the odd feeling she had experienced earlier in the day had faded into a memory.

Anne returned to her desk and opened a case file that she had left there overnight. Her client was Mary Anne MacAdam. Mary Anne was a friend. She was also owner of The Blue Peter, a restaurant and lounge one door down the block. Mary Anne had noticed a recent drop in profits. She suspected that one of her serving staff was steal-ing from her, but she wasn't sure. So she asked Anne to look into it. Anne had just completed her report on that job when she heard the click of the letter drop in her outer office.

Anne scooped up the small pile of mail. She was hoping for a cheque from a previous job. Instead, she fingered through several direct mail advertisements, three bills, and a postcard invitation to a grand opening, and something else. It looked like a piece of litter, but it wasn't. It was an envelope.

The envelope was small. It had been made from good stock and intended for quality personal correspondence when it had been purchased but, somewhere in its journey, it had become mangled and crushed and grimy. The handwriting was barely legible, but, when she looked closely, she saw that it had been addressed to her dead uncle, *Mr. Bill Darby, Darby Investigations and Security*. Anne opened the envelope, unfolded the letter, and began to read:

My dear Mr. Darby,

I can scarcely put these words down because, as I do, I feel as though I am walking through a terrible dream, and putting ink to paper will make it all come true, something I truly dread. Nonetheless, I must do this.

I was nearby when a murder took place. I believe I know who the killer is, and I believe that an innocent man will suffer for it if I do not speak out. I could not bear to let that happen.

I can't go to the police. Please, if you can help me, call 367-0051.

Sincerely yours,

Carolyn Jollimore

The letter was dated October 18th, 2001. Anne stared at it in astonished disbelief.

Oh my god, Anne thought. *That was ten...no, eleven years ago.*

10.

The apprehension that had troubled Anne that morning crept into her bones again. If she were superstitious, she might have attributed her unease to a forerunner, but Anne scoffed at such things as products of ignorance and dim thinking.

Anyway, this restlessness was different. She knew what caused it, or part of it, anyway. It was the suppressed tone of desperation in Carolyn Jollimore's letter, a letter that no one received and that no one had read until today.

Anne tried to imagine how Carolyn must have felt, waiting hours, and days, and weeks, and not receiving a reply. She must have been frantic. Perhaps terrified. And what would she have done then? Given up? Gone to the police? Kept the secret locked away in her memory for years?

And what did she imagine could have kept Bill Darby from contacting her? Did she believe he could be so callous as to ignore her? Did she think he dismissed her as some lunatic?

And how did all this reflect on her uncle? Anne fretted about that, too. Bill Darby had been a man who took pride in his work, someone who worked for next to nothing if he believed in a client's cause. Anne would have been appalled if anyone had thought him cavalier and insensitive when in truth he had been entirely unaware of Carolyn's dilemma. Perhaps that letter had lain, chewed up, in the belly of a mail-sorting machine for the last decade. Or maybe some disgruntled postal worker had dumped it with other undelivered mail on the floor of his woodshed until somebody finally stumbled upon it.

Anne tried, but she couldn't let go of the ideas that churned in her head. They circled like the seamless parade of wooden ponies on a merry-go-round, and they repeated like the never-ending song of a carousel. Carolyn Jollimore's letter had taken a firm hold on her. As a result, she was getting no work done, and she making no progress with her unanswered questions.

Jogging or walking might put her mind at ease, she thought. It had helped in the past. So Anne tied up her running shoes, strode out of her office, and headed up the street along the edge of the business district. She passed a vagrant dozing on a park bench. His cardboard sign read "Will Work for Food." She walked north and east through mixed-class residential and small business neighbourhoods with no special purpose in mind and followed her curiosity into quiet cul-de-sacs, narrow alleys, and dead-end streets. Eventually, she tired, her head cleared of its clutter, and she found herself standing in front of Malone Electronics.

Malone Electronics was the brainchild of Dit Malone, a former local hockey star whose sports career ended after a diving accident had paralyzed him. In the years that followed, Dit displayed an extraordinary aptitude for computers and electronics. Eventually he built a company that developed specialty audio, visual, and thermal surveillance devices for law enforcement agencies across Canada, the States, and several foreign countries.

Anne and Dit had been friends since she came to the Island, but just a year ago, in the course of helping Anne with her first case as a private investigator, Dit was injured and sent to a Nova Scotia hospital. An unexpected side effect of his injury was the occurrence of a slight sensation in his legs, something he had not experienced since his paralysis. Several procedures and months of physical therapy followed but, in the end, his condition improved enough so he could move about with crutches.

Anne walked through the front door into the display room. No one was there, but a voice called out from behind the closed workshop door.

"Come on through." Dit held a button down, the door buzzed, and Anne shouldered it open.

"Hey," she said.

"I know the face, but I can't place the name. Pam? Tammy? Jan. That's it. Jan."

"Is that what you learned in the big city? How to become a smart-ass."

Dit sat in his wheelchair, pulled up to a work bench. A circuit board tilted up on the bench, a large magnifying glass in front of it. Dit chuckled quietly.

It suddenly struck Anne that she'd scarcely seen him in months. Over the last year he had spent long periods in Halifax hospitals. She had visited him several times, but her determination to keep the agency afloat and her teenage daughter from running wild consumed much of her time. As a result, her relationship with Dit, which had been growing, faded, almost without her noticing, and, as she looked at him now, he seemed, though not quite a stranger, not much more than a good friend. She felt awkward standing there. She suddenly realized how much she had missed him, and she regretted the change in their relationship but, for that, she had no one to blame but herself, her own preoccupations and personal distractions.

"You still have the Batmobile?" she asked, pointing to his wheelchair.

"I get pretty tired on the crutches, especially working here. I use them as much as I can, though. Good exercise. The doctors insist. The nurses, too." He winked.

"The nurses are just afraid you might catch up to them."

"No fear of that."

"You're waiting for them to catch you?"

"Now that's a plan. Let me write that down. Still, I have to admit that I'm pretty slow on those things. Last night there was a film on one of the cable channels. I couldn't sleep. So I stayed up and watched it. *Zombies on the Isle of Skye.*"

"I thought you hated those walking dead movies."

"I do, but at three in the morning, there's little choice. Anyway, after a bit, I began to wonder who moved faster, the zombies or me on crutches, and eventually I figured it out. If I was in a foot race with Scottish zombies, I'd probably become their ham and cheese special."

"And how did you arrive at that depressing conclusion?"

"I used a metronome."

"That's the silliest thing I've ever heard," she said with a laugh.

"Blame it on insomnia. Anyway, I could hobble around the room no faster than forty-five beats per minute, but they clipped right along in the mid-fifties. An adagio beats a lentissimo any day. Remembered that from high school music classes. Played trombone."

"That's really pitiful. You know that, don't ya?"

"You got an issue with trombonists?"

"No, just your absurd use of the metronome."

"It's scientific methodology."

"It's demented."

"I think of it as cross-media experimentation. Musical free-thinking."

"And now you've taken music to a place where no note has gone before. Wait a minute! Are you putting me on?"

"Hell no!...except maybe the part about the metronome...though I have to admit that I did think about using one. Great to see you, Anne. What are you busy at?"

"Oh, this and that. You know."

Dit looked at his watch and said, "Do you ordinarily run out of this-and-that by mid-afternoon? The private eye biz must be goin' t' hell."

"I had to clear my head. That's what I meant."

"Do you want to talk about it?" he asked. This time his voice was serious.

Anne opened her mouth to say something just as Dit's wall phone rang. He picked it up and gave Anne a silent indication that he'd just be a minute. "Malone Electronics," he said, and a large smile crossed his face. "Hey, babe. Where are you?... I'm glad...you made good time...yeah...yeah...plenty of room... I would think so...later...sure... not a problem..."

Anne got up and motioned that she had to go. Dit pulled the receiver from his ear and muffled the phone.

"Stick around. I'll just be a minute."

"Gotta go. More this-and-that."

"Are you heading to Mary Anne's later?"

She shrugged.

"Be there...around nine...someone I want you to meet," he said. Then he returned to his telephone conversation and turned toward the wall.

Anne waved noncommittally and vanished out the door.

The walk had done her no good at all. The sun still shone, but her mind was a muddle again. Bits of thought and twinges of emotion whirled in her head like the scraps of debris whipped by wind in an alleyway.

11.

"It was the damnedest thing," said Anne. She sat next to Ben Solomon in the large round booth at The Blue Peter.

Ben Solomon grunted. He read the letter again. Then he pushed it across the table to Anne with the back of his hand.

"Interesting," he said. Ben could be an engaging storyteller at a party but, when it came to uttering a professional opinion, he was as talkative as a Himalayan mystic in a mountainside cave.

Ben had been Bill Darby's best friend. Like Bill, he was a big man. He had short, sparse, greying hair and a stout, firm build. He wore rumpled suits, white shirts, and unremarkable ties. They made him look like a none-too-prosperous sales rep, but all of that belied eighteen years' experience with the Ottawa and the Charlottetown police departments. As detective sergeant he had planned to retire in two years, but those plans changed when the last major case he closed launched him into a top cop position with the Provincial government.

"Interesting? What do you mean 'interesting'? It's more than that. A lot more," said Anne.

"It was written eleven years ago. Three years before I joined the Charlottetown Police. It seems a shame, but it's ancient history."

"It doesn't feel that way to me, Ben. It's been nagging at me all day. When I opened that letter, it was like hearing a scream that had been choked back for eleven years. It brought tears to my eyes. It really did."

Anne fingered the wedding ring that hung from the gold chain around her neck.

"You're reading too much into it, is what I'm saying. You're thinking too much."

"It's not what I think. It's how I feel."

"I think you're spinning wheels over nothing. Take a step back. Look at the facts."

"How is this nothing, Ben?" Anne wagged the letter in his face. She was feeling angry now.

Ben caught the edge in her voice. He leaned back against the leathery cushion of the booth, raised his glass of beer, and sipped, and thought. Then he leaned forward again.

"Okay, let's take a look. What facts do you have?"

"An undelivered old letter to Uncle Bill from a woman who witnessed a murder."

"Now, do we know that it was a homicide...and not the death of someone's family pet...or her imaginary friend?"

"No, but..."

"Is it possible that the woman couldn't go to the police because she was a known pain-in-the-ass? A local kook?"

"Maybe, but..."

"Is it possible that she followed up her unanswered letter with a phone call after no one got back to her?"

"I guess."

"Maybe Bill did handle it or referred her to another agency."

"Okay."

"And, even though she may be a kook, she sounds like an intelligent one. So there's every reason to think she would have followed up in some other way."

"Okay."

"And notice that the woman used the word *believes.* She said she *believes* that she knows the killer and she *believes* somebody else is taking the fall for it. That's pretty fuzzy language. Maybe she heard a rumour from a friend of a friend of a friend."

"Okay, okay, enough. I got it. You're right. But, Ben, I just can't forget about it."

"I never said you should. Turn the letter over to the police. It's their job. Let them handle it. They'll get paid for it. You won't. It's not like it's a real case. Oh...before I forget...one more thing...maybe...*if* it was a real murder...maybe the killer was caught and convicted. There aren't any open murder cases from that time period. So maybe right now he's kicking back and enjoying the ambience of one of those fine cabanas they got over at sunny Dorchester Penitentiary."

"I love it when you get all optimistic like that, Ben."

12.

Anne returned to The Blue Peter that evening. She had left Jacqui at her desk, analyzing the humour of Stephen Leacock stories for an English project. Anne had suggested that topic after a satirical line from *Nonsense Novels* popped into her head.

"It goes something like this," she had said. "'Lord Ronald said nothing; he flung himself from the room, flung himself upon his horse, and rode madly off in all directions.'"

After Anne left the house, Jacqui was still giggling at the theatrical manner with which her mother delivered that line but, by the time Anne arrived at The Blue Peter, the humour of it all had vanished from her mind and, strangely, she felt like a twelve-year-old sitting with the "big people," even though all of those who gathered around the large, round-tabled booth were friends or long-time acquaintances.

Ben Solomon and his wife Sarah had been first to arrive. Brenda Malone and her husband, Dashiell, Dit's brother, came in with Urban Nolan and Eli Seares, two eccentric bachelors who made up what Anne called the "geek squad" at Malone Electronics. Mary Anne Mac-Adam hovered over the group and popped in and out of conversations between her restaurant duties and staff crises. Anne just curled up in the midst of them all, feet drawn up beneath her on the leather upholstery and a half-empty glass of Cabernet in front of her.

Laughter and chatter swelled and fell away and, during a subdued moment, Mary Anne nudged Anne.

"You seem out of sorts," she said. "Not feeling well?"

"It's been one of those days," Anne said, "and I'm not convinced it's over yet." Then she added quietly, "Why are we here anyway? What's going on?"

"Dit wanted us to meet."

"But why? What's up?"

"Well, if I had to guess, I'd say that he has a new friend and wants to show her off. At least, that's what I hope we're here for. He needs a serious upgrade to his social life. All work and no play, if you know what I mean."

"Hmmph," said Anne.

"Speaking of which...," Mary Anne said and bent her thumb toward the door.

Dit pushed through the foyer doors. He had strong, kind features, a muscular build, and brown curly hair. He wore dark trousers with a sharp crease and a cream-coloured sweater that showed off his lingering summer tan. A woman walked next to him, her arm linked loosely under his. She wore high heels and a low-cut, peacock blue dress with one shoulder strap. It shimmered under the dim overhead lights. She carried a white knit shawl.

She's beautiful, Anne thought and straightened up. The sneakers on her feet dangled near the floor. She glanced at Dit. She gave her overstretched sweater a few subtle tugs to imply some shape, but it had no effect whatsoever.

"She's gorgeous," said Ben.

"She's kinda cute," said Anne. "I guess," she added.

Sarah jabbed Ben in the ribs. "You look like an owl," she said. "Stop staring." Then Sarah turned to Anne. "Let me know if he starts drooling, and I'll take him home and lock him in the basement until the next lunar cycle."

"Of course, you must realize that it's against the law to lock up a cop," he said, "...unless it's Saturday night...and bondage gets your motor running..." Ben quickly shifted into the lyrics of a Steppenwolf song and began to sing softly to Sarah, "head out on that highway...lookin' for adventure...in whatever comes our way...yeah darlin' gonna make it happen...take the world in a love embrace..."

Sarah's face turned red.

"Stop it! Stop it!" she growled under her breath. She forced a smile and at the same time poked Ben sharply under the table.

"What? What!" protested Ben.

Anne laughed. Tears came to her eyes.

"Everyone, this is Gwen Fowler. Gwen, this is Ben 'Easy Rider' Solomon and his long, long-suffering wife, Sarah. You know Brenda and Dash. Urban and Eli are my electronics gurus. Mary Anne owns and operates this wonderful establishment and keeps our favourite table reserved, and, next to her, is Anne Brown, fondly named Wilhelmina A. Darby by her parents..."

"The detective?" she asked.

"Yes," said Anne.

"...but as a detective, she now goes by the name of Billy Darby."

"You work under a pseudonym?" asked Gwen.

"I do."

"But why? Wil... Anne's such a lovely name."

"I guess the simple answer...if there is one...is I inherited my uncle's agency after he died last year. His name was Bill Darby. He had a heart attack. It was unexpected. It became awkward to explain to new clients who asked for him that Bill Darby was dead, and that I was taking care of business. Then I'd have to explain who I was and so on. It just became too...awkward...like now."

"I'm sorry...didn't mean to pry. I was just curious."

"It doesn't matter. Anyway, some people think my name change is as odd as a top-hat on a dinosaur. I won't name names, but it rhymes with *Dit*."

"Rings a bell," said Dit. "I probably know the guy."

Anne ignored the comment and went on.

"My birth name was Wilhelmina Anne Darby. It became the endless source of torment in middle school. Later I shortened it to Willy...then Billy. So Billy Darby, the woman detective, was born. End of story."

"Sorry again."

"What's in a name? A rose by any...," Dit mused.

"You're no rose, and you're not Romeo and, as long as you've brought up the subject of odd names, let's look at yours. What kind of name is 'Dit' anyway? It doesn't even have enough letters for a real name."

"The Malones may be an economical gang, for all that, but they've managed to provide me with half the entire Morse code in my good name."

"Actually," interrupted Gwen, "'Dit' isn't his real name."

Anne looked blank. So did Sam and Sarah and Mary Anne.

"I knew that," said Dashiell with a smirk.

"It's 'Diarmuid,'" she said, pronouncing it again more slowly, "DEEar-mut."

"That's even more pathetic than Wil-hel-MEE-na," said Anne. "My condolences. And how did Diarmuid become Dit?" she asked.

An embarrassed grin swept across his face.

"I couldn't pronounce 'Diarmuid' when I was young. "'Dit' came out, and 'Dit' stuck."

"And Gwen," asked Sarah, "how did you uncover this delightful family secret?"

"It was on his wrist bracelet in the hospital. I was one of his caregivers on the spinal trauma ward."

"So you're a nurse?"

"I'm a nurse practitioner." Gwen noticed some blank looks again and added, "It's two steps above an RN and a giant step below doctor."

"Impressive. And how long are you visiting?"

Gwen looked questioningly at Dit. He nodded back in return. Then he pulled himself up on his crutches, stood, and smiled.

"The short answer is...forever. Gwen and I are getting married."

13.

This shouldn't take long, thought Anne, hunched over the desk in her office. She was determined to the set the record straight and set her own mind at ease by locating Carolyn Jollimore.

And maybe Ben was right. Even though the letter pre-dated Ben's time here, he was certain that Charlottetown had no unsolved murder cases, nor did any of the other jurisdictions on PEI. Maybe the Jollimore woman is just some local screwball. An inveterate gossip with an imagination that runs amok. No point jumping to embarrassing conclusions, though. A quick interview with Carolyn would reveal a lot, give her the opportunity to explain her letter, and give Anne the opportunity to explain why no one from Darby Investigations had come to help her if there had been no follow-up after the lost letter.

Anne picked up the receiver and dialled the number Carolyn Jollimore had included in her letter, but a recorded message said the number was no longer in service. So she flipped through the phone directories for a Carolyn Jollimore listing. No luck. Carolyn Jollimore was listed nowhere.

Okay, then, I guess it'll have to be the hard way.

Anne picked up the phone again and methodically called every Jollimore listed. After an hour of dialling, none of those who answered admitted knowing a Carolyn Jollimore. As a last resort, she turned to the computer and opened an online directory for Halifax. A couple of keystrokes brought her a list of Jollimores, a hundred or more.

This is going to take forever, she thought. Then her mind wandered to Dit and Gwen.

Why is he talking marriage? It's so soon. He scarcely knows her. What's the matter with him, she wondered. That's not like Dit. He's practical and down-to-earth and smart...and she's...she's just not right.

She pushed both of them out of her mind, stared at the enormous list of Jollimores as if she suddenly had been confronted by a flash mob of evangelists. Then she dove into it.

Three hours later, she had talked her way from Aaron Jollimore, a musicologist, to Zephyr Jollymore, a Barrington Street stripper. She had made telephone contact with dozens of others and left phone messages for the rest, but, in the end, her efforts seemed futile.

A pang of hunger reminded her that it was past one o'clock. She grabbed a file folder on her desk and headed downstairs to The Blue Peter.

"Club sandwich, dill pickle, water no ice," she told the waitress and sank back into the soft leather seat. Mary Anne approached and slid into the bench across from her.

"Hey," she said, "You're late. What's up?"

"Well," she said and thought for a moment and smiled, "The CEO of Brown Technologies approached me this morning and offered me a contract to do annual background checks on his entire staff. Isn't that wonderful?"

Mary Anne nodded.

"A hundred and thirty-five employees, all males, all professionals, all handsome, all single, all..."

"...fictional?" added Mary Anne.

"You're spoiling a wonderful illusion."

"Real women don't need illusions. I read that in *Cosmo*."

"Oh, yeah? So why do you put on lipstick and blush every morning, huh?"

"So I can look my age, of course."

"And how old are you, Mary Anne? The truth."

"The truth is that real women have real secrets, and I'm old enough to keep mine."

"Aren't some secrets better shared with friends?" asked Anne.

"Some better than others. You have one you want to share?"

"As a matter of fact, I do, but I'm not so sure you want to hear it."

"There's nothing that makes my mouth water more than a secret I haven't been told. Out with it."

"How about the secret of your vanishing money?"

"I'm all ears, hon."

Anne pushed a brown manila envelope toward Mary Anne.

"The details are here...a few surprises, too. First, the waitress you thought was ripping you off? The new one? Genevieve?"

"Yeah?"

"It's not her. Kate, on the other hand, is making a sugary sum at your expense."

"Kate? But she's worked here almost a year...and I didn't notice any drop in revenue until the last couple months. Are you sure?"

"Absolutely. I can't explain why the losses are recent. Could be a weakness for the slots, bills piling up, drugs. Could be a new boyfriend teaching her new tricks...or maybe she was just stealing less back then, and you didn't notice."

"How was she doing it?"

"Under-ringing mostly."

"Whaddaya mean?"

"If a customer orders a double, Kate rings in the cost of a single and pockets the difference. If someone orders a rum and coke, she just rings in the coke. She runs the tab in her head and pockets the grift near the end of her shift."

"Wouldn't I pick up those losses on my inventory check?"

"She probably gets around that by pouring smaller shots for other customers or watering down the bottles when business is slow. I counted her take at $43 from eleven until two in the morning."

"Thanks," said Mary Anne. "Your invoice is inside?" she asked pointing to the envelope.

"Consider it an even trade," Anne said pushing her lunch bill toward Mary Anne. "*Quid pro quo.*"

"Not a chance," said Mary Anne. "Lunch is on me for the next two months."

"That'll screw up your inventory."

"I'll call it a business expense."

Mary Anne waved to one of her waitresses who brought two coffees and set them on the table.

"What's Jacqui up to these days? I haven't seen her for a few weeks."

"High school is a big change, but she's doing well…very well, actually. Oh, by the way, we can't call her 'Jacqui' anymore. It's 'Jacqueline.' 'Jacqui,' she says, sounds too much like a boy's name. 'Jacqueline' is more mature…and sophisticated, so she says."

"Kids change, don't they? Hell, everything changes. Look at Dit. A new woman. New legs. Thriving business. Who would have imagined that ten years ago? And whaddaya think of Gwen?" Mary Anne added enthusiastically.

Anne returned a sour look.

"What's that mean?"

"Nothing."

"Spill it."

"I'm not convinced that they're a good fit."

"How so? She seemed like a pretty good catch to me."

"Well, look at the way she dresses. She's too fancy. Cocktail dress for a night in…in Charlottetown? Come on."

"Are you suggesting that The Blue Peter isn't stylish enough for dress-up? I'm offended."

"You know what I mean."

"Well, she comes from Halifax. It's different there. I'm sure she'll blend in...in good time."

"Maybe, maybe not."

"You weren't much different when you came down from Ottawa, as I recall."

"That was different."

"Maybe, maybe not," mocked Mary Anne.

"I still think that something's not right with her," said Anne.

"Of course. What girl in her right mind would be interested in a handsome, strong, witty, intelligent guy with money? What was I thinking?"

"Now you're making fun!"

"As long as you're talking foolishness, you're gonna give me plenty of material to work with."

"Where is she staying?"

"I didn't ask. At Dit's, I presume."

"Isn't that some kind of conflict of interest? She's a nurse, and he's her patient. It's like that Stockholm syndrome or something. Right?"

"Like I said...'plenty of material to work with,' hon."

14.

"If you're selling insurance, politics or religion, you can turn around right now and go back where you came from."

Edna Jollimore Hibley had received an odd call from an odd cousin in Nova Scotia. Someone was looking for Carolyn, he'd said, and he had given out Edna's home address. Anne had picked his message up on her answering machine, and it led her to Edna's front porch.

Now Edna stood in the open front doorway of her home, her arms crossed in front of her, her feet planted firmly apart, her head tilted like a cat fixated on a mole.

"Carolyn Jollimore?" asked Anne.

"What's your business with Carolyn?" Edna asked.

"It's personal. And private."

"I'm her sister. You can tell me. What's this all about?"

"It's still personal and private. It's also important."

Edna stared at Anne like a fortune-teller at her tarot cards, but finally she stepped aside, motioned for Anne to come in, and led her into the parlour.

The parlour was a stiff, immaculate, old-fashioned room. A red and gold oriental rug covered a square in the middle of the floor. Mid-century black-and-white relatives looked back from ornate frames on the wall. A silver tea service gleamed on a side table. Several straight-back chairs and a matching settee furnished the room. Handmade needlepoint pillows rested on the chairs and settee. Each carried a floral theme and an inspiring word like serenity, courage, or wisdom. Edna ushered Anne to the least comfortable-looking chair, while she took her place on the settee.

"Carolyn is dead," she began. A shudder interrupted the sternness in her voice. It was as if uttering those words would make it true. "It will be eleven years on the nineteenth."

That unexpected news left Anne nearly speechless. All she could muster in the form of words was, "I'm...so sorry."

Edna seemed indifferent to Anne's expression of regret and remained distant and impatient. "What's this about?"

Anne took out the letter Carolyn had written and handed it to Edna.

"This letter was mailed just before her death. But it was only delivered to me by the mail carrier yesterday."

Edna read the letter. Then she leaned forward. She would have toppled to the floor if Anne had not leapt toward the settee and grabbed her. She was conscious but dazed. Anne ran to the kitchen for water and brought it to her. She sipped slowly once, twice, three times and handed the glass to Anne without a word. Then she read the letter again. Her hand trembled. Her eyes were moist. Anne sat beside her on the small couch.

"My name is Billy Darby," said Anne. "Your sister was writing to my uncle, William A. Darby, who died last year never knowing about your sister's plight. I took over his detective agency a year ago. May I ask how your sister died?"

"An automobile accident. Her car went off the road one night after work. She was coming home...here. She was going to relieve me. I was looking after our mother at the time. She had Alzheimer's. I remember being angry because Carolyn was so late, and I needed to get up early for work the next day. I was a nurse. Then the police called and told me what had happened."

"It must have been devastating."

Edna's eyes glared for a flickering second, then softened.

"You have no idea," said Edna. "She was the only family I had besides Mother. My only friend, really." Edna looked up at Anne to see if she understood, but realized that she hadn't. "You see, we're not just sisters. We're twins. Identical twins."

"I was the only child in my family. So I can't begin to appreciate what you...and your mother went through."

"No, you can't," she said. "When Carolyn lived...she was...like my own breath. It was like we shared the same soul." Edna's eyes glazed, sought out a corner of the room, and embraced a distant memory. "After she died, I felt lost...adrift from everything. Sometimes I felt as though I were suffocating...and dying, too."

Anne took her hand in hers and held it. They sat there side by side for a long time in silence. Edna's thoughts drifted again to memories of her sister, memories of herself.

Anne was the first to speak. "Edna, can I get you some more water? Or some tea?"

"No. Thank you," she said, her voice stronger now. She withdrew her hand from Anne's, got up, and walked to the window that faced the street.

"Carolyn mentioned a murder in her letter. Do you know what she was referring to?"

"Yes. It would have to have been the murder of a young woman who worked in the same building as Carolyn. It was a robbery or mugging or something. I don't recall the details. They caught someone, though, and he went to jail for it. It was big news at the time."

"Did Carolyn ever mention it?"

"Why are you so interested ?" asked Edna. She sounded cold again.

"It may sound strange, but...the injustice of it all...the unfairness...it bothers me. A letter goes missing, and a tragedy occurs. I'm sure my uncle could have helped her if he had known. For my part, I think that I'm just trying to come to grips with what happened...to understand it, if that's even possible. But to believe that a simple coincidence can so terribly alter the course of our lives seems almost unthinkable."

"So, Ms. Billy Darby, you have a philosophical bent. Are you a philosopher...as well as a detective?"

"I'm just confused."

"All philosophers are confused. They masquerade at being know-it-alls. What interests me, though, is whether or not you're a confused detective, as well."

"I've got both feet on the ground when it comes to business." Anne's voice had grown a sharp edge in the face of Edna's bluntness. "Why?"

"Because I wish to hire you. I have trouble accepting coincidences, too."

"What is it you have in mind?"

"To carry out my sister Carolyn's wishes, of course. She wanted Darby Investigations to help her with a problem, and...now...so do I. Find out if justice was done...or not. Carolyn suspected something. Find out whether my sister's death was a genuine or a convenient *coincidence*. That's all I ask."

Both women had been unable to discount the close timing between Carolyn's death and the murder her letter alluded to, but neither had spoken of it. Now their cards were on the table, face up.

"You realize, don't you, that after so many years it will be difficult to learn the truth...," said Anne.

"I do."

"...and that it may be difficult, maybe even impossible, to find justice, even if we learn what happened?"

"I can live with that," said Edna, and she smiled faintly.

Anne walked out the door to her car. She hesitated thoughtfully for a moment. Then she drove across the city to the university library.

The University of Prince Edward Island was a collection of brick buildings on the crest of a ridge at the north end of town. The library was a building near the middle of the pack. The grass in the commons area glistened with a fresh soak of rain. Water slowly trickled through deep ridges in the bark of venerable oaks and maples and distorted Anne's reflection in the glass at the entrance to the library.

The microfilm viewer was in a room beyond the check-out and reference desks and beyond the front lanes of computer stations. A librarian retrieved a roll of film and fed it into the viewer, and Anne spun the crank until the date of 19 October 2001 appeared below *The Guardian* newspaper banner. The murder of Simone Villier and the arrest of John Dawson dominated the news on the nineteenth and twentieth. No mention of Carolyn Jollimore's death appeared on those dates, but the morning edition on Monday the twenty-second provided a page-three story and a picture of her wrecked car.

The news story reported that "Carolyn Jollimore, a resident of Mermaid, PEI, died in a single-vehicle accident which occurred shortly after midnight Friday on the Bunbury Road, two miles east of the town of Stratford. Visibility was good, but roads were wet at the time the woman's vehicle left the road and struck a culvert. Emergency response personnel used the jaws-of-life to extract the driver, and paramedics transported her to QE Hospital where she was pronounced dead. Ms. Jollimore was the sole occupant of the vehicle. Alcohol was not believed to have been a factor in the mishap, and an RCMP officer at the scene speculated that the driver may have fallen asleep at the wheel. No witnesses have come forward..."

Despite the reporter's crisp and dispassionate rendering of the accident, Anne felt a queer tingle at the base of her neck that she couldn't account for. She shook it off, finished recording the details in her notebook and left. The afternoon was quickly fading, and she needed a bit more daylight to complete her day's work. When she reached the library's foyer, she saw a familiar figure pass through the turnstile. One hand of the woman supported a shoulder strap attached to a well-laden briefcase. Her other hand carried three books. She was engaged in conversation with a tall dark-haired student wearing jeans and a UPEI sweatshirt.

"Was that Edna Hibley who just came through?" she asked a librarian at the check-out counter.

"Professor Hibley," she replied, correcting her. "Yes. That was she."

"Does she teach here?"

"Nursing Sciences, I believe, and a course or two at the Vet College."

"Can I request some special services?"

"Certainly. What services are you looking for?"

"I need photocopies of all local news stories regarding the Simone

Villier murder from October to December 2001."

"They'll be ready tomorrow morning."

Anne crossed the bridge to Stratford to look at the crash site. As Anne approached the scene of Carolyn's accident, the two-mile mark on the Bunbury Road, she slowed down, her attention shifting to the terrain along the roadway. The accident scene photo in the newspaper had shown a large field in the background, but for the last half-mile she had passed only loose strings of houses and small stands of trees and brush. Suddenly the terrain opened up. Fields appeared on both sides of the road. Several hundred yards ahead stood the bridge over Fullerton Creek. She eased the car onto the shoulder and stopped.

Then she saw something. A small white cross. It was one of those simple memorials that family members sometimes place along a highway where a loved one has died in an accident. She pulled the car a bit further ahead. Her tires sank into the soft shoulder of the road. She stopped and got out.

Anne walked toward the cross. It had been placed on an overgrown path that sloped from the shoulder of the road to a grain field and traversed a tubular metal culvert in the ditch below.

The wooden memorial was old. Edna probably had erected it a short time after Carolyn's death, but the spot had been cared for recently. The wild grasses surrounding it were clipped. A wilted bouquet of summer flowers lay nearby. Even the paths worn into the field by farm machinery suggested that the drivers had kept a respectful distance from the cross.

Anne's eyes fell upon the grey metal culvert. One end was crumpled, likely by Carolyn's car. Once her vehicle left the road, the impact would have been head-on. The stop would have been instantaneous and unforgiving. The end of Carolyn's life probably would have been sudden and painless. *But none of that would have comforted Edna,* she thought.

Anne surveyed the stretch of highway. In each direction it was straight, open, and level. There were no houses, no distractions—just four or five hundred yards of country road behind her and another two or three hundred to the bridge ahead.

The police were right. There was no evidence here to suspect anything but some driver error. But that didn't allay Anne's suspicions. She knew that Carolyn's last letter had been mailed just the day before her death, and that was something the police had not known and couldn't have factored into their conclusion.

And then there were other incidentals. For example, Anne noted that the accident occurred on a straightaway, not a curve; the road was wet, but the rain had ended earlier that evening; and it was not an unfamiliar road to Carolyn, but one she drove each day; also, it was less than a ten-minute drive from her work to the crash site, probably not enough time to drift off to sleep; and her death happened at the end of her regular work day, not after a double shift or some other peculiar scheduling. *Really*, thought Anne, *Carolyn had faced no natural circumstances which would have caused her death*.

It was possible that all of this was coincidence, but Anne had always been suspicious of coincidence, and this prompted a phone call to Ben. Anne needed a favour.

15.

Up until a year ago, Ben Solomon had been Detective Sergeant, had liked his job with the Charlottetown Police, and had intended to retire in a couple of years. Then, he became drawn into a case Anne was working. It had been her first case and what started as a confidential delivery of a client's package turned into an international intrigue involving counterfeit money and an espionage plan gone off the rails.

The result became potentially messy for the governments in Ottawa and Washington, and, in order to avoid public embarrassment, the provincial government agreed to help with the patching-up work, part of which included the creation of a new provincial government post with federal money.

Ben Solomon was appointed to that post, guaranteed his police pension, and given a generous salary, almost double what he made as a cop. Anne's role in the incident was rewarded by the promise of periodic government subcontracts for her future private investigation services. The only catch was that neither of them could speak of the incident again. The entire affair was classified under the Security of Information Act. Both Anne and Ben accepted the terms, although they were quite sure that they had no option. A year later, Anne had seen little to indicate that she would receive any reward for her effort in uncovering the plot and keeping the secret, and the ink had scarcely dried on the legislation authorizing Ben's new post.

Ben's title was Provincial Special Investigator and Liaison for Intergovernmental Law Enforcement Operations. What exactly that meant, he scarcely knew. Nor did anyone else, really, and today was Ben's third day on the job.

Today was also the first day in his own office on the fourth floor of the Jones Building, one of five structures that formed the heart of provincial government operations in Charlottetown. The office was small but bright, and the furnishings smelled new. The walls were bare, and his desktop devoid of pictures or personal items. That morning his part-time secretary, Ida Treat, had shown a technician into the office with a trolley full of computer equipment. The computer was connected in about ten minutes. The technician left, Ida disappeared to her other job down the hall at Pesticide Licensing and Control, and Ben was alone again.

Ben found himself leaning vacantly against a filing cabinet that filled one corner. He opened the drawers one by one. Three were empty. The fourth held a telephone directory and a freshly amended copy of the Police Act. He slipped the book under the desk phone and placed the packet of legislation in the centre of his desk.

The window next to the desk had a view of Victoria Park and a bit of Hillsborough Bay. He looked out over the thin spread of red and orange foliage below and at the dark blue streaks of water beyond and wished he were a detective again at his coffee-stained desk in the drafty squad room with his old friends downtown.

Ben jerked at his necktie as if it were strangling him. Then he sidled into his chair and pulled the copy of the Police Act toward him. He fingered through the legislation until he came upon a sub-section entitled "Provincial special investigator" and began to read.

"I expected that you would have at least a suite of offices," interrupted a voice. A head had poked itself through the doorway and looked around. "You'd need that much space, maybe more, just to fit your job title through the door. What is it they call you now?"

"Provincial Special Investigator and Liaison for Intergovernmental Law Enforcement Operations." Ben forced an embarrassed grin and added, "Bureaucrats. They like big words and big titles. What brings you up here, Chief?"

Jamie MacFarlane flashed a big smile, removed his hat, and sat down in a chair opposite Ben's desk. His hair was short, thinning and grey at the temples. He wore the uniform of Stratford Police Department and the insignia of police chief on his shoulder. Ben guessed that he would be about forty years old. He had known him for six or seven years, and their paths had crossed several times when investigations spanned both sides of Hillsborough River. MacFarlane had grown heavier since their last meeting, thought Ben. Then again, so had he.

MacFarlane put several thick binders onto Ben's desk.

"You...or somebody...called the station and requested an old case file." He motioned toward the binders. "This is it."

Ben leaned forward and glanced at it as if he were uncertain what it was. It was labelled with a serial number.

"The Simone Villier murder," said MacFarlane.

"Oh, yes, I recall it now," Ben said. Anne had asked for the file. It was the first and only official action he had taken since becoming Provincial Special Investigator. "Thanks, but you didn't need to make a special trip."

Ben leaned back in his chair again.

"Not a problem," said MacFarlane. "Consider this a courtesy call to the Island's new top cop."

"Is that what you think this job is?" Ben asked.

"It's what I've heard in various corridors. Should I take all that scuttlebutt with a large grain of salt?"

"I'll let you know after I've waded through all this bullshit," Ben said, picking up the copy of the Police Act and dropping it down again.

"Better you than me. I try to stay away from politics as much as I can. Too much dancin' around...and tryin' not to step in somethin' nasty."

Ben grinned back at MacFarlane, but he remembered rumours of MacFarlane currying political favours himself. *You don't get to be Chief of Police on merit alone, not on Prince Edward Island*, thought Ben.

In fact, he said to himself, *I'd be surprised if he wasn't doing a slow dance right now.*

"Anyway, I won't keep you any longer. You look busy." Ben studied MacFarlane's face, but he could detect neither irony nor sincerity. MacFarlane stood. "Just a courtesy call, as I said. Drop down to the station sometime, and I'll show you around. By the way, what's your interest in the Villier case? You doing historical research or something?"

"Not me. A private investigator. Billy Darby."

"He's dead."

"Bill Darby is. It's his niece, Anne Brown... Billy Darby."

"What's her angle?" MacFarlane sat down again.

"New evidence."

"That case has been closed for a hell of a long time. What evidence could she have come up with that wasn't dug up and examined years ago?"

Ben opened the bottom drawer of his desk, pretended to look for something, and pulled out the only scrap of paper there.

"Here's a photocopy of a letter she received in the mail." Ben handed it to MacFarlane.

MacFarlane read the letter. Ben watched his eyes move back and forth across the page. Then he watched his eyes scan it a second time before he spoke.

"My guess is...it's phoney...somebody's sick idea of a practical joke."

"It's legitimate. I saw the envelope and the cancellation stamp, and the handwriting on the envelope matches the letter."

"I don't know exactly what went on then. I was on other duties with the department when they investigated Villier's murder, but they would have followed the book. They always did. Every lead would have been investigated. Everyone remotely connected with the victim was interviewed, and her killer went to prison. And this letter shows up now? Somethin' smells..."

Ben shrugged.

"So...you're goin' to reopen the case? I think you're making a mistake, Ben."

"I'm not reopening anything...at least I'm not planning to at this time...but, as I said, Billy Darby will be looking into it. I'm just making the file available. Maybe something will come of it. Maybe not...but if you're concerned and have a recollection of what happened, you could offer her your two cents...maybe help her figure out how this letter fits into the Villier murder."

"No thanks. Then two people would be wasting their time, wouldn't they, Ben?"

16.

Anne woke early for a morning run, but the sky was dismal grey, and cold rain pelted the windows. Instead, she took a backpack from the closet and set it beside the front door in case she could fit an hour of gym time into her schedule.

Jacqui was still asleep and would remain so until Anne flicked on the light in her room. In the meantime, she took out a couple of bowls and boiled some water. It would be a perfect day for hot oatmeal, she thought.

By the time Jacqui washed and dressed, breakfast was on the kitchen table. Anne sprinkled blueberries over the oatmeal. Nearby was a dish of freshly cut grapefruit sections, a jar of brown sugar, and a container of milk. Anne was pouring cups of fresh coffee as Jacqui sat down.

"What's the special occasion?" asked Jacqui, looking around.

"No special occasion. I just had a little more time this morning. It's pouring outside."

"And I was going to walk to school with Rada this morning," she said. She sounded disappointed.

"I'll drive you, if you want, Jacqui."

"Please and thanks."

"And it's Jacqueline, not Jacqui, if you remember."

"Right. Jacqueline. I'll try to remember." Anne added a delicate glaze of sarcasm, which Jacqui didn't notice.

"So, tell me about Rada."

"What's to tell?"

"Well, what are her parents like?"

"They don't talk much, except among themselves, and then it's in some other language. They seem nice, though. Mrs. Kikovic gives us treats when Rada comes home. Rada told me what it was, but I can't pronounce it. It was good, though."

"Do they belong to any groups… Are they involved with the school… any hobbies…interests? Does Rada play soccer like you?"

"No, I don't think she's allowed. She can't wear shorts or T-shirts or stuff like that."

"How does Rada feel about that?"

"Like everyone else. It's hard when you don't fit in."

"How about you? Do you think it's important to fit in?"

"Of course, Mom. You can't show up for rugby try-outs wearing hockey skates, can you?"

"I guess not. Okay, comb your hair. It's almost time to go."

Even though the rain had slowed to a trickle, the weather had dampened any desire for conversation and, during the drive to school, everyone in the car retreated into private thoughts. Anne swung the car into the stop-and-drop entrance. Their goodbyes were polite and subdued. As the girls left the car, the wind came up. Jacqui clutched her books and shielded her eyes. Rada gripped her skirt, and her long black hair heaved and swayed in the gusts.

17.

At her office Anne found two messages on the answering machine. The first was from Ben. He said he had a case file for her—the Simone Villier file. Anne had had no hope of getting that police file on her own. So Ben's news was a blessing, and a small thrill leapt through her.

The rain had stopped, and clouds were breaking up in the east as she walked the six blocks to his new office. The door was half-open, and she stuck her head in.

"Hi," she said. "Nice," she added, surveying the room. "Great view up here, too."

"Yeah, but there's no handle to open the window." Ben looked up from an empty desktop. "No fresh air. And if I'm driven around the bend by boredom, I can't jump out. I'll have to find a ground floor way of doing away with myself."

"Good grief! That's a joyful sound. Can't be that bad, can it?"

"I've been sitting here for days. So far, nobody has briefed me on anything."

"You haven't been in the job very long, though," she said. It was a dismal effort at being supportive.

"Maybe not. But I get the impression that the Premier and the Justice Minister would rather not rock any boats."

"What makes you think that? What did they say?"

"Nothing yet. They haven't spoken to me beyond the customary welcome-aboard phone calls. No agenda. No staff meetings. Nothing. I think they'd be happy if I just went away."

"You sure you're not overreacting? Everything takes time in government. You'll see."

"I'm not so sure. I approached the Premier's chief of staff, Wendell Carmody, about the direction I wanted to take with this office, but he got this blank look on his face and mumbled something about it being 'largely a ceremonial post.' Then he winked and said, 'Why don't you investigate the golf courses for a few weeks?'"

"Oh," said Anne. "Is that such a bad idea?"

"I don't golf."

"Well, as I see it, you've got four choices. You can quit. You can play. Or you can work."

"I've never quit anything," he said, "and I'm not starting now."

"And Uncle Bill said you couldn't play golf worth a damn. So that leaves work. Just ignore the bureaucrats. Find something to investigate. They can't fire you for doing your job in spite of them dragging their heels."

"Come to think of it, considering I got this job for keeping a big political secret, I'm not so sure they could fire me if they wanted to."

"Problem solved."

"By the way, there were four choices. You only mentioned three."

"Oh yeah, number four was 'jump.' But I couldn't seriously recommend that option. Up here with the windows locked and all, you would look rather silly. Downstairs, the best you could hope for would be a sprained ankle."

"Here, take this," he said pushing a bulky dossier across the desk toward Anne. "I've got to get back to work."

Anne grabbed the package, gave Ben a mock salute, and headed out.

The case file on Simone Villier was more voluminous than she had expected, and heavier, and when she dropped the bundle on the desk back at her office on Victoria Row, it landed with a noteworthy thump. Anne stared at the enormous case file for a moment. Then she stared at the telephone. Then she stared at the case file again. It seemed to have grown even more large and ponderous.

18.

Then there was that second message on her answering machine. Anne had ignored it. She tried to forget it, and she wished she could, but it came back again and again like a dull toothache.

The message had come from Gwen Fowler, Dit's fiancée.

With any luck, Anne thought as she dialled the phone, *she won't pick up. Hopefully, we can play phone tag until she gets bored or catches on that I'd rather not talk with her...or do anything else.*

Gwen answered on the second ring. "Anne. Hi. I'm so pleased you were able to call back. Dit said that you were usually pretty busy in the morning, but you usually only had 'this-and-that' to fill your afternoons."

"That was Dit's idea of a joke."

"Oh," said Gwen, somewhat surprised and embarrassed. "I didn't know. Sometimes his humour is drier than I'm used to."

"Like day-old toast," said Anne, "and, on special occasions, it comes mummified."

Gwen laughed. Her voice had a clear, musical quality to it.

"What can I do for you?" asked Anne.

"I had hoped that we could do something fun...get to know each other better...talk a bit...shop maybe."

"Gwen, I'm really the wrong one to wander around and hunt for bargains with, and I've got a bit more 'this-and-that' to handle than I would like right now."

"Just talk then?" Gwen's voice quavered, and Anne sensed a neediness in her tone. Perhaps it was disappointment.

"You don't want to drive all the way across town just to talk, do you?"

"I'm not across town. I'm downstairs, actually."

"Downstairs?" asked Anne.

"At The Blue Peter. I just finished lunch. Do you mind?"

Anne had run out of stock excuses to avoid Gwen, and to become blunt would have been rude. Besides, something in Gwen's manner dissuaded Anne from turning her down.

"Come up, then," she said.

Anne scarcely had hung up the phone before she heard footsteps on the stairs. The door to the outer office squeaked. Gwen helloed from the reception area, and Anne called her in.

Gwen seemed to fill the room when she swept into it. She stood taller than Anne had remembered her at The Blue Peter. She wore dark blue jeans and a violet blouse. She set a small purse and a shopping bag on a coffee table and strode to the window behind Anne's desk. She looked out over Victoria Row. The sun had peeked out and dried the cobbled street. It lit up the autumn colours of the trees. Across the street, the stone walls of the Confederation Centre glimmered.

"What a wonderful spot," she said.

"I like it a lot," said Anne.

Gwen turned around. Her eyes fell on Anne and then to her desk, covered with untidy piles of papers and photos and reports. "I guess I did come at a bad time, didn't I?"

"Well, I can't say that there's ever a perfect time, but this is as good as it gets."

"Dit speaks of you often. He likes you. It sounds strange, I know, but it's almost as if I know you."

"I'd like to have been a fly on the wall when those conversations took place."

"It was all quite complimentary," said Gwen.

"Are you sure? Even after every syllable of irony has been scrubbed out of it?"

"No guarantees, but it seemed so."

"Now *I'm* astonished," said Anne.

"I think I detect some irony now, though."

"You've got a good ear. Maybe you and Dit are a match."

"Did you have doubts?"

Anne shrugged and leaned back in her chair. "I always have doubts. That's how I make a living. Everybody has something to lie about, something to hide. Good guys, bad guys...clients, too."

"That seems...cynical," said Gwen.

"I don't let it get to me."

"What about you?" asked Gwen. "What do you lie about?"

"I never lie," said Anne seriously. A hint of smile twitched the corners of her mouth.

"Neither do I," Gwen added, and winked. "So how did you get involved in this business?"

"Necessity. My uncle, who started the business, died. I had a child to support. A door opened, and I stepped through it."

"That's a pretty big step. I'd be terrified."

"You don't strike me as the type who becomes terrified very easily."

"Everyone has fears...and maybe that's why they hide things."

"Perhaps. It was a bit different for me. I had had a bit of experience before I came to Charlottetown. Four years as insurance investigator for an Ottawa company."

"Did you enjoy that?"

"I did, but one of my managers developed a chronic case of roaming hands. I taught him some manners, and he fired me. A while after that adventure, Uncle Billy offered me a job down here."

"But this must have been quite different from insurance investigation."

"The cases are different, but the thinking is similar. Billy showed me how to work cases and stay safe. I think he was actually grooming me for the job, though I didn't realize it at the time."

"What are you working on now, if you don't mind my asking?" Gwen motioned toward the papers on Anne's desk.

"It's a police case file...about a murder ten or eleven years ago. It may be connected to another death around the same time. I've been hired to see if there's a connection."

"That's fascinating. Really. Can you talk about it?"

"Most of it's no secret. It's a closed case," said Anne. Then she went on to describe the murder of Simone Villier in her Stratford office building, the police investigation that followed, and the subsequent arrest, conviction, and twenty-year sentence of John Dawson.

Gwen leaned forward attentively in her chair as Anne recounted what she had learned about the murder. Then Anne reached into her desk and retrieved a separate file folder from which she took out Carolyn Jollimore's last letter. As she read it, Gwen's mouth opened in wonder.

"Oh my god," she said. "What will you do now?"

"A lot of my work is just mind-numbing stuff. I have a pretty thorough idea of how this investigation developed. Next step is crossing t's and dotting i's. Inside the front cover is an index of contents. I like to check that everything is there that should be and that the documents match the inventory...interviews have pages numbered sequentially...and that nothing is missing."

"Can I help?" asked Gwen.

Anne handed Gwen the index sheet. "Okay, dig in. You read out each item on the list. I'll check and sort."

It took forty minutes to verify the completeness of the case file. It would have taken less if Anne hadn't paused the process to scrutinize three of the documents. Two were notable curiosities: Schaeffer's interview of Constable MacFarlane and MacFarlane's arrest report of Dawson. The third document, one that sent a slight chill up her spine, was Constable Best's interview of Carolyn Jollimore. She read it quickly without comment or change of expression and moved on.

"Everything is there," said Anne. She leaned back in her chair and centred the neatly stacked case file on her desk.

"That was fun," said Gwen.

"Fun?" mocked Anne. "...and you said you never lied."

"I'd never seen a police file before. It was interesting. Details are important in my job as well. Loose ends can turn into big problems. While we're on that subject, I have a question I'd like to ask...a rather important one."

Oh god, thought Anne, *is she going to ask me to be a bridesmaid or something?* Anne's mind spun through a flurry of equally awkward options and hoped that the dismay in her mind hadn't wilted the expression on her face. Already her cautious pause was becoming too long and telling.

"Shoot," said Anne.

Gwen looked directly at Anne. She smiled apprehensively, took a slow breath, and asked: "Are you in love with Dit?"

19.

"He is beautiful," she said.

"You mean he's hot," said Jacqui, "...or a hunk...or the bomb."

Rada blushed. Both girls had been sitting together at a table in the school library and were staring across neat lines of desks and tables and carousels toward the blond head of Sig Valdimarsson.

"A bomb," said Rada.

"*The* bomb," corrected Jacqui. "So go over and say something to him."

"I couldn't."

"It's easy. Grab an armload of books, walk by, and accidentally drop them as you pass. He'll have to smile...make a joke...say something... or help you pick them up. That'll be a start. Right?"

"I couldn't."

"It'll work. That's how I met Bobby," she said and reflected on the moment when she pretended to trip near Bobby Fogarty's desk. *Gray's Anatomy*, the biggest book she could find, had toppled out of her arms, struck Bobby's temple, bent his glasses, and nicked his ear, and she ran to the principal's office for a first-aid kit to patch his cut. "We're very good friends now," she added enthusiastically, trying to forget her mortification at the time.

"I couldn't."

"Why? What's stopping you?"

"Mr. Shadi."

Rada's eyes shifted toward the supervising teacher of another class in the library.

"He knows my father, and he would tell him that I am flirting with boys."

"So?"

"It is not allowed."

"...but, if you can't flirt, and you can't date, how can you meet guys? I don't get it."

"In my family, meeting boys is arranged...through friends of my parents, cousins, relatives..."

"That seems like something out of a fairy tale or a Victorian novel."

"That's the way things have always been."

"Are you happy with that?"

"Sometimes I wish I were a Cinderella, and Prince Charming was searching the kingdom for me with a glass slipper."

"Real Prince Charmings are more like Sig over there. You have to dump an armful of books on their heads to wake them up. I could vouch for him to your parents. I've known Sig since grade four."

Rada looked longingly at Sig, and then hopelessly toward Jacqui. She said nothing.

"So much for a social life," said Jacqui as the bell rang.

Both girls jumped up and gathered their books. Rada headed for algebra; Jacqui hurried for art class.

Jacqui grabbed her work-in-progress stored in a cupboard at the back of the art classroom. It was a charcoal sketch of Bobby Fogarty. It was sketch number seven of him. Her closest friends noticed a similarity. So did Madame Desjardins, the art teacher. That made her proud and hopeful. Bobby's birthday was coming up, and she was certain that matting the sketch in a fancy frame would make a wonderful present.

"*Très bien*, Jacqueline," said Madame Desjardins looking over Jacqui's shoulder.

"*Merci*," said Jacqui in her best Island French.

"Jacqueline, I am in need of a babysitter on Saturday evening. Are you available again?"

"Yes, Madame. What time?"

"Seven-thirty until twelve, okay?"

Jacqui nodded.

Madame patted her shoulder and returned to her desk to take attendance.

20.

Gwen's question hovered above Anne's head like a long blade in an unsteady hand. The nature of the question disturbed her just as much as the directness with which it had been delivered. Bluntness was not a common Island trait.

Predictably, Anne had been stunned and silent. Gwen nonetheless sat beautifully poised and silent. She looked expectantly at Anne. Anne's lips parted. Then, something caught her attention, and her eyes were drawn toward the open office door.

Filling that empty door frame was Police Chief Jamie MacFarlane, his uniform crisply ironed and his shoes highly polished.

He stopped short when he saw Gwen.

"The door was open. Bad timing, I guess."

"As I was telling Gwen, there's never a perfect time, but this is as good as it gets."

Gwen stood up.

"Gwen, this is Stratford Police Chief Jamie MacFarlane. Chief, Gwen Fowler, Dit Malone's fiancée."

"A pleasure," he said, shaking her hand. Then he turned to Anne. "I didn't mean to interrupt. We could meet another time."

"I was just about to leave anyway," said Gwen. "We'll talk again sometime soon, Anne." She smiled softly, lowered her eyes, and turned toward the door.

"I'll get back to you on that," Anne replied.

MacFarlane's head turned and followed Gwen as she left the room and closed the office door behind her. His lingering gaze at Gwen had not escaped Anne's notice, and she felt a quiver of envy and agitation. Anne motioned him to a seat, and she settled behind her desk.

MacFarlane was larger than most east-coast police officers. He stood about six-four and had a robust frame. His hair was greying, his features well-proportioned. He had penetrating eyes. He was as daunting as he was handsome, but his most remarkable quality was his voice. It had resonance and depth that commanded attention.

"Is it Anne or Billy that you go by?"

"I'm Billy Darby at work and Anne Brown among friends. What's up, Chief?"

"The Villier case. I have some history with it. I knew Simone, the victim, and I thought perhaps I could give you some help."

"Wouldn't that be a waste of time?" she said. Anne expected some reaction to her echo of his words to Ben: a twitch of lip, a tightening of shoulders, an embarrassed smile. However, she saw nothing but a blink of eyes, and the passing of an extra second or two before he replied.

"You've been talking to Ben, then." He began again in a reflective tone.

"That's right."

"I haven't changed my mind on that," he said. "But I could have phrased it more diplomatically. My concern here is that this case was worked to death eleven years ago. I know. I was there. A suspect was caught, the evidence was clear, the judge agreed, and John Dawson got a well-deserved twenty years for the terrible crime he committed. That leaves me confused. I'm not sure just what more you can achieve by picking away at this case."

"Maybe it'll confirm what's already been concluded; maybe it'll correct a miscarriage of justice. One or the other, that's my hope. That's what an investigation should do, right?"

"I see it opening up old wounds. A lot of people were devastated by Simone's death. Most of them have tried to put the past behind them—not an easy thing to do—and they wouldn't want to relive the agony of those months again."

"Do you mean *they* or *you*?"

"Both, I guess. But I was thinking mostly about Bernadette Villier, Simone's mother. She's had a pretty tough life. Her husband died two years before the murder. He was a construction worker. He fell off a roof he was shingling and broke his neck. Simone was their only child. Bernadette started drinking. She's been sober for a few years now. I helped out some. Hate to see a relapse."

"Why would you do that? Why would you step forward?"

"You've read the police report by now. You know that I had a relationship with Simone, and I also felt some responsibility to Bernadette...as a friend. Simone and I were in love. We were planning to get married. Did you know that?"

Anne shook her head.

"So Bernadette would have been my mother-in-law if things had turned out differently...and...not many know this, but Simone was pregnant at the time. She was thrilled when she found out...she almost glowed...and then it was over...swept away in one senseless act. Now she's dead, the baby, my son, never saw the light of day, Bernadette was nearly ruined, and my personal life became a shambles for a time. And that's why I hope you'll see that no good can come from digging up the past. Nobody wins...nobody."

MacFarlane stared at the floor. Anne saw sadness in his eyes. He struck her as a pathetic figure at that moment, like a distraught child. He may warrant some of her pity, she thought, but Edna Hibley seemed to need and deserve most of it.

"I can sympathize with how you feel, Chief, but new evidence has come to my attention, and I can't ignore it."

"Ben mentioned something about a letter. He showed me a copy, but I didn't put much stock in it. Maybe it's something that Dawson dreamed up in prison. Maybe it's a crank."

Anne fished Carolyn Jollimore's letter out of her desk drawer and passed it to MacFarlane.

"Take a look. Her letter is dated, and the postmark is still visible on the envelope."

MacFarlane looked at it thoughtfully. He stiffened for a moment. Then he said, "It doesn't prove that she wrote this letter, does it?"

"Maybe not, but it raises questions..."

"So far I haven't heard anything that connects Carolyn Jollimore with Simone that isn't complete speculation," he said.

"Simone's murder was the only one at the time. What else could it refer to? This isn't Halifax where there's a couple of murders every Saturday night. And I'm not convinced that Carolyn Jollimore's death was an accident either. It's too coincidental. Something's not right."

"So the author of the letter is dead. Is that what you're telling me? Then there's no evidence that this Jollimore woman was murdered, is there? Maybe she was careless. Maybe she was in some kind of mental state. It wouldn't be the first time I've seen that sort of thing. There's all kinds of explanations. You're not listening to the facts." MacFarlane's voice sharpened, and it reverberated in the room.

"This letter is a fact, and my client wants an answer that explains it."

"Who's your client? What's his connection to this?"

"I'm afraid that's confidential."

"So, you don't want my help, then?"

"All I've heard so far is an argument to quit this case. That's not the help I'm looking for."

"How long have you been a private investigator?"

"What's your point, Chief?"

"When you've been in law enforcement as long as I have, you'll realize that, after the evidence is examined and the pieces fit, you turn
the page. Our evidence was solid, we presented it to the Crown, and
it stood up at trial. The report into Carolyn Jollimore's death. What
were the findings?"

Anne said nothing. MacFarlane stared at her. Then he said, "Right.
They found nothing. It was an accidental death."

"I think this letter may change their opinion on Carolyn's death,"
said Anne and returned the letter to its drawer.

21.

A perky receptionist with a necklace of braided flowers tattooed around her neck led Anne through a maze of beige cubicles and dividers to the office of Davidia Christian, manager of White Cross Medical.

"Ms. Billy Darby to see you," she said and disappeared.

Davidia looked up from her computer screen and smiled. It was an unguarded, inviting smile, and Anne felt suddenly at ease.

"You said you wanted to talk about Carolyn," she said. It was almost a question. Anne nodded, and Davidia smiled even more broadly.

"She was a dear friend," she said. "Probably my best friend at the time. We were older than most of the other clerks in the office. We had more in common, I suppose. But what's your interest in Carolyn? Did you know her?"

"No," said Anne. "I'm a private investigator. I'm looking into the circumstances surrounding her death."

"That was ages ago, dear."

"I'm trying to clear up some loose ends for a client."

"Carolyn's sister?"

"Did you know her?"

"I felt like I did. Carolyn and Edna were twins, and Carolyn liked to talk. They had quite a cross to bear. Their mother was doing poorly. Alzheimer's, you know. Their mother was a bit difficult...I suppose that comes with the illness...but it was hard to keep caregivers to look after her. They'd come and go. The girls had to work out a schedule between themselves to care for her. That's when Carolyn started her flex hours. White Cross was pretty progressive with things like that, even then."

"How did that change things for Carolyn?"

"She had already worked here for several years...and she was an excellent worker, too...but, when things became difficult at home, she arranged an evening shift, four o'clock until midnight."

"Why those hours?"

"It was a full shift, but it overlapped an hour with the regular shift. That way she could get up to speed on that day's workload...and get up on the office gossip," she giggled, and then added wistfully, "...and maybe for a little frivolous human contact, too. It also worked well with Edna's nursing schedule. Carolyn would relieve Edna when she got home."

"And that worked out?"

"Unless one of the daytime caregivers quit...which is what occurred just a couple weeks before Carolyn's accident."

"Do you recall what happened?"

"Well, she worked the week before Thanksgiving. I remember that, but Carolyn was out for most of the following week."

"Wasn't that around the same time as the Villier murder?" asked Anne.

"It was the Friday after the murder that she returned to work."

"You have a remarkable memory, Davidia. I can scarcely remember where I was last Friday."

"Neither can I, most of the time," she laughed, "but the circumstances were different. It was comical actually...in a way. She came in for her evening shift as usual. I asked her what she thought about the murder, and she didn't know what I was talking about. She said she hadn't heard. I told her that it had happened over the long weekend. Too busy with her mum, I guess. I teased her about that, I tell ya. Told her that if it had been the end of the world, God would have to send a telegram to let her know. The murder happened right downstairs, ya know. Not here, of course, but over in Stratford where we had our offices then."

"And you say she worked before Thanksgiving?"

"Yes, the whole week."

"How could you possibly remember that?"

"I phoned her every evening she worked."

"What on earth for?"

"Carolyn was a Corrie fan. You know, *Coronation Street*, the British soap opera. If she was on evening shift, she'd miss the telecast. So I phoned to let her know what had happened."

"When's the telecast?"

"Six-thirty."

"So you called her at seven or so."

"No, not until a little after eight. I like to watch *The Price Is Right* and *Jeopardy*. I always called after they were over. Not much on TV after that, just cop shows. Besides, that's halfway through her shift. She always liked to take a little break...grab a bite of lunch then."

"You're absolutely sure of the time."

"Like clockwork."

"How did the office staff react to the murder of Simone Villier?"

"Everyone was concerned because it happened so close to home. The office was all abuzz with gossip."

"Had anyone in your office been close to Simone?"

"Not that I knew, but on PEI you're only a step or two away from knowing someone who knows anyone else."

"Was there gossip about Simone?"

"A bit. She was flashier than most of the girls in our office and, where there's flash, there's fire, they say. She was pretty, and she flirted. That might have drawn out a few talons, but our staff and Tidewater's never really mixed. In spite of that, everyone was relieved when that crazy homeless man was arrested. He was unpredictable. He would shout crazy things at people on the street. Throw things. The girls were scared of him."

"And Carolyn? How did she react to all this?"

"She felt sorry for the poor girl, of course. She was the compassionate sort. Later, though, after it had sunk in, it must have hit her harder, that and her troubles at home, because she took a few more days off before she returned to work...and a few days after that, her car went off the road."

22.

The empty board room displayed an impressive view of the city on two sides. It was a long room, carpeted. Dark cherry wood panels covered a third wall and a large rear-projection screen dominated the fourth. A security guard unlocked the door, flipped several switches. The soft drone of fluorescent lights broke the stillness. Another switch illuminated the screen. The guard stepped aside and made way for the fifteen or twenty suits and skirts which arrived for the scheduled ministers' meeting. The ministers took their places at the table, and the stenographers and assistants filled the rows of plush chairs behind them along the wall. The initial flood of chatter quickly settled into a blend of subdued murmurs and quiet laughter. A few just stared reflectively into the empty projection screen.

The chime of a cell phone drew attention and silent disapproval to the man in the navy blue sport coat at the table. Others surreptitiously fingered the off button on their phones before the premier arrived.

"I've got to take this," he said to the Fisheries Minister, a handsome woman in her mid-thirties, and removed himself to a nearby ante-room. He locked the door behind him. "This is a bad time. What is it?"

"A private investigator is snooping around."

He recognized the voice. It belonged to Chief MacFarlane.

"Is this a concern?"

"She's been digging into things she shouldn't be. She has the case file, and she's working her way through witnesses."

"Why are you calling me?" His tone shifted from agitation to anger.

"You have as much to lose as I do."

"As I see it, the road doesn't go that far."

"Nice choice of words, my friend. Maybe you should do some reflection."

"Can't you handle it? I can't get involved in such things!"

"And I can only do so much. Some help from your corner would ease the situation. She's getting a boost from Ben Solomon."

"How far along is she?"

"She's not there yet, but she's beginning to put two and two together. By then it will be too late for the usual nudging. Listen to me. I'm trying to avoid drastic measures here, but it's coming to that if we can't stop her. You know what that means, don't you."

It was not a question. It was the illumination of a fact, and it held strength enough to quell the unease that churned inside him and to replace it with a grudging conciliation.

"I'll see what I can do."

23.

Anne finished the supper dishes and settled Jacqui into her studies. By then it had grown dark, but she still had one more task to complete—her interview with Bernadette Villier, Simone's mother.

Each time Anne drove across the Hillsborough Bridge, her eyes were drawn downriver. Each time, the view was a pleasant surprise, like a new painting on a living-room wall. This evening was no different. An oil tanker, moored to concrete piers in mid-channel, was awash with deck lights. Farther away and closer to the harbour mouth, a few white sails near the yacht club tacked in the gentle drafts. Splotches of light marked the Charlottetown skyline. Old groves of trees masked the light on the Stratford side of the bay.

Anne turned right onto a winding road. It branched off into darker streets, one of which led to the Meriwether subdivision.

Bernadette lived there in a small, neatly kept, older residence with a covered front porch. Her home sat on an oversized lot. That made her house look smaller. Luxurious, newly built split-level homes surrounded it, and they made it look out of place.

Anne pulled to the curb in front of Bernadette's house. On the corner, a red fox, stoic and attentive, watched her. Then, startled by the halogen headlights of a car, the animal fled toward the creek and a golf course that bordered the rear of the property.

Anne mounted the stairs to Bernadette's front porch and was about to knock when the door opened.

"Come in, dear," she said.

Bernadette was short and trim. She had clear grey eyes and a young complexion that brought doubt to any guess at her age, but she spoke with the crispness and plainness of older women in the country villages.

"Come in," she said again and led Anne down a short hallway to a living room off the kitchen and pointed her toward a pillowed chair. "Make yourself comfortable. Tea's near ready. Won't be a minute."

The living room was tidy and had the lemony scent of household cleaners and furniture polish. It was simply furnished. A sofa and chair framed a space in front of a brick fireplace. A china cabinet fronted a wall to the kitchen. A drop-leaf dining table and two padded straight chairs stood alongside another.

Anne didn't sit. Instead, she looked over the framed photos on the mantel over the fireplace. Staggered among the old black-and-whites and a sepia were two faded colour pictures of Bernadette and her husband. They looked happy. She was young and pretty. Her husband was sturdy and sandy-haired. His arm draped over her shoulder. One hand held a beer, and he mugged for the camera. A photo next to it showed Simone with her arm around a girlfriend. Another shot captured her alone on the pier at Rustico.

"That's Simone," said Bernadette, pushing through the door with a tray of tea and sugar cookies. "She had just turned fourteen."

"She looks older," said Anne.

"It's the curse that every young girl wishes for...and every mother dreads. When she was fourteen, she looked seventeen. When she was fifteen, she passed for twenty-one. The cookies are homemade. You must try one. You said on the phone that you wanted to talk about Simone?"

"I don't mean to dredge up troubling memories, but I'm investigating a case. A few of the details overlap Simone's death, and I thought you might be able to help me understand them."

"I'll help if I can. What would you like to know?"

"Well, first, can you tell me a little about Simone? What was she like?"

"I suppose the polite gossips in the community would call her 'a wild child'...and they wouldn't be far from the truth, I s'pose. But she comes to it honest enough. She took after my husband in some ways. Luc, my husband, god luv 'im, was a rebellious and independent young man. He was a carpenter from North Rustico; I was a farm girl from Kelly's Cross. He drank a bit. He got into trouble from time to time, but he wasn't a mean man, and he was exciting. Maybe that's what drew me to him. He worked hard, joked a lot, and most people liked him in spite of his faults."

"Was Simone well-liked, too?"

"When she was young, sure, but as she got older, she changed. We never had much, you see. That never bothered Luc and me, but Simone was different. I think we embarrassed her. Eventually she moved out. She wanted more than we could give her."

"More?"

"More money, more things."

"Did her boyfriend, Jamie, fill that need?"

"Jamie was handsome, and funny, and being a policeman he had a touch of glamour to him. But I couldn't see Simone waiting for a young cop to get her what she wanted. Now have a cookie, dear...and your tea's getting cold."

She poured Anne a second cup of tea, and Bernadette chatted blithely about her old life in Rustico with Luc. She recalled fond memories of community lobster boils, dancing at the Legion hall, buying fresh cod and herring at the wharf, and being cheered by the houses all lit with Christmas lights. Then she turned to sadder memories—Luc's fall through rotten planks in a roof he was reshingling, catching his neck on a ragged edge, and bleeding to death.

"Two tragedies within a few years must have been devastating. Did family and friends help you through it?"

"The community was good to me. Luc had no insurance, of course. But I was offered a job as bookkeeper in a local store. I was always clever with numbers. I got by. After Simone died, I moved to Stratford, a better job."

"I don't see a picture of Jamie and Simone together," Anne said, pointing to the mantelpiece.

Bernadette thought deeply for a moment, then looked baffled, and said, "I don't recall her having one."

"Have you kept in touch with Jamie since?"

"He took a place in the receiving line at Simone's wake and visited once or twice afterwards. That was about it. He never seemed comfortable, though, and we were never close. Everyone grieves differently, I s'pose. Anyway, he married a year or two later. Some Dutch girl from eastern PEI, but I hear they're split up now."

"From what I heard, Simone and Jamie had been heading in that direction. Sounded like they were planning a future together, marriage even."

"Newspapers played that up after her death. Don't know where they got it from."

"It wasn't true?"

"Can't say it was...or it wasn't."

"But you weren't convinced?"

"On the surface everything looked fine, but, call it mother's intuition or what, I think she may have had her eyes on someone else."

"Any idea who?"

"No."

"When Simone learned that she was pregnant, how did she react? Was she excited? Confused? Worried?"

Bernadette became silent. Rigid. Her face paled, and her eyes filled with tears.

"I'm sorry. I thought you knew."

After she left, Anne sat in her car for a few minutes and reflected on what had happened. Things had changed. Now there were two conflicting sides to the Jamie MacFarlane–Simone Villier love story: Jamie's romantic recollection of Simone as a textbook Cinderella, and Bernadette's suspicion that Simone was in the process of trading up.

Which could be trusted, she didn't know. MacFarlane was egotistical enough to fancy that Simone could only love him, but was he so egotistical that he missed any warning signs that she was cheating on him? Bernadette suspected her. Why wouldn't MacFarlane? For cops like him, attention to detail and suspicion go together like a pair of handcuffs.

Then, too, if MacFarlane suspected that Simone was playing around, how would he react? Dump her? Humiliate her? Hit her? And the other man? If there was one, what was his role in this drama?

MacFarlane's description of his relationship with Bernadette was skewed as well. He had depicted Bernadette as a lonely, distraught mother grieving for her daughter and husband almost to the point of alcoholism, but that wasn't the same Bernadette Anne had spoken with. That woman was resilient, stable, and self-reliant. Had MacFarlane deluded himself? Had he reinvented his self-image as a more generous and altruistic person than he had ever been? Or was he just lying?

Something else bothered Anne, too. Her reaction to Simone's pregnancy was surprising. Perhaps Bernadette didn't know her daughter as well as she thought.

A lot of questions, thought Anne, *not many answers.*

Anne started the car, turned around, and headed up the street. A breeze had come up and stirred a drift of leaves across her path. Another car turned up the avenue behind her. Its headlights illuminated a cold, bluish path ahead of it. She hated halogen lights. They were bright and glaring. Even in her rear-view mirror, they were distracting. She speeded up. So did the driver behind her.

Anne's hand reached up to flip the dim switch on her mirror at the same time as a large red fox darted in front of her. She slammed the brake pedal. Her car skidded and slid to a stop, but Anne's eyes locked on the glare in her rear-view mirror. She saw the cold blue lights of a car hurtle toward her. She heard the screech of its tires, and she braced for collision, but the other car stopped. Just inches from her bumper.

The driver, impatient or angry, slammed his gear shift in reverse, spun tires, and squealed backwards until he intersected a side street and roared away.

Anne's hands trembled. The fox had vanished into the night.

24.

Anne pulled into a no-parking space near her Victoria Row office building. It was early morning. The sun was low and carried little warmth. Dew dampened squares of grass along the street. The few cars parked overnight reflected the hysterical flash of red and blue lights from a Charlottetown police cruiser.

Mary Anne MacAdam was waiting at the curb.

"What happened?"

"I came in early to check last night's receipts and noticed your door ajar. I thought you might be up for a cup of coffee. I went upstairs, I pushed the door open, but you weren't there. Then I phoned the police...and you."

They reached the second floor. Inside were Constables Frieda Toombs and Jeremy Willis. They turned when they heard footsteps.

"I'm Billy Darby. This is my office. Whaddaya got?"

"A mess," said Constable Toombs with a sweep of her arm.

Anne looked at the overturned furniture and ransacked filing cabinets. She looked past them into her private office. It was the same there.

"What've you found?"

"There's tool marks on the front door and the door to the office inside," said Willis.

"...and more on the safe," said Toombs. "But their pry bar couldn't open it."

"Any ideas?"

"Most break and enters are drug-related."

"Well, that narrows it down to a few thousand suspects," said Anne. "What now?"

"We'll make some inquiries. There's a couple of security cameras in the area. Maybe we'll get lucky. For now, we need you to check what's here...and what isn't. Make a list. The sooner we get it the better."

The police left. Anne walked into her office, stood by the window as the police car pulled away, turned around and stared back at the trail of debris leading back toward the front door. She felt like hitting something. Anger welled up, and like a passing wave, it sank into dejection. Mary Anne rested a hand on Anne's shoulder.

"Come down for a coffee. You can deal with this later," she said.

"I'll be there in a bit," Anne replied.

Anne heard a scrape against the fractured doorjamb as Mary Anne closed it behind her. By then, the anger had diminished. The dejection had dissipated, and Anne began her clean-up in the reception area.

Chaos, she thought. *Friggin' chaos.*

The filing cabinet and her desk had been ransacked. Notes, memos, invoices, notices, manuals, bills, directories, and magazines littered the floor. Cabinet drawers dangled open, and the contents had been strewn about. Knick-knacks had been swept off tables and desktops. The more fragile ones were broken. The bulb in a lamp had shattered, and the shade had twisted.

The scene in her private office followed the same theme: overturned furniture, a shambles of paper from files, and damaged bric-a-brac, but it took less time to put back in order than the reception area. Anne went to the safe. It was a large floor safe, something that could have come out of an old payroll office. She noted the tool marks on the door. She spun the dial and entered the combination. The door swung open.

She reached for a file labelled "Carolyn Jollimore." It was intact, and Carolyn's last letter was inside, where Anne had last put it.

Mary Anne brought a fresh coffee to Anne's table in The Blue Peter and slipped a Danish on a small dish alongside it.

"How ya feeling now?"

"This helps a lot," said Anne taking a long sip. "Thanks."

The Blue Peter was empty except for the wait staff preparing lunch. Mary Anne had brought a coffee for herself and sat down across from Anne.

"Anything missing?" she asked.

"Don't think so."

"Well, that's a relief."

"It is, and it isn't."

"I don't follow."

"If it were druggies, like the cops say, something would be gone... computer...something. I'm not sure I buy that story. First of all, an upstairs office like mine isn't an ideal target. What's to steal in an office? No cash, no jewellery, no guns. No fancy electronics."

"I suppose."

"They'd make a better score here," said Anne with a sweep of her arm. "A quick smash and grab. Most places leave a little float of cash in the till. Take that, grab a ham sandwich from the kitchen, a sackful of cigarettes, and an armload of liquor from behind the bar, and they could be out of here in a couple of minutes."

"Great idea but, please, don't spread it around. Keep it between yourself and your closest friend. That would be me, by the way."

"A drug-related B and E just doesn't seem right..."

"...unless they're complete dough-heads," said Mary Anne, "...and that's not unheard of."

"But there was something else, too," said Anne. "The place was trashed."

"So?"

"Why trash a place?"

"If you're a lunatic, or a drunken kid on a rampage...then, yeah..."

"That would be chaos then," said Anne thoughtfully.

"You're losin' me now. This is only my second cup of the day."

"Madmen or drunks are chaotic."

"We're still on different floors, girl."

"There's no order in chaos. It's random."

Mary Anne looked blank.

"Let me explain. When I straightened the reception area, everything was everywhere. It was a job to sort. It was the same in my office *except* for the contents of my desk. Sure, the files, papers, invoices were dumped. So were the drawers. But when I began to put things back, I noticed that they were, for the most part, all together."

"The caffeine still hasn't kicked in, girl."

"Don't you see? The only place where I found a pattern in either room was at my desk. If I reconstructed how the intruder would have created that same exact pattern, only one scenario makes sense: they opened the top drawer, removed the contents, and tossed them on the floor. They did the same with the middle drawer and dropped those papers on top of the others. The bottom drawer was next. Its contents were on top."

"I get it, but it seems like a stretch."

"The last thing they did was pull out the drawers. The drawers were tossed on top of the papers that had been inside them. To remove the desk drawer, however, means releasing a catch. That would have had to have been a deliberate decision and an extra step...unnecessary... unless somebody was doing a detailed search of my desk for some-thing...and that's what I think happened...and I think the rest of the place was trashed afterward...for window dressing...to cover up their real purpose."

"So, who would do something like that?"

"I have an idea. I just don't know why."

25.

Jamie MacFarlane wore sneakers, blue gym pants, and a zipped-up matching jacket when he left his Stratford home. He drove across the Hillsborough Bridge toward Charlottetown. Early-morning traffic had thinned. The day had brightened. His mood was sour.

He turned up Riverside Drive, exited at the first roundabout, and turned into a long, little-used, dirt lane that led some distance behind an old warehouse.

MacFarlane pulled over and stopped. An empty road stretched a few hundred yards ahead and behind. The warehouse on his left threw a great shadow. A berm, topped with brush and stunted trees, extended along his right.

Beyond the berm and out of sight lay the oval track of the Charlottetown Driving Park. A dozen stables stood at one end. Horses whinnied and hooves beat rhythmically on the turf. Sounds carried in the autumn air. So did the smell of manure. MacFarlane rolled up the window, lit a cigarette, and checked his watch. It was nine-thirty.

MacFarlane's eyes fixed expectantly on the road ahead. As he did, a memory of last night flashed across his mind. The rear of Anne Brown's car loomed in his windshield. He flinched involuntarily, and he felt a rush of panic just as he did when he had been tailing her.

The devil was in the details, he thought. He speculated on what Bernadette may have told Anne. And what small confidences Simone may have told her mother so many years ago. At the very least, Anne would come away with an impression of Bernadette quite different from the one he had painted in her office.

MacFarlane's contemplation fell apart when his eyes registered the movement of a car turning onto the dirt road ahead. It was a shiny blue Camaro. It fishtailed on the damp clay, steadied up, roared ahead, and stopped abruptly, window to window, alongside his.

Windows rolled down.

The driver of the Camaro was Michael Underhay. Most people called him "Cutter."

Cutter operated a bar and headed a local biker gang. Thefts and drugs had been his special criminal interest, but recently he had ventured into racketeering with regional gangs. MacFarlane had arrested Cutter in the past. In recent years, though, the two had developed a convenient arrangement. MacFarlane turned a blind eye to many of Cutter's under-the-radar Stratford activities in return for

Cutter dropping information on competitors and others, especially those who became high-profile and newsworthy in his jurisdiction. As a result, the arrest record of Stratford Police Department looked good, crime was down, and local voters and town councillors remained content.

"You got the letter?" MacFarlane asked.

"No," said Cutter.

"No?" MacFarlane's face was reddening.

"You need a hearing aid, old man?" Cutter grinned. His smile flashed a broken tooth and revealed drooping facial muscles, damaged in a severe prison beating.

"You stupid sonofabitch, I even told you where it was."

"It wasn't there. They couldn't find it." The grin faded. His tone chilled.

"They? Who's they? Weren't you there? I told you it was important. That's why I wanted you to handle it personally, not some stoned flunky."

"You think I'm going to stick my neck out for you? Or anybody? My lawyer advises against it. Says it's likely to cut into my leisure time."

"Don't get wise with me. It had to be there. I saw it there."

"It wasn't there," Cutter snarled. "They knew what they had to do, and they did it. Like I said...there was nothing there."

"Why should I believe you?!"

Cutter's rage finally burst through.

"I've got nothing to gain by holding out. If I could screw that Darby bitch, I'd do it in a heartbeat. She cost me thousands after that run-in last year...thousands! And a couple of my boys are still doing time. Nothin' would make me happier than dancin' on her grave and pissin' on her tombstone."

Cutter fell into a silence. When his rancour abated, he continued: "I did what you wanted. And I don't work for nothin'. So, we still got a deal?"

MacFarlane's first urge was to reach out, grab Cutter's windpipe in his hands, and crush it, but he had seen too many first urges land people in penitentiary cells. He relished his violent image for a moment more. Then he nodded slowly.

"That evidence will disappear?"

"It won't disappear. I can't make that happen, but it will be compromised. It won't be admissible at trial. The case will fall apart. The problem will go away...and as for your problem with Anne Brown... I may have a way to solve that, too. I'll let you know."

26.

Anne stood by the elevator at the Jones building, a cup of coffee in her hand. She pressed the button for Ben's office on the fourth floor.

The unexpected start to the morning had thrown her off—breakfast skipped, morning run cancelled, and office trashed. The coffee at Mary Anne's had worn off, and she had needed another, one with more bite. She gripped the second coffee lightly. It was large, still hot. Double sugar, double cream.

She took a guarded sip and stared at the lit elevator button. Then she stared at the coffee and felt a twinge of guilt. So she turned and headed toward the door to the fire stairs.

Just as Anne reached for the handle, the door burst open. It struck Anne hard. The momentum drove her back. She staggered, lost her footing, and tumbled across the floor.

When Anne recovered, she found herself slouched against the corridor wall, still gripping the coffee cup, but most of the contents had spilled, some dripping down the wall, much of it pooling beneath her. She felt the sticky, warm liquid soak through her slacks and sensed the sting from a burn on her hand.

The man who had flown through the door halted abruptly. He looked stunned and then embarrassed.

"You clumsy idiot! What the hell are you doing?" said Anne.

"I'm terribly sorry."

The voice belonged to a well-dressed man in his forties. He wore a grey tailored Italian suit and carried a black leather briefcase.

"It was my fault," he said.

"Ya think?" said Anne. "I'm a mess!" she said looking at herself.

She shook her arm. Her sodden sweater sprayed a line of coffee toward his dress shoes. He backed up guardedly. Then he stepped forward and extended a hand to help her up.

Anne ignored him and lifted herself from the floor. She moved toward the stairwell door, but the tiled floor was wet. She slipped, lurched forward, clutched his still outstretched arm, and fell headlong into his chest. His arms closed tightly around her. Her head buried itself in the scent of a freshly pressed shirt and a pleasant cologne.

She pulled away in embarrassment.

"Thanks."

"Not at all. It was entirely my fault...trying to get someplace unimportant too quick."

"Now I've ruined your jacket," she said pointing to his sleeve, stained with coffee from her sweater.

"Nothing to be concerned about. I'm clearly the cause of my own misfortune...and yours. Again, my apologies. My name is Fenton."

"Anne."

"Do you work in the building?"

"I'm visiting a friend."

"Well, if your friend isn't offering lunch, then perhaps I could persuade you to join me...as a way of my making amends...or supper, if you prefer."

"And how would your wife feel about that?" asked Anne pointing to his wedding ring.

"I'm sure she could be convinced of the harmlessness of it."

"I'd bet that even my teenage daughter would raise her eyebrows at that suggestion."

"You're married?"

"A widow. Thanks for the offer, though, harmless...or otherwise."

"I understand. Still, I can't let you go without redeeming myself in some way. Let me at least cover your dry-cleaning costs."

"No. I'll just toss these in the wash."

"Surely not the sweater," he said and quickly pulled several bills from his pocket. He pressed them into her hand. "I insist," he added, "and perhaps if we meet again, it will be under more pleasant circumstances."

Then he turned and rushed off before Anne could object.

Anne watched him disappear through a door. Then she trudged up four flights and poked her head through Ben's open doorway.

"Hey," she said as she walked in.

Ben smiled at the sound of her voice and finished signing a letter. Then he looked up. His smile drooped.

"What happened? You've sure gone to hell since I last saw you."

"Yep. Just got back. They were askin' about you."

Ben laughed and wagged a finger at her.

"You're sharp this morning...for a person that looks like they've been dumpster-diving."

"I was up early. My office was ransacked."

Anne dropped into a deep comfortable chair facing Ben's desk and curled up on the seat. She looked washed out and suddenly felt rather tired.

Ben's smile faded into attentiveness. He leaned forward.

"Tell me about it."

She shrugged. "Police think it was a drug-related B and E."

"And you?"

"I think it was something else."

Anne described how she had found the office, and she explained the inconsistencies that made her doubt the police explanation.

"And you think someone was looking for the letter?"

"That's the only conclusion I could draw from the pattern of litter near my desk."

"Who knew it was there?"

"Only two people. Gwen Fowler and Chief MacFarlane."

"Not the usual suspects," said Ben.

"Well, we can rule out Gwen. She has no connections to anything. MacFarlane, however, is beginning to smell a bit."

"I'd tread carefully before I turned over that rock."

"You sayin' I should leave him alone?"

Ben noted an all-too-familiar edge creep into her voice. It had always reminded him of the low growl a terrier makes before it snaps at your finger. It brought a smile to his mind, but he managed to stifle it before it slipped onto his face.

"I'm sayin' follow the evidence before you get bit by whatever might be under that rock. He may be a small-town police chief, but he has a lot of influence. By the way…"

"Ben, we need to meet," a voice interrupted. "I need some input on that staffing report I sent you." The man who poked his head into Ben's office wore a red and grey silk tie and grey trousers. His grin forced its way through an impatient expression, and it took a few moments for him to notice an elbow on the armrest of the chair in front of Ben's desk.

"Didn't know you had company."

"That's quite all right. I'd like to introduce someone, if you have a second. Mr. Peale, this Anne Brown. Anne, Fenton Peale, Minister of Justice…my boss."

Anne craned her head around the back of the chair and said, "Good morning again, Fenton."

"Anne?" He said with surprise.

"You two know each other?" asked Ben.

"We met over coffee," said Anne.

"Anne runs Darby Investigations and Security in Charlottetown. She's a private investigator."

Peale looked suddenly confused and said, "Yes, I believe I saw the name on an application for renewal of her license. Nice to see you, Anne."

"You, too. I'm sure we'll bump into each other again."

"Ten minutes, Ben?"

Ben nodded. Peale disappeared, his footsteps clicking down the hallway toward his office.

"Guess I have to get back to work. So what's your beef with Mac-Farlane?"

"A number of loose ends. First of all, he was Simone Villier's boyfriend. She was murdered, and he wound up arresting the man who would be convicted of her murder. He's too close to everything."

"Was he a suspect?"

"He was interviewed. His alibi held up, apparently."

"Anything else?"

"Sam Best, another Stratford officer, interviewed Carolyn Jollimore. But Carolyn lied to him about being in the office at the time of the murder. A co-worker is quite clear about talking to her on the phone on the evening of Simone's murder. Carolyn was at work when she made the call. A week later Carolyn was dead."

"...and Carolyn said that she couldn't go to the police about the murder."

"Right. It's also occurred to me that the only connection between the two deaths is that letter. We have photocopies, but they can't be introduced in court. The only real piece of evidence is the original."

"So you think he killed both women?"

"That's my guess."

"Motive?"

"Not yet, but solve the first murder and the second is a slam-dunk."

"Just be careful, and don't stick your neck out, okay? And by the way, before I forget... John Dawson is out of prison."

27.

The Charlottetown Police had no current address on John Dawson. In fact, they had no knowledge of his release—at least that's what they claimed. The Parole Office was reluctant to release personal information, but they agreed to pass on any information to him if he should glide into their radar. Anne left her card.

The halfway house for Queens County was in Charlottetown. It had been a large residential home in the twenties. It was in good repair, large enough to accommodate at least half a dozen clients, most of them parolees with a lingering taste for alcohol, amphetamines, and popular drug cocktails. Three of them were sitting in wicker chairs in the shade of the front veranda when Anne pulled into an empty parking space. The veranda faced a busy street. A table had been set between them, and they passed the time by watching the stream of city cars, moving the pieces on their checkerboard, and blustering about grandiose plans for the future.

The bluster sank into a surprised silence as Anne strode up the pavement toward the steps to the halfway house. Parole officers, medical staff, counsellors, ministers, and relatives often dropped in. Of course, most of those who visited did so only out of professional necessity or some guilt-fuelled compassion. Even the pizza delivery man sported a strained grin when he balanced his blanketed trays at the front door. Those passing on the street avoided eye contact. For the average person, a visit to a halfway house would have been tantamount to visiting a lepers' colony. So the sight of an attractive young woman with no briefcase walking toward them with a bright smile on her face was not only unexpected and startling, it was also disarming.

"Hi, guys. Who's winning?" she asked, looking down at the checkerboard.

"I believe Tipper has the edge in this game," said Pun'kin.

Pun'kin had an enormous head, and the unruly shocks of orange hair that covered it made it look even larger. *It looks like a pumpkin on a fencepost*, a boyhood friend had once said, and the nickname stuck. Anne had never met Pun'kin, but she recognized him from the streets of Charlottetown. He had been a drunk, a petty thief, and a brawler. Tipper, on the other hand, had run over his dealer half a dozen years ago because the pouch of drugs he had bought contained more filler than fun. It was an "accident," Tipper had claimed, but he served time for vehicular manslaughter anyway.

Anne didn't recognize the third man. He moved a checker thoughtfully, but it was promptly taken by Tipper. Then Tipper took two more pieces. The third man just chuckled.

"Maybe you should get a student loan for checkers college?" Anne said.

He chuckled again.

"Barry's an accountant," said Tipper.

"For real?" asked Anne. Barry nodded.

"Do you work here?"

Then Tipper and Barry laughed. Pun'kin bent over in his chair. Both hands supported his laughing convulsive head, and from Anne's perspective it looked as if he were gripping a bowling ball.

"I didn't think white-collar criminals did real jail time anymore. What was so special about you?" said Anne.

"I specialized in estate management for seniors and took care of the accounting for a big retirement villa. Gambling took hold of me—casino roulette, poker, online and off, sports lines, slots, pretty well anything and everything. I lost it all. It wasn't pretty."

"Shoulda got your MBA instead. Look guys, I'm trying to get in touch with John Dawson. Maybe you know him? I hear that he's out, but those who know aren't too anxious for me and him to link up. Any ideas?"

"He's not here, if that's what you're askin'," said Pun'kin.

"Dorchester?" asked Tipper.

"Yeah."

"I recall the name. Never met him, though. He'd been shipped to Nova Scotia. Some minimum security facility. That's all I know."

"Thanks and good luck, guys."

"Don't ya know some cop or politician that can help ya find him?" shouted Pun'kin.

Anne waved her thanks without looking back.

28.

J. Dawson lived off Mt. Edward Road in Charlottetown's north end. It was a respectable neighbourhood. Houses were spacious and well-maintained, and mature hardwoods shaded adjacent streets and muffled the traffic from nearby thoroughfares. It had taken Ben less than a minute to peg the location of John Dawson and to send a copy of his release document to Anne's iPhone. She read it quickly. Then she picked up a copy of Dawson's mug shot from a folder on the front seat of her car.

The photo showed a scruffy character with hair matted in long, thick clumps. His mouth gaped through puffy lips. His eyes seemed vacant. If he had not been standing for the shot, Dawson's features could have been that of a corpse. Add shabby, stained clothes, impulsive behaviours, and the stench of a homeless drunk, and Anne could well understand why Davidia Christian, Carolyn's friend, and her co-workers might have been frightened by him. Anne shuddered.

Twenty-eight Joiner's Street was a small boarding house. Anne rang the doorbell. Irene MacLeod, the proprietor, opened the front door. Irene was an elderly woman with sagging jowls and a weathered face. She took one limping step toward Anne and peered closely at her through weak eyes.

"I'm looking for John Dawson," said Anne. "Is he in?"

"No one here by that name," said Irene. In spite of a vaguely polite smile, Anne read suspicion in her eyes. Anne pointed to the bank of mail slots in the foyer next to her.

"Says J. Dawson on the letterbox."

"That belongs to Jacob Dawson."

"Is he in, then?"

"He doesn't receive visitors."

"He'll see me."

"And who are you?"

"Billy Darby. I'm an investigator."

"Do you have identification?"

Anne produced her license.

"You're a *private* investigator." Irene sounded as if she had just smelled the stench in something vile. "No, I'm sorry, but you'll have to leave."

Irene started to close the door, but Anne blocked it.

"Maybe we could come to an understanding. Tell him who I am, and tell him that I have some information which will very much pique his interest. If he's still not interested in speaking with me, then I won't bother him anymore. Just tell him that, please, if you will."

Irene MacLeod said nothing. She left Anne waiting in the foyer and went up the stairs with a slow limping ascent. Anne heard knocking. Inaudible words were exchanged. Then Irene descended even more wobbly, a hand and forearm tightly gripping the banister, and motioned her toward a nearby reading room.

Anne waited five minutes, picked up a magazine, and was working her way through the vocabulary quiz on carnival slang when she sensed a presence. She looked up and gave a start. She had heard nothing, and suddenly he was beside her.

"Good afternoon," he said.

"John Dawson?" she asked.

"Jacob, he replied. "John Jacob Dawson. I don't go by John anymore... for obvious reasons."

"I'm Billy Darby. I'm a private investigator, and I'm working a case which dovetails with your arrest. I came to discuss it with you, but I didn't think I'd get past your executive assistant."

"Irene is very protective. She got tapped by the cops in Ottawa back in the sixties. She had just got out of hospital and stopped to visit friends. Her friends were hosting other friends. They were smoking grass. She wasn't. As a matter of fact, she never did drugs. The cops busted in. Everyone was arrested. Her friends had parents with dough. She didn't. At the end of it, she spent a year in Kingston, and her friends skated."

"Tough luck. But times have changed since then. You've changed, too. Your mug shots don't do you justice."

The man who stood before Anne could have passed for a young professional. He was clean-shaven, fit, and displayed an alert and intelligent presence. Dawson wore jeans and an unbuttoned sports coat over a T-shirt. A small gold cross on a gold chain hung from his neck. He had brown hair, trimmed and loosely combed back. Only flecks of grey and a weathered face suggested the hard use of his past.

"Never saw them myself...and never wanted to...but I can imagine. I was a different person then."

"How so?"

"First, what do you have for me? Irene mentioned some...information?"

Anne explained the letter that Carolyn Jollimore had sent. She told of its misdelivery, her recovery of it eleven years after its posting, and that Carolyn had died shortly after writing the note.

Dawson listened thoughtfully, then asked: "Did it suggest any more about the killer?"

"No, it didn't," said Anne, "but Carolyn's death in a car accident and your conviction shortly after seem curious. My client asked me to follow up. That's why I'm here."

"So you're not looking at my case per se."

"No, but there seems a connection. I'd like to find out. So I'll get right to the point. Did you murder Simone Villier?"

Dawson seemed to wilt as he sat in the chair across from Anne. His eyes buried themselves in a corner of the past, and his mind followed.

"You've got nothing to lose by telling the truth now. You were convicted and did your time," said Anne.

Anne waited patiently. Long moments elapsed before Dawson returned to the starkness of her question. He looked up, his mouth trembling faintly.

"I don't know," he said. "I just don't know."

"Then...why don't you start by telling me about your life at that time? Maybe we can pull some things together. Where are you from?"

"Down east. Georgetown."

"Parents?"

"Dad was a trucker when he was sober, which wasn't often. He lost his driver's license, abandoned us, and headed for Winnipeg. He sent money a few times. Then that stopped...last we heard from him."

"We?"

"My mom and my brother and sisters. Mom was a moody person... couldn't hold a steady job. Everyone thought she was a bit odd...and I suppose she was...but, when you're fourteen or sixteen, that can be pretty embarrassing. Welfare took us after Mom killed herself. Then they broke us up and sent us to foster homes."

"That must have been difficult."

"For a long time I felt bad about her suicide. I was the oldest of the kids. I always wondered that, maybe if I could have stepped up a bit more, she wouldn't have done it." He disappeared again into his past for a few seconds. Then he continued on.

"The day I turned sixteen, I took off. I got tired of bein' the cheap labour on somebody's boat. So I headed for Charlottetown, got a few odd jobs, lived with friends, and started drinkin'...like father like son, eh? After that, everything spiralled out of control. The more I drank, the fewer friends I had, and the more I felt sorry for myself. So I drank even more and, when the kick from that didn't work, I started on cocaine."

"Expensive habits," said Anne.

"And there's no such thing as a free lunch," he said. "So I panhandled, shoplifted, broke into stores and houses. I was so strung out on whatever was on the go that I can't remember a lot of what I did. Strangely enough, I never got busted for the drugs or burglaries. Police took me to detox a number of times, but that was usually the result of disturbing the peace, scuffles with other drunks, or urinating in public. Stuff like that."

"Were you ever violent? Any fights?"

"Push and shove stuff...drunk on drunk...that's about it."

"You were arrested at Stratford supermarket for theft, destruction of private property, assaulting a police officer, and resisting arrest."

"That's what they say. I don't remember."

"Drunk? Stoned?"

"Probably. I had started having blackouts by then. My world turned strange. Sometimes I saw things. I was pretty out of it."

"What do you remember about your arrest?"

"I remember the psych ward more than the arrest. I was there for a day or so. Then I was sent to detox. After that, it was jail, where they grilled me for hours and hours on end. They told me they had evidence that I murdered some girl. I said I couldn't remember doing anything like that, but they kept at me. Funny...as jammed up as I was, all I could think about was getting another bottle. Eventually, I was charged with murder. My lawyer, court-appointed, suggested that I elect a trial by judge alone. Apparently, the press had launched a hate campaign against me and the other street bums. Public sentiment was running high, and he worried about a jury trial. Later the charge was amended to manslaughter."

"Why manslaughter? They had the murder weapon...they found her jewellery in your pocket."

"They couldn't find my prints on the murder weapon or anywhere else in the office."

"Then how did they connect you to the crime scene?"

"That office building is near the bridge I slept under. Sometimes I panhandled in front of it. That was no secret. So perhaps I was there that day."

"Anything else?"

"As I said, the interrogation was relentless. Cops must have gone over the details of the murder a hundred times or more, so often that I could picture it happening and..."

Dawson stopped mid-sentence. It seemed as if the words were choking him. Then he burst out, "... I may have admitted that it was *possible* I hit her."

29.

When the bell rang, doors burst open, seven hundred students spilled out, and the roar of them filled the corridors like a thunderstorm floods gullies. Students jostled and streamed toward half a dozen exits, in spite of the admonitions of their teachers trying to negotiate safe passage to their lounge.

Only a fifteen-minute break separated the two afternoon classes. Locker doors banged and rattled. Books thudded as they were hurled inside. Locks clacked. Mobile phones lit up. Then, quickly as it had begun, the rush abated. The hallways began to thin out and the remaining students clustered in small pools of laughter and chatter. Some pumped change into vending machines. Others found their customary refuge outside the school and lit up. Jacqui grabbed a juice pack, jabbed a straw into it, and waited until she saw Rada.

"Guess what?" she asked, and not waiting for a response added, "I'm babysitting Saturday night. Madame Desjardins'. You want to keep me company?"

Rada brightened. "Of course...but I have to ask permission. What time?"

"Seven-thirty until twelve...twelve-thirty."

A doubt clouded Rada's face and she asked, "Will Madame Desjardins allow me?"

"She won't mind. I'm sure of it. I could stop at your house, and we could walk over...and I could walk you home after, so your mother needn't worry. Okay?"

"Okay."

"We'll talk later," said Jacqui. "I have to meet someone in the library."

Jacqui smiled to herself as she grasped the door to the library. She had a plan, she thought, a marvellous plan. The hardest part was in place. The second piece sat at a computer terminal and looked intently at the screen.

Bobby Fogarty was researching an essay on whether or not visualizing a sports performance was a valid method of practice. Actually, the idea for it had come from Jacqui. He had been grumbling about how poorly he had played in the soccer game against Souris. He was feeling sorry for himself. Jacqui chastised him at the time, saying "Do you think Pelé or Beckham wallow in some woe-is-me mood like you're doing? Of course not. They keep running perfect moves in their head until their bodies finally get the message."

Jacqui's comment stuck in Bobby's head but, actually, Jacqui's idea had come from her mother. Anne had been an athlete, too, something Anne's own mother, Hazel Darby, had hoped would never, ever happen.

Anne had been a late addition to the family of Frederick and Hazel Darby. One miscarriage was followed by the birth of their son, Richard. He succumbed to crib death. Hazel's third pregnancy and second successful birth ten years later was a surprise. Hazel always referred to Anne as her "miracle child." As a result of her tragedies, Hazel became an overprotective mother, something Anne struggled against for years.

Eventually Hazel began to mellow. She still forbade Anne's involvement in rugby or hockey, but she allowed Anne to try out for soccer, secretly believing that she was too small to make the team. However, Anne had speed, stamina, and determination. That impressed the coach and won her a spot on the team. Anne knew that her size was a handicap. As a result, she developed an ability to read the fluidity of the playing field.

"It's like being a quarterback on the football field," Anne once told Jacqui. "If you don't want to get creamed, then learn to read the moves. Uncle Bill told me the same thing when he was a cop: every time someone approached him on the job, he'd anticipate every nasty little thing they might try, and he'd picture what he could do in response. If you practise reactions in your head enough times, you won't have to think when something happens. You'll act automatically."

"Bobby!"

Fogarty jumped in his seat. His arm jerked as he turned. A notebook and pencil toppled to the floor.

"Geez, Jacqui...you scared hell out of me."

"Jacqueline," she corrected.

"Right... Jacqueline. What's up?"

"Happy birthday!"

"It's not until Saturday."

"I know that...but I'm babysitting on Saturday. So I won't be able to swing by for that birthday cake your mother's making."

"How do you know she's making a cake?"

"She made one last year. It was delicious. Vanilla. Homemade. And she cut up little chunks of fresh peaches and baked them inside. Creamy lemony icing! Yum!"

"You aren't coming over, then?"

"'Fraid not. And I won't be able to give you your present until Monday, I guess…"

"You got me a present?" Fogarty seemed disappointed and surprised.

"I did. It reminds me so much of you."

"What is it?"

"Can't tell you before your birthday, can I? But, if you have no other plans, you could come over to Madame Desjardins' Saturday night, keep me company, and I could give it to you then."

"I could do that," said Fogarty. He seemed intrigued.

"Oh, by the way, is Sig coming to your get-together?"

"I think so."

"Bring him along, too." Bobby leaned back in his seat and looked at her suspiciously.

"Why him? Three's a crowd, isn't it?"

"Ordinarily, but it won't be in this case. Please…unless of course you're jealous of Sig…"

"I'm not jealous of him," he said, squirmed in his chair, and reached down to pick up his notes and pencil.

"Remember. Special birthday present. Saturday only. Private viewing."

Fogarty's eyes brightened.

"Yeah, okay. I'll see you there."

"With Sig?"

"With Sig," he said, but bewilderment swept over his face. The bell rang.

30.

Anne looked thoughtfully at Dawson. He avoided eye contact and slowly massaged one hand with the other. It seemed to soothe him. He looked at his wristwatch and massaged again.

"I shouldn't have said that," said Dawson. "...that 'I might have hit her.'"

"Why?" asked Anne.

"I don't believe it. I don't believe I killed her."

"You had serious mental and alcohol problems. You had blank spots. You can't be sure of your state of mind. What makes you think that?"

"Like I said, it's just a feeling."

"Something to hang on to anyway. I suppose you're lucky. It could very easily have gone the other way...first-degree murder and a life sentence...instead of ten to twenty."

Dawson loosed a hard glare. Muscles in his jaw flexed.

"Lucky? It's not the word I'd choose." Despite the lingering glare, his words were calm and controlled.

"How would you look at it?"

"How do I look at it? You're right, it could have been worse. But it wasn't luck. Luck would have been getting a full psych evaluation before the trial. Luck would have been having a lawyer with the resources and experience to prepare a solid defence. Luck would have been some grounds for appeal before the deadline."

"What I'm trying to say is that the judge must have seen the weaknesses in the case. And he did cut you a break. That counts for something, doesn't it?"

"It does...yes...it does."

"But you're still bitter."

"It comes and goes." Dawson reached up and clutched the crucifix on the chain around his neck. "This helps."

"How so?"

"We've got things in common. Christ was considered dangerous and a lunatic, and he got railroaded. So did I."

Anne let that thought sink in for a moment or two, but she wanted to keep Dawson calm and on track, so she moved the topic along.

"Would you feel comfortable filling me in on the last ten years, Jacob?"

"Sure. I guess. Where do I begin? Oh yes, it all started at Springhill Prison...spent a month-and-a-half at their Intake Assessment Unit. They dug around in my background...figured out I was a drunk and a druggie and a social misfit. Then I was shipped off to the Atlantic In-stitution...sounds like a college campus, doesn't it... That's the fancy name for a maximum security prison in Renous. A notorious place. I was there for two years. Then they decided I wasn't very dangerous or an escape risk. So they shipped me to Dorchester Pen. After five years in Dorchester, they thought I was turning into a real nice fellow and transferred me to the "farm" at Westmorland...a minimum-security facility. I was released three years later. That's the *Reader's Digest* version of my coming-of-age story."

Dawson looked at his watch, looked up at Anne, and smiled. She didn't return one.

"So you did ten years of a twenty-year sentence. The minimum. That's pretty impressive. They must have felt that you were rehabili-tated. How did that come about?"

The glibness and irony of Dawson's recollections suddenly fell away as he began talking about his addictions, and Anne sensed that she was drawing closer to the real John J. Dawson.

"As I said, I was a drunk and a junkie and a social outcast when I was young. At Renous, they had the results from my original intake assessment, and they had programs to help me get my head above water. A twelve-step program led me off the booze. Coincidentally, it also led me to Christ again. He had always been there...somewhere," he said pointing to his heart, "but I couldn't hear him anymore. Don't get me wrong, I didn't turn into a full-blown Bible-thumper...but it put me on a different road. Counselling helped, too."

"New heart, new eyes, new man," said Anne.

"Except that that's about the time I found out that I was crazy."

"How do you mean?"

"I had been a bit odd before my great plunge into the abyss, but after my addiction rehab I turned a bit strange again. I felt energized... thought I could conquer the world. Funny idea to have in prison, eh? I decided that I wanted to get an education. So I signed up for a GED. I got the books and dug into them. I was so excited I couldn't sleep. I couldn't sleep at all. I was sure I could complete the coursework in a week or two. Started preaching, too...at the same time...testifying in the yard...and proclaiming the Bible so everyone could hear it from my cell...saw myself as Christ's apostle in jail. I got thumped a few times for my trouble, but that just made me feel like a martyr. So I got beat up again and that landed me in the infirmary. Looking back, I guess I was driving everyone else crazy."

"How did you deal with that?"

"I didn't. I got pretty down about it. I felt like a loser…a fraud. I felt like my life had lost all meaning again. Then a nurse at the infirmary spoke to a doctor there. They checked me over and ran some tests. It turns out that I have bipolar."

"Did you get treatment?"

"Psychotherapy and drugs. It took a few months to get the right mix of meds, but I'm fairly stable now. After that, I kept up the education. I still read the Bible…to myself. It's a matter of balance, apparently."

"So you're on parole now?"

"I was released in Nova Scotia last year. Now I'm on full parole, but maybe that letter you have might lead to a statutory release." He glanced at his watch.

"Thanks, Jacob. I really appreciate your taking the time to talk with me. I won't keep you any longer. You obviously have an appointment."

"An evening class."

"For your GED."

"No, Sociology. I'm finishing my third year."

"University?"

"Yes," he grinned. "You can get through a lot of courses in ten years… with no place to go."

31.

Anne's visit and interview with John Dawson had been interesting to say the least, but it had not added anything to her arsenal of evidence against MacFarlane. *A smoking gun would be nice*, she thought. However, smoke drifts, especially after ten years. She had a pile of suspicions and not much else, at least nothing that would bring MacFarlane to his knees at trial. She figured that he was troubled with her snooping around, but if he kept a low profile, shut his mouth, and did nothing, he would ride out her digging about in the dust of the past.

Maybe it's time to kick the hornet's nest and see what pops, she thought.

She picked up the phone, hesitated, then put it down again. A surprise might be the better choice, she decided. Then she thought the better of it. She would need some leverage first. She picked up the phone a second time and called Mary Anne.

"Mary Anne, have you any information about Chief MacFarlane's ex? Know anyone who runs in her circle? I think her name is Lydia something."

"You came to the right store, hon. What do ya need?"

"I want to pump her for information about MacFarlane, and I may need some leverage if she's reluctant. Any deep dark secrets...things she'd like to hide?"

Mary Anne explained that before she opened The Blue Peter, she had been manager of a restaurant and lounge downtown. It was a popular place, and she had got to know most of the patrons, especially those who liked to party. Lydia Vandermeer had been one of them. Lydia was about twenty-one at the time. Beautiful, popular, talented, and pretty well-off. Her parents had been industrious farmers who immigrated to PEI and started a tobacco farm. They prospered, sold their farm to a corporate group, retired, and returned to the Netherlands, but Lydia remained on PEI. It's where she had gone to school and where her friends still lived.

"She married MacFarlane a few years after that," Mary Anne said. "They seemed a good match. At the time he was the 'golden boy,' so to speak. Old Chief Quigley had taken a heart attack, and MacFarlane stepped into his job. The publicity he received after the Villier murder made him high-profile, I guess. But I heard he had the backing from the deal-makers in town as well."

"I take it they didn't live happily ever after."

"No, MacFarlane had a wandering eye. He even flirted with me, and I was married at the time and a good deal older than the usual cupcake he nibbles on. Something about him, though. He always seemed like he was above it all. No fear. A turn-on for some, but not me. Anyway, Lydia comes home early from work and finds him in the sack with some young blonde. She was pissed...and hurt...and filed for divorce."

"How long had they been married?"

"I'd say about five years."

"Good to know, but she may still have some feeling for him."

"That ain't the half of it. She got her divorce and not much more."

"I thought property settlement was fifty-fifty on the Island. Like California."

"It is. She was in here a while back. We chatted about the old days, had a few glasses of wine, and she got 'round to her not-so-lovely love life. Turns out she's broke. Her husband had always handled the household finances, and it seems he managed to hide most of their assets. She never found out how or where or even when. He had some private business dealings, but he was vague about them. He must have been expecting this to happen for some time, though. It's not something you could pull off in a week or two. She even lost some prime waterfront land and a nest egg her parents had given her years ago."

"Sleazebag or what!"

"Tell me about it! Go see Lydia. Tell her I sent you. You won't need leverage."

32.

Jacqui had stuffed her bag of soccer gear in a closet and settled into homework by the time Anne arrived home. Anne hung up her jacket, sniffed at the gear bag.

"Beans and wieners and a salad," she shouted toward Jacqui's door. "I'm in a rush. That enough?"

"Fine," Jacqui hollered back.

"And that soccer bag smells. Did you put all your clothes in the wash?"

"I'll do it after supper, Mom."

"Don't forget."

Supper was on the table twenty minutes later. Jacqui was still in a studious and preoccupied state of mind. She wasn't really following her mother's recount of her day and broke into the middle of one of Anne's stories: "By the way, I'm babysitting Saturday. Madame Desjardins'. Won't be too late."

Anne was jarred, not by Jacqui's surprise notification, but because she had completely lost track of what she had been saying to Jacqui, and the dinner table fell quiet for the remainder of the meal. Then Jacqui casually broke the silence as if she had not noticed it: "By the way, it's Bobby's birthday Saturday. I can't go, but I have the perfect gift for him."

"I wanted to torch his car. Then I thought some firefighter might get hurt. So hiring a hit man crossed my mind, but that wouldn't have the same satisfaction as doing it yourself. I'm not too handy with guns. That's a man's solution. Women prefer poisons. Did you know that Catherine de Medici poisoned half a dozen former lovers and rivals? And there used to be schools in medieval Italy and France that taught the art of poisoning? It was quite the rage."

Anne grinned at Lydia Vandermeer. She was much of what Mary Anne had described: beautiful, charming, and clever. She had thin lips and a narrow nose. She had bright brown eyes and an enviable figure.

"I can't tell you how many scenarios I ran through my head after he screwed me over."

"Was it as bad as Mary Anne suggested?"

"Worse. He even maxed out the credit cards. He knew that our debts would be split as well as our assets. So he charged a lot of high-end items. Then he sold them at a discount to friends and pocketed the cash. Me, I was forced to cough up half. He even charged a luxury cruise to the Mediterranean, where he and his new trampy blonde girlfriend partied for a couple weeks. I had to bankroll half of that, too."

"Why did he go so far?"

"He wanted me to suck it up...and let him have his fun on the side. I wouldn't, and a divorce would smudge his public image, he said. Jamie had two sides: Mister Charm and Mister Bastard, and he was a vindictive bastard at that."

"Did he talk much about his time on the job before you married?"

"Some."

"What about Simone Villier?"

"He liked to talk about how he busted the guy that killed her. He got a lot of publicity from that. He got right puffed up whenever he had the chance to tell someone about it. I thought it was cute at the time. Now it just seems farcical."

"What about Simone?"

"Strangely, he never mentioned her, and if I brought her name up he got distant, quiet, and touchy. She wasn't a welcome topic."

"Didn't that seem odd? I'd heard they were engaged or about to be engaged...that it was getting serious."

"I'd heard that, too, from other people, but it wasn't something I was comfortable pressing him about, and, frankly, I wasn't that interested."

"Under the circumstances, it was fortunate the two of you never had children."

"To say the least! I always wanted children. It just wasn't in the cards. A good thing in hindsight."

"I've heard a lot of good things about fertility treatments and in vitro. You might want to explore those options the next time around. Jamie must have been disappointed."

"About what?"

"Not having kids."

"Why?"

"When I spoke with him a few days ago he seemed almost heartbroken about having lost his child."

"What are you talking about?

"His girlfriend, Simone Villier, was pregnant when she was murdered. It seemed to impact him quite strongly."

"She was pregnant?"

Anne nodded solemnly.

Lydia sat astonished for a moment, then her lips twitched. Her eyes crinkled in the corners. Anne expected her to burst into tears. Lydia, who obviously had difficulty conceiving, was now confronted with her own physical inadequacy. Lydia's hand reached up to cover her mouth, and she bent forward. A long high-pitched expulsion of air and sound escaped from her throat. It resonated like a howl of excruciating pain, and Anne's eyes widened with concern as Lydia's slender frame heaved uncontrollably.

"Oh my god!" cried Lydia. Anne's hand reached out to comfort her but fell away when she became aware that Lydia was convulsing, not with anguish, but with laughter. "Oh my god!" she repeated, and she repeated it again and again between gasping breaths and volleys of laughter.

Anne's confusion slipped into awkwardness and then into mortification as Lydia seemed unable to control herself.

"Was it something I said?" asked Anne, her cheek and throat turning crimson. Lydia's head nodded, her finger pointed toward Anne, and she went into another spasm.

Anne took several sips of the sweet, creamy herbal tea she had been served and tried to recover some dignity in the circumstances.

Lydia finally gathered some control and said, "Oh god, you're hilarious," but her face was still contorted from laughing and her eyes watered.

"I don't get it," said Anne, somewhat miffed.

"Sorry, Anne, but here's the thing: Jamie can't have kids. Never could."

"Are you sure?"

"Absolutely. He told me so. He had a severe case of mumps when he was a kid. Swelling in the groin affected reproduction. I was forever the optimist, though. I insisted that he see a doctor again…get a second opinion. I thought maybe it was reversible or something. It wasn't, and his sperm count was near zero."

"And you're so happy about this, why?"

"Sad to say, but his misery becomes my joy. And I've had so little to crow about lately. This makes up for the delay."

"How do you mean?"

"It means that somebody other than Jamie knocked up Simone Villier."

"That must have been a blow," said Anne.

"A proper kick in the nuts," said Lydia.

33.

The damp coolness of October struck Anne as soon as she stepped outside the little house Lydia Vandermeer rented in Pownal, a village fifteen minutes east of Charlottetown. She pulled onto the road and followed a dim meandering path toward the city. It was eleven o'clock. Hers was the only car on the road.

She looked toward the blackness of the shore and the greyness of the sea beyond and turned over Lydia's revelation in her mind. *A kick in the nuts*, she had said.

No doubt, thought Anne, but it could be more than that. It could have been the motive for Simone's murder. MacFarlane discovers that Simone is pregnant—perhaps she even told him. Simone wouldn't have known about MacFarlane's sterility. He knows he's not the father, becomes enraged at her infidelity, and kills her. Simone's mother had suspected that her daughter was cheating on MacFarlane.

On the other hand, maybe Simone's new lover had killed her. For what motive, we could only guess. Blackmail? The burden of child support? A wife? Social consequences of some sort?

Anne was drawn to suspecting MacFarlane much more than Mr. Anonymous. First, MacFarlane had a massive ego, and the thought of her dumping him would have been inconceivable. He may have overreacted, struck out, realized she was dead, and found someone like Dawson to blame. Second, MacFarlane had lied about the child being his from the get-go. Police had recorded his statement that she was pregnant in an early interview, and he had played that sympathy card with Anne when he dropped into her office to persuade her to drop the investigation. All deceptions. Intuitively, he kept that information from Lydia, who was smart enough to put two and two together. Third, he had frightened Carolyn Jollimore so badly that she lied about her proximity to the crime. Perhaps she had recognized him somehow.

Anne's cell phone buzzed. She glanced at the call display. It was a private number. The highway forked just ahead at the base of a hill. Anne pulled off at the junction onto a grassy area. As her wheels left the pavement, she felt the car dip to the right. The steering was sluggish and she noticed a wobble. She grabbed the cell phone just before the last ring would send it to voice mail.

"Who? Edna?" she said. "Wait a minute. I'm in the car...can't hear you...hold on."

Anne got out of her car and wandered about the grassy lot to find a stronger signal.

"How's this? Better? Good. What can I do for you? I can meet you first thing in the morning. An update? Of course. Where? Okay, I can be there."

Anne returned to her car. It was still running. The headlights cast enough illumination for her to see that the right rear tire was flat.

"Shit! Shit! Shit!" She stomped her foot with each invective she hurled.

It took a minute for her frustration to settle. *Ben would be asleep*, she thought. *A tow truck might take a couple of hours. To hell with it. I'll do it myself.*

Anne popped the trunk, located the spare. She thought it looked like a toy. The operator's manual was in the glove compartment. She sought it out. It would explain where to put the jack.

She was paging through the manual when high beams from an approaching vehicle enveloped her car. It had come from behind and stopped. She heard two creaky doors open. She looked back. She caught the outline of a pickup truck. Two figures emerged. They walked toward her, just silhouettes in the glare of the truck lights.

"Having trouble, missy?" said the larger silhouette.

"A flat," said Anne.

"Need help?"

"I could do it myself," said Anne, hesitantly, "but...if you're offering..."

"Say no more. Glad to be of service. Just stay right where you are, missy. We'll take care of it. I'm Buddy, this is Frank," said the bigger of the silhouettes.

Buddy was medium height and bulky with the lumbering gait of a truck driver. Frank was taller, younger, and more fluid in his movements, but Anne could not clearly make out either of them in the glare of their truck lights, and she was content to remain in her car while they worked.

Frank pulled the jack from under a flap in the trunk. The spare thumped as it hit the ground. Frank loosened the lug nuts as Buddy placed the jack under the frame and cranked. Anne felt the car slowly rise.

"Excuse me, do you have a cell phone?" asked Buddy. "I have to make a quick call to my woman," he said.

"Sure." Anne handed him the phone.

Buddy reached for the phone. He took it and slipped it into his jacket pocket.

"You won't be needing this for a while," he said. "Just stay right where you are...and you won't get hurt. Don't want this jacked-up car to drop on your foot or anything, right?"

Anne felt a chill. It wasn't the October air. It was fear, creeping up her spinal column. It tingled, and she shuddered. The numbness of adrenaline coursed through her body. Her eyes darted about the front seat for something sharp. There was nothing. Her left hand slipped down into a storage slot in the driver door. She felt a ball point pen and gripped it tightly out of sight.

"Ya know, Annie girl, some people have the idea that a woman should stay at home and mind things there and bring up the kids." Buddy knelt by Frank on the other side of the car, but she could clearly hear his voice. She heard the pop of a hubcap.

"Not me, though. I guess I'm more liberal. I think a woman should do whatever she needs to do to feel good," he said. Anne felt the chill of the night air brush her neck and the stickiness of the sweat on her hand as it squeezed the pen.

"Now, my woman, she loved to dance and she kept a great house, but one time she convinced herself that she wanted to do more outdoorsy stuff. I didn't try to talk her out of it, no sir. She's kinda headstrong. Frank, put those lug nuts in the cap so ya don't lose 'em."

The car quivered a bit as Frank pulled the wheel off the studs. Anne heard the clatter and clank of the spare.

"So one time, she takes the notion to cut out some brush behind her garden. I say I'll do it. She says no, no. She wants to do it herself. That's fine, I say. So I show her what she needs to know. She goes at it. An hour later she runs into the house covered in blood. It was awful. That chainsaw caught a branch, kicked back, and took a chunk out of her leg. Had to call 911. Paramedics patched her up, but she don't dance like she used to. Never will, I expect."

Anne heard a soft squeal from the jack as Frank turned the crank. It sounded like the mouse she once caught by its foot in a trap. At the same time she felt the car dropping to the ground. That small motion was strangely dizzying.

"Snug 'em down good. Wouldn't want the little lady to have an accident on our account?" he said to Frank.

"Too bad," he said, his voice raised so Anne could hear him. "A hard lesson to learn. But that was her. This is you. I expect you'd be different. I expect you'd be smarter than that. You look smart. Like you went to college. Smart people learn their life lessons early. Others only when it's too late."

Anne jumped in her seat when she heard a thud. Frank had hurled the flat tire into the trunk. He roughly tossed the jack in after it.

"A pretty young woman like you still wants to dance and have fun, right? An old aunt of mine used to say, 'A man who is warned is half saved.' Clever lady. Lived to be ninety-three. I always liked that one."

"Have you finished your phone call?" asked Anne. She heard the fear in her own voice, but hoped that Buddy had not.

Buddy took her phone from his pocket and tossed it into the back seat.

The pickup truck backed onto the highway and returned the way it had come. Mud obscured the license plate number. Anne found herself shaking when she dropped the pen from her hand. She reached back for her phone.

"Dit, I know it's late, but I need to talk to somebody. Are you alone?"

34.

Dit lived on a groved estate across the harbour from Charlottetown. His house was a two-storey brick with a mansard roof and resembled the old manor houses of Provence, but Dit had redesigned it with a modern interior and all the amenities needed by a paraplegic in a wheelchair. His surgeries the previous year had minimized his need for a wheelchair, and he greeted Anne at the front door on crutches.

Dit was alone. Gwen had gone to Nova Scotia to pick up some things from her apartment. She would be returning tomorrow or the next day depending upon other business she had to clear up.

Anne stood in the doorway. She looked like a lost puppy that had endured great misadventures before finding its way back home. He knew something had seriously upset her. He shifted a crutch to his other side and held his arms out. Anne rushed in, encircled him with her arms, and buried her head in his chest. Slowly his arms closed around her, and neither said anything.

After a moment, Anne loosened her grip, took a step back, and looked up at Dit. She wanted to burst into tears, to let everything just come flooding out, but she fought the impulse. It was something she might have yielded to years before, but in her more recent life as a private investigator she knew that she had to keep her "game face" on, even with friends. Otherwise, she would look too emotional and weak, the stereotypical woman, and then someone would inevitably suggest that she find something else to do, meaning "women's work."

Already, in the eyes of the public, she had two strikes against her. One, she was female, and two, she was small and looked vulnerable. Some would go so far as to say three strikes were against her, Jacqui being number three, a child to protect and raise, though at sixteen Jacqui was hardly a helpless, needy child. Even Dit, who had been her supporter and rock when times had gotten tough, had from time to time backslid into that state of mind.

Instead Anne tucked her impulses behind a forced grin and a distracting remark: "I had a really, really, sucky day, and I need a friend. Any recommendations?"

"I think I have Rent-A-Buddy on speed dial. I could call. Or, Jack Daniels, Jim Beam, and Captain Morgan are in the library. I believe they're having a quiet chat."

With a sweep of his arm Dit motioned her in. They passed through the living room, spacious, open, and furnished in a smart, simple style. The skyline of Charlottetown glimmered beyond the window. It was the perfect room for dinner parties. It conjured up civility, good manners, cordiality, and fun, but Anne felt an odd aversion to that room tonight, and Anne was relieved when Dit led her past it.

The library was warmer, smaller, and furnished in leather and dark wood. A light scent of furniture oil hung in the air. The lamp was on when they entered. This was Dit's favourite room and where he spent much of his time at home.

Anne sank into a large supple chair, her legs curled up underneath her like a parlour cat. Music filled the room. It was a habit of Dit's, perhaps a need, a way to fill the quiet of an empty house. Frenzied rhythms flowed from unseen speakers.

"Who's your friend tonight?" asked Dit.

"I love a man in uniform," said Anne.

"Captain Morgan it is then," he said and grabbed a bottle of rum from a cabinet. "Straight?"

"I've never had that bad a day. Coke. Ice. A twist?"

"Can do," he said. He finished mixing her drink. He poured himself one as well. Anne felt the rum tingle and her body slowly warm. Dit pressed a button on a console, and the music changed to Cuban.

"Better," said Anne. Her eyes brightened for the first time since she came in.

"You don't like Monk."

"He's like...too many fireworks at once. I don't want my head pulled in so many directions, not tonight, above all, not tonight. I don't want to think anymore."

"This kind of music," she said, her arm circling vaguely toward the salsa rhythms that enveloped the room, "makes me want to get up, dance, and have fun." Anne became abruptly conscious of her words. They conjured the ugly familiarity of Buddy's words. She turned cold, and her voice flattened. "I feel like I just got off the stress express."

"So...you want to tell me what happened?"

"I didn't know if I was going to be raped or beat up or killed," she said.

She looked up toward Dit. His lips parted with surprise, but he said nothing. Instead, he looked expectantly for her to explain.

Anne recounted the incident from the time she left Lydia Vandermeer's farmhouse. The dark road. The telephone call from Edna. The flat. Buddy and Frank's timely arrival, their offer to help, and the taking of her cell phone. Buddy's story of his woman, her chainsaw accident, and his disturbing application of it to Anne.

"It was like the nightmare I used to have as a kid. Being trapped, unable to move while shapeless, evil creatures swooped around me."

Dit noticed a tremor in her hand, and he could hear the soft chatter of ice in her quivering glass. Anne noticed none of that. Her eyes remained fixed and wide as she relived the episode.

"Are you sure you weren't imagining the threat? Just about everyone would be uneasy in those circumstances. A benign remark, a sloppy choice of words, could spark an old fear."

"You don't believe me?" Anne snapped back.

"Of course I believe you, but everything they did and said could be interpreted as your imagination magnifying the circumstances." Dit felt pleased that he had preserved a calm, soothing, reassuring tone. He knew that Anne could "fly off the handle" from time to time. She had done so in the past, and he couldn't understand it. For that matter, he could never quite understand why so many other women he knew reacted the same way.

"He knew me by name," said Anne. "He called me 'Annie girl.' He did it just once, a slip of the tongue. That isn't a local phrasing. It's not a colloquialism. He knew who I was."

"That's something, I suppose…but you didn't phone the police. Why?"

"Police couldn't do anything. The threat was implied. They would say that all they did was help some woman in distress on the highway. Good Samaritans with simple minds and maybe lousy social skills, the cops would say. I couldn't tell the cops, but I had to talk to someone. So here I am."

"What next?"

"Just carry on as usual, I guess. And you?" Anne said, finished her drink, and stood up.

"The band plays on," he said.

"Are they playing 'The Wedding March' or '50 Ways To Leave Your Lover'?" As soon as Anne heard the words fly out of her mouth, she regretted them. She was tired and stressed. Dit's enumeration of possibilities, his unbearable parsing of Buddy's words, and his sparing support of her take on the evening had upset her. She didn't want analysis. Not now. She didn't want thinking. That could wait. Tonight she just wanted a shoulder to cry on. Tonight she just wanted to feel sorry for herself and for someone else to feel sorry for her…for ten or fifteen minutes anyway. Was that too much to ask?

"What do you mean by that?" Dit asked. He looked confused, and he sounded defensive.

"I think it's pretty clear," said Anne. She felt trapped, but there was no way out.

"Are you questioning our relationship?"

"I guess I am."

"What gives you that right?"

"We're friends, aren't we?"

"Say what you have to say, then."

"I don't think you and Gwen belong together."

"You're making no sense. Do you know that? None whatsoever."

"How can you say that? You and Gwen are worlds apart. Anybody can see that."

"Like who?"

"Anybody. You were pretty well confined to that hospital bed for months with surgeries and physio. You came to depend on her. After a while that became like a drug. That became your whole world. Now you can't see anything past your next fix of pretty attention. And she's in the business of caring about patients. It's not a quantum leap to imagine that she would be drawn to you after a while. I don't blame her, but I see this relationship falling apart in a year or two. Getting married so soon is like an act of desperation. Open your eyes! Look at reality!"

"The reality is that she's in love with me, and I'm in love with her. I think you're just jealous. I'm happy...really happy...for once in my life and you, my so-called best friend, try to snatch it away."

"I'm doing nothing of the sort!"

"You're jealous of my good fortune and can't stand to let me enjoy it. I thought you were above that sort of thing, Anne. I guess not. Your own personal life is a sham and has been for years. Talk about dependency, you've hid behind your widow's shield for fifteen years. You've pushed away every man that got near. And, whether you realize it or not, you've even used your daughter as an excuse to put them off. You have a job, but you've got no life, and now you don't want me to have one either. Go! Go, dammit! Just go! Get out!"

Even after the door slammed behind her, Anne could still hear the *cubano son* rhythms of the Buena Vista Social Club. She had heard that song many times. The lyrics told a sad and tragic love story, but the beat was buoyant and filled with life and steeped in hope.

Anne cried for most of her drive home.

35.

The next morning Anne hovered between sleep and consciousness, and she hid there restlessly. It wasn't a hangover. She'd had only one drink. But something intangible and troubling had restrained her, and she lingered in this twilight, avoiding the resolution. Anne's head ached, her eyes were gritty, her mind reluctant, her body limp from a dulling paralysis, and she wanted to stay in bed, sleep the rest of the day. Only Jacqui didn't let her.

A litany of *Mom, you're going to be late! Mom, it's time to get up! Mom, I need some lunch money!*

Anne rolled over in bed, her eyes still closed, and her body convinced that it was the middle of the night. She swung at the snooze alarm, but it had no effect on Jacqui's nagging mantra. Finally, her mind roused and slowly began processing.

"Mom! Mom! Are you awake?"

Jacqui's voice was loud, annoying, and very close at hand. The light switch snapped, and Anne's last refuge was exposed. Jacqui hovered over her bed.

"Mom! I have to go and I need a lunch or lunch money."

"What time is it?" asked Anne groggily.

"Quarter to eight. Are you sick? Are you taking today off? Don't you have people to see or appointments or anything? Don't you have to work?"

Anne sat bolt upright and leaped onto the floor.

"Oh my god, I have to meet someone…at nine. What time is it?"

"Nearly eight. Lunch money?" said Jacqui, sounding disgusted and impatient.

"Take some…in my purse."

"Thanks," she said, and added as she fled out the door, "I don't know what you did with my Mom, but I'd like her back sometime today."

Anne saw a crooked smile trying to wriggle its way onto the dopey face staring back at her in the bathroom mirror, and then her memory stirred up the incidents from the night before. She had tried to bury those memories in her sleep, but there weren't enough hours in the night to finish the job. There never are.

The flat-tire incident was dodgy and nerve-racking, but that was part of the job. The thing with Dit, though…that was…

What an ass I've been, she said to herself. *What a stupid ass!*

By eight-forty Anne had washed, dressed, eaten, and was driving toward the University and her appointment with Edna Hibley. Her frantic morning had pushed Buddy and Frank and Dit out of mind until she exited her house and eyed the spare tire on her car.

On her way, she pulled into a service station next to a shopping centre, collared the attendant, and told him she had a flat in the trunk and needed it fixed. She'd be back in an hour or so to see about it. Anne had five minutes to spare as she walked across the campus toward the meeting place with Edna.

Edna seemed more relaxed on campus than she had been when they met at her house the week before. Edna had arrived at the student centre before Anne arrived. She had seated herself at a table in the cafe. She was sipping coffee and nibbling on a blueberry muffin when Anne approached.

"Good morning," she said brightly to Anne. "Coffee's over there if you need one. You look like you might."

"I do. Late night. Very late."

"Party?"

"Work, I'm afraid. Barely time to see my daughter…yesterday or this morning."

Anne poured a fresh cup of black coffee, returned to the table, and sat down opposite Edna.

Edna's light brown hair was loosely pulled back and fastened with a pin behind her head. Anne thought she looked about fifty, closing in on fifty at least, she thought. She was plain but not unattractive, sturdily built but not plump, neatly presented but not primped.

"I have to apologize," said Anne. "I wasn't aware that you were a professor. Nursing?"

"I teach the odd course to the nursing students, but most of my teaching is in veterinary medicine."

"That's quite a shift. What took you in that direction?"

"Like the paths of so many others…fate. Carolyn and I graduated high school in '83. We both received entry scholarships to UPEI, me in nursing… Carolyn in business. Dad died the summer of our second year, and that derailed us somewhat, I'm afraid. Mother was an invalid with early-onset Alzheimer's, and we shared her home care until 2001."

"How did you manage to finish college?"

"Determination. Education was important to both of us. We took night courses or day courses, depending on what kind of schedule we could coordinate between us. Dad's insurance money kept us afloat for a while. Carolyn and I always worked well together. We worked part-time, too, she as a bookkeeper and me at a vet clinic. After Carolyn's death, though, I couldn't handle Mother on my own. Her health was deteriorating...mentally and physically. I had to put her in a nursing home. By then, I had got my nursing degree."

"You married, too."

"A hapless marriage, as it turned out. He was a lovely man, ten years older than I. He suddenly died in his sleep. Completely out of the blue. We had been married for just eighteen months. An undiagnosed heart problem. At that point I'd had my fill of dealing with human complaints and sicknesses and death. So I moved on. I pursued a Master's in pharmacology and a Doctorate in veterinary medicine. I've been associate professor for half a dozen years now...and I like it very much."

Abruptly, Edna's tone shifted from personal and reminiscent to direct and businesslike: "So where do we stand? Have you made progress?"

"I have. There's a connection between the Villier murder and Carolyn's death. The common thread is Simone's boyfriend, Jamie MacFarlane. He was a police officer at the time. Now he's Chief of the Stratford Constabulary. I may have uncovered a motive for him to have murdered his girlfriend. I've caught him in a string of lies about his testimony and his relationship with Simone and others. I'm following up on them now."

"But what's his connection to Carolyn's death?"

"She was interviewed as part of the Villier investigation, and she lied. She said she had gone home early the evening of the murder when, in fact, she had worked until quite late."

"You think Carolyn would have been a witness? Surely not. I would have known. She would have told me something."

"Carolyn wasn't aware of the murder until several days later. She probably never actually witnessed anything, but she may have some-how concluded that MacFarlane had done it. That's the only reason I can think of that would explain her lying. If MacFarlane somehow became aware of her lie, then he might have felt compelled to kill her to prevent her from coming forward."

"Will you be able to establish that?"

"I'm working on it. I think I'm stepping hard enough on his toes to make him very nervous. When people become rash, they make mistakes."

"How much longer?"

"Hopefully a few days. I can't say for certain."

"Then you'll have proof?"

"I can't promise anything. Like I said, it's been a very long time since the crime was committed. I'm confident I'll have enough to discredit him, but a conviction for murder will be difficult to substantiate. The reality is that the only way to get him for Carolyn's death is to get him for Simone Villier's. The two are tied together. Sorry."

"I can give you two more days. That's the most I can do. Two days."

Anne returned to the service station. The mechanic rolled out her tire, jacked the car, and replaced the spare.

"That'll be ten dollars," he said.

"Nail?" asked Anne.

"Core in the valve stem."

"I've had valve stems replaced but never a core."

"Wasn't replaced. Just tightened it, pumped her up," he said.

"Did it vibrate loose?"

"Not by accident." Anne looked at him expectantly. He got the hint and continued. "Used to be a common high school prank in the day." He took a small tool from his pocket and held it up. "This part fits in the stem hole. Twist it counterclockwise. If you twist just a little, air leaks out slowly."

36.

"Let's go! Let's go! Let's go, ladies!"

Phys Ed teacher Fred Mueller shouted into the showers. Steam billowed, spray cascaded from two rows of shower heads, students hooted and shouted and laughed, and their echo was deafening.

Mueller waited a minute and stuck his head 'round the corner into the shower room and shouted again, "Let's go, ladies. The bell's about to ring. C'mon! Get a move on!"

Sig Valdimarsson rushed past him out of the cloudy haze and into the locker room. William Larsen was right behind him. He loosed a ninja cry and snapped his towel. It cracked like a whip against Sig's ass. Sig yelped.

"Knock it off, Larsen! Get dressed," shouted Mueller.

Sig's long wet blond hair clung to his neck. He was slender, but broadly built and muscular. He towelled off and started dressing for the second class. Larsen's locker was next to his.

What's up this weekend?" he asked.

"Birthday party."

Larsen's ear perked.

"Birthday party? Whose?" he asked.

"Bobby... Fogarty...at his house," said Sig, grunting between tugs at the clothes he was rushing to put on.

"A big seventeenth blowout, huh?"

"Nah, just a few friends. A family thing. His mother's got something planned."

"Oh," said Larsen.

"... Then I think we're going over to Madame Desjardins'."

"Whoa, she's pretty hot for a teacher. I bet Bobby's mom didn't plan that."

Sig gave him a disdainful look.

"Jacqui Brown is babysitting. She can't come to the party, but she wants to give him something. I'm tagging along. Might do something afterwards, though."

"I know what she can give me for my birthday," he laughed. Sig ignored him. "So it's a party, and then a party after the party. Cool. See you at practice."

37.

Ben Solomon felt just like he had been when summoned to Mrs. Bell's office. Mrs. Bell had been principal at the junior high school he attended in Ottawa. That time, he knew what the summons was about. Fighting again. Rudy Fitz had called him "bagel baby." It wasn't the first time. So, at recess Ben popped him with a volleyball shot to the face. It swelled like an overripe tomato. A supervising teacher had seen the whole thing.

Rudy could blubber with the best of them, and at thirteen he had mastered the art of lying. So he denied his provocation. The teacher believed Rudy's whimpering explanation. So did Mrs. Bell. Ben was suspended for the day. His parents were called.

"It won't happen again," said Ben's mother.

"No, Mrs. Solomon, I'm sure it won't," said Mrs. Bell crisply.

"Benjy, what's the matter with you? Haven't you learned anything?" scolded his mother as she left the office with Ben. Her hand swatted the back of Ben's head as they descended the broad stone steps of the schoolhouse. "You're a bright boy, Benjy. Next time, act smart. Don't let anyone catch you. Here. Here's three dollars. There's a matinee at the Odeon. Be home for supper, and don't be late."

Serpico was the main feature that day and later that evening Ben Solomon imagined himself as Al Pacino, cleaning up a corrupt Canadian city from the forces of vice, greed, and cruelty.

The premier's office was on the fifth floor of the Jones Building, one floor above his. Premier Thane Clark had not summoned him, but his chief of staff, Wendell Carmody, had. He was the premier's go-to man for problems he'd rather distance himself from.

The door was open. Premier Clark and Carmody were talking. Ben knocked politely on the door frame and entered. Both men turned toward the door.

Premier Thane Clark always looked taller than he actually was. He had a full head of grey hair, casually combed back on the sides, always a touch long for the professorial, liberal-thinking look, and always meticulously arranged. He was quick to step forward and greet Ben.

"Good morning, Ben. It's good to see you again. Wendell tells me that you're beginning to settle in. That's wonderful…and I'm hearing good things about you. Someday soon we'll get together for a longer chat.

It's wonderful to have you on our team." The premier glanced quickly at his watch. "Another meeting," he said with a smile and returned to his office, closing the door behind him.

"What's up, Wendell?"

"Have a seat, Ben." Wendell motioned Ben to a chair. "Won't take long. I've been made aware of an irregularity that we need to take care of. More of a nuisance really."

Wendell didn't take a seat. Instead, he leaned against the edge of his desk in front of Ben's chair. The smile on Ben's face grew weaker.

"Yes?" said Ben noncommittally.

"Actually there's been a complaint, unofficial of course. It's about a police file that you requested. I understand that it's fallen into the hands of a private detective, a Ms. Billy Darby. We need it returned."

"Why?"

"Only peace officers or officers of the court can have access to those files. They're confidential. As a matter of fact, it's a personal privacy concern, too."

"I authorized it."

"You can't do that."

"She came into new evidence relating to the case."

"Then she should have requested it through a proper application."

Ben felt the steam rising and his chest constricting as he watched Carmody's lips move through his playbook of political hoops and bureaucratic red tape. Ben took several long slow breaths to control his breathing. He couldn't count how many times he'd seen contents of a police file slipped into the hands of an outsider, and he knew that he had the authority to widen the circle of access to the file in spite of Carmody's declaration. He took a few longer, controlled breaths until he felt some calmness return. *There is something else going on here*, he thought.

"Who initiated the complaint?"

"I can't go into that. It's confidential."

"I can find out."

"I'm sure you can, but as I mentioned, it's unofficial at this time. No one wants to draw any more attention to it. If it's ratcheted up to an official complaint, it may come back on you. And let's face it, Ben, you knew it wasn't kosher."

Ben winced at his choice of words and wondered if it was an unconscious choice or a mindful one.

"No problem. I'll get it back. And I assume there won't be any fallout for Ms. Darby."

"Nothing permanent. As I understand it, though, a separate privacy complaint has been made, and that will have to work its way through the system. I'm sure it will be done quietly, though, and expeditiously."

"I'll do what I can to help, Wendell. You know that. Perhaps, though, if you can spare a moment, you could explain how everything will 'work its way through the system.' I'm a little muddy on this administrative stuff."

Wendell Carmody stood up and returned to the chair behind his desk. His posture relaxed. The tautness in his smile faded.

"Coffee?" he asked, pointing to a fresh carafe at a side table.

"Perfect."

"Sweetener?" Wendell asked as he held up a bottle of liqueur.

"More than perfect."

Carmody poured two cups, brought one to Ben, and settled into a chair next to him. He took a quick slurp, and then he began: "According to the legislation governing private investigators, here's what usually happens..."

38.

"Anne? Listen. You've got problems."

At first Anne didn't recognize Ben's voice. It was abrupt, sharp, and impatient. Anne was about to ask him how he heard about the flat-tire incident so soon, but Ben gave her no chance to interrupt.

"Where are you right now?" he asked.

"Just got into the office. Why?"

"You're going to have company."

"What do you..."

"Just listen."

"Do you have a photocopier?"

"Yeah."

"Photocopy the Villier police file."

"Yeah."

"Photocopy any notes you've made on your investigation so far."

"Yeah. Why?" said Anne finally able to squeeze one word into their one-sided conversation.

"They may be serving a warrant for your files. Also, that letter from Carolyn?"

"Yeah, what about it?"

"Put it in an envelope and mail it to yourself. All photocopies you make? Remove them from your office right away."

"You're kidding, right?"

"Wish I were. Get on it now. I don't know how much time you have. I'll meet you for lunch and fill you in."

Ben returned the phone to its cradle on his desk. Immediately he picked it up again, thought for a moment, and replaced it. He got up and walked quickly from his office to the office three doors down. The placard on the door read "Ministry of Justice." The door was open. The secretary looked up from her typewriter just in time to see Ben move past and through the open door of Fenton Peale's office. Peale was startled by the looming figure entering his domain, and it took a second for his eyes to focus on the grim face of Ben Solomon.

"Ben? I didn't know we had a meeting."

"We don't. Your door was open. I need a second."

"Go on, then. What is it? You look flustered."

"More confused than upset," said Ben. It was as close to conciliatory he could manage at that moment. "Question. Were you aware
of a complaint about a police file I requested regarding the Villier
murder?"

"Never heard of it."

"Were you notified of a warrant issued to seize the files of a private
detective, Billy Darby?"

"No."

"Your office licenses private investigators and security officers."

"Oh, I see. Let me explain. Our ministry's legislation covers the police and other peace officers. PIs and security guards operate under
Department of Industry legislation. Industry regulates the private
sector. Justice does criminal background checks on their applicants
and rubber stamps Industry's submissions for licensing. It's more
efficient that way."

"Who investigates PIs that violate the legislation?"

"Industry."

"And warrants?"

"Industry. Anything else, Ben?"

"No. Thanks. Sorry for the intrusion." Peale said nothing. Ben turned
and left the office. Embarrassment followed closely behind him.

39.

Anne picked at her lunch and fidgeted in her seat at The Blue Peter. Every time she heard the whoosh of the front door opening, she looked up anxiously. *Where the hell is he*, she wondered. *What's keeping him?* When he finally came through the door, she sprang out of her seat at the round table, and rushed over.

"Ben, what's going on?"

"Same question I was going to ask you. You pissed somebody off. Can I guess who?"

"MacFarlane?"

"I expect so. I tried to warn you. Slow, quiet, methodical investigations don't stir up big stinks, and from the odour floating in the halls of the Jones building, you've set fire to the entire outhouse."

"The trouble with slow investigations is that they're slow," she said. She sounded defensive. She hoped that Ben didn't perceive it, but she knew that she'd been backed against a wall. "You never know if you're making progress. It's like those British TV detectives. Always tiptoeing around, afraid they're going to offend someone. At least I know that I struck close to home, and I know it's MacFarlane at the grassroots level, but who's helping him in government?"

"Hard to say. Industry is doing the kicking. Justice seems to be out of the loop. MacFarlane knows and has worked with pretty well everyone who's connected and can pull strings. He owes favours, and lots owe him. Easy to cover his tracks. So what happened exactly?" Ben asked. "Who showed up? What did they say?"

"They didn't say much really. Some bureaucrat from Department of Industry arrived, knocked, and came in with the sheriff who served the warrant. It was only about an hour after your heads up. Thanks for that, by the way. They even made me open the safe."

Ben raised his eyebrows.

"I know what you're thinking and, no, they didn't find my .32. But they were surprised at Uncle Billy's little arsenal. The sheriff checked the paperwork. Everything was up-to-date, he said. He looked closely at the box of .32 cartridges stacked with the others. Then he looked at me and said, 'You know that .25 and .32 calibre handguns are prohibited weapons in Canada, right?' I told him I thought that Uncle Bill had a .32 a long time ago, but I hadn't gotten around to cleaning out all his odds and ends."

"Where was the .32?"

"In my purse. I knew their warrant wouldn't cover a personal search."

"What was the basis for the warrant?"

"Supposedly, I had passed myself off as a police officer in order to get information from someone. They didn't say who filed the complaint, but I have an idea who. I was looking for John Dawson yesterday. I stopped at the transition house and talked to three parolees on the porch. I'm guessing somebody leaned on one of them."

"And I'm guessing that someone has been keeping a close watch on your travels in this case. Did you get everything photocopied that needed to be?"

"Yes. Everything that was important."

"Where are the copies?"

Anne tilted her head toward Mary Anne's restaurant office.

"And Carolyn's letter?"

"With Canada Post again," she said lightly, but her levity was short-lived. "You know that I'm out of business, don't you? They've suspended my private investigator's license."

"A temporary setback. They'll investigate the complaint. After a few weeks they'll find that it was bogus, and you'll be back in business again."

"In the meantime...?"

"In the meantime, give it a rest. MacFarlane's not going anywhere." Ben smiled and patted her hand reassuringly, despite knowing that she would not take his advice.

40.

"He said what?"

Ben's voice rang sharp and loud. He grew livid. His face glowered.

Fenton Peale wasn't used to anger, confrontation, or anyone questioning his suggestions, and he felt suddenly trapped and helpless. For a real moment, Ben had frightened him, and he shrank back against his chair as if someone had thrown a punch, but, after realizing that Ben had kept his distance, Peale recovered enough composure to respond.

"Don't shoot the messenger, Ben. I'm just passing along what Carmody shared with me: he wants you to take a step back from the Billy Darby situation…at least for the short term. Personally, I like the girl. She's got a lot of spunk. Realistically, though, Carmody's got a point. He's received allegations of improper conduct, and the government can't be seen to take sides or assist her. You're a part of this government. If she's tainted in some way, you will be, too and, in the political arena, so will Carmody and Premier Clark and me and Bob MacEwen at Industry. When Carmody speaks, he speaks on behalf of the Premier, and he makes sense. We all have to step back and see what plays out. That's how things are done around here, Ben. That's how we survive."

"Bullshit," said Ben. He backed out the door of Peale's office and passed his secretary's desk. One of her hands gripped the phone. Her other gripped the desk. Her face was pale, her mouth agape, and her mind uncertain whether to phone security or flee.

Carmody's office was one floor up. Ben took the stairs, rather than the elevator. He wanted to be sure that Peale had time to phone Carmody but, before he hit the stairwell, he was intercepted by his part-time receptionist, Ida Treat. She huffed as she passed him a bundle in an interdepartmental envelope. She disliked her services being shared by several offices, and a sour expression on her face revealed that mindset. Ben took the envelope, noted that it came from Department of Industry, and handed it back to her.

"File this under 'political interference,'" he told her. She huffed.

"Now," he said. She huffed again, but headed toward Ben's office.

Carmody's door was open wide. The door to the Premier's office was ajar. The Premier's personal assistant sat at her workstation next to it like an edgy guard dog. Her eyes flicked quickly up at Ben and down again to her computer screen. Her hands rested on the keyboard, but they scarcely moved.

"Hey, Cathy. Deputy Dog in?" In spite of the rebuffs by Fenton Peale and Ida Treat, Ben's tone had become warm and cordial.

Cathy Doiron relaxed. She looked up and smiled timidly back.

"If you mean Mr. Carmody, he's out of the office at the moment." She cocked her head and threw a glance toward the crack in the Premier's door.

"Is he expected back anytime soon?"

"Hard to say. Something came up quite suddenly, and he had to step out. Is there something I can do for you?"

"If you had a moment, could you scribble down a note for him?"

"Sure."

"I want to start it off like this:" Cathy picked up her steno pad. "Dear Mr. Carmody, It's come to my attention that you are either a sonofa-bitch or the messenger of a sonofabitch, both of which put me in the undesirable position of having to inform you that it is...inadvisable to tell any peace officer in the execution of his legal duty to 'take a step back.' As the chief peace officer in this province, I am obliged to carry out...my obligations and duties under the legislation that empowered me. Remember that I am not an elected official. Remember, too, that I was offered this position by...a higher authority, which shall remain unnamed, and subsequently appointed by the current government. Be advised, therefore, that the only circumstance in which I might find myself 'taking a step back' would be...to better position myself to direct a proper kick to the balls of anyone who makes such a sug-gestion in the future. Thanks for the opportunity to make my views clear, and...by all means feel free to share this point of view with colleagues who might find it useful. Signed, Benjamin Solomon."

Cathy's eyes had grown merrier as she continued recording her shorthand. At the end, she stifled a snicker and rolled her eyes again toward the opening in the door. "After I type it, do you want me to send it down for you to sign, Ben?"

"That probably won't be necessary. My signature won't make it anymore true or heartfelt than it already is. Just see that he gets the message. Oh...and use your discretion with the wording. I'm told I can be a bit too blunt at times. My wife Sarah probably would say 'crude.' It's a cop thing," said Ben. He winked and headed out the door. He had a smile on his face. He felt energized. Feigned outrage had always been his favourite investigative tool. No laws governed it, and one was always surprised at the reaction it produced.

Carmody slowly opened the door of the Premier's empty office. He emerged when he perceived that Ben had gone. He stepped warily past Cathy Doiron's workstation.

"How many copies of Ben's letter would you like?" she asked.

Carmody scowled.

"Just asking," she said and shrugged.

"Not a word about this," he said savagely. "Not a word."

"Of course not, Mr. Carmody," she said and smiled to herself.

41.

Anne was shattered at the suspension of her license. She sat alone in her office and stared blankly at the phone as if anticipation somehow would make it ring and the incoming message would make everything all right again. The power of wishful thinking was fleeting, though, and after the last trace of it vanished, she slumped into a morass of gloominess and self-pity. In a short twenty-four hours she lost her best friend, her private investigator's license, her client, and the prospect of any income.

She'd hurt Dit terribly. She had read it in his face. He would never forgive her. How could he? She had demeaned the most important segments of his life, and he had lashed back, and rightly so.

Then the investigator from Industry had said that her suspension would likely last for two weeks while their enquiry process took its course, but who knows? It could just as easily drag on for a month...or more. Why would the bureaucrats give a damn? They're still getting paid.

And Edna, her one big client, had given her two days to clear things up. Edna didn't have an unlimited bankroll for detective services, and she was counting on tangible results for her investment in Anne. Now, all of that seemed elusive and a colossal waste of time, energy, and money.

And that wasn't the end to the fallout from this disaster. It would take no time at all for gossip to spread, true or not, that she was employing dodgy tactics. Her enemies, and she had made a few over the past year, would leap at the chance to spread lies about her. Her methods would be under a microscope. New clients would be less likely to call. Reputation was essential in her business, and especially so on a small island like PEI where word of mouth was the measure of a trustworthy enterprise.

The more she contemplated the ill luck that befell her, the more her focus returned to how it all came about, and it was that which confounded her most. The allegations claimed that Anne had passed herself off as a police officer to pry information out of someone, but the name had been kept from her. That was the key to moving ahead— knowing who had been tossing kerosene on the fire. She knew it had to be someone she had spoken to in the last few days. But who?

Anne turned over the names in her head. *Edna Hibley. Davidia Christian. Bernadette Villier. None of them seemed likely candidates. Neither would have had a reason. Jacob Dawson? No again. If anything, he would have more cause to support me than deceive me. If I find he was falsely convicted, there may be grounds to have his conviction overturned, and that could open the door for a lawsuit. Irene MacLeod? Not interviewed, but the gatekeeper to Dawson and others. She was a possibility...more of a wild card. She may have loyalties apart from Dawson. She could have a closet full of secrets, for all I know. Then there were the boys on the porch. Pun'kin, Tipper, and Barry. Each of them a parolee. Each exposed to pressure from up the food chain, legal or otherwise. Four possibilities altogether*, thought Anne, *but which one?*

Then it suddenly dawned on her. It may not matter. The investigation would continue at a snail's pace until it was resolved regardless. What did matter, though, was that some key player had to know that she had talked to these people. To put pressure on one them, Anne must have been followed and seen talking to them. Anne had been extra careful to avoid surveillance. So following her would have been difficult, but not impossible. On the other hand, no one could have followed her to Lydia Vandermeer's home in Pownal. It was a two-lane county road with little traffic. She would easily have spotted another car.

No, she thought. *I wasn't being followed. Someone knew where I was going...or where I had been.*

Anne had stared at the phone long enough. She picked it up and dialled. The number rang.

"Dit, don't hang up! Just listen! I behaved like an ass last night. I did. But I was stressed and tired and frightened. You know that. And a lot came out that shouldn't have, and I'm sorry. Really, really sorry! I didn't mean any of it! I don't want to lose you as a friend! I really wish you all the best. Okay? Can we talk about it? My day yesterday was shitty, and today has been worse. My office was searched. I'm facing bogus allegations of posing as a police officer. My license has been suspended, my files have been seized, and I think my car or phone has been bugged, and I need some help. So if you can, that would be great. If not, that's okay, too."

"I'll tell him you called."

The voice belonged to Gwen Fowler. Her reply was civil, but cool and impersonal. Then she hung up.

42.

Ben felt wonderful. It was a splendid October morning. The sky was a deep, rich blue. Only a cluster of puffy clouds gathered along the eastern horizon as he walked from the parking lot toward the Shaw building and his office in the neighbouring Jones building. Behind him the bay reflected the sky. Ceremonial cannons pointed decoratively toward the harbour mouth, and the Lieutenant Governor's mansion on a grassy knoll behind him was a resplendent white in the strengthening sunlight.

Yesterday he had snarled and snapped like a new dog in the kennel. Today the old dogs would be wary and keep their distance, and today he planned to mark his territory. If worse came to worst, though, he still was on an extended leave of absence from the Charlottetown Police. He could return there. Or he could pack it in. Retire. He was a bit young to spend the rest of his time on Earth mowing the lawn and painting the trim on his house, but there would always be something he could do with the skills he'd developed over the last twenty-five-odd years. Security consultant, retail investigator, instructor at the police academy in Summerside.

Then he thought of Anne landing on her ass, unexpectedly, for no justifiable reason. It was a precarious, uncertain profession for sure. Then a picture of himself shouldered its way into his head: him struggling against an unkillable jungle of garden weeds, him shining up old war stories with other ex-cops at Tim's coffee shop, him shovelling the monotony of forever-drifting snow from his driveway. Images like that made him cringe. No, he would never retire, he thought to himself. He took one long, last, fresh, cool lungful of fall air into his lungs before he stepped through doors into the Jones Building.

Donnie Chamberlain, the uniformed commissionaire, greeted him at the entrance. He looked rather frail and small, white-haired, a crackling voice: "Good morning, Mr. Solomon."

"A great morning, Donnie." Four ribbons, one with a bronze oak leaf, identified his Korean War service. Ben stopped abruptly and asked, "How the hell old are you, anyway, Donnie?"

"Old enough to know a few things…and young enough to give you a thumpin' if you get rowdy," he said and winked.

"Ever think about retiring?" asked Ben.

"I'm havin' too much fun to retire. You aren't after my job, are you, Mr. Solomon?"

Ben still had the grin on his face when the elevator opened on the fourth floor. He walked past the closed door to his own office and into the reception area for Ministry of Justice.

"Is the minister in?" he asked the receptionist. She nodded as she looked up from her keyboard.

The door to Fenton Peale's office was open partway. Ben knocked politely. He heard Peale's invitation to enter, and he did.

"Good morning, Fenton."

"Ben. What's up?"

"I reached out to Carmody, and I think we've come to a mutual understanding."

"You spoke with him yesterday?"

Ben hesitated for a moment. "Indirectly," he said and then added, "He got my message, though."

Peale looked puzzled and then brightened. "Then everything worked out. That's wonderful. So you can live with the suspension of Ms. Darby's license?"

"Of course. You had no control over it. Frankly, I'm not sure that Carmody did either. If there are allegations, they have to be looked into. That's the way it goes. She'll survive it. My knowledge of her suggests that she's squeaky clean. She'll land on her feet. She always does. Luck of the Irish, I guess."

"I'm glad you see things that way, Ben. People I've talked to were of the opinion that she was stepping beyond her authority with that Villier case. Too much enthusiasm narrows a person's focus, and that can lead to errors in judgment. In the end, I would chalk her troubles up to…inexperience."

"You may be right, Fenton, and that's why I have decided to open my own investigation into the connection between the Villier murder and the death of Carolyn Jollimore."

Peale looked genuinely stunned.

"This is a surprise."

"I thought it might be. That's why I wanted you to be first to hear about it."

Peale looked away in thought and then said, "What brought this about?"

"Billy Darby may have been overenthusiastic. We'll wait for the outcome of the inquiry on that point. But there's no denying that she came across new evidence which can't be ignored. I'm not sure

if you're aware, but it's a letter from Carolyn Jollimore posted to
Darby Investigations just a day before she died in what was labelled a
'single-car accident.' The letter apparently was lost for over ten years
before it reached Darby Investigations. The contents of the letter
suggest that Carolyn was aware that someone other than John J.
Dawson had killed Simone Villier."

"It sounds to me like something the police could better handle,
doesn't it?"

"Ordinarily I'd agree, but, in this case, the letter Ms. Darby received
in the mail suggested that Carolyn Jollimore felt that she could not
confide in the police. That's why I am handling it personally."

"I see. This won't interfere with your regular duties?"

"Absolutely not."

"Good." Peale reached into a tray of incoming memos, retrieved an
email, and read it to Ben.

"This came this morning. It pertains to your orientation with other
Canadian law enforcement agencies. It's been difficult to cobble this
schedule together, but we've finally worked it out. You're to meet with
RCMP at their headquarters in Ottawa day after tomorrow and with
ranking CSIS personnel the following day. Third day there's travel
to Orillia for a meet with the Deputy Commissioner of the Ontario
Provincial Police, et cetera. The following day is another travel day to
Montreal where you've been scheduled into meetings with the Sûreté
du Québec. Any problem?"

The Minister passed a copy of the email to Ben. Ben glanced quickly
over it.

"I... I guess not," he said.

43.

Habit had kick-started Anne's morning. She had launched herself out the door at six and forced herself to complete her run along the boardwalk at Victoria Park. The water was still, the air was cold and damp, the sky was breathless, and the gulls seemed frozen against the grey tableau of a twilit morning.

In spite of the dour atmosphere, however, and at the end of her run, she felt energized and ready for whatever the day promised. She felt alive.

But that sentiment was short-lived. Anne arrived at work at her usual time, but she wasn't really sure why she went there. She had no job to work at, no client to pursue, and she had one less friend to keep her spirits up, so what was the point, she thought.

By the time she put her key into the locked front door of her Victoria Street office, she had sunk into a depressing funk. She hated moping; she despised moodiness; and she loathed idleness, but now she was aware of each of those weaknesses taking hold of her, just as inevitably and insidiously as decay claims a fallen tree.

Perhaps this was a mistake, thought Anne. Perhaps she shouldn't have come here. She stood, anxiously paced the office, and returned to her desk. For a while she stood there, looking out the window. Victoria Row was bright and cheerful. Tourists, fresh from a Dutch cruise ship in the harbour, pointed cameras, clutched each other's arms, laughed, and strode briskly past and toward Province House. A flicker of their liveliness touched Anne, but with little effect. She fell again into a self-absorbed isolation.

On the street below, a wheat-coloured van pulled cautiously to the curb. Anne recognized it as Dit's van, the one he used at work. He must have got my message, she thought, and pulled away from the window lest he look up and see her there.

Anne suddenly felt excited and hopeful. She pulled a sheaf of papers from a drawer, scattered them about her desk top, and pretended to study them. She could feel her heart beat as she waited. It beat so hard that she fancied, rather foolishly, that Dit would notice it when he came through the door. Then, even more crazily, she believed she could hear the beat of her heart. A soft thump, thump, thump, thump that frightened her. Again, a soft thump, thump, thump.

She realized that the sound came from her outer door. A muted rapping.

Why would Dit knock, she asked herself. *He wouldn't*, she concluded.

"Come in," she shouted. Her voice had turned uncharacteristically loud and sharp and unreceptive.

Who the devil is it? Now...of all times.

Anne had wanted at least a solitary moment with Dit to make amends, to assure him that she had been out of sorts, that she had not meant what she had said the night before.

The door to her inner office was open wide and, from her desk, she watched the door at reception pushed in with an irritating sluggishness. A head peeped timidly from behind it. Anne recognized that it was Eli Seares.

Years before, Dit had hired two researchers for his electronics company. At the time Dit's decision caused some eyes to roll and blank stares to linger, because each of the young men had peculiarities. Urban Nolan had a degree of autism, and Eli Seares had a chronic shyness. Dit had not hired them for charity's sake, though. He knew that they had talent and ability, qualities many others viewed as curiosities, and that they were dismissed, underestimated, or masked by behavioural oddities that often accompanied them. Dit saw through all that and was among the first to perceive the potential of Eli and Urban in his business environment.

Later Dit became aware that Eli and Urban were not just good, reliable workers. They were brilliant in applied electronics and were making significant advances in the research and development of the electronics surveillance devices Dit was manufacturing.

Although Anne had desperately wanted Dit to walk through the door, her disappointment vanished when she saw Eli. Of the two researchers in Dit's shop, Eli had always been her favourite. There was something endearing about him. Perhaps his crooked little smile. It seemed to peek out reluctantly, but uncontrollably when he was happy. And he always seemed pleased when Anne visited Dit at Malone Electronics.

Eli was still half-hidden behind the front door when she beckoned him in. He smiled shyly. His glance ricocheted from her face to her shoes and then away toward the window.

"Come in, come in, Eli. I'm so glad to see you. Are you here on an errand or do you need the services of a private investigator?"

Eli's bashful giggle sounded like a stifled cough. But Anne's cheerful invitation led him away from his protective place at the door frame, and he edged into the room. His left hand toted a leather satchel. His right arm raised up to display a small black metal box. A black cable plugged into it, and at cable's end dangled a silver rod.

"An errand, then, is it? What exactly does it do?" Anne knew very well that it was a sweeping device for r.f. signals. Dit must have decided to send Eli to check for hidden listening devices instead of coming himself. He was still angry, Anne concluded.

Eli's lips moved, but no sound escaped. She saw a flicker of fear in his eyes. She smiled encouragingly at him.

"Take your time. I'm in no rush, Eli."

Eli took two long, deep breaths. Each time Anne could hear the breath expelled. All the time, Eli's eyes were fixed at a corner of the room as if searching for something. Then he began to speak.

"...*mumble* 'tronic *mumble* surveillance *mumble* 'vice." Eli spoke in soft, muted tones almost impossible to hear. His face flushed.

At work Eli had always spoken rather sparingly to Urban and Dit, just what was necessary, little more and, prior to this visit, he had managed to utter only a few words to Anne. So this venture was a new challenge.

"An electronic counter-surveillance device?" repeated Anne. He nodded jerkily.

"Yes," he whispered.

"You're going to sweep for listening devices?" she asked.

"Yes."

"Would you be more comfortable if I went away while you work... or shall I stay?"

"You can stay," he said and smiled benignly.

Eli turned the detector on and made a few adjustments.

It took less than two minutes for Eli, silver wand and cable in hand, to sweep the reception area and Anne's office. Eli displayed the bug he retrieved from her telephone and set it on her desk.

"Good one, Eli!"

Eli looked confused, then said, "...*mumble* more to do."

Anne must have had a puzzled look on her face when Eli said, "Your car." He pointed out the window. "Need to examine it." A modicum of strength had slipped into his request.

Anne's car was in a parking lot around the corner. She and Eli walked toward it. Anne unlocked the doors and got behind the steering wheel. Eli circled the car pointing the wand toward possible transmission spots. Then he climbed into the back seat with his gear. Anne watched him through the rear-view mirror. He waved the silver probe slowly around, but the r.f. detector revealed no transmission signal. He shook his head.

"Excellent," said Anne and grabbed the door handle to get out.

"No...more," he said, loudly, almost a shout from Eli's perspective. The sound of his own voice unnerved him. He recoiled, the sweetness of his elfish face dissolving into a cowering tremble, his breaths short and shallow.

"My mistake," said Anne, anxious herself for him and trying to calm him. "Sorry. What do you want me to do?"

"Drive someplace...please."

Anne drove a few blocks east and north. Eli expelled another slow deep lungful of air in an effort to control his breathing. "Yes...," he said, and more excitedly, "...a...GPS tracker."

In his own timid way, Eli made clear to Anne that he had found a second device, a latent battery-powered GPS tracker that transmitted only when the car was moving and was impossible to detect otherwise. This model could transmit signals to a remote computer or smart phone that overlaid the data onto a Google-like map image, showed the route taken and the stops made, and recorded the date and time of each.

Eli retrieved the tracker from the steel frame underneath the plastic rear bumper of her car. He dropped it in her palm as quickly and deftly as a wary pigeon nicks breadcrumbs from a hand on a park bench. Before he left the office, he gave her a weak smile, but Anne believed that he was quite worn out from the efforts he had put forth communicating with her. She thanked him profusely again and waved as he left.

From the vantage point of her window Anne watched Dit's van pull away, Eli at the wheel. It was obvious that Dit was still angry with her, but she didn't know what she could do about it. Perhaps time would heal their relationship, she thought. Or perhaps nothing could ever put things right again.

A gust of wind engulfed the Confederation Centre Library building across the street. Maple trees on the terraced courtyard quivered. A handful of red, orange, and mottled green leaves were torn from their tenuous hold on limbs and drifted onto the street.

44.

"I've got good news and bad news," said Ben. Anne was on the other end of that telephone call, still at her office, and still looking out her window.

"Shoot," she said.

"Good news is… I'm officially opening an investigation into the Villier and Jollimore deaths."

"That is good," said Anne, and then added somewhat sarcastically. "Do I get to watch?"

"Ha, ha," said Ben flatly. "You can look, but don't touch…for now."

"Thanks a lot. I'll clean up my rose-coloured glasses, too."

"Much appreciated."

"And the bad news is…?"

"I'll be out of town for a week or so."

"You never watched many Westerns when you were a kid, did you, Ben? If you had, you'd have known that good guys don't leave town 'til *after* they round up the bad guys. Cooper, Eastwood, John Wayne, Gregory Peck… Lee Marvin…et cetera, et cetera."

"They didn't work for the Province of Prince Edward Island."

"Well, thanks, Ben. That image just sucked all the life right out of my 'home on the range' fantasy. Maybe I should just go shoot myself now."

"That would be illegal…besides, moviegoers prefer happy endings."

"So what's this trip about?"

"It's been in the works for a while. A sit-down with the gold braid at various law enforcement agencies off-Island. We just got the schedule this morning. I leave tomorrow, early. I'll be gone five or six days. Kinda looking forward to it… Sarah might come, too. If I'm lucky, I might even catch a Raptors home game."

"So you'll be able to dig into *my* case when you get back?"

"Actually, with my laptop and wifi, I may be able to dig into something while I'm away. Here's the thing though. I want you to keep a low profile. Don't rock the boat. Get it?"

"Don't rock the boat," she said. "I got it."

"I mean it now. There's no need to rush ahead. None of the players are going anywhere."

"Okay, okay, I can live with that…for a while. By the way, Eli was here."

"Dit's Eli?" Ben sounded incredulous.

"Yep. He swept my office and car. Guess what? Telephone was bugged. Car had a tracking device."

"Figured. Check with Dit. See if he can assess the devices he recovered. Are they high-tech? Low-tech? Law enforcement issue? Or off-the-shelf junk? Serial numbers. They might lead somewhere, too, and could be that the program used by the tracking device is managed by an online company. If so, we might get a warrant for the account." Ben was becoming excited. So he was surprised to hear only dead silence on Anne's end. "You still there?" he added.

"Yeah, yeah, I'm still here. Sounds good but, better yet, why don't you check in with Dit on that?"

"Yeah… I guess I could handle that, if you want."

"Thanks."

Ben caught a tone in that one word that sounded troubled. He had sensed something out of tune earlier in their conversation, but had ignored it. Anne had joked and teased, much as she always did, but he perceived an edge to her humour that was not customary. It was not mean, but it was dispirited and more callous than he would have expected.

"Mind if I make a suggestion?"

"If you feel the need."

"Look, Anne. I know that you've had a rough few days…and no doubt you're going to have a few more. It's happened to me more times than I want to admit, but, whenever I've been in a fast game, and I couldn't make the moves I wanted, sometimes I'd slow things right down… change the pace big-time. It throws the other team off. Know what I'm sayin'? Think about it."

"Didn't know you played basketball, Ben."

"Never did. I'm Jewish. Remember? I'm talking chess."

45.

Anne changed the message on her answering machine to indicate that she would be out of the office for a few days. She locked the door, dropped the key into her coat pocket, and walked down the creaking wooden stairs to the main level and Victoria Row. She headed toward The Blue Peter. It was almost lunchtime.

Mary Anne's restaurant was only a few steps up Victoria Row from Anne's office but, in that short distance and in the time it took to get there, Anne had reached a conclusion: Ben's advice made sense. Maybe it was a good time to change the pace, do something different, let the dust settle on the case until she could find a side door into its secrets. There were still several pieces missing, and maybe they would fall into place with a little distance and perspective. Like Ben said, the players aren't going anywhere soon.

By the time Anne withdrew from her thoughts, she had reached the intersection at Grafton Street and, rather than backtrack to The Blue Peter, Anne turned left and headed down the street toward the waterfront. Maybe try something different for a change. *Something new*, she told herself, and *something borrowed, something blue*, echoed in its wake.

The eye-catching displays in the store windows were a welcome distraction from annoying echoes. So was the heightened bustle of lunchtime foot traffic on a mild, sunny October day. The old business district of Charlottetown, through which she walked, had been transformed wondrously since her childhood memories of the place.

She could remember holding her father's hand as they walked. Longhaired hippies and their bizarre attire were commonplace then, but still a curiosity to a five-year-old from a conservative family. A craft shop and a fancy restaurant had recently displaced the shoemaker's narrow workplace, as well as a tailor shop her father used to frequent. And an art store with paintings of landscape and seascape hanging in its window had opened. Some looked like a child had painted them. Her father had laughed and swore that the shop wouldn't survive the year, but it did.

Since that time, a large hotel had risen on the site of the old waterfront. Alongside it were the yacht club and a marina and the memorial park. Long gone were the decrepit wharves, rundown sheds, and nighttime gathering places for local drunks, layabouts, and vagrants.

By half-past twelve, Anne found herself at the water's edge. Construction of a new convention centre had begun. The noise and dust were disturbing. So Anne edged away and followed a waterside boardwalk. The tide was rising. Waves lapped playfully against the rock breakwater and, in that watery chatter, Anne imagined children's laughter.

The sound of laughing children faded while Anne stared across the bay toward Stratford and along its shore. Simone Villier and Carolyn Jollimore and Jamie MacFarlane came to mind. Dit, too, his lavish home visible there among the trees across the water.

Something borrowed, something blue echoed again, and Anne felt a cool wind draw in with the tide from the harbour's mouth.

Anne abandoned the boardwalk, cut up through the yacht club, past the half-dozen boats already hauled up and trussed securely in carriages for winter storage. She turned again and strolled between the brick of the new courthouse on one side of the street and a row of brick lawyers' offices on the other. Grafton Street lay just ahead. She had come full circle.

Anne stopped at the corner and waited for the light to turn. She heard footsteps padding softly behind her. She looked back and saw a familiar face.

It was Jacob Dawson.

"Jake," she said, greeting him. It took a few more steps before he reached her. He recognized her, stopped, but struggled to remember her name.

"Billy... Darby, isn't it?"

"It is. What brings you down here? Break from school?"

"A bit of old business," he said, gesturing vaguely back toward the brick buildings up the street. "And you?"

"Just a walk to unwind before lunch." Anne checked her watch. It was pushing one o'clock. "I suppose you've already eaten," she said.

"No, not yet. Irene... Ms. MacLeod...usually makes up a bowl of soup and a sandwich if I'm not too late. I'm on my way back now."

"Sounds like she takes an interest."

"She's had troubles with the law...like me. She tries to reach out."

"A good friend. Well, I'm on my way to the restaurant just around the corner. You're welcome to join me."

"No," he said hesitantly, "I don't think I can..."

"It's on me, of course. Great food there, and it beats soup and a sandwich...or cafeteria cooking."

"Well... I guess a student can't refuse a deal like that, can he?"

The Crown and Anchor was less than a block away. It was a popular restaurant decorated with a blend of nautical and regal motifs. Poses of famous and unremembered aristocrats wearing white wigs and buckled shoes and holding ornate swords decorated wood-panelled walls. Ships serenely at anchor in soft pastel mists or in close engagements at sea joined them. Comfortable, high-backed booths gave the feel of privacy and softened the voices from other tables.

The Crown and Anchor was half-filled at the end of the dinner hour. Dawson, dressed in jeans and a university sweatshirt, looked around somewhat uncomfortably while Anne studied the menu.

"Grilled salmon, asparagus tips, and baked sweet potato is the special. Sounds yummy. What would you like, Jake?"

"That sounds good," he said absently.

"Are you sure?"

"Yeah, sounds perfect," he said, this time with confidence.

Anne placed the order with the waitress. Water and coffee arrived promptly.

"How's school going?" Anne asked in order to stir up conversation and put Jacob at ease.

"Very well," he said.

"Sociology, isn't it?" asked Anne. Jacob nodded.

"Why that major?"

"Circumstances," he said. "I would have preferred following a science curriculum, but it's pretty hard to complete lab assignments in prison." He smiled for the first time. "'Please pass the potassium nitrate and sulphur' always draws suspicious looks from the guards."

"You have a year left? What'll you do after you graduate?"

"Social worker, addictions counsellor. Something along that line. I have a lot of experience to pass along there."

"Was it difficult getting started with university courses? Did the government pay for it?"

"The government will pay for GED and trade courses, not college courses so much, but I got some financial help from the John Howard Society once I convinced them I could handle the material. They funded a couple courses. I had access to tutors at Dorchester, and I could write to a student advisor at the school to keep me on track. Fortunately, I had a brother and sister who were luckier than I growing up. Maybe they felt guilty about it. Anyway, they split the cost of my correspondence courses between them. It didn't amount to a lot of money all at the same time, and I pulled together a few dollars myself from my work in prison. Only a few bucks a day, but I didn't smoke...and had nothing much else to spend it on."

"And now?"

"The University was impressed with my progress," he said proudly. "They gave me a late-entrance scholarship to cover tuition for the courses I have left...and I work some evenings and weekends at Milton Springs. I'm on the front desk. It's slow, but I can catch a few hours of study between calls or check-ins. Thank you," he said to the waitress. She had slipped a plate in front of Anne, another in front of him. She was young, dark-haired, pretty. Her eyes were lively and her smile warm, and her attention lingered on Jacob.

"Looks like you have a fan," said Anne after the waitress left.

"It's an illusion, Billy. Once they learn *my* history, I'm history."

"That will change," she said, "and you must have made some friends by now." Jacob didn't respond, and they continued their meal with little more than the clink of forks and knives to cut the silence.

The first sign of alarm rang in the frozen expression on John Jacob Dawson's face. He stared toward another booth as a couple was preparing to leave. The woman was in her late twenties, dark-haired, and dressed in a mocha business suit. Her low-cut blouse was not businesslike. She moved gracefully and sensuously across the room, quite accustomed to the gazes that followed her.

The man was tall and solidly built with short, greying hair. He was good-looking, confident, and dressed informally in tailored slacks, a button-down shirt, and a lightweight Hudson's Bay sweater. Unlike her, his eyes roamed the room casually and continually and unconsciously. His roving eyes stopped when they touched the table at which Anne and Jacob sat.

Anne turned and looked. She watched Chief MacFarlane approach their table. Quickly, she turned to Dawson: "Take a deep breath, and act normal...don't talk."

"Billy Darby," said MacFarlane. "What a coincidence. Heard you weren't around anymore."

"Sorry to disappoint, Chief. I don't disappear very easily."

"A resilient spirit," he said and then looked Dawson in the eye. "I don't recognize your friend."

"Jacob. This is Jamie, Stratford's Police Chief. Jamie, Jake. Jacob is a sociology student at the university. He's writing a paper on law enforcement and is looking for a private investigator's perspective."

"You'd make better use of your time if you interviewed real law enforcement officers, Jacob." MacFarlane stared closely at Dawson. Anne fought back an impulse to match MacFarlane's demeaning remark. Dawson took hold of his glass of water and sipped. "Do I know you?" MacFarlane asked.

Dawson finished off his water. He put the glass down, a big smile blossomed on his face, and he chuckled.

"I really doubt that we travel in the same circles, Chief, but it's a pleasure to meet you."

Dawson extended his hand. MacFarlane shook it firmly, smiled back, and returned his attention to Anne.

"Heard about your...unfortunate situation," he said. "Heard, too, about your taking a vacation, so to speak."

"You've got big ears, Chief. Vacation? I prefer to think of it as a moment to pause and reflect on the evidence I've pulled together... loose ends...like false statements in a police report...like a potential suspect who lied about fathering a dead girl's baby."

"A harmless embellishment to protect her reputation, no doubt..."

"...or a bit of smoke to hide a crime...," Anne said. "And I seem to find more smoke the longer I look."

"Sometimes the smoke you see has drifted from somebody else's fire," he said. MacFarlane leaned over the booth, one arm clutching the back of her seat, the other planted firmly on the table. He loomed over Anne and added in an ominous whisper, "And sometimes people get burnt, when they look in the wrong direction too long."

Then MacFarlane straightened up, stepped back, assumed a relaxed stance, and smiled.

"But good luck with that...," he said calmly. Then he turned toward Dawson: "...and good luck with your paper, Jake. Ms. Darby has my number if you need a professional point of view."

46.

"I wanted to plunge my fork right through his windpipe. I wanted to hear the gurgle of his blood every time he breathed. The fork was still in my hand."

"Why didn't you?"

"I thought of prison. It'd be a life sentence for certain this time. But I could have killed him...just like that," Jacob said, snapping his fingers. "It all came flooding back...the relentless interrogations...the stink of the officer's breath...the ache inside me...my need for a drink...so strong that all I could feel was my thirst and they all knew it. MacFarlane knew it even though he wasn't in the room. He wasn't stupid. He knew how to get around things at the station. He had leverage."

"You can't kill him. Not now, anyway."

"But I could have," he said. Irene MacLeod couldn't decide whether his answer indicated repentance for the urge or disappointment at the missed opportunity.

Irene took away the untouched bowl of soup she had placed in front of Jacob when he returned home. She took it to the kitchen, and she poured it down the drain.

Meanwhile Jacob stared at the empty white place-setting on the table in front of him. His hands trembled; his thoughts were a jumble; and he needed a drink.

He longed desperately for a drink.

Anne texted Jacqui that she would pick her up after school. She stopped at the Bottom Dollar Market, picked up a few sale items, and pulled into the pick-up lane at the high school. She was still a few minutes early, time enough to pick over the bones of her unlucky encounter with MacFarlane at The Crown and Anchor.

So much for keeping a low profile, she thought. *Ben would be pretty crabby if he knew, but it wasn't my intention...or my fault. Meeting Jacob was a coincidence...and coming across MacFarlane, in that place, was a terrible fluke.*

The shocked expression on Jake's face flashed through Anne's mind. She was amazed at how quickly he recovered. MacFarlane hadn't recognized him, but that didn't mean he wouldn't pull things together later. Obviously something twigged in MacFarlane's memory, and that was a worry. Another worry was her revelation about him getting Simone pregnant. That stirred something in him, too, but exactly what and how important it was, she couldn't calculate.

The school bell jarred her out of the reflections. Streams of students poured through every exit door in a blurry explosion of energy and movement and noise and colour. It was a bit dizzying, but the thump against the side of Anne's car startled her. Unable to brake their run soon enough, Jacqui and Rada had fallen against it. A burst of chattery laughter, a thud of books, and the solid clunk of a closing rear door followed.

"Hi!" both girls shouted out, almost in unison, and laughed at the coincidence.

"No school for a couple days, huh?" asked Anne.

"Nope," both girls said, simultaneously again, and fell into convulsive giggles. "Teachers' Convention," added Jacqui.

"I got some downtime the next few days, too. So what would you say to some driving lessons tomorrow?"

"Super. Can Rada tag along?"

"Don't see why not."

47.

A solitary crow clung to a limb, topping the elm tree a few houses up from Anne's home. The crow was motionless and barely visible, a shadow among shadows at four in the morning. Its head cocked perceptively at the soft grind of footsteps along the stone walkway below, but it kept silent, its black eyes peering through grey skies and mottled leaves at the dark figure beneath it.

The figure was practically imperceptible as well, blending with darkened houses, the pre-dawn gloom, and street-front shrubbery. It stopped at Anne's driveway, looked around carefully, and listened until the sound of a light truck on an adjacent street faded completely. Then it moved up the driveway toward a car parked within the deep shadows of her house. He slipped beneath Anne's vehicle. The narrow beam of a small Maglite illuminated the undercarriage and traced the line of the exhaust system back to the manifold.

There was just enough room for the man in black to work his arms and hands and shift his head. He fitted two plastic cable ties loosely around the pipe. He took a pre-cut half-section of radiator hose from his overalls and slipped it between the plastic ties and the pipe. He carefully bedded a stick of industrial dynamite into the rubber hose, plugged both ends with cloth, and cinched the cable ties until the explosive and primer fuse were tightly secured in the rubber casing around the pipe, just behind the exhaust manifold.

The man removed himself from beneath the vehicle and looked carefully around. Suddenly, lights flashed at the corner and illuminated the street. His heart began to pound. A car roared toward him. Its muffler had broken. A pipe on its undercarriage scraped and squealed when it struck the pavement, and it spat a stream of sparks with every bounce.

The man in black sank into the shrubbery of a nearby house. A light snapped on in a bedroom window across the street. Perhaps others had been awakened, too, he thought. So he remained motionless in his shadowy hiding place.

Ten minutes past. Then fifteen. Twenty. By that time, all the lights in all the houses had darkened, the birds had become still again, and an unbroken peace had fallen over the street. Only then did the dark figure emerge from cover and steal away.

48.

"Girls, come on! Time's a-wasting!" Anne shouted. She grabbed her jacket, slipped shoes on, and snatched her car keys from a pegboard in the pantry. A clatter reverberated in the upstairs bedroom and travelled down the stairs toward the living room. Choruses of laughter and indecipherable girlish gibberish preceded Jacqui and Rada's near-collision with Anne at the back door, followed by a timely but not altogether convincing "sorry" from both girls.

"All set?" asked Anne.

"Yes," both replied.

"Learner's permit?"

"Got it," said Jacqui.

"And you're sure your mother knows what we're doing?"

"Yes, Mrs. Brown. I told her that you were taking us for a drive," she said and glanced furtively at Jacqui.

Anne paused for a moment, wondering whether or not Rada's mother would equate that with Jacqui learning how to pilot a car in a parking lot. She thought not but shrugged it off.

"Okay, hop in," Anne directed.

Anne glanced in the rear-view mirror. Rada looked somehow different, she thought.

"Seat belts? Okay," she said and turned the key in the ignition.

Pius and Germaine Arsenault would celebrate their fiftieth wedding anniversary in two more days, but they wouldn't celebrate at home in Tignish. Instead their five children had chipped in and arranged a vacation in New Orleans. It would be a pleasure trip. Music and delicious food were to be expected. But they were looking forward to more than that.

Germaine had acquired an interest in genealogical research. In fact, she had become the unofficial folklorist and historian for both the Arsenault and the Gallant families.

Great-great-great-great-great grandparents on both sides of their families had been transported to New Orleans by British occupiers of Isle Saint-Jean during the Acadian Expulsion in the mid-eighteenth century. A few family members had stayed and managed to escape the purge by fleeing to New Brunswick or hiding in the deep woods of Prince Edward Island until such time as the British gave up their madness or French troops retook the settlements, something which never came to be.

Germaine's research had turned up distant cousins still living in Terrebonne and St. Charles parishes in Louisiana. She had corresponded with them on several occasions, and they were anxious to meet face to face. Everyone was looking forward to that reunion and the festivities they knew would surround it.

"You've got your passport?" Germaine asked.

"Yes, yes, you ask me already two time," he said.

"And your pills," she added.

"Yes," he replied simply. There was no point in arguing.

"And you took them this morning," she said.

"Yes, yes," he said. This time he became gruff.

Germaine wriggled in her passenger seat as if to make it more comfortable. It didn't. This was Germaine's way of indicating that she was angry with Pius.

That man always forget something, she thought.

"I know what you are thinking," he said. Germaine looked at him sternly. "Don't think so loud. I can hear every word...and not very nice to me either. What kind of language is that from a lady!" he said and shot a leathery-faced grin at her.

Germaine laughed and poked her fist in his side.

The Arsenaults' car sped through Cornwall and North River. Only another two or three more miles and they'd reach the airport.

"Where are we going to practise?" asked Jacqui.

"I think maybe the high school. It has a long access road with no ditches and no buildings and a huge parking lot. No cars there today. The teachers' meetings that have set you loose from school are in Summerside and Montague."

"And we wouldn't want to hit a teacher during practice," laughed Jacqui.

"Except maybe Mr. Shadi," said Rada, who blushed at her own boldness.

"Who's Mr. Shadi," asked Anne.

"Just a teacher," said Jacqui. "Hey, you missed the turn."

"Need gas," said Anne. "And some extra-strength aspirin for later."

Anne stole a quick look in the rear-view mirror. Jacqui had caught her meaning and smiled back, more of a smirk really. Then Anne glanced at Rada again. *Something different*, she thought. *Ah, yes, a hint of lipstick...and a little makeup has brightened her eyes.*

"Here we are," she said and swung off the road into a gas station at the intersection of the Trans-Canada Highway. She glided into an empty spot at a pump and turned off the ignition. She popped the fuel cap, activated the pump, and squeezed the handle. Her fuel was low, but it seemed to take forever to fill the tank. She stared off toward the intersection absentmindedly and then back at the girls who were busy texting someone.

It was a busy location, this close to the highway. Several vehicles were stacked up and waiting for an open pump. So, when she had finished, Anne backed out and parked the car out of the way along the curb of a walkway and went inside to pay. It was busy there, too. Three people had lined up ahead of her. Another stood behind.

Anne's car chugged merrily along the curb. The girls texted friends from the back seat. Anne waited in line with dwindling patience. The first customer started to pay for his gas and a special on milk and bananas but had to exchange the whole milk he had grabbed for 2%. The second customer bought scratch-and-win tickets, scratched a small win without leaving the lineup, and used that to buy more tickets.

That's when it happened.

"Pius, you look like you chew on a lemon."

"Heartburn. Gas," he said. "You bring those Tums or Rolaids or whatever they are?"

Germaine dug around, grasping for something in her bottomless purse. Her hand found a roll of something. She picked two tablets from it and handed them to Pius.

"Here," she said.

Pius said nothing. His sunburnt face was turning grey. His eyes were closing. His fingers gripped the steering wheel. His chin nudged his chest, and his car hurtled toward a red light at the intersection.

Germaine's eyes grew wide. She dropped the tablets and tried to wrestle the wheel from Pius's hands, but she could not do so. Luckily, no one had stopped at the light ahead. But Germaine looked with horror at two cars just past the intersection, approaching and preparing for a left turn in front of them. Germaine desperately hung onto the steering wheel. She pushed it up, counter-clockwise, but it wouldn't turn. She pulled down on it, and their car sprang across three lanes. Germaine watched the widening eyes of the first driver, in a little white pickup, as he entered the turn. He hit his brakes quickly enough, but the driver behind him was slower to respond, rear-ended the truck, and drove it forward so that it clipped the rear fender of Germaine's vehicle.

Germaine's hand slipped from the wheel when her car spun round and round, but, when it straightened, it pointed toward the corner of the gas station, the corner where Anne had parked. It picked up speed. Pius's foot had remained on the accelerator, and Germaine was too shaken and disoriented to respond.

49.

Ben would describe himself as robust; his wife, Sarah, would describe him as overweight. Not more than fifteen pounds, he would argue. Day to day, his size was not a problem. But for Ben an airline seat always felt like being bound in a straitjacket. Fortunately, on this day and on this flight, the seat next to him was empty. Sarah had decided that she had too much year-end gardening to attend to. So she had stayed in Charlottetown instead of travelling.

He missed her but still nodded to divine providence for the small kindness that now his arm and elbow could sprawl wherever it wandered, and it could still share the empty seat with the Simone Villier case file, the part of it he had brought with him anyway.

Time to boldly think where no cop has thought before, he reflected as he paged through the file. Then the urban sprawl of Montreal Island broke through the clouds, the seatbelt sign illuminated with a ringtone, and the pilot announced the descent. *Okay, Scotty, time to beam me up a lead.*

Ben repacked the papers and reports and looked at his watch. It was twenty after ten. He must remember to change to Eastern Time after the plane landed, he thought.

The scratch-and-win woman was getting on Anne's nerves. Another small win and another ticket taken in exchange. Anne looked at her watch—almost ten-thirty. She had hoped to complete a solid hour of driving practice and pick up a few groceries before lunch. That was not so probable now, and Anne was about to clear her throat loudly and wave her charge card in the air, but the clerk suddenly straightened and stared past her out the window. She almost produced an expression of profound bewilderment, but horror displaced it. Then terror struck with a resounding crash, the shattering of glass, and an explosion.

Everything unfolded in a slow motion for Anne. *Not a myth*, she thought. It was a peculiar observation to punctuate a horrific experience, but it was her last thought before she lost consciousness.

The Arsenaults' car had hurtled across the station lot, grazed a gas pump, and struck Anne's car. It exploded in a blast that lifted it off the ground, shattering the windows of the station. Shards and splinters of debris flew in every direction. Shrapnel tore across the room. So did shredded racks of newspapers, candy boxes, and chintzy souvenirs. The fragments punctured plastic bottles and pressurized aluminum cans, and they sliced through shirts and hats and the flesh of those trapped inside the building. Then a huge fireball erupted in the midst of the wreckage of the two cars outside. A wave of intense heat singed nearby parked cars, and billowing smoke drifted into the station.

Screams and shouts followed the trauma, heard outside first and faintly inside. Shrieks and sobbing followed the recovery of one's senses, the sight of fallen bodies, the spectacle of blood dripping from wounds and seeping through clothing, and the dread of unspeakable consequences.

Paramedics and firefighters arrived on the scene within five minutes. They found that most of the damage and most casualties had been very near or inside the building.

The scratch-and-win woman had just stepped away from the counter when the explosion happened. She had turned toward a wall of flying glass and was splattered with fragments. One splinter caught her throat and nicked the jugular vein. She bled heavily. The store clerk escaped serious injury. Her position and a solid counter had shielded her.

The man behind Anne was critically injured. The force of the blast had thrown him into Anne, and she was driven headfirst into the service counter. Several others, browsing the displays nearer to the source of the explosion, were hospitalized for severe wounds. One never recovered consciousness and died of burns. It could have been much worse, news reports later claimed, if the station clerk hadn't pulled the emergency fuel shut-off switch for the pumps.

Anne was the last of the injured to be transported by ambulance to the Queen Elizabeth Hospital. She was semi-conscious at the time and rode alone.

50.

Dorval Airport. A three-hour layover. What a waste, thought Ben. He could almost walk to Ottawa in three hours. Now he was stuck, just a taxi ride from historic Old Montreal, the site of the finest international cuisine in Canada. Nothing focuses the mind better, thought Ben, than the hope of a magnificent meal in a world-class restaurant. One of his favourites, an Indian restaurant, hung temptingly in his memory. Should he risk a taxi ride in? Then he recalled once spending two hours in a snarl of traffic on a Montreal expressway. Perhaps he shouldn't.

The Dorval layover wasn't a complete waste, though. Ben worked through it and uncovered two lines of inquiry that might be worth following up on. The first was *Tidewater*, the organization Simone Villier had worked for. Very little of it had been mentioned in the case file, other than a brief interview with Simone's immediate superior, a Dale something-or-other. The second was a deeper look at Chief MacFarlane himself. Stratford wasn't his first job as a peace officer. As a rookie he had been assigned to Bridgewater, Nova Scotia, where he would have to have stirred up a bit of paperwork or been evaluated or remembered. Perhaps something worthwhile might turn up there. Or maybe, with a little luck, his new about-to-be-friends at RCMP headquarters might be able to dig deeper for him.

Ben felt pleased with himself, and the craving for food had slipped temporarily from his mind. Ben repacked the file in his carry-on bag and headed for the boarding gate. His Ottawa flight had been called.

The Queen Elizabeth Hospital was unprepared for the influx of victims at Emergency. The waiting room had been near capacity with walk-in patients when ambulances began to arrive. The critical and seriously injured were whisked into the trauma centre. Anne and several others with lesser injuries were placed on gurneys and left in a hallway for an available doctor.

Anne regained consciousness there but remained dazed and disoriented until she recalled the circumstance that had led her to the gas station: Jacqui's driving lesson.

"Jacqui! Jacqui!" Her voice was weak and hoarse from the smoke she had inhaled. Her cough rattled with phlegm.

Is she not here? Where is she?

Anne called out again: "Jacqui!" Her voice broke again. She turned her head, saw no one, and tried to sit up, but a passing nurse intervened, urged her to remain calm, and asked her what she needed.

"My daughter," she said, "and her girlfriend...were there." Her eyes were filled with fear and unanswered questions, but the nurse assured her that she would inquire, even though she'd not seen any young people brought to Emergency.

Anne's heart leapt hopefully at the news. *Thank god they're okay,* she thought. But a short while later, a bit less confused, her mind reprocessed the meaning in the nurse's words in a different way: *If they're not here, then they must be dead.*

"Where is she? Where's my daughter? Jacqui!" Anne screamed and raised herself up on the gurney. Her feet touched the ground, but her legs collapsed beneath her. Two nurses hurried to her side. Anne weakly resisted. An Emergency-room doctor calmly filled a syringe.

51.

Constable Timothy Foley had graduated the Summerside Police Academy earlier in the year. He was lucky to have been offered a job so quickly. He was thrilled by it, but he was bottom man in seniority, slightly above station gofer, and trusted with little beyond the ABCs of his duty assignments with the Charlottetown Police force. It was a small blow to his ego. He was eager to do more. He wanted to use his skills and prove his worth. But that wouldn't happen today.

His day had started lazily. A few hours into it, the call came in—an explosion and fire at the service station on the Trans-Canada Highway. Both City Police and RCMP responded. His adrenaline surged. An exciting hour of drama followed. His role, however, proved to be little more than that of spear-carrier in a high school Shakespearean tragedy. Then, almost too quickly, it pretty much ended, except for traffic control and following detectives roaming the scene.

He started the engine and pulled away from the devastation of the gas station. Smoke still lifted from a few hot spots in the ruins. Firefighters kept a spray on them as well as the gas pumps. The acrid smell of burnt rubber and melted plastic hung in Foley's nostrils.

He looked in his rear-view mirror at the two women in the back of his cruiser.

"First, we'll head for admissions at the QEH. Hopefully, your mother will there, Jacqui."

Perhaps I should have said "likely," Foley thought to himself...*or "I'm sure she'll be...."*

Jacqui said nothing. Nor did Rada. And the rest of the trip to the hospital passed without words. Jacqui was numb, and, if she had dared to hope that her mother was alive, her hope was crushed by the indelible image of their twisted and burnt-out shell of a car.

Foley inquired for Anne Brown at the Emergency desk. The nurse on duty wrote a room number on a slip of paper and explained that she had been admitted a few minutes before. That was Jacqui's first good news since the explosion. The second was the floor nurse who reassured her that her mother was well but resting.

After reassurance that the girls would be all right, Foley took his leave. Jacqui sat by her mother's bed and watched her breathe. She looked small and pale and fragile, almost like a child, she thought.

"Mom?" Jacqui spoke when she saw her mother's head move and her eyelids quiver.

Anne heard the words as if part of the dream she was having, a bizarre dream, none of which she would later remember.

"Mom, wake up. You're all right. We're all right."

Now Jacqui sounded as if she were weeping, but she couldn't see her and, despite the soothing words, believed that Jacqui sounded troubled and needed help. Anne struggled, her arms felt trapped, and something covered her face.

"Nurse, I think she's waking up."

It took a few minutes for Anne to orient herself to her surroundings, a bed in a general ward of the hospital. Jacqui was sitting in a chair next to the bed. The nurse slipped through the curtain divider and removed an oxygen mask from Anne's face.

"Won't need this anymore," the nurse said. "You're doing just fine. And you've got some company. So I'll let you two chat. I'll be 'round again in a few minutes."

"Don't cry, Mom," said Jacqui, bending down and wrapping her arms around her mother.

"I'll cry if I want to. I thought you were dead."

"And I thought you were," said Jacqui. Both laughed and cried at the same time.

"What happened?" asked Anne. She struggled to sit up, still a bit fuzzy-headed. Jacqui placed a second pillow behind her.

"Rada wanted to try my mascara. It would have been awkward in the car, and the lighting would have been better in the washroom, and you had been in line for so long...anyway, we were only in there for a minute when we heard a crash and an explosion. The light went out in the washroom, and we tried to get out. We didn't know what was happening. We were so scared. But the door wouldn't budge. We couldn't get out. We were stuck there. We pounded and pounded, but nobody came. All we heard was screaming and sirens and..."

Jacqui started to shake and cry again at the retelling. She was sitting on the edge of the bed. Anne reached out for her and she dropped down on the bed next to Anne. Anne held her there and soothed her.

"That's okay, babe. You don't have to talk about it."

Jacqui sobbed for a few minutes in her mother's arms and, without moving, began to speak again.

"... And then someone must have heard us. The firefighters...they tried to get us out but couldn't. A few minutes later they used some kind of grinder or saw to take the door off. We couldn't believe what we saw. Our car…was hardly there…and you weren't…"

Anne felt her daughter's squeeze, and she hugged her back and held her safely against her. "It's okay, baby."

"The firefighters took us to a paramedic, and the paramedic took us to a police officer, and he drove us to the hospital. That's about it."

"That's plenty for now. And Rada's okay, too?"

Jacqui nodded.

Rada had remained at a waiting area near the ward and called her father. He arrived twenty minutes later.

Ahmed Kikovic was a deskbound engineer and designer, and, like most men in a sedentary occupation, he carried a noticeable waistline. Ahmed was in his early fifties and always wore a coat and tie to work, in spite of a very relaxed company dress policy. His hair was full, trimmed and swept straight back, greying at the tips. His eyebrows were bushy. They gave him a fierce look, especially when he was distressed, and this was one of those times.

"Rada," he cried as he entered the waiting area. The place was empty except for his daughter, who looked dishevelled, tired, and dejected, alone at the end of a cushioned bench. He grabbed her by her shoulders and looked directly at her. "Are you all right? It was on the radio, too."

Rada nodded but began to cry and put her arms around his neck. He held her gently for a few moments and then stood up.

"Where is your hijab?" he asked.

"It must have burnt in the car," she said. She sounded apologetic and embarrassed. Her hand rose to her head as if it might still have been there.

Ahmed took another step back and looked at her more closely.

"What change is this?" he asked, surprised.

Rada's glance dropped to the floor.

"What is that on your eyes?"

"Eyeliner?" she said. "It is allowed."

"The other?" said Ahmed, still pointing. His voice had risen. His tone had grown harsh.

"They call it mascara."

"And is it halal?" he demanded. "And perfume? I can smell it. Is it halal? And where do you get this mascara and this perfume?"

"From Jacqui."

"And those clothes?" he said pointing to her skirt.

"It's Jacqui's. We just play. We exchange clothes. We were just play-ing," she said and tugged at Jacqui's skirt, but it wouldn't pull down more than a few inches above her knee.

"This is not playing. You are not a child any longer. You are a young woman. A Muslim woman. Soon you will be ready to marry. But what righteous man will find you worthy to be his wife if he sees you like this? You will bring shame upon yourself and your family.

"All this is haram!" he shouted and waved his arms. Two nurses emerged from the doorway to another ward. At the raised voice of Ahmed they directed severe stares and walked past.

"I did no harm," Rada said. "I did no wrong."

"So, now you rewrite scripture. Yes? What a wise child you have become in that school of yours. At sixteen, you speak on tradition. At sixteen, you interpret the Quran."

"I did not mean that."

"Perhaps not, but you have become wilful and grown weak...and *you* have led her to this place," he said. His finger pointed at Jacqui. She had just pushed through the doors from the general ward to see if Rada was all right. She froze in place at the condemnation Rada's father had levelled at her. Then Ahmed turned fully around toward Jacqui. Both alarm and dismay swept over her.

"You teach her to be bold and shameless and to display herself like an ornament in a shop window. A pity you have no father to instruct you. And your mother...she works and provides and that is right... but she pursues labours which are unsuited for a woman...and we see how that path has served her today...the visitation of chaos and destruction. It is a sign and a warning."

Jacqui wanted to shout out that it had been an accident, nothing more, but she could not make herself speak. Only her eyes could speak and that was to tell Rada she was sorry. Tears were streaming down Rada's cheeks. Her eyeliner and mascara had weakened their hold and were staining her cheeks. Her father took her arm and led her down the long corridor toward the stairs to the exit.

52.

"You had a rough day at the office, haven't you, my dear?"

Anne was sitting up in her hospital bed, waiting for Jacqui to return with a real cup of coffee from the cafeteria when the woman entered her ward and drew back her curtain.

"Edna, what are you doing here?"

"I was visiting old friends when the ambulances started to arrive. They needed help obviously...especially with all these government cutbacks...so they pressed me into service, so to speak...as a volunteer."

"But you're a vet."

"I was a nurse...," she said. It was a rebuke, but a gentle one and well-meant. "...and still am."

"So you are."

"Besides, no classes today...no meetings...nobody at home to nag... and glad to help out. Saw your name on a list and thought I'd pop in."

"I appreciate that, Edna. It was very kind of you."

"How are you feeling? Really."

"A bit achy and tired...the gash on my shoulder is sore. A few stitches. So, no strapless evening gowns for a while. But well enough to go home."

"A head injury?" Edna asked, pointing to a bandage on Anne's head. Anne nodded.

"Did you lose consciousness?" Anne nodded again and shrugged it off. Edna returned a rather sober gaze without comment.

"I come from a long line of stubborn, hard-headed Irish and German stock. I'll be fine."

Edna seemed temporarily distracted, and then caught herself and replied: "I'm sure you will. Anyway, I brought this. Thought you could use it." Edna drew a slip of paper from her handbag and handed it to her. "If I've underestimated, let me know."

Anne looked at it thoughtfully. It was a cheque made payable to her. Anne put the cheque on the food tray next to her bed and pushed it back toward Edna.

"Thanks. It's fine...and generous, too. A bit premature though. The case is incomplete, and I dislike billing for half a job."

"No matter. I was very satisfied with your efforts. I've gotten my money's worth, I'm sure of it. I'm also sure that I don't want to put you at any more personal risk."

"You don't believe that all this is related to my investigation, do you?"

Edna opened her mouth as if to speak, but found no words.

Anne continued: "This was clearly an accident...a one-off...not related to anything but chance."

"And the suspension?"

"You heard about that?"

"It's in this morning's paper. A small article."

"Oh my god. Those bastards. They're determined to destroy my business, aren't they? Edna, don't let that discourage you."

"It won't. Perhaps some time in the future we'll continue the investigation. As for right now, I think I want to step back a bit and get some perspective."

"If it's about the money, don't..."

"It's not that. Even going this far has been quite hard on me emotionally, and I need some distance. For now, anyway, our business is over. Thanks again, Anne."

Edna gently shoved the cheque a bit closer to Anne. Then she patted her arm, turned, and left.

When the privacy curtain around Anne's bed swung shut, she could hear the little sounds from occupants of the five other beds in her ward: the coughing, soft dialogues among friends, the shuffle of slippers across the tiled floor, the bustle of nurses coming and going. But none of it was a tonic for the emptiness Anne now felt. Her client had quit, and that meant she no longer had a valid claim to investigate on her behalf. *The Guardian* news story would soon dry up any current business, and probably that would poison the well of potential clients. On PEI business had always been fuelled by word-of-mouth references. Now, as far as Darby Investigations was concerned, only a lingering bad taste would prevail.

Jacqui pushed through the curtain to Anne's bed.

"How's Rada?" asked Anne.

"Her father picked her up," said Jacqui. She sounded disheartened. Anne's natural instinct was to somehow spring Jacqui from her blue mood, but Anne had no energy for it now. She had her own mudhole to wade through. So, for a long while, both women remained silently together, each retiring within her own contemplation and solitude.

Numerous minutes passed. Finally, Anne could stand it no more. Her stillness, her self-pity, her inaction overcame her. She felt as if she were being buried under their stifling weight. She sprang up. A wave of dizziness struck her but quickly passed.

"Jacqui, hand me my clothes."

The sharpness in Anne's voice roused Jacqui from her self-indulgent reverie. She handed them to her mother, and Anne began to dress.

"And where are we going in such a rush?"

Dr. Peter T. Little passed through the curtain veil into Anne's cubicle and nearly tripped over Jacqui who had squatted down to retrieve her mother's shoes. Jacqui glanced up and saw an owl. Dr. Little was a short, wiry man with a ruddy complexion and short red hair. His round eyes looked through round, wire-framed spectacles. They fixed on Anne.

"Time to go. I'm feeling much better now."

"Sorry. Can't let you go." Little spoke coolly and decisively.

"Why not?"

"A couple of reasons. First of all, you'll scare the devil out of hospital visitors."

Anne stared back with a puzzled expression. Dr. Little stuck out his arm and pointed.

"First, the blood all over your jacket and blouse. Second, you smell like a jumble of fuel oil and Girl Guide campfires."

"Thanks, Doc. You sure know how to make a woman feel special."

Dr. Little ignored her.

"Third, we need to keep you overnight. For observation."

"I'm feeling great. What's to observe?"

"You may or may not have a concussion."

"Like I said. I feel great."

"It's a precaution. You were unconscious for a bit. Somewhat disoriented. I can't let you go."

"I like you, too, Doc, but I'm fine. Trust me."

"Let your...sister...go home, get you...and maybe her...some fresh clothes, have a good rest tonight, and maybe you can leave in the morning."

Jacqui's face soured in disgust. Anne forced back a grin.

"I'm liking you even better now, Doc, but no thanks. Got things to do."

"Perhaps I haven't been clear. You will not be discharged today. Period. I'll look in again tomorrow. Then we'll talk." Little paused a moment in order for his words to sink in. Then he turned and left.

"Is this a hospital or a prison?" Anne shouted after him.

Little's head popped back through the curtain. Anne detected an owlish grin.

"Welcome to 'Hotel California.'"

53.

From the Hilton Garden Inn where Ben had spent the evening, it had been a fifteen-minute taxi drive along the Rideau River to the new national headquarters building of the Royal Canadian Mounted Police. During last night's phone call, Sarah had told him about the gas station explosion. He would have caught the next plane home, but Sarah reassured him that it wasn't necessary. Anne was okay. She would keep an eye on her and keep him updated.

The new billion-dollar building rose out of the autumn landscape southwest of the capital. The glitter of glass and the silvery gleam of the great structure immediately caught one's eye. Its grounds spread across fifty acres, most of it grassy patches, avenues, and immense parking areas.

Ben passed through security and was escorted through an atrium and down a wide corridor to a small amphitheatre. Already seated were eighteen men and four women, some in police or military uniforms, some not; some Canadian, others foreign.

Ben received an information packet and an individualized agenda. RCMP Commissioner Keith Whately greeted the ensemble. A fifteen-minute introductory video rolled across the screen. A half-hour guided group tour followed. After that, a small cadre of escorts sorted and gathered those with similar agendas and led them to their scheduled orientation sites. Ben's group included a police superintendent from Nova Scotia and a chatty senior public servant from Newfoundland.

The RCMP's Deputy Commissioner of Specialized Policing Services met Ben's group before their first session. He was tall, angular, and lanky. His hands seemed disproportionately large, and his piercing stare was a peculiar match with his calm, easy-going manner. Ben knew him almost at once. It was Bill Truman.

"Ben, good to see you again. It's been a long time," he said, shaking hands.

"Eighteen, nineteen years."

"Saw your name on the roster. It brought back a lot of memories. Ottawa...the police academy...walking a beat on Bank Street...," said Truman, chuckling at some memory.

"Yeah," said Ben, "...at twenty below..."

"...good times..."

"They were," said Ben, "...most of them. I never heard that you made the big leap from city police to the RCMP."

"Took a chance. Turned out to be the right choice for me." A finger beckoned from down the hall, and a hand to the ear signalled a phone call. "We'll talk later," he said and turned.

Ben's two morning workshops covered updates to the Canadian Firearms Program and new courses at the Police College. After a twenty-minute break, Ben was taken to Forensic Science and Identification Services.

For Ben, FS&IS was a jaw-dropping look at their biological, chemical, and engineering labs, testing facilities, information repositories, and computer technologies, almost entirely staffed by civilian scientists, specialists, and engineers, who analyzed and processed vast quantities of potential evidence: chemical traces, DNA, currency and banknotes, tool marks, poisons, criminal identifications, ballistics, crime-scene analysis, and so on.

Dr. Calico Fernandez headed the Trace Evidence lab and led Ben's small group around her world of Bunsen burners, computers, separators, and spectral analyzers. Calico was a short, tired-looking woman with mixed brown hair and sharp bony features whose enthusiasm and thoughtfulness more than compensated for her plainness. As she spoke, she could read the faces of her small group like litmus paper, and, when she sensed that her scientific terminology and depth of field had reached saturation point, she quickly put on her middle-school science teacher hat. She had had several years' teaching experience before being recruited into the RCMP's Laboratory Services fifteen years ago, and she replaced the glazed stares of her group with a glint or two of wonder.

"I loved *Anne of Green Gables*," said Calico, having learned where Ben hailed from. "Anne was a bit of a know-it-all, but still... In fact, I read all of Lucy Maud's books. Have you read any?" she asked Ben.

"'Fraid not," he said. "I'm from Ottawa, actually."

"But you live and work on PEI."

"Yes," he said.

"You're so lucky...so-o-o lucky. That's where I got my undergraduate degree. UPEI. Anyway, our labs are a wonderful resource for local police agencies there. If we get a paint chip, we can identify the car's make and model, and sometimes the year and even the manufacturing plant which turned it out."

"When I worked with the Charlottetown Police and referred samples for identification, we were very satisfied with the outcomes."

"Thank you. We got a few samples just couriered in this morning, as a matter of fact. From that explosion yesterday. You know, the one in Charlottetown. Have you heard about it?"

"I have. A friend of mine was one of those injured."

"Oh, I'm so sorry!" she said.

"What will you test for?"

"Explosive residue," she said. Ben looked surprised. Then a flutter of disquiet dampened her countenance.

"But it was an accident," said Ben. "One car rear-ended another."

"Well, there you go," she said. "We'll chalk that test up to overzealous investigators. It sometimes happens. Now, through that door, gentlemen, is where we will find..."

Ben scarcely heard the words. His mind was already overwhelmed with a flood of not-so-pleasant possibilities.

54.

Jacqui had been uncharacteristically withdrawn all afternoon. Anne thought she needed a break, and Anne herself needed a distraction from the boredom of an enforced convalescence. So she sent her to the hospital gift shop to pick up a few things. Jacqui returned half an hour later with a couple of magazines, *Cosmo* and *Good Housekeeping,* as well as a Harlequin romance novel. Anne looked at the selection sceptically and wondered if Jacqui were trying to send her some kind of message.

After supper, Anne sent Jacqui home by cab. She skimmed through "How to Get Lucky at the Office" in *Cosmo* and "Taking the Horror Out of Kitchen Stains" in *Good Housekeeping* before she dozed off. Her cell phone roused her. It was Ben.

"How are you feeling? What happened?" he asked.

"It was pretty terrifying..."

Anne elaborated on the accident, as well as her worry that Jacqui and her friend had been killed.

"And what about you?"

"I'm okay. Took some smoke and got a cut. They're keeping me for observation. I get out tomorrow."

"Ya know, Sarah and Mary Anne were in to see you," Ben said.

"I guess I was asleep then."

A flash of colour caught her eye. Anne looked up. Her privacy curtain was open enough to see the door to her ward. She stiffened uncomfortably. She recognized the person walking through it and toward her bed.

"Gotta go. Visitor coming in. Good luck with the big meetings tomorrow. See ya in a few days," she said and closed her phone.

Gwen Fowler strode toward the foot of her bed and smiled.

"Hi," she said. "Feeling better?"

Anne was just as surprised at her cordial smile as she had been about her appearance in the doorway a moment before.

"Well enough. Tired," she said, feeling somewhat sheepish, and added, "Surprised to see you here, though. Visiting someone?"

"Just you."

"I thought you would have had better things to do."

"Why would you think that?"

"As I recall, our phone conversation the other day was rather chilly."

"I was feeling more sorry for Dit than I was for you at the time."

"Is he still pissed off?"

"He doesn't take offense so easily, but you caught him off-guard. He was simply defending me."

"So you know how I feel?"

"Yes."

"And yet you still came? Why?"

"Well, I'm not going away. And you and Dit have some history. So we've got to work through this...or come to some understanding...at least for Dit's sake, don't you think?"

"So, if he's not angry with me anymore, why didn't he come here with you?"

"He's in Singapore. Has been for the past two days."

"Singapore?"

"Some contract negotiations with the local police force for surveillance and monitoring systems."

A puzzled expression swept Anne's face.

"So how did Eli know about my...?"

The words dribbled away. Anne stared at Gwen. She shrugged knowingly.

"Why would you do that?"

"Dit would have wanted me to. It's what friends do. So, getting back to my question... Are you in love with Dit?"

55.

Perhaps she was still suffering residual effects. The words had just popped out her mouth as if propelled, and, when they spilled into the light, she wondered where they had come from. Nevertheless, there they were, laid bare in front of both her and Gwen.

"I don't know," she had said. "I don't know if I'm in love with Dit or not."

"Thanks. That's all I needed to know," Gwen had said. "I think now we can be friends."

That had doubly confused Anne. Enigma followed enigma. She no more understood Gwen's reply than she had understood her own admission, and Gwen was no more help in the matter. She just smiled, turned, and left the ward.

"We'll talk later," she said before disappearing down the corridor.

That's how Anne remembered it the next morning. As she awoke, it seemed like an unsettling dream, one in which you are unsure who anyone is and are still baffled by their actions and confused by their words, but not frightened. Perhaps it was a dream, Anne speculated, and half-believed it until she saw the magazine and box of candy that Gwen had left for her.

It was mid-morning before Jacqui arrived at the hospital. She sat on the edge of Anne's bed.

"Overslept," she said. She sounded apologetic.

"You needed the rest. You've had a rough time of it as well." She patted Jacqui's leg.

Jacqui handed her mother a copy of *The Guardian*.

"We made the front page, Mom."

A banner headline read: "Blast Rocks City." A two-column sub-head added: "3 Dead, 8 injured; Police Investigate."

"You're looking well this morning," said Dr. Little. He had appeared like a magician, suddenly out of nowhere, it seemed. He startled Jacqui, who was still absorbed in the news article.

"Do you mean 'captivating' or 'captive'?" asked Anne.

"Let's take a look, shall we?" Little examined her chart. "Okay... okay...okay...," he said mentally ticking off high points of her overnight observation.

"I take it everything's *okay*. Can I go now?"

"Do you remember how you got here?"

"By ambulance from the gas station."

"Who brought you this magazine?" he said picking one off the food tray.

"Gwen Fowler."

"What's my name?"

"I'm sorry, doctor. I must still be a *little* forgetful. Do lucky guesses count?"

"Who won the Stanley Cup last year?"

"The Maple Leafs."

"Forgetful...and delusional," he mumbled, as he pretended to write on her chart.

"My doctor, the vaudevillian," said Anne to Jacqui.

"Okay, pack up, Ms. Brown. We've got really sick people waiting for that bed."

"Next time I get blown up, I'll book into a Holiday Inn. Better room service," said Anne with a grin.

"By the way, there are some people here to see you. I'll ask the nurse to show them in once you've dressed. Good luck."

"Break a leg, P.T.," she said with a wink.

Anne hustled into the clothes that Jacqui had brought from the house. She wanted to out-distance her nurse, whom she knew would be obliged to trundle her to the exit in the obligatory wheelchair but, in her rush to leave, she had quite forgotten about the visitors who were waiting to call on her. They greeted her just outside the door to her ward.

"Ms. Brown, we'd like a few minutes of your time if you're feeling up to it."

Anne nodded. They wore no uniform, and their dress was casual-sloppy, but Anne knew they were police officers, detectives with the city police. They led her and Jacqui toward a small empty visitor waiting room just past the nurse's station and closed the door behind them.

They needed her account of the mishap, and Anne led the detectives through events leading up to the explosion, where she was, where the girls were, and what she remembered about the aftermath.

"Is there a Mr. Brown?" asked one detective.

"I'm a widow."

"Boyfriend?"

"No time for one."

"Employed?"

"Self-employed. I run Darby Investigations and Security."

"You must have ruffled some feathers there once in a while...unhappy clients, husbands caught with their pants down, cashiers with hands in the till. Anybody come to mind?"

"I don't quite see what my background has to do with a motor vehicle accident...even a very tragic one like this."

"We don't believe that it was an accident."

"Suicide? That's a helluva way to get even. Besides, I never heard of the people who rear-ended me. The Arsenaults. And I haven't had any clients up west. Doesn't make sense."

"The rear-end collision, we believe, was accidental, but we think it triggered an explosion in your vehicle."

"I don't see how that's possible. Couldn't the other car have hit a fuel pump before hitting my car?"

"It not only could, but it did. Nevertheless, video surveillance recovered from the gas station's camera suggests it, and we have reports from eye witnesses and additional video footage from the hotel parking area across the street that confirms it. The Arsenaults' vehicle vaulted a curb into the gas station. It nicked a pump and struck the left rear panel of your car. Your vehicle exploded, and that explosion set off the spilled fuel from the gas pump. You had just filled the tank. Full tanks burn if they're ruptured. They don't explode on contact. There was a fireball, but that was after the fact. The sequence looks suspicious to us and to the Fire Marshal who reviewed it."

"You mean someone was trying to kill my mom?! And me and my friend?!" Jacqui said.

"We're considering that possibility. Officially, it's still considered an accident. We're still collecting evidence and processing the scene. All the results aren't back yet from the lab."

"So, with that possibility in mind, what cases have you worked recently?"

"Currently, none. My client withdrew from the contract to investigate the death of her sister, Carolyn Jollimore, who died eleven years ago. Also, my license has been suspended pending a review by the Department of Labour. There were allegations—false ones—that I posed as a police officer to secure evidence. The Jollimore case also had some links with the Simone Villier murder of eleven years ago."

"Any threats?"

"Just Buddy and Frank. Maybe not even their real names."

Anne walked the detectives through her roadside encounter and the bizarre conversation that passed between them that night.

"Anything else?"

Anne thought about mentioning Chief MacFarlane's name but put that thought away. Cops tend to stick together, and a slur on a senior member might be interpreted as a smear of them as well. She shook her head.

"What about the break-in?"

"Your boys have the report. Anybody do a follow-up on it? Or is it just a statistic for year-end tally?"

"Any ideas?"

"Sure, the trashing of my office was a smokescreen to cover up an attempt to steal some documents I had securely locked up. That's my theory."

"What kind of documents?"

"That's confidential."

56.

Ben had met up with Deputy Commissioner Bill Truman in the afternoon after completing his orientation sessions. Ben had wanted to drop everything when he learned of the forensics concern and book a flight back to PEI. Truman had talked him out of it.

"Wait 'til tomorrow," he had said. "The results will have been processed by then, and you'll have a clearer picture of what you're faced with." Ben agreed, but cancelled his appointments with CSIS, OPP, and Sûreté du Québec and arranged a flight home.

Truman invited Ben for supper at his home that evening, and they chatted about Ben's new position with the PEI government. Truman had a great laugh when he learned Ben got the job as a result of his association with old Bill Darby's niece and her entanglement in a bizarre case of blackmail, murder, counterfeit bills, and the intelligence community. Ben also laid out details of the current investigation that Anne had begun into the deaths of Carolyn Jollimore and Simone Villier. Ben mentioned Anne's suspicions and his. Truman looked thoughtful but said nothing.

The next day Ben and Bill met at an old watering hole. The location was Ben's third choice. The first, a hotel lounge they used to frequent, had been bulldozed and replaced by a condominium. The second had burned.

Choice number three, His Majesty's Horse, had been a traditional British pub for many decades. In the early seventies, though, its clientele had shifted from English transplants to Quebec activists and Irish immigrants. It was a peculiar mix unless one considered that the turmoil in Quebec and the "troubles" in Ireland shared a common goal: separation from the Crown.

The entertainers who played there shifted as well from Brit to folk, but the atmosphere remained rollicking. The sign above the pub remained, but the patrons never referred to it as His Majesty's Horse. Instead, the new clientele dubbed it His Majesty's Arse, with the exception of people like officers Solomon and Truman who, having sworn to uphold the constitution as well as the Crown, never felt comfortable referring to the place by its colloquial name. Instead, as a compromise, they called it The Horse's Arse.

Although Ben never shared the separatist goals of the clients, he did love the camaraderie and lively atmosphere, especially on weekends.

This was not a weekend, nor was it the seventies. So Ben was disappointed to find the tables at the pub filling for lunch with suits and ties from the nearby government buildings.

Truman arrived a few minutes after Ben.

"Not the same, is it?" he said.

"Hasn't been for the last fifteen years, I guess. The most radical activity you'll find around here is some NDP volunteer spouting rhetoric about the evils of fracking. What time's your flight?"

"One forty-five."

"Have you ordered?"

"Yeah, two specials on their way. That's what you always order, right? Or has the leopard changed its spots?"

"Some things change, some things stay the same."

"Any developments?" Ben asked.

"It definitely was a bomb. A stick of dynamite, to be exact. With a blasting cap. No timer or remote detonator. A crude device wired to the exhaust manifold and cradled in a length of rubber hose to hold the heat from the pipe. When it hit 300 degrees, it would ignite. Your friend made a couple of stops. So it never reached its ignition temperature. However, the impact of the collision triggered the explosion. Blasting caps are sensitive to getting knocked about. It blew. At least, that's what the crime-scene investigators are suggesting. They're still following up on details and testing other bits of debris. That's about it."

"Thanks for the help, Bill."

"No problem, Ben. Glad to help, and I'll give our staff in 'L' Division a personal call. You'll have their complete cooperation and be kept up-to-date on our end of the investigation."

The waiter placed the bill on their table. Ben took a coin from his pocket.

"Call it," said Truman.

"Okay, heads PEI wins, tails Feds lose."

"With decision-making skills like that, you could have been a senator."

57.

John Jacob Dawson slipped quietly through the front door and into Irene MacLeod's boarding house. His backpack weighed heavily on his shoulder, and he headed for the stairs and his room. He heard the shuffle of Irene's slippers in the kitchen. Guilt and shame stalked him like a nagging shadow. He felt like a thief sneaking up the stairs, but he was at the end of his tether, and that was the stronger pull.

"Is that you, Jacob?"

He stopped cold. His throat constricted. He felt trapped but held on to a thread that gave him the strength of mind to answer and not to bolt up the stairs straightaway.

"Yes," he said faintly, and again, more clearly, "Yes, it's me."

"Sit in then. Lunch is on the table." said Irene with a holler. "Hungry?"

He descended and slung his backpack into a corner of the sitting room. He smelled beef vegetable soup and followed the sweet aroma to a table in the dining room.

"A bit, maybe. Have to hit the books, though. Mid-terms next week."

Jacob looked distracted and tired, and he fidgeted. He sat in front of a steaming bowl, a buttered biscuit on a side dish, but he sampled nothing. His spoon swam through the broth as if to dispel the heat. He took a taste or two and pushed it aside.

"I made a sandwich, too, if you'd rather that."

Jacob didn't respond. His mind had drifted elsewhere.

Irene left the room and returned a few minutes later. She found Jacob still brooding.

"I guess I'm not hungry after all," he said, pushing away from the table and getting up.

"I'll save it for a while. I can heat it when you're ready," she said, then added, "Something bothering you?"

"I'm fine," he said. "Just tired."

He rose from the table, grabbed his backpack, and headed to his room. A few minutes later Irene heard a rumble of footsteps descending the stairs. It was Jacob. His face was twisted and ferocious when he confronted her.

"Where is it?" he demanded.

"What do you mean?"

"You know what I mean, goddammit. The bottle."

"It's where it should be. Did you think I wouldn't recognize the clunk of a whisky bottle...or catch the signs of a dry alcoholic? I've been in this business for twenty-five years, Jacob. I've seen it all, and I don't put up with any of it. You know that."

"Where is it? Did you pour it out? What'd you do with it? I need it."

"I know you need it, and I will tell you where it is, but you don't need it this very instant. So, sit. I want a word with you first."

Irene sat down at the table. Jacob remained standing. His fingers snaked through his hair frantically, and he spun full circle as if unable to find a way out. Then he just stood there in the middle of the floor, staring at Irene, and contemplating whether or not he should tear the kitchen apart looking for it. Irene remained calm and resolute, and then she began to speak.

"What's the first step to sobriety?"

Jacob was dumbfounded, then angry.

"What is this? Twenty questions?" he asked.

"You've taken it. You've been to AA in prison. You went to it in Nova Scotia, and you started here, too. So tell me. What's the first step? You won't find the bottle. I guarantee it...and I won't give it to you until you answer."

"I admitted that I was powerless over alcohol...that it had made my life unmanageable."

"Was that true?"

Jacob nodded.

"What changed you? How did you stop?"

"It's pretty easy in prison. The bars are closed."

"No smart answers now. Something else. What was it?"

"I prayed."

"Did that work?"

He nodded again, but again he became angry. "But seeing MacFarlane again was too much. Now I can't get him out of my head, and I just want to get blind drunk and maybe...forget him...for a while anyway. If I can't kill him, at least I can flush him out of my head."

"Jacob, just think. Drinking and drugs isn't the way out. It's the way in. Think about it. Way back when, it was you that decided to get stoned. MacFarlane didn't make you do it. You did. You slid to the bottom. You got caught between a rock and a hard place, and you were so out of it you didn't know how you got there. You, not MacFarlane, are to blame. If he left you with a bad hand, it was because you dealt him the cards. You were so greedy for a drink that you even talked your way into a conviction. You did that, not MacFarlane."

Irene paused to let her words sink in. Jacob sat, reflective and in pain.

"Who pulled you out of that awful hole, Jacob?"

"God," said Jacob, his answer hovering somewhere between question and statement.

"He may have made the way easier, Jacob, but it was you, mostly you. God didn't make you a drunk any more than He made you sober. The question is... Are you going to let MacFarlane sucker you again... without putting up a fight?"

Jacob shook his head with a slight resolve. He took a deep breath and held it for a long time before he expelled it. His eyes had softened a bit.

Irene held out the telephone.

"Here," she said. "Call your sponsor. If you still want it, the bottle's in the trash can on the porch."

Jacob took the phone.

58.

Jacqui said nothing until they left the hospital and stepped into the cab that was waiting for them. Ben's phone call just after noon still resonated in her ears. He had confirmed the lab results: a crude bomb had blown up her car. He told her to go home and stay there until he got back. She was considering it.

"What are we going to do, Mom?"

"Go home," said Anne. "Just one stop first."

The taxi took them to Kelly Rentals, and they completed their trip home in a late-model blue Ford sedan.

"Mom, I'm scared."

"I know you are, and until this is cleared up, you can't stay here… or around me. It'll just be a couple of days. How 'bout Aunt Delia's? You liked visiting her there in the country, and it would be pretty this time of year."

"I can't. I'm babysitting. I promised Madame Desjardins, and she's depending on me."

"How 'bout Mary Anne's? She'd love to have you, too, and I wouldn't be far away."

"Okay, but I promised Madame."

"Great. Pack a bag. I'll call her and take you over. Lunch first, though."

Anne took Jacqui to The Blue Peter. Mary Anne helped Jacqui gather up her things, and they headed toward a back room that served as Mary Anne's office.

Anne headed for her office, too. A small pile of letters had accumulated below the mail slot inside her door. She shuffled through them, looking especially for a letter of reinstatement from the Department of Labour, but to no avail. She hadn't really expected one. The rest she left unopened on her desk.

The thought that someone was trying to kill her had never left her mind, but she had avoided the subject and played down the gravity of the threat as long as Jacqui was around. Mary Anne had read that message in Anne's eyes, and she, too, had kept mum about it while the girl was there.

Now, alone for the first time, it was a time to make decisions and put together a game plan. Whoever had been tracking her movements throughout the investigation had attempted to cripple her progress and had been pretty successful. Anne was even uncertain whether Edna's withdrawal of support from the case arose from a personal decision or as the result of outside pressures.

Anne's options were limited. Legally, she couldn't engage a new client. Nor could she conduct surreptitious activities or follow up her previous case regarding the death of Carolyn Jollimore. What choices did that leave her? She could say "to hell with it" and violate the regulatory restrictions. The downside to that was the likelihood that she was still being watched, or tracked with new surveillance devices. If either were true, she would be stopped again pretty quickly, detained by the police, or worse.

Doing nothing wasn't an option. She was too pig-headed for that, and she knew it. Even thinking about doing nothing, willingly or not, made her angry and bolder. The trick was to do nothing, break no laws, get some answers, and not get killed. Piece of cake, she thought glibly. But how?

Then it came to her. Perhaps having no client presented another opportunity, not a road block. Technically, the Simone Villier murder had nothing to do with Carolyn Jollimore's death. Legally, she could still dig around in that backyard. No one could fault her for asking questions about a closed case, and it might prove useful to see what alarm another wild card tossed on the table would stir.

She picked up the phone and dialled.

"Bernadette? Billy Darby. I'd like to speak with you. It's important. Not over the phone."

In her hurry to leave her office, Anne collided with the two detectives who had interviewed her at the hospital that morning.

Detective Iris Caine appeared to be the senior of the two. She did most of the talking. Detective Will Bryant stood behind her. Caine said they needed a word with her. Anne ushered them into the outer office and shut the door.

Caine had a long, though not prominent, nose and small eyes, which gave her a bird-like appearance. She stood six inches shorter than Bryant, but she moved with a muscle-bound stride.

"Do you know Michael Underhay, Ms. Brown...or is it Darby?"

"Yes, and I answer to both...my married and single names. Why?"

"He may have a role to play in the attempt on your life."

"I can't see why. We have some serious history, but that was over a year ago."

"What kind of history?"

"I had a valuable package from a client that had to be delivered. Cutter's men stole it. I got it back. He didn't like it, and a couple of his boys are doing time for a related abduction."

"Anything else?"

"In the course of retrieving my merchandise, the bar he runs caught fire. It was closed for a month. He didn't like that either. What makes you think he had something to do with the explosion?"

"We viewed some surveillance videos of Victoria Row for the night of the break-in at your office. Underhay's Camaro was spotted on those tapes. It circled a couple of times."

"Interesting, but I don't see a connection between him and anything that may have been in my office."

"He and his gang have connections with Hell's Angels. They've used dynamite to settle scores in Montreal that way. It's a crude method, but they're not big on subtleties, and they're indiscriminate when they're targeting the competition or people who get in their way. It sends a big message."

"It seems like a tenuous link."

"We're still gathering information, but there is one more connection. The dynamite wired to your car was partly encased in a rubber hose. RCMP crime lab has just identified it as an old radiator hose. It came from a Camaro, same year as Underhay's."

"Are you going to pick him up?"

"We will be...now that we have a motive. Revenge."

Michael Underhay was a vicious sonofabitch, no doubt, but Anne never took him for stupid or ostentatious. He had always been more direct in his brutality, a hands-on kind of thug, but maybe he had changed. Maybe he was learning a new thing or two, Anne thought, as she drove across the bridge toward Bernadette Villier's home.

Anne didn't have to ring Bernadette's doorbell. She was watching as Anne pulled up, and she invited her in.

"Thank you for seeing me," said Anne.

"You didn't give me much choice, dear. Your news sounded urgent and, frankly, you sounded desperate, too. Come in. Sit down."

Hospitality was a time-honoured tradition in many homes, especially among older residents, and that was evident in Bernadette Villier's welcome. She led Anne into the dining room. Table was already set with a pot of tea, two china cups, saucers, and small silver spoons with an old pattern. Homemade sweets were stacked on the glass dish between them.

"Tea?" Bernadette asked. Anne nodded and thanked her again, and they sat. "Help yourself. They're fresh," she said, pointing toward the pastries and scones.

It was evident to Anne that Bernadette wanted company. She was a working widow, childless, living alone with few relatives or friends to pass the time. So Anne hadn't the heart to rush her through the formalities of a tea and, for the next half-hour, Anne and Bernadette chatted about the fall weather, speculated on the severity of winter, and found a common thread in acquaintances they both knew slightly. Anne had felt the urge to brag about her daughter, Jacqui, but caught herself on two occasions. Instead, they ate sweets and lamented the doings of several local legislators and, at what seemed an appropriate lull, Anne shifted topic to more serious business.

"You were right earlier, Bernadette. My business is urgent, and I am desperate. In the last four or five days, several people have threatened me, my office has been ransacked, my business has been shut down... and yesterday someone tried to kill me...and anyone near me."

"Oh my!" said Bernadette. The shift in topic from the mundane to attempted murder stunned her. She looked genuinely horrified.

"What made it even worse was that my daughter and her girlfriend almost lost their lives as well. All of this followed my investigating the connection between your daughter Simone's death and Carolyn Jollimore. Someone wants to stop me one way or the other, but now I'm running out of options. That's why I've come here today. I have to ask you to do something...something that will be extremely painful for you."

59.

"Back in about an hour, hour and a half. I have an appointment," said MacFarlane. The office administrator nodded and kept writing on a notepad as the Chief walked by and out to his car parked outside the Stratford police station.

MacFarlane drove home, changed out of his uniform, and crossed the bridge to Charlottetown. He pulled into a strip mall, stopped at a pay phone, and dialled a number.

The voice at the other end was more of a bark than a greeting, but MacFarlane recognized it.

"Don't say anything," said MacFarlane. "Just listen."

MacFarlane heard the crack of cue balls breaking up on one of the pool tables in Cutter's club, The Hole in the Wall. He heard a roar as more than one ball found a pocket.

"Pipe down," roared Cutter. "I'm trying to talk here, godammit."

"Yeah," he said as he returned to the phone.

"You're going to be arrested in ten or twenty minutes. You're being set up. My ears tell me that one of your boys planted evidence. It points to you. He plans to take over while you're away. Three people are dead in the commission of a felony. That's murder, and no bail with your record. I can tuck you away in a safe place for a few days... or you can tough it out on your own. But I won't be able to help. RCMP Major Crimes is involved."

A tense silence followed as Cutter processed the news that MacFarlane had thrown at him. Then he said, "Okay, how do you want to do it?"

"Say nothing to anyone. Leave now. Act casual. Drive to our meeting place. I'll wait ten more minutes."

"What's in it for you?"

"The continuation of a mutually profitable relationship. I like stability...and, more than that, I want a bigger slice of the pie when the dust settles. Ten minutes."

The phone went dead. Cutter stood straight and carefully examined each of the men bent over the pool table and those huddled at the bar. Rage churned inside him. He felt like his head would burst. He wanted to kill one of them. He wanted to kill someone, anyone, just to demonstrate the lengths he'd go to maintain discipline, and he wondered which of them found the balls to try and take him out.

Whoever they are, they're dead, thought Cutter. *Even if I do go to prison, I'll find out who's behind it and make sure they're fucking dead.*

They're fucking dead men, he screamed, but that sound could only be heard inside his own head.

Bernadette Villier leaned forward rather timidly and anxiously after hearing Anne's worrying remark. Her slender fingers froze on the handle of her tea cup.

"I don't believe that John Dawson had any part to play in Simone's death," said Anne. "I can't say the same for Jamie, however. No hard evidence links him, but there are numerous inconsistencies and several lies that cast suspicion his way."

"What do you mean?"

"When police interviewed him at the time, he disclosed that Simone had been pregnant and that he and she were very much looking forward to having a child together. But I interviewed the woman he later married, and she told me that Jamie was infertile. His sperm count was too low, the result of a childhood illness. He couldn't have children. If that's true, then someone else was romantically involved with Simone. You suspected so yourself. As far as the investigation is concerned, that 'someone else' may have killed her."

"But what reason would he or anyone else have to do such a terrible thing?"

"He may have been married...not wanted a child to support. Or... Jamie could have killed her in a jealous rage, knowing that the child couldn't have been his. It's also possible, a long shot though, that the baby was Jamie's, beating the odds against his ability to father a kid. In that case, he could have killed her because he wrongly thought she was having an affair."

"I see," said Bernadette. She was still leaning attentively forward. Anne wasn't sure whether fear or astonishment was staring back from Bernadette's face. "I still don't know what you expect of me," she added.

Anne took a paper from her purse and handed it across the table to Bernadette.

"I need you to sign this document. It allows authorities to exhume Simone's body and test the DNA of her fetus. It will go a long way toward learning the truth."

Bernadette held the paper at a distance as if it were tainted and stared disdainfully at Anne.

"How can I permit this to happen? Disrupting her grave after all these years. No, no. I can't do that. Let the poor girl rest in peace. She had so little of it when she was alive. Let her rest."

"Do you really think she rests in peace, Bernadette, knowing what you know now? Do you? And what would Simone have wanted more? Rest or justice? And what would the child she carried have wanted? Your grandchild."

The disdain in Bernadette's eyes shifted slowly from the document in her hand and fixed itself on Anne. Bernadette's lips tightened unpleasantly, and Anne braced herself for a burst of anger.

But then it all unravelled. Bernadette's lips quivered and trembled. Her eyes filled with tears. She buried her face in her hands and sobbed without restraint.

Anne reached across the table and placed her hand over Bernadette's.

"There's nothing shameful in doing what you think is right...whatever that may be, Bernadette."

Anne's touch returned Bernadette to the immediacy of the moment. She reached for her napkin. She dabbed her eye. Then she looked at Anne once again. Bernadette's countenance had changed. She reached out for the document. Then she reached for the pen.

60.

Anne couldn't risk Bernadette having second thoughts about exhuming Simone's remains. So after she left Bernadette's Stratford home, she headed straight for the Coroner's Office in Charlottetown. It would probably be several days before the papers were processed and arrangements were made for the digging and examination. Anne didn't know how she would pay for it. The government wouldn't, the police wouldn't, Bernadette wouldn't, and she had no client to bill for it either. But it had to be done, she reasoned. After all, she had always believed that Carolyn Jollimore was her real client, not Edna. It was Carolyn to whom in a strange way she was emotionally connected, and it was her Uncle Bill Darby to whom she felt indebted and owed satisfactory closure to this bizarre case.

Anne had just left the Coroner's Office in the Sullivan Building when her phone buzzed.

"Ben, you're back."

"Staying out of trouble?" he asked. Anne sensed his humour in the question.

"Not a chance."

"Well, we need to talk, and I have an appointment. Want to come along?"

"Sounds fascinating. Are you gonna tell me what and where, or is this meant to be a surprise?"

"Meet me at University and Richmond. The Island Business Development Association. Dale Quinn's office."

"Who's she?"

Anne heard Ben's phone click off before he heard her question, but she was only a few blocks from that location.

MacFarlane left the main road fifteen minutes after he picked up Cutter. Cutter wasn't happy when MacFarlane popped the trunk of his car and told him to get in. He balked at first. MacFarlane told him that he couldn't be seen riding around with a known felon and that, if he didn't like it, he could find his own way out of his troubles. Cutter swore viciously but crawled in, and MacFarlane slammed the trunk shut.

The gravel turn-off was bumpy. MacFarlane could hear Cutter swearing at every pothole and rock the car struck. MacFarlane made another turn, this time onto a narrow path through a wooded area and a fallow field. His car moved slowly toward its destination, but occasionally it skidded on the wet grass, and it pitched and rolled violently in and out of old ruts. Strangely, Cutter's epithets became quieter, if no less offensive and threatening. Finally, the car came to a rest.

"We're here," Jamie shouted. Cutter gave no reply.

Jamie popped the latch on the trunk, left the car, and went around to the rear. The lid was half up, Cutter struggling to get up and out.

"Where the hell are we?" Cutter sounded groggy and disoriented and was unsteady on his feet.

"An old cabin."

"Where?"

"Almost two miles in any direction from anywhere. Nobody will find this place."

Cutter looked around. He could see nothing but trees. More importantly he could hear nothing. No cars, no boat engines, no tractors. Nothing. Still he sensed a vague familiarity about the place.

"Let's go inside. It's not fancy, but comfortable enough."

It was nearly five o'clock when Anne arrived at the Island Business Development Association offices to meet Ben. Three or four of the office staff, including the receptionist, already had their coats on and were rushing to leave. Ben stopped one of them.

"Dale Quinn's office?"

"Down the hall," she pointed. "Second door on your left. She's expecting you."

The lettering on her door read *Deputy Director*. The door was partly open. Ben knocked and entered. Anne followed.

Dale Quinn was a handsome woman in her late forties. Her long blonde hair was pulled back in a rather severe manner that gave her a no-nonsense appearance. She wore a navy skirt and a pink floral blouse. A matching navy jacket had been slung over the back of her chair.

"You must be Ben," she said warmly and shook his hand. "And you..."

"Billy Darby."

"Please, take a seat," she said. "Ben, you said you worked with the Ministry of Justice?"

"Yes, I'm the chief provincial investigator and law enforcement coordinator." Ben leaned forward, his identification in hand. Dale Quinn examined it closely and smiled.

"How can I help?"

"I've reopened an investigation into the murder of Simone Villier, and I'm looking for background information on her and the Tidewater Group. The case file was a bit sparse in that regard. I believe you were office manager at the time of the murder?"

Dale's smile slipped away, and she tilted back in her chair.

"Yes."

"What can you tell me about the Tidewater Group?"

"A group of Island businessmen who had planned to develop Stratford."

"What kind of development?"

"Waterfront mostly. Quite a grand scheme actually. Dredge out the shallows on the south side of the channel, build piers for passenger liners, hotel, a new marina, boardwalk, tourist shops."

"Big money was involved?"

Dale nodded.

"Privately funded?" asked Ben.

"The directors all had money...or political connections...or properties on that side of the bay...but they didn't part with money if they could avoid it. In the beginning, the project was visualized as a joint capital venture. The directors would put up a third of the capital. The rest would come from a provincial and federal split."

"But it didn't work out."

"No. Federal and provincial money had begun to trickle in first, but for their part the directors invested more energy than cash."

"How much was the total proposed capital expenditure?

"A hundred and fifty million."

"Were they on the payroll at the time?"

Dale nodded.

"Expense accounts?"

She nodded again.

"From what I see on that side of the river, not much was developed. Didn't that raise eyebrows?"

"Oh yes, but don't get me wrong. Nothing illegal transpired. The press got antsy, the public grumbled, but the negative publicity just wore itself out."

"Politically?"

"There was smell enough on both sides of the aisle to keep the peace."

"What happened to close it down?"

"Environmental concerns and Aboriginal objections. Shellfishers said the silt from dredging would destroy their fishery. The Mi'kmaq on the reserve by the Narrows weren't consulted about the project. So they dug their heels in and joined with the fishers in a lawsuit. That dragged on for a couple of years. An injunction blocked construction. Then the courts found that the project would violate Federal regulations. So the project was shelved."

"And after?"

"After that, everyone was happy, except maybe the Feds. Their purse strings had opened first. On the local side, the directors made money: land acquisitions, start-up money, related business ventures, consultation fees, lawyers. Fishers continued to harvest their clams and oysters, and the Mi'kmaq rejoiced at having been recognized by Ottawa."

"You did well yourself, too, I see."

"I was a highly efficient office manager, and I took good notes," she said and smiled.

"What can your notes tell us about Simone?" asked Anne.

"Simone? Not much to say really. She was young and pretty and coquettish, and all the men flirted and joked with her."

"By 'all the men' you mean the directors?"

"Usually them. They were in and out frequently, but there were other visitors to the office, too."

"Anyone particularly interested?"

"Not that I recall. Most of them were married, you see, and, if tempted, they'd be rather guarded about indiscretions, if you know what I mean."

"Were any Tidewater directors contacted or interviewed during the investigation?" asked Anne.

"Not that I heard, and I can't imagine that they would have been."

"Why do you say that?"

"Would you interrogate your boss if you were a local cop?"

"Do you have a list of directors handy?"

"I'm sure I do somewhere," said Dale. She stood and headed for a filing cabinet. She bent over a bottom drawer, shuffled through several folders, pulled out a sheet of paper, and handed it to Anne.

Ben looked over her shoulder. The pained expression on his face reflected his surprise and discomfort.

"Impressive," he said, "...and what were your activities on the day Simone was murdered?"

"I had no office appointments booked that day. I didn't go in. I had several meetings to attend in Charlottetown and didn't return to the office that day. In fact, I didn't return until after the Thanksgiving holiday weekend. Simone was there mostly to mind the phone and finish up some correspondence. It was a light day."

"Thank you for your time," said Ben, standing up to leave.

"One other thing," asked Anne. "Why would she have been in the office that evening?"

"No reason, unless she came back," said Dale with a shrug. "Maybe she forgot something."

61.

"Or maybe she was meeting someone, someone she couldn't be seen with in public," said Anne as she and Ben walked toward their cars.

"Maybe," said Ben. "The names on that list read like they were taken from *Who's Who on Prince Edward Island*."

"Do you think the investigators would have been too intimidated to interview them in a murder case?"

"Not the RCMP, but the Stratford Police? Hard to say. One thing I know for sure. They'd be walking on eggshells to avoid losing their jobs. Half those directors are current or former top bureaucrats or ministers. The rest are high rollers in business. I'd say the absence of any documents in the case file is telling. A lot that may have been said could have been off the record, but that doesn't do us much good."

"Eat yet?" asked Anne.

"Nope."

"Is Sarah making dinner?"

"She's at some club meeting. She didn't expect me home so early. I'm on my own tonight. The Crown and Anchor or The Blue Peter?"

"Definitely The Blue Peter. After yesterday and today, I just feel like curling up in the corner of my comfort zone."

"Sounds good."

As soon as they walked through the doors of The Blue Peter, they felt a warmth radiate from the chatter of six o'clock diners that half-filled the place. House lights glowed with intimacy and geniality in spite of the early autumn darkness. Ben and Anne headed toward the high-backed round table where they were accustomed to sit but were surprised to see several others already seated there. As they got closer, they saw Gwen Fowler. Next to her sat Jacqui and Mary Anne, rapt in some hilarious story of Gwen's. Ben brightened, but Anne felt a sudden twinge of discomfort.

A flicker of embarrassment passed Gwen's lips, but it diffused quickly behind a broad smile.

"Hi," Gwen said. "Thought you'd be resting up after your ordeal."

"There's no rest for the forcibly unemployed."

"Or unemployed workaholics," replied Jacqui.

"Thanks for your support, dear."

"Glad to help in your search for the truth, Mom."

"How do you know that I wasn't chilling out at home...or unwinding at the gym...or shopping for some small delight to make up for yesterday's incomplete driving lesson, Miss Smart-ass?"

"Mary Anne drove me over to pick up a few more things. Nobody was home. Your gym bag was in the closet. Your cell phone was turned off, and my call to your office went to voice mail."

"Sounds like there's a bit of detective in her," said Ben.

"An attractive, single woman disappears mysteriously for a big part of the day...hmmmm...sounds more like an afternoon assignation to me," said Mary Anne.

Anne blushed.

"Dr. Little had been asking about her," said Gwen.

"He looks like an owl," said Anne. "Besides that, he can be quite rude."

"You know what they say about owls," said Ben.

"No, please tell me," said Anne, her arms folded in front of her.

"Absolutely no idea," said Ben. "The words just popped into my head," he said sheepishly.

Anne gave his arm a slap. "You're not helping," she told Ben. Then she turned her attention to the others.

"If you must know," said Anne, "I had a meeting with Bernadette Villier, the murdered girl's mother. I had another meeting with the girl's former supervisor. I also filed papers to exhume Simone's body for a forensic examination."

"Yuck," said Jacqui.

"What for?" asked Gwen.

"She was pregnant at the time she died. There's a chance we can get DNA from the fetus. That may lead to the father...and that may lead to her murderer."

"What makes you think she was pregnant?" asked Gwen. She seemed genuinely interested.

"Her boyfriend said that she was three months gone."

"When?"

"Several times. First in his police statement eleven years ago, then to me at the office that time he dropped in. You remember. You were there. You left just after he arrived."

"That's odd."

"I don't understand. What's odd?"

"That she was pregnant. There was no mention of it in the autopsy. You showed it to me when we verified the contents of the file."

"Why would they mention such a thing? That's pretty personal, isn't it?" said Mary Anne.

"Autopsies of suspicious deaths are comprehensive investigations and produce quite detailed documents," said Gwen. I've seen a few at the hospital in Halifax. The coroner would have checked for amniotic fluid and noted it in his report—at least most would."

"Even an early pregnancy?"

"In my experience, coroners look for everything and inventory everything they find."

"You're suggesting that she wasn't pregnant!" said Anne.

"If amniotic fluid wasn't mentioned, I'd be very surprised if she were."

"Well, I guess I stepped in it this time," said Anne. "It was difficult enough convincing Bernadette Villier to sign the application for exhumation in the first place. And now I'll have to backtrack and break this news to her...that it was all for nothing." Anne slowly sank into disappointment and a deep reflection.

"Don't get too upset just yet," said Ben. "Who was the coroner on record?"

"Rogers... Redding...something like that," said Anne.

"Remington?"

"Yeah, that's it."

"Dr. Roger Remington. I know him. Let me give him a call. He's retired now, but he may have memory of the case. Just hold on."

Ben got up and walked to a quieter spot at the back of the restaurant. He checked his address book and tapped the number into his cell phone.

A few minutes later he returned to the table.

"Did you speak to him?" asked Anne.

"I did, but I'd forgotten. He was a crotchety man when I knew him years ago. Now he's a crankier old bugger than he was then. But he was always meticulous. Very sure of himself."

"What did he say? Did he remember the case?"

"Don't know if he did or didn't. All he said was 'If I didn't state amniotic fluid, then she wasn't pregnant. Simple as that.' Then he hung up on me."

"Oh boy," said Anne, looking at the hole she had dug for herself. She contemplated how she could extricate herself from it and still maintain some level of dignity.

62.

Could my life possibly get any more screwed up? The concept was there; the sentiment was there, but those words had not completely formed in Anne's mind. She was still asleep.

It had been in a downward spiral for the last several days. There had been no signs of it letting up. She had slept in, though it seemed more like a state of suspended life in which she was awake but unable to move. Through some half-sense, though, she perceived that her mind and body were telling her that today would be no better. *So why open my eyes*, she wondered? *Sleep on. Forget about everything. Rest beneath the warm blanket and all will be well.*

Then she felt a cramp in her calf. The blankness in her mind curdled into a sour headache. She could sense the minutes creeping by and somewhere in her consciousness she recognized a piece of paper passing mysteriously from one hand to another and, with each exchange, her path ahead became more impeded, as if she were entangled in a mess of rope. It frightened her, and she awoke.

Anne stared at the clock. It was ten o'clock, but it took some time for her to believe that it was so. She had rarely slept so long as this. It startled her, and she leapt from the bed as if it were on fire and, less than an hour later, she stood awkwardly on Bernadette Villier's doorstep, ringing her doorbell.

"May I come in?" she asked.

Bernadette looked puzzled, but stepped aside to let Anne in.

"Would you like some coffee or tea?"

"Not today, thank you. Look. Bernadette, there's no way to sugar-coat what I have to say. So here it is. I made a mistake." Bernadette's face became grim and taut.

Anne continued: "Simone was not pregnant. Jamie, in his statement to police, said that she was, but the coroner's report says otherwise. We contacted the coroner last night. He confirmed what he wrote in his report. So there will be no need to exhume Simone's remains after all."

Bernadette remained stone-faced. Then she said, "Why are you doing this do me?"

Anne's lips parted and her mind stumbled for an answer.

Then Bernadette's eyes swelled with tears.

"Why are you doing this to me? Why are you doing this to me!" Bernadette's voice had risen to a shriek.

Bernadette stepped toward Anne. Her face was frightfully distorted. Pained. Her arms raised as if to grasp some understanding of her confusion and hurt, but there was no such satisfaction to grab onto. Instead her fists struck down on Anne's shoulders. Again and again they pummelled Anne, but they carried little force and no malice and struck at the anguish that she could not drive out of herself.

"Why?" she sobbed. "Why?"

Anne grasped Bernadette firmly, pulled her close, and held her. Bernadette's arms lost their strength and purpose and fell limply by her side, but her sobbing continued. Anne said nothing. She could say nothing, but she continued to hold onto her comfortingly.

"I was forgetting," said Bernadette. "I was finally putting the dreadfulness of it behind me. Then you confused me. Then you brought it back. It all came back. Why?" Bernadette asked and pulled away from Anne. Bernadette's tears had dispelled her shock, but the dismay that remained hardened into a resurgent anger and bitterness.

"I was looking for justice," said Anne, "...for everyone...for Simone... for Dawson...and for Carolyn Jollimore, the woman who died as a consequence of Simone's murder."

"I don't care about justice anymore. I just want peace of mind. I want peace of mind."

"I think that the one needs the other, Bernadette."

Bernadette took another step back.

"I want you to go. Now. No more of your words. No more of your theories. Just go...and don't come back."

Anne stroked Bernadette's arm sympathetically once more. Then she turned and left the house. Anne found it difficult to drive across town with tears in her eyes.

Anne pulled her car into a parking space outside the Sullivan Building. Her eyes had dried by the time she reached the Chief Coroner's office. The receptionist was a gaunt woman of sixty-something. Her hair was short, wiry, and badly dyed a rich black. Her lips had been coloured too red for a pasty complexion.

"I delivered an application to exhume human remains on behalf of Bernadette Villier, the mother of the deceased, Simone Villier, yesterday. Mrs. Villier has had second thoughts and wishes to withdraw the application."

"Just a moment, please," said the receptionist as she tapped keys on the computer console at her desk. "Are you Mrs. Villier?"

"No, my name is Billy Darby. I'm acting on her behalf."

"I'm afraid that only Mrs. Villier can withdraw the application, and she must do it personally or submit a formal letter with her signature properly witnessed."

"That won't be possible. Mrs. Villier is too distraught for that."

"That's unfortunate."

"There must be some other option."

"The application has already been processed by our office," she said looking down at her computer screen. "It's been passed on for approval of two other regulatory departments before the final okay. These things move rather quickly. That should happen by the end of the day. Then the onus returns to Mrs. Villier. She could choose to continue with the exhumation...or to do nothing at all, in which case the permit will simply expire."

"Good to know. Thank you."

"It just gets better and better," said Anne. She slumped into a chair in Ben's office and, like a cat, curled her feet up underneath her.

"It does," said Ben. "It does. Fenton Peale came in this morning. Red-faced. Thought he was about to take a stroke."

"Yeah? What about?"

"He thinks you're trying to do an end-run around your suspension. Are you?"

"Of course, but what business is it of his? That's between me and the Labour Department."

"Can't say. Apparently, Bob MacEwen is talking about a restraining order, maybe charges of one sort or another."

Anne uncurled from her comfy chair and sat up.

"Thought that might get your attention," he said.

"Can they do that?"

"Charges? Criminal, no. Regulatory, not likely. Restraining order? That's possible."

"Why is Fenton in the middle of this? What's it to him?"

"Your application for an exhumation permit? It touches base with Justice before approval."

"Is Justice going to block the application?"

"Fenton was talking about it, but I don't think it can be done. Justice has no hold on it. The case is closed. Besides, it was Mrs. Villier that made the application, not you, right?"

"Technically," she said. Ben raised his eyebrows suspiciously.

"Good enough. Don't give me details. Don't want to hear them. Got some good news for you, though. Michael Underhay has gone to ground. Police tried to serve the warrant for his arrest, but he's disappeared. He'll be too busy dodging police to trouble you."

"I like the sound of that," she said.

"So...you've yanked enough chains for today. Why don't you go home and take the rest of the day off?"

"I like the sound of that, too, actually," she said.

Anne sounded sincere. Ben looked sceptical. Anne left the office with a wave. She looked tired and weary. It had been a rough week for her, thought Ben.

"I don't like it at all. She's still causing trouble. She won't stop. She's like a fucking rat terrier. Something has to be done!"

The caller was frantic and sounded desperate.

"Which phone are you on?" asked MacFarlane.

"My other cell," said the caller. MacFarlane nodded.

"Good, but there's nothing to worry about yet. Can you stop the application?"

"No. But if they dig her up they'll know that it was mine. I can't go to prison now. I've got too much to lose."

"You're talking stupid now, dammit. Do they have a sample of your DNA to match it against?"

"No."

"Is there anything that connects you to her personally?"

"No."

"So there's no grounds to suspect you, and if there's no grounds to suspect you, then there's no reason to take your DNA to find a match. You're being ridiculous. Just calm down. Calm down. You have absolutely nothing to worry about...except me...if you lose control and tie me into your problems. Then you'll have a problem...a big one...maybe your last one."

There was no reply, but MacFarlane paused a moment for his words to register as forcefully and as terrifyingly as he intended them. Then he continued in a more reasonable and calm tone: "But let's not dwell on that. We've had a pretty good working relationship so far, haven't we?"

There was no reply.

"Haven't we?" MacFarlane's voice became sharp.

"Yes."

"I've helped you and you've helped me, right?"

"Yes."

"I have something in play. It will take care of most of the loose ends. So you don't need to worry."

"What is it?"

"You don't need to know either. It won't affect you. Just keep your head on your shoulders."

63.

The sound of her vacuum cleaner had masked the opening and closing of both the outside door and the entry to the main room of her boarding house, but she had caught a stray shimmer of light from that direction and that's when she turned and saw Jacob Dawson entering.

"Where were you last night?"

Jacob looked well but sheepish, almost as if he was being reprimanded by his mother. Irene MacLeod was no mother in the real sense, but she did feel a maternal draw toward Jacob. The two other boarders in the house were older men, more independent and hardened by life. Jacob exhibited a veneer of toughness sometimes, but Irene viewed him as an innocent when it came to the real world. He was accustomed to its travails, but had enjoyed few of its joys and, having walked so often along the paths of his troubled life, he had no reliable compass to guide him toward happiness. And this worried Irene.

"I'm okay, if that's what you mean," he said smiling at her. "I smell soup."

"Are you hungry?"

Jacob nodded.

"It's in the kitchen. Wasn't sure if you'd be here, but I made some on the chance."

Jacob dropped his backpack near the door and headed for the kitchen. He looked hungry.

"Did you have breakfast?" she asked.

"I did. I stayed at my sponsor's overnight."

"Is that customary?"

"No, but I had a lot of stuff to unload. It was good to have somebody to listen...somebody who's been there."

Irene ladled a bowl of beef barley soup into a bowl and set it in front of Jacob. She set a ham sandwich next to it. She added half a pickle. Then she sat down and watched Jacob wolf down the food. She felt happy.

"Feeling better?" she asked.

His mouth was full, and he nodded vigorously.

"We talked half the night. Then we worked out a way to take some pressure off."

"Good. So...what shall I do with that quart of whisky? Toss it?" Irene asked.

"Or give it to somebody who doesn't need it."

Ben wouldn't have believed it if someone had told him that Anne had taken his advice, but she had. She would have vigorously denied that she frittered away an afternoon, but that was what it amounted to, at least by her standards.

Ordinarily, she would have followed her pattern of jogging from home toward Victoria Park and following the boardwalk along the water. The rhythmic padding of her feet and the ever-pleasing and ever-changing vista of Charlottetown harbour had always been refreshing, but she couldn't follow that routine today. The car explosion had not seriously injured her, but its effects had left her worn and uninspired.

Instead, she headed for the gym. Only a few others shared the recreational equipment with her that afternoon. She had a routine there, too. Stationary bike for cardio; bench press, leg curls, and arm curls for strength; and then the speed bag.

She forced herself through her strength regimen and felt rather satisfied with herself when she matched her last weight and rep count. Then she slipped on a pair of light boxing gloves and strode over to the speed bag.

She set up a slow one-two rhythm, then picked up the speed and shifted to double hits when she felt comfortable. Then she shifted back and forth between the two, the bag thumping hypnotically all the while. Occasionally, she lost the rhythm, but brought it back again and again. The rhythms were mesmerizing and soothing, and one could almost drift into mindlessness within the pattern.

Eventually, Anne grew tired and self-aware, but she also became more agitated and angry as if something ugly were working its way up from deep inside her. She abandoned the cadenced punching. Hard jabs and crosses took its place. Her attention to the bounce and gyrations of the bag grew more intense and focussed because Anne saw something that no one else could see in the bobbing, elusive leathery bag. She saw the smug leers of Buddy and Frank—the ones who had terrorized her on that dark country road. She saw the frightening sneer of Cutter Underhay who had tried to kill her and her daughter. She even saw the duplicitous faces of MacEwen and Carmody and Peale whose political goals had obstructed her investigation.

After she had finished, her chest heaved and her arms felt like lead. Beads of sweat rolled down her face and neck. Her T-shirt was damp, but somehow she felt strangely pleased. It wasn't until she had spent ten minutes in the sauna that she felt a wave of exhaustion sweep down upon her. She showered, changed into street clothes, pinned back her half-dried hair, and drove home.

The house was quiet with Jacqui away. Too quiet, thought Anne. She turned the TV on for company. She flicked through the channels, but nothing caught her interest. She thought about making supper, but, with Jacqui's absence, there was no point. Besides, she felt too exhausted to eat. Perhaps later, she thought. Then she lay back on her couch, pulled a blanket over her, and descended into a deep sleep almost at once.

The sun was lowering. The TV fluttered. Commentators and show hosts jabbered away, but Anne was oblivious to it all.

"She sent me packing," said Walter Bradley, Chief Investigator with the Department of Labour.

"What did she say?" asked MacEwen, his boss's boss.

Walter Bradley had been around politics long enough to know that he had better choose his words carefully or his future might become suddenly very unpredictable, and he was just five years short of retirement.

"I knocked on the door, identified myself, and asked her if I could enquire about her application for exhuming the remains of Simone Villier."

"Go on," said MacEwen impatiently.

"'Can't you leave me alone?' she says. Those were her exact words. Then she tries to shut the door. My foot was already halfway in and caught it. I say, 'I'm conducting an official investigation for the Province and need to know if anyone pressured you to file that application. Ms. Darby, for example. Did she urge you to file the papers?'"

"And did she?" asked MacEwen.

"The woman wouldn't give me a straight answer. She kept saying 'What difference does it make? I don't give a care for the paper. Do what you want with it? She wasn't pregnant.' I say, 'What do you mean?' and she says, 'It doesn't matter anymore. Simone wasn't pregnant. Nothing matters now. So get your damn foot out of my door and go away before I call the police.' So I leave. And that's what happened," said Bradley, and he looked closely at the Labour minister to determine if he had given the proper answer.

MacEwen said nothing. He got up and left the room, tossing back a quick "thank you" on his way out.

MacEwen returned to his office, closed the door behind him, and picked up his desk phone.

"Wendell, just wanted to get back to you on the matter we were discussing. The mother was distraught. Not much to go on yet. But it seems she's lost interest in exhuming the body. No. She just keeps on saying that she wasn't pregnant, and she doesn't care anymore. So it's good news. Pass it along to Fenton? Right."

MacEwen hung up his phone and breathed a sigh of relief.

64.

Madame Desjardins gave instructions to Jacqui, left an emergency number, and told her that she would return around twelve, but not later than one. Her seven-year-old son, Luc, gave her a hug and returned to watch the end of a Disney special on cable. He was snacking on a plate of orange slices when Madame Desjardins left.

Jacqui sat down beside him on the carpet. She chatted about the TV programs she had watched as a child, and she pointed out the high quality of graphic effects in the film that he was watching, but Luc was more interested in the pleasure of the experience than Jacqui's childhood memories or qualitative analysis. Then the doorbell rang.

Jacqui opened it to Rada. The sight of her was a surprise.

"Hi."

"I didn't think you'd be coming," said Jacqui. "after what your father said."

"I didn't know if I'd be coming either," said Rada. "May I come in?"

"Sure," said Jacqui, and waved her into the room. "This is little Luc Desjardins," she said.

"I'm not 'little,'" he said without looking up.

"Luc, this is Rada. She's my friend, and she'll be visiting a while. Is that okay?"

Luc looked at Rada, nodded, and returned to his program.

"He's almost ready for bed...not quite as sociable as usual. Did your father change his mind?"

"No. Neither have I. We had an argument, and he told me I couldn't leave the house for the whole weekend. I told him I promised to help you babysit. It made no difference. He never changes his mind."

"What did you say?"

"Nothing. I went to my room, locked my door, changed, and went out the window."

"I'm not so sure that was a good idea."

"I have the right to opinions, don't I? I have the right to make my own friends, don't I?"

"I guess," said Jacqui. She couldn't recall Rada ever speaking so harshly or angrily before.

Rada removed her hijab and sat down on a large armchair. Her cheeks were damp with tears.

The TV movie had ended, and a series of tasteless, loud commercials flashed across the screen. Luc looked up and over toward Rada.

"Why is she crying?" he asked.

"Rada is having a sad day," said Jacqui.

"Why?" he asked.

"Maybe she'll tell you another time. Right now, it's bedtime. Your mother said. Remember? Right after the show. So off we go." Jacqui laughed, scooped him up, and carried him off to his bedroom.

Jacqui tucked Luc into bed, kissed him good night, and returned to the living room a few minutes later. She heard water running in the washroom. Then the doorbell rang again, and she ran to answer it.

Bobby Fogarty and Sig Valdimarsson stood in the open door frame looking very uncomfortable.

"Ya know, it just doesn't feel right, knocking on a teacher's door in the middle of the night," Bobby said.

"It is kinda creepy," added Sig.

"It's not the middle of the night. It's eight o'clock. And what's to be scared of? Madame Desjardins is a nice teacher."

"Yeah...but still..."

"Well, don't just stand there. Come in. Sit," she said, pointing them toward the sofa.

Jacqui started to giggle.

"What's so funny?" Self-consciously, Bobby examined his clothes. Perhaps he had spilled something on them, he thought.

"You both look so-o-o guilty right now. It's funny, but cute, too. Happy birthday, by the way."

"Thanks. You've been out of touch with everyone for a couple days. Didn't know what was up. Heard rumours. You all right?"

"Nothing serious. Just shaken up. Mom is overprotective. So she boarded me with a friend of hers. I'll be back on Monday. Miss me?"

"Sure." Bobby sounded uncertain, but Jacqui didn't notice.

Instead, she looked admiringly at Bobby. Then she looked confused. Bobby's eyes and the eyes of Sig were fixed somewhere else. Jacqui swung her head around. Rada had just entered the room. She, too, looked confused.

"I don't think you've met. Rada, this is my friend Bobby Fogarty, and this is Sig Valdimarsson. You may have seen them at the school. Boys, this is Rada Kikovic, my buddy."

Rada took a seat in the other armchair, across from Sig. She clasped her hands together and cradled them in her lap. Her eyes avoided the boys on the sofa and alternated between Jacqui and the oval coffee table and the paintings on the wall.

"Can I get anyone a coke?" That seemed to get Sig's and Bobby's attention, and that was good enough for Jacqui. "Rada, would you like to pour a few glasses? I'll have one, too. I brought a bottle. It's in the fridge. Ice in the freezer, glasses over the sink, first cupboard on the right."

Rada felt not only ill at ease but physically ill as well. She felt like a rabbit caught in an open field. She could scarcely move, and her thoughts had broken apart into glittery bits that defied repair. So Jacqui's request of her was a relief. Any excuse to leave the room provided a respite.

Sig felt self-conscious as well. He had been staring at her, but he couldn't help himself. Something about her compelled his eyes to follow her. He saw a serenity and dignity and quiet beauty that he had never experienced before, and it was intoxicating. He imagined that she had caught him staring at her, and he looked quickly away. Until now, his glances had been fleeting, but, when she stood to leave, their eyes met and lingered momentarily and, for each fraction of that second, both of them experienced a trembling of undefined emotion and fear.

Sig's eyes lingered a bit longer and bolder than hers. They followed her as she left the room and headed into the kitchen. Her eyes were bright, her skin was smooth, and the way she moved seemed both naive and sensuous. Sig felt uncomfortable when he found himself staring at the empty doorway through which she had disappeared, so he returned his attention to Bobby and Jacqui.

"Big party?" asked Jacqui. Bobby shrugged.

"No. Just Sig and me, my sister, mom and dad."

"What'd you get?"

"A really good pair of soccer shoes. Interchangeable cleats."

"Cool."

"And clothes," he said, gesturing toward the zip-up sweater he wore. "Part cashmere."

Jacqui reached across and ran her hand over the sweater.

"That's so-o-o soft," she said. "I love it."

Jacqui heard the clink of glasses in the kitchen and motioned to Sig.

"Would you give Rada a hand in the kitchen with the drinks, please, Sig? Thanks."

Sig blinked, faltered, and managed to nod. Sig had an athletic build and played on two varsity teams throughout the year. Nevertheless, he felt unusually awkward and ungainly as he stood and walked toward the noises Rada was making in the kitchen.

"Here's something else," she added. Jacqui reached into a cloth bag next to her chair and pulled out a rectangular package. It was wrapped. A red ribbon encircled it. A bow fronted it.

"What is it?" Bobby gave it a little shake.

"You have to open it to find out," she said.

Bobby gave her a little grin, and then he attacked the wrapping with a disturbing vitality. The ribbon, bow, and wrapping paper fell to his feet, and Bobby held the present in his hand, at a suitable distance away in order to scrutinize it. It was a picture, matted and framed, and signed by the artist.

"Cool," he said. "What is it?"

"It's a picture...," she said. "...of you... I sketched it myself."

"Thanks, Jacqui. That's real nice."

Sig and Rada walked into the room, glasses of pop in their hands. The ice clinked with each step. Both were smiling. "Look," said Bobby. He held up his present.

"It looks kinda like you," said Sig with uncertainty.

"It is him," said Rada.

"That's what I said."

Then the doorbell rang several times, and there were impatient knocks on the door.

65.

MacFarlane took his time circling the block. At this hour the occupants of neighbouring homes had settled into sedentary routines, and the streets were quiet. On his first pass MacFarlane had seen only two people abroad, a woman following her leashed dog and a shaggy-haired teen with a guitar case strapped to his back. He passed Anne's house a second time. Then he eased his car to the curb, and waited in the dark. The pale glow of a cell phone lit his cheek.

"Stratford Police Department. Constable Williams," said the voice answering.

"Williams. Chief MacFarlane. Anything going on that I should know about?"

"No, sir. Quiet all afternoon and pretty quiet so far this evening. How'd your meetings go?"

"...well...very well. Just tying up some loose ends. By the way. I got a tip on the possible location of Michael Underhay. I'm following up on that. So I may not be available for a while...maybe not until tomorrow afternoon. If there's an urgent matter, call Sergeant Deale. Got that?"

"I do...and have a good evening, sir."

MacFarlane clicked off, rolled down the windows of his car, and scrutinized the nearby houses. He heard nothing, and he saw nothing out of the ordinary. MacFarlane would have preferred to do this late at night as he had when he planted the explosives in Anne's car, but events were developing more quickly than he had anticipated. Time was running short. The timeline had to be compressed.

MacFarlane had always been concerned about timing. He didn't like rushing into action. He believed that's when mistakes were made. He had witnessed it dozens of times in the criminals he had arrested over the years—good planning undermined by hasty implementation. But now, as he thought about this present modification, he concluded that it may even be more advantageous. His car was a common model and, parked where it was, it should draw no attention and, if someone should see him, there was little chance anyone would recall the particulars of anyone passing by at eight or nine o'clock at night.

He got out of his car, retrieved a large hockey equipment bag from the trunk, and closed the rear hatch soundlessly. Then he walked toward Anne's house, two doors up the street.

MacFarlane wore black sneakers, blue jeans, a bulky navy pullover, and a Boston Bruins cap. He blended well into the mottled blotches of a shadowy street. As he approached Anne's house, he looked around carefully. The outside light was off. He looked for a motion detector, but found none. Then he turned up her driveway. Her rental car was parked at the upper end, just beyond the side entrance.

The house bordering Anne's driveway was dark, just as he had found it the last two evenings he had driven past. Newspapers sticking out from their delivery box suggested that the neighbours were away. The large maple trees along their property line cast deep shadows on Anne's home. But the foliage had blocked him from seeing a small light burning in a downstairs side window of her home.

The light in that window didn't discourage MacFarlane. He had planned to take her by surprise anyway, hopefully with very little struggle, and he knew that, if he had to, one quick blow could render her unconscious. However, one thing did raise his concern—the sound of voices coming from Anne's living room. Visitors would scotch his entire plan.

MacFarlane heard the mutter of mixed voices, but not clearly. He had to know what was happening. So MacFarlane moved more closely and stealthily alongside the building just beneath the lit window. He raised himself up to a corner of a pane and peered in. Anne was asleep on the sofa. The voices had come from the TV, where broadcasters were discussing a weather forecast on a news channel.

MacFarlane checked the physical layout of the room and moved toward the side entrance. He set the equipment bag down and tried the handle. It was not locked. The handle turned, and the door opened soundlessly into a tiny entry with two steps leading to the kitchen. The inside door was ajar. MacFarlane worried about the steps, but they were firm. He crouched on the upper tread and nudged the door. It opened a crack, enough so that he could see Anne clearly.

Quietly, he removed a flask and a cloth from the pocket of his pullover. He removed the cap, doused the cloth, and pushed the door again, but this time the door squeaked. Anne moved restlessly on the couch. He remained frozen for several minutes. Then he pushed the door open wide enough for him to slip through the frame but, at that moment, the door loosed a mournful groan. The noise jarred Anne from her sleep, but she was too late. She glimpsed a looming black shape enveloping her. Her arms went up defensively, but the weight of the man was too much. She felt the wind driven out of her. She attempted to scream but something jammed her mouth and nose. She gasped for breath and smelled something sweet and pungent. Then consciousness slipped away.

MacFarlane taped her ankles together, then her hands, and added a firm strip across her mouth. He recovered the hockey equipment bag from outside. Then he laid Anne inside, zipped it closed, carried her to his car, and placed her in the trunk.

Anne was unaware of how long she had been unconscious but, when she awoke, she felt sure that she was in the trunk of a car and, from the smoothness of the ride, she was confident that it was a main highway. For a while she struggled against the bindings that held her, but it was futile, and gradually she became aware that escape had become secondary to a more immediate threat to her well-being. Nausea.

Anne could still taste the drug that had knocked her out. It lingered in her nostrils and throat. A sickening sweetness clung to it. The odour inside the canvas bag was appalling, too, but in a different way. It was rank with the indelible stench of old sweatshirts and rancid footwear. Together, the odours churned her stomach, but she fought back the urge to vomit. She realized that, with her mouth still taped shut, she would asphyxiate if she threw up.

The car suddenly swerved off the main highway onto a secondary road. She half-rolled inside the equipment bag. The blackness disturbed her sense of balance. She felt disoriented and lightheaded, and she felt the initial twinge of a spasm.

Something, she did not know what, brought to mind her long-ago pregnancy, her birthing of Jacqui, and the discomfort and pain she endured during that traumatic ordeal. Controlled breathing was a godsend of a technique that had been taught at prenatal classes she and her husband, Jack, had attended. It had eased the hurt then. Perhaps it would do the trick now.

Anne twisted herself into a more comfortable and stable position. She blanked her mind as best she could, focused on willing the muscles in her body to relax, and fell into a slow rhythmic pattern of breathing.

Five long minutes passed. All that while, she staved off a string of involuntary surges from her stomach. She was beginning to feel more comfortable and confident until the car veered off again.

MacFarlane slowed to a crawl along the new road, but the first bump was a head-banger. It was frightening. The vehicle lurched to the left and then to the right, all along the rutted pathway. Fear jostled the controlled breathing completely from Anne's mind. The succeeding bumps and shocks were irregular, unexpected, and Anne struggled unsuccessfully to brace herself.

A short smoother period followed. Anne had been knocked about and beaten up in the trunk. She felt the bruising and assessed the soreness that would come tomorrow—that is, if tomorrow came for her at all. In spite of that, however, she realized that her nausea had vanished. Fright and pain had vanquished it.

Then the vehicle stopped. She heard the driver door open and heard the pop of the trunk latch. Someone hoisted her from the trunk by the handles of the bag that held her. Her captor said nothing. She heard his footsteps crossing a short porch and the creak of an old door. She heard the zip of the equipment bag that held her and squinted into a shaft of flashlight too bright for her dilated eyes.

MacFarlane tipped the bag on its side and rolled Anne out onto the bare wooden floor.

"I brought you a playmate," he said.

66

"Hey, people! Let's get this place rockin'."

William Larsen pushed his way past Jacqui. He ducked as he came through the door, a case of beer tottering above his head. It barely cleared the opening. A corner of the case grazed Jacqui's cheek as he passed, and she caught the sour smell of alcohol on his breath. Four or five more rushed in after him and disappeared into the kitchen. For a moment, surprise and disbelief overcame her. Then she hurried after them.

"Wait! This isn't my house! I'm babysitting! You can't stay!"

The uninvited visitors also caught Bobby and Sig unexpectedly. Both felt awkward and unsure of what, if anything, they should do, and, within minutes, a dozen more streamed past them. Party-crashers filled the house. The din increased. Noise in one quarter competed with noise in another, and chatter and laughter escalated to shouts and manic roars. Someone plugged in a portable stereo. A strident rap song pumped out a muffled defiant lyric. The atmosphere became unrepressed and shrill. More people came through the door.

Rada became alarmed by the growing crowd. The press of so many people so quickly had startled her. So she abandoned her armchair and shrank into a corner near the stairs. Sig moved to her side.

In the kitchen, an already drunken William Larsen and his troupe in the kitchen were draining all of Jacqui's energy. There was no reasoning with them. They only half-heard what she said, and they laughed at her frustration as if it were some comical routine meant to entertain them. Jacqui hadn't heard the other cars pull up outside or the pickup truck that had jumped the curb and found a parking space on the front lawn, but she did hear the music rumbling from the living room. Finally, she threw up her hands and retreated.

Jacqui was alarmed at the transformation that had taken place in the living room.

"Bobby! Do something!" she said. Bobby couldn't hear her from where he stood, but he could read her body language and sensed what she wanted. He looked around blankly.

Even Jacqui found herself at a loss to know where to begin or what she could do next. A swirl of light-headedness swept over her, and she fought to keep it in check. It was the first taste of fear and a precursor of panic, and Jacqui struggled to refocus.

She saw several people descending the stairs from the second floor, and she remembered little Luc who was up there in bed. She bounded up the stairs two steps at a time. Jacqui had closed up all the upstairs rooms when she had put Luc to sleep. Now, two of the doors were ajar, one of them being Luc's. Jacqui pushed. It slowly opened. She peered into the semi-darkness. He still lay in his bed, tucked in, eyes closed, and fast asleep.

She closed that door and headed down the corridor toward the other. She stopped abruptly when she heard small noises inside. She gave the door a slow shove. A shaft of light from the hallway revealed two bodies on the floor. The scruffy beard belonged to Hank Stillwell. The blonde mop of curls suggested Missy Metcalfe. Her bare breasts and his boney thighs suggested something else entirely.

"Out you two! Out! Find a hotel room, for god's sake!"

"We're kinda busy," said Hank. He sounded half out of breath and a bit whimsical. Then he laughed.

Missy moaned in agreement.

"Now!" said Jacqui. "Get out of here now!"

"Come back in ten minutes. You and your boyfriend can have the room then."

The moaning of Missy and the renewed enthusiasm of Hank infuriated Jacqui. She turned her head away as if to find some resolution and saw Rada, standing just outside the doorway and looking in. She must have sought refuge from the mob downstairs and followed her up, thought Jacqui.

The expression on Rada's face was troubling to Jacqui. It shifted between tears and fright. The sight before her was sordid and embarrassing, and Rada was appalled. Jacqui felt the anguish and confusion that confounded Rada at that moment. This wasn't her reality. Rada was an innocent, she thought, not too much different from little Luc in regard to worldliness. At that moment, the thought struck Jacqui that the blame for all this could fall on no one but herself.

An uncontrollable knot of anger overcame Jacqui. She turned back toward the entangled and writhing limbs of Missy Metcalfe and Hank Stillwell. Instinctively she drew back her leg and delivered one of her better soccer kicks into Hank. In their shadowy clutch Jacqui couldn't see where it landed, but he flinched and squealed in pain like a little boy who'd fallen from his bike, and he rolled away. Missy's eyes grew large and frightened. Jacqui sent a second kick toward Missy. Despite the faint light, Missy saw a glint of white as Jacqui's sneaker hurtled toward one of her swaying breasts. She shrank back. Jacqui's foot fell short of the mark and caught the recoiling side of Missy's left shoulder.

"Do I have to repeat myself...," Jacqui said, "...or are you getting the picture?"

By then Hank and Missy had scrambled a few feet away. They cast angry, yet guarded, stares at Jacqui as they hurried into their clothes and made for the hallway, hopping and dressing as they left.

"Come on," said Jacqui to Rada. "We've got to get you out of here."

She grabbed Rada's arm and led her along the now-empty hall and down the stairs. Sig had remained in the corner near the foot of the stairs.

Jacqui gazed around as she descended into the main room. It was frightening to see the house so full. Many she recognized from school. Others she had never seen before and, from their dress and demeanour, she would never care to see again.

Once more she shouted at Larsen to leave, but Larsen and his group were still too drunk and self-absorbed to make sense out of what she was telling them, and Jacqui's voice sank beneath the deafening music and a pumping sub-bass that sent tremors into the beams of the house.

At the bottom of the staircase, Jacqui grabbed hold of Sig's neck and tugged until he bent down toward her. She cupped her hands to his ear.

"Get Rada out of here. Walk her home. This is no place for her."

Sig nodded and took Rada's arm. He broke through the crowd and led her toward the front door.

More beer was being passed around. Some drank from their own pints of whisky. Jacqui winced when she saw someone butt his cigarette on the floor. The smoker wore a varsity football sweater she didn't recognize. Jacqui didn't know him.

"What are you doing?" she shouted. "Get out! Out! Don't you have any respect?" She pointed at the crushed cigarette butt.

The footballer stared at her. He looked incredulous. His girlfriend snickered. Both were glassy-eyed.

"Who the hell invited you to this party? Get lost," he said, putting the palm of his hand on Jacqui's face and shoving her away.

Jacqui's foot caught. She stumbled back, lost her balance, and tumbled into a cluster of people behind her. Jacqui and two others sprawled across the floor. Beer spilled. Glass broke. Someone swore at Jacqui.

"Her right brain doesn't know what her left foot is doing," said the footballer to his girl. He turned toward a group of his friends, pointed toward Jacqui, and hooted.

Bobby leaped over Jacqui and the two others on the floor. He drove his right fist into the footballer's belly, just below his rib cage, knocking the wind out of him. He doubled over. His beer bottle fell to the floor. Bobby's arm encircled the boy's neck. His other hand clenched it in place, and rendered him helpless. Bobby led him out the front door and threw him off the porch onto the front lawn.

Jacqui had recovered by then. She pulled herself up, shoved her way through the amused crowd, and yanked the plug from the disc player. The wall of sound crumbled into a stunning and somewhat sobering quiet. The voices and shouts that had been competing for space in the din now seemed garish and shrill and out of place. There was an embarrassing lull.

Jacqui seized that moment, stood on a chair near the centre of the room, pulled a cell phone from her pocket, and held it above her head.

"Hey!" she shouted loudly enough to get the crowd's attentions. "None of you were invited into this house. I want everyone to leave. I'm calling the police. Anyone here when they arrive will be arrested. So get out now," she said.

Then she tapped in the emergency 911 number.

67.

"I brought you a playmate."

Anne could see nothing in the stark darkness of the room. But she heard the words, and her skin crawled. She recognized the voice. Jamie MacFarlane's.

Anne heard the snap of a match and saw the flicker of a kerosene lamp. Then she heard a roar of anger. Her eyes hadn't quite focused, but her head turned toward the sound. A hairy tattooed arm lunged toward her. Behind it she saw a ragged tooth and the weathered face of Cutter Underhay. Instinctively, she rolled and skittered away but fetched up against a cabinet. She shut her eyes and braced for the clasp of hands around her throat or the thrashing of his fists. Then she heard a metallic clatter, a sharp clank, and a litany of vile profanities and foul oaths.

"Nice reflexes, Ms. Billy Darby," said MacFarlane. Then he turned to Cutter. "Play nice, Cutter."

Cutter's vulgarities and curses dwindled into unintelligible hate-stoked grumbles. It was only then that Anne gathered the courage to turn around and face him. He glared at her from across the room. Looking around for the first time, Anne found herself in a small, crude cabin that, at one time, hunters or woodcutters might have used as a refuge. Now it was abandoned and in disrepair. A single kerosene lantern illuminated the interior and threw creepy dancing shadows whenever a draft of air breached a crack in the flimsy wallboards.

A rusted wood stove stood by a side wall. The pipe from the firebox had disconnected from it and dangled from its hole in the roof. The floor was water-stained and soiled with animal droppings and bits of pine cones shucked by squirrels. An old beer case lay in a remote corner. Several beer bottles littered the corners. A few had been broken. And there was a dearth of furniture. One wood table stood in the centre of the room. One usable chair was pulled next to it; the only other seat had a broken back. An ancient metal frame bed butted the long wall opposite the door. A dank mattress lay on top.

Still cringing against an old floor cabinet, Anne's eyes remained fixed on the bed. Cutter had retreated there. He sat on the floor, leaning against the side of it, his right arm crooked on the frame as if poised to leap, his left arm bent to grasp the tubular metal headboard. One handcuff held his wrist; the other encircled both bed and post. His failed attempt to attack Anne had been just inches beyond his reach.

MacFarlane chuckled a bit at the rage in Cutter and the terror in Anne. Then he reached out and pulled the tape from her mouth. He grabbed her shoulders and pulled her across the floor to the other corner of the metal bed. He snapped a cuff over her left wrist and secured the other cuff to frame and post, just as Cutter's had been.

"There," he said. "Get comfortable. You'll be here until tomorrow."

"What happens then?" she asked.

"You'll find that out tomorrow," he said, removing the tape from her hands and her ankles.

"That better?"

Anne nodded. "Can I have some water?"

"No," he said flatly. Then his cell phone rang. When he looked at the caller display, his brow crumpled in thought and displeasure. The phone continued ringing. He glared at it as if it were a personal affront, but he took the call, answering brusquely, "Wait."

With a satisfied glance at his two prisoners, MacFarlane walked outside. The sagging door dragged across the threshold. With a final lift and jerk, he slammed it shut and walked toward the car. The evening was clear and moonless. A damp air had drained vigour from the blackness of the sky. The dim stars had disappeared. The strong ones had grown indistinct and dull. MacFarlane put the phone to his ear and listened to the tirade his caller had launched against him. He feigned patience and said nothing. The rant finally lost some impetus and spiralled into pointless repetition.

Finally, MacFarlane spoke: "I'll meet you in half an hour. Don't be stupid! You're up to your ass in this, too."

MacFarlane never returned to the cabin. Anne and Cutter heard his car start and listened curiously to the rattly sound as it backtracked over the path. The sound grew fainter, and finally it disappeared below the rustle of leaves and the scraping of branches in the October breeze.

The day had been balmy and pleasant, but as the evening progressed, the balminess turned damp, and the agreeable temperature grew chilly. The lamplight fluttered madly in the drafty cabin. Both prisoners had grown quiet and reflective. Cutter stared somewhat blankly at the shape-shifting of the shadows. He looked like a wound spring. Anne's fear had subsided, but the foreboding atmosphere of her tenuous situation replaced it. It was almost as if she could hear a clock ticking, like dedicated footsteps, toward an ill-fated hour. She couldn't afford to wallow in the luxury of feeling sorry for herself. She needed answers, and she needed them soon. Anne became consumed with uncovering those answers. It was a curiosity bred in desperation. It was undirected and unquenchable, and Cutter's continuing, sullen silence fanned her anger and determination. Finally, she could stand his indifference no more, but she took care to choose her words and tone judiciously.

"'We're going to find out tomorrow.' What did he mean by that?"

"You're the detective," he said. He responded slowly as if her inquiry had diverted him from an important engagement. "You figure it out."

"Look, Cutter, getting in each other's face may be an amusing way to round out the evening, but we've got more important troubles to work out. Things don't look so good."

"Ya think..."

Cutter's sarcasm rankled Anne, but she suppressed the urge to snap back and replied as calmly and as low-key as she could manage.

"You got a plan?" she asked.

"Yeah, I have a plan."

"What is it?"

"Kill you...kill MacFarlane...or vice versa."

Cutter turned away and sank into some dark private thought. *So much for the voice of reason*, she thought. She needed a different tack. *What if I provoked him?* she thought. *That might open him up.*

"You're so full of shit, Cutter. Kill me? You had your chances. You blew them all. You had me pinned down in your own club just over a year ago...and what happened? I got back what you stole from me. Oh yeah, and there was that fire I started that almost burned your club down. Remember that? And you tried again two days ago. You blew up my car and almost killed my daughter! You aren't smart enough to kill me, are you?"

"You got lucky last year. A fluke. And that explosion? That wasn't me. MacFarlane engineered that fiasco. Then he framed me for that job."

"So you say. Why would he do that?"

"I don't know, but we've done a lot of business together over the years. He tipped me off. Said that the cops had a warrant and one of my boys framed me. He said he could hide me until the dust settled."

"Why would he double-cross you? That doesn't make sense."

"I said I don't know, but it had to be him." Cutter sounded genuinely perplexed. "All I know is that he wants you dead and me dead."

"You know his plan?"

"Bits and pieces. He likes to show how smart he is."

"You want to fill me in? Maybe we can figure something out."

"He took me up here in the trunk of his car."

"Sounds familiar."

"Soon as he opens the trunk I know where I am. This is my cabin. My uncle left it to me in his will along with his business at The Hole in the Wall. I haven't been here since I was a kid." Cutter grinned and sounded almost excited.

"Forget the memory lane flashback."

"Anyway, he pulls his gun and handcuffs me. Later he gets braggin' and tells me about the frame. I ask him what he's goin' to do. He says his story is going to be that he got a tip about my whereabouts, which is here, and that I had grabbed you, but he arrives too late. Supposedly I've already killed you. Then he kills me in the shootout. You're dead… I'm dead…and he becomes a big hero again and lives happily ever after."

"Why hasn't he killed us already then?"

"Every detail has to match his story. He planned it for tomorrow morning. If he kills us tonight…"

"…the time of death wouldn't make sense," said Anne.

"That's all I know."

"So that's why you made that dumb attempt to kill me when he dumped me out of that bag?"

"Takin' you out would screw things up for him…buy me a little time maybe."

"Perhaps I can pay you back sometime."

"You'll need a plan first."

"I've got a plan," she said. Anne spoke with an air of confidence that surprised Cutter. His surprise drifted into scepticism. Then he laughed at her.

Anne pulled the bobby pins from her hair. She pushed the fingers of her free hand through her long hair as if she were modelling and shook it out. "Much better," she said and smiled.

68.

"You've had a very busy week."

"The worst one ever. Madame Desjardins is going to kill me when she finds out."

"As far as we can determine, you weren't at fault. You did what you could under the circumstances. It'll all be in my report," said Constable Foley.

"There's going to be a report?" Jacqui was surprised. "Ohmygod, is it going to be in the papers?"

"That's unlikely to happen." Constable Foley spoke with an officious certainty, but Jacqui wasn't convinced.

Constable Wilkins, his partner, returned from a walk-through of the house and property and stood next to Foley and Jacqui.

"No drunks left inside or out," said Wilkins, "and there's more mess than damage. You're a lucky lady," he said. He sounded very satisfied with himself.

"Yeah...lucky," she echoed. The faces of her disappointed mother and a dismayed art teacher haunted her imagination, and Rada's humiliation and her father's frustration intertwined with them until the unmusical tinkle of glass coaxed her attention back to reality.

Bobby Fogarty swept the fragments into a dustpan. The glass in his framed present had shattered, but the picture was not damaged. He picked it from the floor and examined it carefully.

"I can fix that," said Jacqui. "Don't worry."

"The birthday boy?" asked Wilkins. Bobby nodded. "Right then. I guess we're done here. If any latecomers show up, call."

"Thank you."

Constables Foley and Wilkins headed for the door. Foley turned and started to speak, but stopped. He nodded encouragingly toward Jacqui. Jacqui waved a goodbye.

The door closed behind them, and Jacqui looked at her watch.

"I have an hour, maybe a bit more, before she arrives."

Jacqui surveyed the living room. Disgust with the look of the place and discouragement with the task ahead overwhelmed her. Tears dampened her eyes. She blinked repeatedly to clear her vision and dispel any evidence of what she was feeling.

"Why don't you head home? It's getting late, and I've got some work to do around here," she said purposefully to Bobby. She turned away, bent down, and scrubbed at a spot on the floor with her fingernail.

She wet it and wiped it. The mark left by the cigarette butt disappeared. Only a small smudge remained.

"Can I help?" said Bobby.

"If you want?" Her words were hesitant, but her heart brightened. She waited a second or two for some qualifier from Bobby, but none came. "Okay then. Open all the windows. Let's get some fresh air in here. Then gather up the bottles and garbage. I'll grab the mop and pail."

Jacob Dawson hunched over his workstation in the periodical section of the Robertson Library at the University. Two open books spread across his desk. The storage ledge above his carrel held three bound volumes: *Youth and Society*, *Symbolic Interaction*, and *Discourse and Society*. The library would close in an hour, and he rushed to add notes onto a lined pad and highlight passages in a stack of photocopies.

"You still on?" she asked. Sami Smith's perfume somehow had swept ahead of her person. It quickened Jacob's attention before she spoke. Jacob seemed startled by her sudden interest but quite pleased with her intervention. She was very attractive and smart. She was also charming. And her eyes burned with a hint of mischievousness, a trait accented by the bright pink streak in a forelock of her blonde hair. Her avant-garde airs fascinated him.

Jacob leaned back in his seat and stretched. Three straight hours of study under his belt had wearied him, and the major group presentation tomorrow meant a long night ahead. Still there was much to do. Tonight's study session weighed just as much on his mind as it did on Sami's. Their group results would count significantly on mid-semester grades.

"I'll be there. The others on board, too?"

Sami smiled brightly and shook her head in affirmation. Jacob secretly marvelled at the perfect cherubic shape of her lips and the stunning whiteness of her teeth.

"You?"

"Absolutely."

Jacob returned to his studies and note-taking, but he was slowly losing his initiative and his will to continue in earnest. Part of the fault was his weariness; part was Sami.

Sami was a delight. She brightened his otherwise solitary life. He was drawn to her, but she knew almost nothing of his past, and experience had convinced Jacob that her knowing about it would put an end to dreams he had envisioned with her. But the truth of his past was only one stumbling block, he thought. Real and present demons circled like birds of prey...and they were growing hungry and anxious and impatient to be satisfied.

Jacob's pencil point snapped. He stared into the imitation wood veneer of the carrel in front of him and saw his future and his past—a small box, a cage, a storage locker, a prison cell, but perhaps that small world was simply his fate, its tentacles reaching out from every corner. There was no escaping—fate, destiny—whatever one might call it. At one time he had accepted Christ and the hope of redemption, but he could not dispel his long-held disposition that all of time had already been written. The future had already been scripted. The play had begun. Everything else—plans, expectations, dreams—was sham and illusion. A cruel joke.

Twenty minutes elapsed. His attention suspended. His mind drifted. He closed his books and gathered his notes. Then his cell phone buzzed. It was a text message: *"need u now."*

Anne rotated around to the foot of the bed. She still believed that Cutter would try to kill her, but she didn't think his arms could stretch far enough to reach her where she was now. Nonetheless she preferred caution, and, from her new position, she could keep him in her line of sight. She could also prevent him from observing her too closely. She did have a plan, and it involved picking the lock on her cuffs.

In theory it was simple; in practice, a little more challenging. She had done it before—a few times. But that was when Anne was fifteen. Her tutorial, though, had begun when she was eight or nine.

At that time, her uncle, Billy Darby, was a cop with the Ottawa police. For a while he lived in the same house as Anne, her mother, and her father. Often, when Anne's parents went out for an evening with friends, they enlisted Billy to babysit. Anne loved it when he watched over her. He played games and did card tricks. He even showed her how the tricks worked and, with his help, she would practise his sleights of hand to astonish her school chums.

Sometimes after Uncle Billy arrived home, he would let her play with his night stick, a collapsible baton. There was something wondrous about the baton. A flick of the wrist would instantly deploy the telescoping parts from the length of a ruler to almost the length of a yard stick. She felt powerful with it and waved it about as if it were a Star Wars lightsaber. Then, after having vanquished a dark-side stormtrooper or two, she would tap the baton's tip on the hardwood floor, and magically the whole thing would collapse into its short, stubby handle. Again and again Anne did this, and again and again Uncle Bill would rock with laughter.

His handcuffs had been among her temporary playthings at those times, too. But they had been more of an intellectual puzzle than an exciting implement of action. Of course, when Uncle Billy snapped that cuff around her wrist, she was so small at the time that she could slip right out no matter how tightly they encircled her hand, and she giggled with delight each time she set herself free. In turnabout, she handcuffed her uncle, and he made a show of struggling with them until he retrieved his spare key and made his escape.

Something about the mechanics of the handcuffs had fascinated Anne. It rivalled some Lego sets in complexity with its keyed mechanisms, spring releases, and ratchets, the smoothness of its movements, and the decisive sounds of its engagement. It was shiny and solid and substantial and, because it was one of Uncle Billy's tools, it seemed important and grown-up.

Five years later, Anne's adventures with batons and handcuffs were remembered only as a bit of childhood fun and distraction. Playacting the Jedi knight had lost its zest, but Anne still treasured the spirit that had empowered her. As a teenager, Anne played that spirit out more practically on the high school soccer field. So, one evening when Uncle Billy snapped handcuffs on himself in her living room after dinner, handed her the key, and asked her what would Princess Leia do if she were in this predicament, she was divided between laughing him off for his presumption that she was still a little kid or accepting his foolish challenge simply to humour him. Anne chose the latter, but she couldn't determine whether she had done so because of kindness or a habitual respect for her seniors.

Anne played along, but she did so reluctantly. After all, Uncle Billy was getting old, she thought. His hair was greying on the sides and thinning like a parched field on top. He must be at least forty, forty-five, she guessed. So she made an effort to be kind. She suggested three or four thoughtful answers—a few of them quite inspired, she believed. Then she became tired of the game and proffered half a dozen wild guesses, none of which satisfied Uncle Billy's quest for... *For what?* she wondered. It was all becoming rather silly and tedious.

"What's the trick?" she asked.

"The trick is the key," he answered in his best Alec Guinness voice. Anne's failure to guess right, as well as Uncle Billy's faux mystique and, in her mind, unrelenting reply, frustrated Anne, and she threw up her hands.

"The trick is that you can't get out of a cop's handcuffs," she said. "That's no trick. That's just common sense."

"You must use the Force, Luke," said Billy continuing his Obi-Wan Kenobi impersonation and pointing his forefinger toward the side of his head. Uncle Billy wasn't suppressing a laugh as he sometimes did before he delivered the punchline to a joke, and fifteen-year-old Anne staunched the impulse to call his bluff a second time. Perhaps his clue is a real clue, she thought.

"Reproduce the key?" she said, half-expecting his great guffaw to upstage her. Instead, he smiled. But it wasn't amusement. It was satisfaction.

"Might make a cop out of you yet...if you don't make the cut for the World Cup team."

"And the answer is...?" Anne's short reply was a confusion of frustration, sarcasm, and ill-defined pleasure.

"Let me show you," he said. "Give me one of your bobby pins."

Billy took the key from his pocket. He put the bobby pin next to it on the table top. You turn this pin into this key," he said. "You need to recreate the tip, the shank and the pick lever to do it."

"Don't you need tools?"

"They're all in your hand...and head. You know what the key looks like. You make the tip first." Billy stuck the end of the bobby pin into the keyway of the handcuff and bent it back. He withdrew it and showed Anne an eighth-inch crook in it. Billy wiggled it back into the keyway at an angle and bent a second short crook in the opposite direction. He withdrew it and showed Anne.

"The rest of the bobby pin is a lever," he said and inserted the homemade lock pick into the keyway. "Be careful to turn it slowly but firmly. You'll feel pressure coming off the ratchets. There. See?" he said, and the handcuff opened and fell from his wrist.

Anne had never forgotten Uncle Billy's lesson, and, in the flutter of kerosene-fuelled light in her cabin prison, she worked her bobby pin into the keyway of her handcuff, hoping that it was stiff enough to take the load of releasing the spring.

It was.

69.

It had begun to rain, not a heavy driving rain, more of a thick mist, which obscured vision, fogged the glass, and made it difficult to judge distance. Fenton Peale turned on the wipers and redirected the warm airflow to the windshield.

He drove past MacFarlane's house and continued slowly along Bunbury Road. He wasn't absent-minded. He hadn't been distracted. He was preoccupied. His well-planned life was unravelling, and he was losing control. He could feel it. He could see it in his own reflection. In his rear-view mirror, a worn, aging man stared back at him. He had a deeply receding hairline, prominent wrinkles, and lacklustre eyes and, more troubling, a complexion drained to a paleness so haunting that he conceived of himself as slowly disappearing, fading imperceptibly into oblivion. And it all seemed to happen in just days.

His personal habits had been neglected, too. He smelled of sweat and the stink of whisky. He was dishevelled and untidy as an old bachelor. His suit jacket and trousers were wrinkled. He had clawed his necktie away from his collar. The knot was misshapen, the collar unbuttoned, and wiry chest hairs sprouted in the breach.

Peale winced at the tightness in his waist. He felt trapped. A whiff of fear and desperation swept over him in a flash of heat. He unbuttoned his jacket and rolled down the window halfway. The renewed air was cool and fresh. He breathed more freely. But the wind suddenly loosed a nasty gust. It blew the front of his suit jacket open. The oiled wooden handgrip of the Webley .455 revolver sticking from his waistband glinted in the light of a passing streetlamp.

Peale had not travelled the upper Bunbury Road in eleven years. What he had done there had repelled him too much, and he had struggled to put the deed behind him. *Out of sight, out of mind* was a lie, as it turned out. But the passage of time helped blunt his conscience and deaden his memory and, for short periods, allowed him to rationalize his crime, but the ghost of it never departed. Its presence, in some form, was always there, and, like a boil beneath one's skin, it wanted to work its way out.

It had happened eleven years ago this month. On 19 October 2001. It had rained that night, too. He had not wanted to be there, but Mac-Farlane had him over a barrel. It had been foolish of him to agree, but he saw no other way out. So he borrowed a pickup truck, smeared mud over the rear plate, and waited in the parking lot of a fast-food restaurant near her workplace. MacFarlane had provided him with Carolyn's work schedule and a description of her car.

Peale sipped coffee in the cab of the truck but tasted nothing. The coffee was hot, but he felt nothing. His nerves were ragged, his mind detached. Then he spotted her. Carolyn's black Saturn coupe passed Peale's position exactly three minutes after midnight, the scheduled end of her shift. He put the truck in gear and followed her down the street, past the intersection to the Hillsborough Bridge, and onto the Bunbury Road. A battered red Ford Ranger bolted from a side street and cut off his truck. It drove maddeningly slowly, and Carolyn's Saturn disappeared around a bend in the road. He couldn't pass. When the Ford finally turned off, Peale tromped on the gas to catch up. The speed limit changed to highway limits as the city houses began to diminish, and he hoped that she hadn't made it too much farther.

The highway glistened from the rain that had fallen earlier that evening, and the moon had not shown signs of rising. He increased his speed, and several minutes elapsed before he caught the glimpse of her tail lights.

A good scare will do.

Those were MacFarlane's instructions.

Run her off the road. She'll get the picture.

Peale felt the knot in his stomach as he approached the designated spot. A long stretch of road. No houses in sight. No traffic. No witnesses.

Do it quick. Don't give her a chance to think about braking.

Peale quickly glanced ahead and behind for other vehicles. There wasn't a glimmer of light. He turned on his truck's high beams. Their brilliance framed her head in the rear window. He overtook her car, blasted his horn, and eased across the dividing line into her lane. He saw the fear in her eyes as the side of his cab loomed toward her, forcing her to the road's edge. Suddenly her car jerked to the right. Her tires caught the shoulder, softened by the rain. The wheels dug in and dragged her toward the ditch. Her car fishtailed on the edge, straightened momentarily, then hurtled off the incline and into a culvert. The force of the impact crumpled the front end.

Then don't stop. Get the hell out of there. No witnesses, no problem.

Peale noticed an orange glow from the wreckage. It was short-lived. Darkness followed quickly and completely. *This wasn't supposed to happen*, he thought, and touched his brakes. *What if she's badly hurt?*

Peale saw a dim glow of car lights somewhere far behind him. It reignited his fear—fear that MacFarlane would reveal his affair with Simone, fear that Simone's pregnancy would point to him as a suspect, and fear that he would lose his family, his reputation, and his business. He had too much to lose. Hairs bristled on his neck. His foot hit the gas pedal. His truck lurched forward and vanished beyond the thicket of trees lining the dark country road.

Eleven years later, Peale's neck hairs bristled again. Peale's stomach convulsed, but there was nothing to toss up. It happened as his car passed the white cross that Edna Jollimore Hibley had erected and tended as a memorial to her sister Carolyn's "accident." The moment passed. Then his thoughts turned to the present, his rendezvous with MacFarlane.

Peale was late for the meeting, but he didn't care, and it would have been quicker to backtrack, but he vowed never to travel that stretch of road again. So he drove on, circled around, and arrived at MacFarlane's home by another route. Sickness and guilt no longer plagued him. Hatred stood in their place.

Peale buttoned his jacket and pressed the buzzer. He saw a curtain shift. Then he heard the click of the front door.

MacFarlane filled the open door frame. He wore dark sweats and a white T-shirt. His arms and neck were muscular, and his waist solid, but lacking the trimness it had once had. He stood a head taller than Peale and presented a formidable, if not intimidating, figure to him. MacFarlane scrutinized Peale, took a step back, and smirked.

"You look like shit," he said. Peale pushed by him in silence.

"You've been blackmailing me for over a decade, you sonofabitch!"

"Congratulations. I've got your ten-year pin around here...somewhere," he said, looking around the room mockingly.

"And it's all been a lie. You conned me."

"Don't know what you're talking about, Fenton."

"She wasn't pregnant. You convinced me that she was. Lies! All lies!"

"I didn't lie. She did. She told me she was pregnant, and I believed her. If you've been conned by anybody, it was her. Now get a grip on yourself."

"You can't push all this off on Simone. It was you who was blackmailing. It was you who forced me into this godawful mess."

"You wouldn't be in a mess if you had stayed home and played with your wife and not someone else's woman...especially mine. You must have had a death wish back then. You could have guessed what would happen if I found out. You're lucky I was satisfied with blackmailing you. I had a better idea at the time...shoulda killed you."

"Why didn't you?"

"I decided to give you a break. She was just a slut after all..."

"I would have been better off dead. At least then I wouldn't have become a murderer."

"The price you pay," said MacFarlane.

"Well now's the time for you to pay!"

Peale reached for the revolver in his waistband. MacFarlane jumped forward, grabbed his wrist with one hand, and drove his other fist into Peale's belly. He crumpled to the floor gasping for breath. MacFarlane removed the Webley from Peale's belt and set it on the end table next to a reading chair behind him. He sat down in the chair and waited while Peale blubbered and whimpered pathetically on the floor.

"Did you think I wouldn't notice that bulge? A bag of carrots would have been less obvious."

Peale was too stunned and shaken to be aware of MacFarlane's sarcasm. He pulled himself half-up and leaned against a sofa. His shoulders slumped, and he stared emptily at nothing.

MacFarlane continued: "At the time, I hadn't intended to harm that woman. That culvert being where it was...that was just fate. But it *was* a bit more leverage on you. I hated you, your money, and your arrogance, and when you killed Carolyn Jollimore, you became my own little marionette...and you still are."

Peale had ended his pathetic little noises of pain and despair. He looked up at MacFarlane. The fear had left his eyes. A helpless emptiness remained.

"I don't hate you anymore, Fenton. Time puts things in perspective. Simone played you just like she played me. Simone loved Simone, no one else. And her text messages? They prove that she was still workin' her way up the food chain even when she was bangin' you. Didn't know that, did you? You were just the last pig at the trough."

"What are you going to do?"

"Like I said, Fenton, I don't hate you anymore." MacFarlane pointed to a second chair and motioned Peale to take a seat. Peale rose from the floor, still gripping his stomach, and limped painfully toward it. He eased himself down. Hopeless exhaustion coloured his face.

MacFarlane continued: "I never used those text messages against you, did I?"

"No, but I can read between the lines."

"And who brought out the vote when you were running for town councillor and for the legislature?"

"In return for my support for your appointment to police chief."

"You win, I win. Nobody loses. And that's how it will continue to work, Fenton. You continue to do what you do. I keep those messages stashed away and, while I'm alive, nobody will find them. Win, win. So clean yourself up, and get a grip, and I'll continue to cover your political back. Win, win. Forget and you'll lose everything...lose your family...lose your job...lose your reputation...your legacy...your freedom...everything. Understand?"

MacFarlane had a gathering urge to laugh at Peale. The more he had talked, the more shrunken Peale had become. He looked pathetic. He looked small. He looked broken. But MacFarlane quelled the urge with the satisfaction of knowing that he had defeated him.

"Understand?" he repeated.

Peale's nod was subtle, almost nonexistent, but there nonetheless. He stood slowly and hobbled toward the door.

"Wait!" said MacFarlane. "Aren't you forgetting something?"

Peale turned. MacFarlane pointed toward the pistol on the end table. Peale offered a blank look. MacFarlane picked it up and tossed it toward him, but his reflexes were slow. He fumbled, and the gun fell to the floor. Peale jumped fearfully at the noisy clatter it made. MacFarlane chuckled. Peale bent slowly, picked it up, turned, and headed out the door. It had begun raining again.

MacFarlane smiled. He hollered after him: "If you feel the urge, kill yourself someplace quiet and out of the way...save the family from scandal."

70.

"I'll send someone back for you," said Anne as she stood up. Cutter turned and stared with the same surprise as someone viewing an apparition of the Virgin Mary.

Anne held up her unshackled arms. "Tada!" she said, confirming her achievement with a vocal flourish.

"Get me loose," he demanded.

"Can't do that," said Anne. "You haven't earned the trust."

"What if he comes back?"

"Then the first part of your plan has been accomplished. I won't be here to bait his trap to frame you. Anyway, I'll be quick about it. Gotta be a phone somewhere near here."

Anne took a few steps toward the cabin door. A sudden gust disturbed the air, and the flame in the kerosene lamp on the table fluttered wildly. Shadows raced across the walls like a disturbed colony of bats. They distracted Anne. She hesitated. Cutter lunged. This time his steel bed didn't catch in a loose floorboard and fetch him up.

"You're going nowhere!" He sounded desperate and menacing.

He heaved up his end of the bed with his cuffed arm and hurled himself toward the door like a football lineman. The bed followed. His strength and speed were surprising and unexpected, and his sprint left him within arm's reach of the door. He blocked her escape.

"I haven't finished with you yet."

Anne was alarmed at his agility and strength, and she would be no match if he grabbed her. She froze in place, closer to the other end of the metal frame, nearer the middle of the room. Cutter's eyes burned with rage as he assessed his next move. The lamplight glowed harsh and yellow. Cutter's skin took on a sallow, oily cast. His eyes were blood red, but unkind shadows turned the hollows of his face as black as a spider's hole.

Anne took another slow cautious step back. Her foot came down on a dried spruce cone. She faltered, and Cutter attacked again. Awkwardly, Anne threw herself back and spun further away. As she did, she heard the shattering of glass.

Cutter's last lunge had carried the bed with him, and it collided with the table. The table shook, and the oil lamp toppled, rolled, and crashed to the floor. For a fraction of a second, near-total darkness consumed the cabin. Then a spark in the wick caught the spilled kerosene, and the room filled with light. Anne and Cutter watched as the pool of oil spread thinly in every direction. Flames followed the trail. The blaze flared hungrily and smoked. It fed on kerosene and scraps of tinder and bits of trash scattered about the floor and, having fed, spit out an even more malevolent flame.

Cutter abandoned his vengeful assault on Anne and backed away from the fire. He tried frantically and unsuccessfully to free his hand from the bed, but managed to pull himself closer to the cabin door. Freedom was only a few taunting inches away. His eyes blazed wildly with fear. The smoke thickened. It gripped him, and he hacked and coughed to spit it out.

Anne was amazed at the speed with which the fire grew, and her eyes scoured the room for a way to escape. Within a minute or two the flames had formed a wall that spanned the width of the room. She could scarcely see Cutter through the gathering smoke. So even if the door was undefended, she could not reach it now. Instead, she hurled herself once or twice against the boarded wall of the ancient cabin, but the boards were sound and the nails stubborn. Her only other option was at the end wall, a fixed window to let in morning light. It was the only one in the cabin, but it was high, too far up for Anne to reach.

Cutter's screams paralyzed Anne. Her thoughts fell apart. At first his screams were ones of horror, as if he had just stumbled into a nest of snakes, their eyes glinting in the moonlight, their movement against his clothing shrivelling his skin. When the first of the flames touched his trousers, they danced with orange delight. Then horror turned to terror with the first bite of their searing tongues. Then his shirt caught, and he recoiled at the lunge of death toward him. He twitched and shuddered and beat against the lapping of death against his flesh. Then he loosed a scream so wretched that Anne nearly collapsed with dread. More screams. Gasps. Whimpering groans. And a final shrieking litany of gibberish and paradox spilled from his mouth: "O god, o my god, o god, ohmygod, godammit, o god, godamn you...you... you...godamn you...o my god damn you...oh, oh...ohhh!"

Cutter's long hair caught and burned with a distasteful smell and crackle. He screamed a long, tortured howl. Then he gasped to wail once more but, with that second breath, his mouth and throat and lungs filled. He tasted the flavour of pain, and his agony quenched itself in a writhing death.

Anne remained transfixed by the horrors before her until a sharp crackle of burning wood snapped her attention back to her own perilous condition. Her thinking became crystal clear. The window was her only escape route. Anne seized a wooden cabinet and dragged it to the wall below the window. Still, she could not reach the glass after she stood on the cabinet. The chair with the broken back was nearby. So she grabbed it and climbed once again onto the cabinet, hauling the chair up with her. Above floor level the air was thick with smoke. She retched and coughed. The fire grew closer. The heat flashed toward her in waves. It became intense.

From her cabinet-top perch, Anne swung the chair above her head and beat the window as savagely as she had strength to do. The first swing shattered the glass and, as it broke, Anne heard a startling whoosh. The fire was vented. A stream of oxygen flooded in and fed the conflagration. The flames roared with a fresh vengeance and, in a ghastly flight of fancy, Anne imagined Cutter's dead soul somehow driving the ravenous sweep of fire toward her. Anne shuddered at her own madness, but fear bristled inside her, fuelled her despera-tion, and she swung the chair with renewed force. Her second and third swings cleared shards of glass and jagged splinters from the window frame.

Anne set the chair on the cabinet top and climbed carefully up on the chair. From that height she could easily grip the newly made hole. Anne muscled up until her head stuck out the hole. She took a long breath of fresh air. Then, with a firm grasp on the empty frame, she rolled forward. She lost her grip as she tumbled out, but her fall was softer than she had expected, and she managed to land on her feet.

Anne staggered, stumbled, and crawled from the foot of the cabin toward a semi-dark cluster of withered spruce trees. She leaned against scarred, coarse bark and drew a deep breath. It was cool, clean, and fresh, and she felt exhilaration, the electrifying euphoria of being alive. It lasted for a few short moments. Then her hands began to tremble. Palsy gripped her, and the horrors she had endured the past evening forced themselves once more into her mind.

Anne was helpless to defend herself. She felt as if she had been viciously slapped and forced to acquiesce and live through it again: the terror of rousing from sleep at home, a dark figure enveloping her, choking her, drugging her; her desperate efforts to control her body, to quell the nausea that would lead unquestionably to asphyxiation; the dread at finding herself face to face with death at the hands of two brutes; the horror of Cutter's pitiful screams as he burned; and the eerie haunting echo of Cutter's last utterance, his last wish—his final desire to send her into the fiery hell with him.

Anne curled into a ball on the damp ground, the horror, the anger, and the hatred of it all swirling in her mind. Tears streamed from her eyes. Her body convulsed with sobs, and her hands shielded her eyes as if they could shut out the debilitating impact of her experience. For a while Anne had felt as if she had left her body altogether and was floating freely and terrifyingly in a sea of all-too-real memory, and she had wondered if she were going mad.

But those feelings were dissipating now—like the back side of a wave—and she could feel herself once again. Her fingertips sensed the texture of the ground beneath her. Her ears heard the crack of burning timbers, and again she drew strength from the feeling that she really had survived.

Then a sudden roar, like a speeding car passing too closely, startled her. The sound had come from the cabin. The fire had broken through the roof. Smoke billowed. Flames shot skyward. The ground all around her glowed with a yellow-orange light, and shadows danced eerily beside spruce saplings and blueberry bushes.

The roar of the fire had heightened Anne's vigilance. Her attention leapt from past terrors and present reprieve to future survival. First, she had to get out of there. MacFarlane would be back soon, and if he found her he would have to kill her, and the woodlands surrounding her were vast enough to hide a small body. No one would find her remains...ever.

Anne quickly gathered herself together and made for the rutted trail that led out of this place. Her ankle ached as she hobbled up the path. She was confident she could walk it off. If she was going to die, she would go out kicking and screaming, she thought.

Once the cabin dropped from sight, the path she took cut through thick stands of spruce and endless acres of reforested white pine. The light from the cabin fire gradually diminished. Darkness closed in upon her, and it wasn't until then that she realized it had started to rain. The rain was light and soft and welcome. It was clean and cool. Refreshing.

Anne moved slowly and steadily along, careful not to turn her ankle again, but the road was uneven and seemed never to end. Darkness had dimmed her sense of time and distance, and she stumbled around for almost an hour. Impatience started to dog her. Then she spotted the intersection, a few yards ahead. At the sight of it, her pulse quickened, and expectations mounted. Even this late at night, the odd car would be travelling the road. A house would be near at hand.

The paved road, however, was a disappointment. Anne peered to the right and then to the left. There was no sign of civilization in either direction, but a glow of light against the overcast sky suggested that Charlottetown was southwest, and that was the direction she chose.

Anne trudged along. The highway cut through endless fields of potatoes and the stubble of freshly cut grain. The few houses she encountered were summer residences, unlit and unoccupied. Several long laneways branched from the highway, but they promised nothing but darkness. No porch light or barn lamp offered hope, and there was no assurance that a house lay at the end of any of the lanes. Anne heard the occasional barking of a dog. She also heard the baying of coyotes and, for that reason, she resolved to remain on the road and await the chance of a passing vehicle.

The ache in her ankle had not yet worked its way out. Running, if she had to, was not possible. Add to that, the rain. It was still light, but it was no longer refreshing. She felt the cold creeping into her bones. Her hair was dripping and her light sweatshirt was heavy with dampness.

Then, at a downcast moment, Anne saw the lights of a car rounding a bend in the road. She felt a jolt of elation. The car was heading her way. Its cold blue halogen lights raked the trees on the bend. Anne waved excitedly. Just as quickly, though, a pang of fear swept over her.

What if it's MacFarlane? He'd use the same route to return, she thought, *and he was due back. Long overdue*, she thought. *What if it's him?*

The car's headlights had not yet illuminated her figure on the side of the road. Fear won out. Anne limped off the shoulder and slid into the ditch, and the car passed without incident.

It might have been MacFarlane...and it might not have been.

She couldn't tell.

Anne climbed the bank and resumed her hapless trek and, like a gambler walking empty-pocketed, she dreamed the sweet victory of a win, but felt only the cold regret of loss.

71.

Linda Moore was finishing her evening shift at the Kings County Hospital. She was an RN, a transplant from Toronto, and had lived for the last two years with her husband in Savage Harbour. She had never had the inclination to move to PEI, but her husband, a computer technology specialist, had been offered a job in Charlottetown and a salary he couldn't refuse.

You go where the work is, she rationalized.

She missed many things about Toronto. Big city life was exciting, diverse, and cosmopolitan. It bustled with opportunity, and the night-life was compelling.

Other things were less missed—the assembly line of weekend stabbings and beatings at the hospital where she had worked; the unbearable traffic; the cost of a decent apartment; and there was detachment there, too, a loneliness, which she could never quite define.

PEI was different from Upper Canada, and Savage Harbour was no Toronto. Moving to Savage Harbour...as Linda's old friends phrased it...*was like a Londoner being posted to Nairobi*. Savage Harbour conjured images of 1930s films of small-town America or prewar English villages in Agatha Christie tales, where everyone knows everyone... and personal business is popular gossip.

No doubt, the place was culture shock for Linda. She had grown up in a Toronto where few residents could name more than a couple of their neighbours. A passing hello or nod of recognition was as close as she had ever got to neighbourliness. So, if renegade Mayor Rob Ford and cult-leader Charles Manson had been smoking crack two apartments away, she would never have known. And *not knowing is not dreading*, one friend had said.

But, as Linda eventually learned, the imposition of village life wasn't always a bad thing. She learned that the day her water pump broke.

It happened on a Tuesday, her day off. Husband Frank had gone to work. Baby Michael was cranky and teething. She turned the kitchen faucet and...nothing. A limp dribble. Her heart sank. She was helpless around mechanical devices, and she didn't know a plumber. So, in desperation, she knocked on the door of neighbour, Mary Murphy. Mary had dropped off a kettle of chowder and fresh biscuits the same day Linda's family moved in. Linda had received the food graciously but with a spoonful of suspicion.

Come in, dear. Bring in the child. Never mind yer shoes, said Mary.

Linda apologized, told her about the broken water pump, and inquired about plumbers.

Sit down, and we'll sort things out, said Mary.

Mary waved Linda toward the kitchen and showed her to a seat. Then she opened the back door, and hollered: *Colin, come in for a minute, would ya? There's need of yer plummin' services.*

An hour later, after a second cup of tea, a home remedy for teething, and a summary of local gossip, Colin reappeared at the door, a box of tools under his arm.

All done, he says. *Not the water pump, neither. The pressure tank was waterlogged. Nothin' to it. And if that's you, thinkin' of reachin' fer yer purse, I'll chuck this whole lift of tools right at ya.*

Linda smiled whenever she remembered that day.

Linda headed for her truck in the hospital's staff parking lot behind the power plant. It was one a.m. She waved at the embers of two cigarettes glowing in the shed, now the only refuge for the smokers on staff. There was a chill in the air and a misty rain, too, and Linda pulled her sweater more tightly around her shoulders.

Her Toronto Suburban had been traded for a Dodge Ram. The truck roared to life. The wipers swept the windshield but left streaks. It was hard to see. Linda pulled away regardless. She missed her husband. She missed her son. She hadn't seen either today, and perhaps both wouldn't be asleep when she got home.

The road to Savage Harbour cut cross-country, secondary roads the whole way. It was a sleepy, empty road most of the time, but especially so at night, and tonight she poked along even more slowly than usual. She was worn out for one thing. For another, the road was still hard to see. A film of dirt still clung to the glass. A veil of blurry mist materialized almost as soon as the previous one had been wiped. Linda pushed the washer button, and cleaner fluid spurted across the windshield. She increased the wiper speed and pumped the washer button a few times.

The wipers swept most of the streaks away. The glass was clean, clean enough now for Linda to see a woman standing in the middle of her lane waving arms for her to stop.

Linda had no time to brake. She swerved the wheel hard left, skidded around the woman, then swung the wheel right, and steadied up in her own lane. Linda's heart was pounding as she looked in the rearview mirror at the receding image. The woman was still standing, so she knew she hadn't struck her. Linda said a quick *Thank god for that* and continued down the road.

Linda didn't pick up hitchhikers. She never had, nor had her parents since their hippie days. Times have changed since those carefree days, they had warned her. And Linda had acquired her own experiences to back up that advice. In Toronto she'd nursed a woman who'd been brutally beaten after stopping for a hiker who robbed her and jacked her car. And in news reports and through co-workers, Linda had heard of similar experiences and frightening close calls.

Why tempt fate? Linda asked herself.

Still it was a wretched night for a young woman to be on a deserted road by herself. And where was her car? How did she get there? A small mystery to consider during her drive home. Did she run it into a ditch? Had some bastard of a boyfriend kicked her out of his car? Maybe a drunken husband beat her up, and she was on the run from him. Or was she just good bait for some simple-minded driver like her to stop? What if someone was waiting in the shadows?

The wind kicked up out of the northeast. The mist increased to a light rain, a cold rain, and leaves shook themselves loose from the poplars and scattered over the roadway. Linda wished she were home in bed. She drove another mile toward home thinking of little else than the face of the mysterious woman in the middle of the road.

When the first niggling tugs of guilt arose, and Linda felt their presence, they were not welcome. In fact, Linda felt that such knee-jerk sentimentality flew in the face of common sense. Clearly nothing could justify the intrusion. Nothing rational anyway. Yet in spite of rationality and past experiences, a disquieting degree of culpability and shame continued to weigh upon her.

In one sense, Linda believed she was betraying herself. In another, she felt that she had no choice. But the reasoning that drove her to that decision kept rattling around in her head like a mantra: *This isn't Toronto...it's different here.* Linda wasn't convinced any of that made sense, but she couldn't help herself. She stopped, turned around, and headed back.

The woman hadn't walked much further from the spot where Linda had first seen her. The woman seemed dazed or exhausted. Her clothing was soaked through. She smelled of wood smoke, and she shivered uncontrollably. Linda retrieved an emergency kit she always kept in the truck. She wrapped a wool blanket around her, led her to the cab, and helped her onto the running board and inside. Linda turned up the heat. A blast of warm air flooded the cab.

"Are you all right?" she asked.

The woman nodded, a movement almost indistinguishable from her cold tremors.

"I'm taking you to the hospital in Charlottetown. It's closer. What happened? Can you tell me?"

The woman's mouth moved, and sounds came out, much of it inaudible, but the words, *fire* and *dead*, were clear enough, and Linda made a call to emergency services on her cell phone. "You're going to be okay. I'm getting help. Try to rest."

The woman said nothing, and Linda glanced over. Her head rocked gently against the side door window. Her eyes had closed. She had fallen fast asleep.

72.

At ten past two Ben's phone rang. He reached blindly toward the night table beside his bed. The phone rang twice before he answered.

"What."

His tone was more bark and complaint than inquiry and interest. He listened. Then he sat up and swung his legs onto the floor.

"Who was that...at this hour?" said Sarah, groaning from the other side of the bed. "What time is it, anyway?"

Ben's attention remained fixed on the phone call.

"I'll be right there." He hung up the phone.

"What was that all about?"

"A fire and a fatality," he said and got up. He had dumped his clothes in an orderly heap on top of a nearby chair. Now he sorted through them and began to dress.

"What's that got to do with you? Isn't that the Fire Marshal's job?" asked Sarah, half-sitting up now.

"Yeah, but this is different," he said and gave her a quick peck on the cheek. "I've got to take a look."

"Why?"

"I'll tell you all about it when I get back," he said, already half out the bedroom door and reaching for the railing on the staircase.

Ben pulled up at the scene. The press had already arrived. A minivan with a CBC logo and a cheap coupe that belonged to *Guardian* reporter Tommy Townshend were parked just outside the police barricades up the street, but the fire was less chaotic, less dramatic, than the press had hoped. There would be a story, of course. The victim was prominent enough, but no spectacular picture would showcase it.

Ordinarily that street would have been rather quiet and dark. Now an array of flashing lights broke the darkness for half a block. A pumper truck from the town's fire hall had pulled up in front of the damaged building. An emergency response vehicle had parked behind it. Each was ablaze with lights. The fire had been doused, but smoke hung in the air. Several firefighters milled around their vehicles. A few others searched for hot spots inside the building.

Behind the fire trucks was a Stratford police car. Rapid blue and white flashes burst from its roof. The officers on duty had set up the traffic barricades. Now they were waiting for firefighters to release the scene to them. Ben recognized both of them. Both threw puzzled looks in his direction and mumbled to themselves.

Ben broke out his cell phone, made a quick call, and packed it away.

Melvin Dickieson, Chief of the volunteer fire department for the Stratford region, stepped from the house, saw Ben, and walked over. He removed his helmet, stuck it under his arm, and ran fingers through his short black hair. It glistened with perspiration. A strong odour of grease and smoke wafted from his gear.

"Thanks for the heads-up," said Ben and glanced around surreptitiously.

"Not a big fan of the guy, but not happy to see anyone end up like this."

"It's him?" asked Ben. Melvin nodded.

"He's dead?" Melvin nodded again.

"Paramedics confirmed it. They responded as soon as the call came in."

"Who phoned it in?"

"Neighbour across the street," said Melvin pointing. "Maude Quinn. She couldn't sleep, got up, and saw a lot of smoke."

"Any ideas?"

"Looks accidental. We found him slumped over in an armchair in the living room. The fire originated in the kitchen. A pan of potato slices were deep-frying on the stove. Looks like he dozed off, the oil caught, and he was overcome by smoke."

Sergeant Ryan Schaeffer of the Stratford Police suddenly appeared next to Ben and Melvin. It seemed as if he had stepped out of nowhere.

"Ben. Melvin," he said, nodding to both men. Then he turned to Melvin. "You fellas finished?"

"Won't be long."

"Let me know. My officers will secure the site."

"That won't be necessary," said Ben. "I've already arranged for the RCMP to handle the investigation into MacFarlane's death."

"Look Ben, you may throw your weight around Charlottetown and with the provincial bureaucrats, but not around here. This is ours." His arm scribed a vast arc, and his countenance shifted to an angry grimace. His reaction was swift enough to suggest unresolved animosities. "This is our town. It's our jurisdiction, and it's our investigation."

Ben faced Schaeffer, glowered, and was about to square off verbally with him when he heard a voice a few feet behind him.

"I agree."

The voice was familiar. It belonged to Fenton Peale, MLA for Stratford-Kinlock and PEI's Minister of Justice.

"Mr. Peale," said Ben assuming a formal, public posture. Ben stared silently and waited stoically for the minister's clarification.

"I see no reason for you to get involved. I don't have to remind you that this is my legislative riding. I know Sergeant Schaeffer well. He's competent and experienced, and he has my complete confidence."

"I have nothing against Schaeffer, Fenton, but this incident is complicated. In the first place, the investigation of Chief MacFarlane's death by Schaeffer may be a conflict of interest. An independent investigation has to prevail here."

"I disagree. There's no evidence of foul play and, from what the firefighters told me, it's obviously accidental. There's not even the hint of a conflict of interest. I say there's no problem here."

"Mr. Peale, pardon me for reminding you...sir...but cause of death hasn't been determined. You're not a peace officer, and you don't have the authority or experience to make that call. You don't have official standing here, sir."

Peale bristled at Ben's insolence and obstinacy, and Ben watched Peale's eyes harden and narrow with mounting, suppressed rage.

"I want you to stand down...or else I'll have you detained by the Stratford police."

"That would be a mistake," said Ben flatly.

"Schaeffer," said Peale. Schaeffer looked baffled and hesitant.

"What do *you* think, Tommy?" Ben had directed his words at Tommy Townshend. Tommy had been standing eight or ten feet behind Peale, close enough to hear the heated exchange. Peale's head snapped around, and he saw Townshend, his notebook open.

Peale felt a bolt of alarm. For a moment, every thought and image and political wile in his head dissolved into an iridescent blank emptiness.

Townshend had been recording details of the conversation with keen interest but, at the sound of his own name, Townshend started. He looked up with a bemused grin toward the quarrelling group. Schaeffer had already ventured one cautious step toward Ben, but Peale held him back with a firm arm.

"Who...me?" said Townshend in reply. "I don't have opinions, Ben. I'm just a journalist," he said and returned to the notes he had been compiling.

Peale recovered quickly. If Townshend were to publish this squabble, Peale knew that he would find himself juggling a political hot potato that could kill his chances in the upcoming election.

Peale put his hand on Ben's shoulder and leaned in toward his ear.

"Ben, let's take this somewhere private." Then he took Ben by the arm and led him toward a solitary darker corner of MacFarlane's front yard.

"Maybe I was a bit too brash…"

"Maybe…?" said Ben.

"All right…all right… I shouldn't have come on that strongly, but it is my riding. My responsibility is looking after the interests of my constituents. MacFarlane's, the police department's, the community's. How do you think it will look if I turn the accidental death of a prominent citizen over to another jurisdiction? What will voters read into that? People will think that I've lost confidence in my own people, or they'll think there's some kind of cover-up. I'm just trying to save face here, Ben. You know how it is."

"I'm not sure if I do…not in this case…not in these circumstances."

"Okay, then I'll tell you, but it's confidential. Just you and me. Right?"

Ben said nothing, and he levelled a long, inconclusive, grim stare at Peale.

"It's this way," said Peale. "Years ago, when I was town councillor, I pushed for MacFarlane to be appointed Chief. It was a backroom deal. Quigley had retired by then. MacFarlane was a golden boy at the time. I had planned to run for provincial legislature and figured his appointment would give me an edge when I threw my hat into the ring. And it did. MacFarlane reciprocated. He got the votes out for me during two elections but, as I got to know him better, I didn't like what I saw."

"Did he pressure you?"

"Some, but lately he's been coming on strong, suggesting that he's been accumulating some dirt on me. It might get leaked to the press, and I'd be done."

"What kind of dirt?"

"Some money may have been diverted to my campaign from a questionable source."

"Where did the money come from?"

"He wouldn't say, but it was none of my doing, I swear. Could've been an overzealous campaign worker. Could've been MacFarlane himself. I don't know. Still, if the smell of corruption hits the air at election time, it'll stick to me."

"What have you done for him in the meantime?"

"Nothing. Nothing, really. I swear. So far I've been able to stall him."

"So what was all this nonsense about tonight?"

Peale hesitated. His eyes shifted uneasily as if he were searching for an answer or contemplating whether he should tell the truth. Then he looked Ben straight in the eye.

"If it's a local investigation, I could probably convince Schaeffer to let me recover whatever documents MacFarlane had that could hurt me, but if the RCMP get involved, no telling what might happen to them. Now, I know that things between us haven't been running smoothly, but maybe we could start again, and we could trust each other. I need you to believe me, Ben. Do you think it'd be fair to have my name unfairly dragged through the gutter? Do you? I've got a family to think about. I know it's asking a big favour, but it's something I'd never forget either. Give me the opportunity to look. Please."

Peale smiled apprehensively, sadly, and hopefully at the end of his solicitation.

Ben had had some history with Peale, and the man had made a few cogent points, but Ben had a great deal more history with policing and criminal behaviour. Perhaps Peale was being honest with him, perhaps not. Perhaps he was reacting just like every other cornered and desperate politician. That business can get as dirty as any larceny or sleazy con but, as possible as all that was, Ben admitted to himself that he'd regret seeing anyone, even Peale, take the blame for one of MacFarlane's intrigues.

Ben weighed his options. There appeared to be two. If he let Peale run with his plan, and it turned out badly, he'd get burnt. And if he got burnt, *he'd* lose *his* job, not Peale. Politicians were like cats. They always landed on their feet somewhere happy. On the other hand, if he did things strictly by the book, and it turned out badly, he'd still lose his job. Political appointees, and Ben fit into that category, were like barn mice. Eventually, they land on some cat's dinner plate.

After what seemed like an extraordinarily long reflection, Ben looked up at Peale. Peale licked his lips nervously. Ben's face softened.

"Here's what I *can* do. The RCMP will take over the investigation as I said they would. I'll supervise their operation myself. If anything turns up that may be politically damaging but doesn't tie you to illegal activity, I'll see that it never becomes public."

"Thanks, Ben, but you may not recognize what MacFarlane might have. You may overlook it without knowing. I should be there. I'm really the only one who could know the political fallout of a document."

"Sorry, Fenton. You can't be there."

"Ben, that's not enough. If you want to help, let me look. I have to do it myself. I can't take the risk that something significant may be discounted."

"Best I can do, Fenton."

"Dammit, Ben, you're being unreasonable." Peale's conciliatory posture was falling apart, anger very near the surface.

Ben looked over Peale's shoulder. Two RCMP constables waited at a distance. He brushed by Peale and headed toward them.

Peale shouted after him: "Ben, what about the press? Townshend?" Fear and desperation had returned.

"*He's* not an unreasonable man. I'll have a reasonable word with him," he said without looking back.

73.

Anne couldn't remember her trip to the Queen Elizabeth Hospital in Linda Moore's truck. She had slept through most of it, and she only vaguely remembered the initial examination and transfer to a general ward for observation. She was awake and alert but physically played out. Her throat was raspy and dry, and she coughed a weak cough. A tendril of hair fell across her eye. She whisked it away with her hand and felt gauze graze her face. Her hands were bandaged. Both of them. She stared at them uncertainly and sighed deeply and sadly as if she had lost a part of herself. She fidgeted in her hospital bed while trying to find a comfortable position. A twinge in her ankle recalled the turn she had taken. She recalled the fire, too, but another fresh memory of it was thankfully interrupted.

"Well, well, Ms. Brown. You're having a busy week. Two visits in three days, isn't it?" said Dr. Little. Anne had no time to respond. The doctor tilted her head back and shone a bright light into each eye. "Good, now open," he said, inserting a tongue depressor into her mouth and examining her throat. "All good."

"What's so good about this?" she said sarcastically, holding up her gauze mitts.

"A few stitches. Nothing to be concerned about. What I suppose I meant was…a few more of your accidents, and I can afford another trip to the Caribbean…that is, if you don't bankrupt the national health care system in the process."

"Piña coladas, warm sands, steel drums, and eager señoritas, I get it."

"No, actually, it's more like dysentery, AIDS, malnutrition, and open sores. I volunteer at a medical mission a couple times a year, and now that you've re-entered the land of the quick and sharp-witted, there are a couple of people who would like to say hello. We'll chat later."

Detectives Iris Caine and Will Bryant were familiar faces to Anne. They had interviewed her two days before while pursuing the theory that Cutter had been behind the bombing at the gas station.

"What happened?" asked Caine.

Anne's recitation of events began with her kidnapping by Jamie MacFarlane. Her recollection was cold and dispassionate like reading aloud from a high-school history book. Anne loathed dredging up details of the experience. She knew the pictures would come out dripping with emotion and pain. So she buried them beneath a mask of indifference.

Caine took notes, her face expressionless as well, her eyes intent, and her body scarcely moving, but she didn't interrupt. Nor did her partner.

Finally, Anne stopped speaking. Caine looked up and saw that no more was forthcoming.

"Is Cutter dead?"

Anne nodded.

"You're sure?"

"I watched him cook," said Anne. Her words were flat and devoid of sentiment. Her expression was distant and solemn, and Caine squirmed uncomfortably in her chair.

"And you never saw MacFarlane after he left the cabin?"

"No," said Anne.

Anne dozed for another hour after the police left. When she awoke she found Ben and Sarah sitting next to her bed.

"Feeling better, dear?" asked Sarah.

"I think I am," said Anne. She stretched and yawned. She felt rested, even if not completely alert. She remembered everything from the night before, but now it all stood at arm's length. Her grim adventure had not become diluted, dismissed, or reworked. Now it seemed more like an improbable dream, too fantastic to have occurred, yet too real for a fiction.

"Have you been here long? How did you find out?"

"About half an hour," said Sarah.

"City Police phoned," said Ben.

"He's dead," said Anne.

"I know," said Ben. "So is MacFarlane. A house fire as well."

"Ironic," said Sarah.

"He got a phone call at the cabin," said Anne. "Then he left. He was coming back. I'm sure of it."

"We'll check the phone records tomorrow. That may fill in some blanks."

Anne's new-found clarity dimmed with confusion. "Why tomorrow?"

"Today's Sunday. Fat chance finding anyone to run with the ball today...especially when it appears to be an accidental death. Plenty of time to get the facts. No rush. Get some rest. Okay?"

Ben's cell rang. He took the call. He said nothing, but his face lost some colour and turned as stony as his attitude. "Gotta go," he said.

"Ben?" protested Sarah.

"It's important."

"Not again."

Ben left Sarah at Anne's bedside. Sarah was quietly angry, and Anne was puzzled, but Ben was in too determined a rush, and he bolted from the room.

A ribbon of yellow police tape shimmered in the sun and fluttered in a cool, light, autumn breeze. Several vehicles stood in front of MacFarlane's damaged residence. The grey Lexus belonged to Fenton Peale. The two others were police vehicles—one RCMP cruiser, the other from the Stratford Police Department.

The two Mounties stood on the front doorstep. They looked embarrassed and uncomfortable as Ben strode up the concrete walk. The fury in his eyes made the Mounties even more apprehensive.

"I said, *nobody, but nobody gets in the house*! Why wasn't that clear enough?"

"Did everything we could but shoot them, Ben. They wouldn't listen. Peale is Minister of Justice for the Province. He brought them in."

"He's a politician. Not a peace officer."

"But he authorizes who is and who isn't, and it's his signature that renews RCMP contracts on PEI. What else could we do?"

"I'll show you. Let's go."

Ben brushed past them and stormed through the front door. The Mounties followed.

"Peale!" Ben shouted and the sound of the name resonated throughout the house. Peale was descending the stairs from the second-storey bedrooms. Ahead of him were Sergeant Schaeffer and another police constable. The constable carried a small cardboard box. It was half-full.

Ben blocked their exit.

"Schaeffer, I told you that the RCMP would be in charge of this site…," said Ben.

Schaeffer didn't respond.

"…and the RCMP secured it."

"Justice Minister Peale countermanded that order. He authorized me to take over the investigation."

"That's not going to happen. You," he said, pointing to the constable, "put that box down."

The constable froze, but Schaeffer gave him a shove to move ahead and pushed him past Ben.

"You had your chance, Ben." Fenton Peale's voice rang with a clear air of authority and determination. "A little cooperation goes a long way. Schaeffer...," he said, addressing the Sergeant, and nodding for him to keep going.

Ben grabbed the constable with his right hand and shoved Schaeffer back with his left.

"Arrest them. All of them," said Ben.

The RCMP looked at each other and shrugged. Schaeffer pulled away and swung his fist at Ben. Peale recoiled in surprise. The constable shrank back, stumbled over a carpet edge, and dropped the cardboard box. Ben blocked Schaeffer's swing and countered with a right to Schaeffer's mid-section. It went deep into a soft belly, and Schaeffer crumbled to the ground.

"Okay, Ben, you can keep the damn box. It was inconsequential anyway, but this isn't over yet. I can guarantee that," said Peale. "Sergeant Schaeffer, constable, c'mon, let's go."

"Not so fast. Fenton Peale, Sergeant Ryan Schaeffer, and Constable Whatever-your-name-is—oh yeah, Sam Best," said Ben looking at the man's name tag, "You're all under arrest. Suspicion of tampering with evidence and interfering with a police investigation."

Ben motioned to the RCMP constables. They appeared slow to react until Ben walked over to Peale, turned him to the wall, handcuffed him, and searched his person. Then they fell into a familiar protocol with the other two. Schaeffer and his constable were disarmed and cuffed.

Ben's final act was to snap a humiliating picture of the handcuffed trio against the wall in MacFarlane's house. The RCMP constables read them their rights and led two of them to their cruiser. Ben led Peale to his own vehicle.

Out of hearing range of the detainees, Ben gathered the two RCMP constables.

"What's the plan?" asked the one.

"We'll take them in, hold them for questioning, and let them go when they're penitent enough," said Ben.

"Are we going to lose our jobs over this?" said the other.

"Not a chance. You did what you could under the circumstances. They couldn't have applied more pressure if they tried. But if anything does come of this, it's all on me. I was the last and most senior peace officer to give you a legal order, and you carried it out. That's all that can be expected."

"I hope you're right," said the first.

"That snapshot I took is proof they crossed a police line without authorization. If they get amnesia, the photo may magically turn up on page one of *The Guardian*. By the way, did you get a chance to toss the place?"

"You said look for anything that doesn't fit, right?"

Ben nodded.

"Wasn't much, but we found an old tin candy box."

"And?"

"It was on top of a floor joist brace in the basement near the furnace."

"What was in it?"

"Just a couple of old cell phones and a few trinkets."

"Why did that catch your eye?"

"First of all, it was a peculiar place to store something. Second, one of the cell phones was pink. Don't think it was MacFarlane's," he said and snickered.

"Where is it now?"

"In the trunk," he said and pointed toward the cruiser. "Had no time to check the rest of the house."

"Good work, fellas, and thanks for the timely heads-up."

They nodded.

"Instruct your reliefs to finish the search...and...and I'm sorry I came down so hard on you earlier. A lot happened last night. You did a great job."

74.

Fenton Peale's mind raced like a mouse trapped in a maze. A mouse probably could find an exit. Peale couldn't. His schemes led him round and round in shifting patterns, but they always revisited the same frightening dead-end—arrest, disgrace, prison; arrest, disgrace, prison. And time was not on his side.

With MacFarlane alive, he thought, at least there had been some glimmer of a hopeful future, even if it kept him in thrall to a manipulative, cruel, unscrupulous snake of a man. At least then he could have held onto his comfortable lifestyle and the leverage he wielded as a prominent leader. He could have kept the accolades, the respect, and the public esteem that came with it.

MacFarlane's demise, however, was like a curse reaching back from the grave—a malevolent vine, creeping toward and clinging to the wickedness it had propagated. Peale could sense the sucking grasp of its tendrils. A disquieting chill touched him. Everything worthwhile in his life seemed as if they were bleeding ever so slowly away.

Somewhere MacFarlane had hidden Simone's text messages with him. Their discovery would link him to her murder, the scandal would ruin his career and marriage and, Carolyn's death linked to it all would suggest his clumsy effort to cover it up.

His attempt to find the text messages had failed, and, inevitably, they would be uncovered. How long it would take, he didn't know, but the minutes until their discovery were ticking away. That he knew. The RCMP would conduct a thorough search. His shame and weaknesses would be uncovered. And now, locked up in a holding cell, he could neither protect himself from ruin nor flee from danger.

Peale paced back and forth tediously in his narrow cell. Thoughts trickled through his mind. Fragments of plans formed. Bits of hope fell away. He paced continually and purposefully. He felt like a caged animal and, like a caged animal, his footsteps led him nowhere, and his instincts pounced on no resolution.

Two hours later, a guard brought a tray of food. The guard seemed jovial and curious but said nothing beyond a cheerful greeting. Peale responded with an anxious flicker of eyes. The tray lay untouched. An hour after that, Peale had ceased pacing and was reclining despondently on his bunk. He heard footsteps on the shiny concrete floor. Then a voice.

"Smart move, not calling your lawyer," said Ben, his suit looking especially rumpled, his face haggard and unshaved. "No point stirring up more dust than necessary. Time for a talk."

Peale sat up slowly. He slumped back like a wilted plant against the wall behind his bunk. His mouth remained inexpressive, but his eyes were expectant, curious, and suspicious.

"Peale, you're a stupid sonofabitch, pulling a stunt like that. I don't know what was behind it, but I'm going to find out. Meantime, I'm giving you a chance to redeem yourself. I'm considering holding off on formal charges at this time...at this time...," Ben repeated slowly with emphasis.

"Why would you do that?" asked Peale.

"I want you to come clean about what you were up to. I told you I'd protect you if I could."

"I wasn't sure where your fine line stopped. What shade of grey is too dark, Ben? Or do you even know yourself? I couldn't take the chance. Sometimes when a fellow goes so far and stops and turns around, he realizes he's already stepped too far...without even noticing it. That's politics...that's business...and I expect that's law enforcement, too. It's all a judgment call."

"What was your judgment call, Fenton?"

Peale ignored the question and turned toward a blank wall.

"What next?" asked Peale after a handful of reflective moments.

"Nothing. You're free to go," said Ben.

"What's the catch?"

"You behave yourself. Don't go near MacFarlane's house. Don't interfere with me or Anne or anyone I designate as an investigator. As for the future, there's an old saying: 'Hew to the line, and let the chips fall where they may.' The line I'm talking about is my line. It's the only one I understand. The fallout...what happens to you...what you may or may not have done...well, that's a job for pundits, lawyers, and philosophers. After all is said and done, I'm just a cop."

"What about that picture?"

"It's packed away somewhere. Might be hard to find. Maybe it won't be found."

"And Schaeffer and Best?"

"They're licking their wounds and contemplating their future. Something to think about."

75.

Mary Anne and Jacqui picked up Anne at the hospital after her discharge and drove her home. Home was solidly built, practical, and rather small—two bedrooms, bath, and a large linen closet upstairs; the kitchen, living room, washroom, pantry, and dining room downstairs. Anne did little entertaining. So the dining area off the kitchen had evolved into a room for television, reading, or chatting. Mary Anne and Jacqui naturally gravitated toward the family room, but Anne balked. That was the place from which MacFarlane had abducted her, and the memory was too fresh and hurtful. She headed instead for the living room.

Jacqui followed her mother down the short passageway. Mary Anne remained in the kitchen to make fresh coffee. Anne and Jacqui heard the clamour of cupboard doors and the clinking of cups and Mary Anne's scurrying about the kitchen as they settled into the puffy upholstered chairs and sofa set. The floral pattern of the furniture had long been out of fashion, but that had never been a serious concern for Anne. Nor could she let it be, not with her income.

"I've never liked this room," said Anne. "It's so dark in here."

"Neither have I," said Jacqui, "and look at that pattern. It belongs in an old lady's house. It's depressing."

"Maybe we could rent it to some film company that needs tacky period furniture from the seventies."

"Or donate it to the Salvation Army."

"Don't think they'd take it," said Anne. "There's Barry's Barter Barn. They say they'll take anything for something." Then she quickly added second thoughts: "No, even Barry wouldn't take a risk on this stuff."

"We could break it up for kindling. It'd make a great fire."

The words were scarcely out of Jacqui's mouth before she regretted them. She caught the flicker of recollected terror in her mother's eyes. Then the flicker disappeared. Anne said nothing.

"Sorry," said Jacqui. "I wasn't thinking."

Anne smiled weakly. "You had a pretty rough night, too," she said.

Jacqui had already related most of the details of her babysitting fiasco to her mother. That revelation had been intended less as a confession and more as a distraction from her mother's truly horrifying evening.

"How did Madame Desjardins take it?"

"She didn't explode. She looked around a bit. Checked on Luc. He'd slept through the whole thing…but she didn't say much of anything. It was kind of weird, actually."

"And Rada?"

"I asked Sig to walk her home. I didn't know who might be lurking around after the party. I was worried…and Bobby was helping me clean up. Later she told me that Mr. Shadi, the teacher, had seen her walking with Sig…"

"You've been talking to her?"

"She phoned this morning. Mr. Shadi called her father and reported it. She had sneaked out of her house last night. I didn't know that. Her father is very upset, her mother is ashamed and disappointed with her behaviour, and they say she's forbidden from associating with me anymore."

Tears filled Jacqui's eyes. Her lips quivered, and her composure quickly disintegrated into sobs.

"She was my best friend, Mom."

Jacqui's voice had become broken, pitiful, and pleading. Anne beckoned with her hand, and Jacqui rushed across the room. Jacqui's arms enfolded her, and Anne held her close, and slowly, silently, rocked her.

"World's finest brew of coffee. Straight from Mary-Anne-land," said Mary Anne, strutting into the living room with a tray of cups and a carafe. She stopped short. The china tinkled. Her words stammered to a halt.

Mary Anne's cheeks blanched. Displays of emotion always unnerved her. Each time she found herself in the midst of a teary crisis, she felt stupid, powerless, and awkward.

Mary Anne's face reddened self-consciously. Hurriedly, she set the tray on a table, turned, and fled back toward the kitchen.

"You're gonna need sweets to go with that, too," she said on her way out. "Don't get up. I've got it."

"What did I tear you away from?" asked Ben.

Mary Anne had just rushed in through the front door of her restaurant. Her wait-staff was busy preparing and serving Sunday brunch. Eight tables were occupied. The special was waffles with raspberries and whipped cream and scrambled eggs.

"Coffee and angst," said Mary Anne. Ben's face mirrored his confusion. "Don't ask," she said. "What was it you needed?"

"I'll have one of those," he said, pointing to a passing plate of waffles and eggs.

"Anything else?"

"The big file that Anne left in your office for safekeeping."

"That you can have. The waffles not so much. Sarah says you're on a diet."

"Then hold the whipped cream and add a coffee. I'll be over there," he said pointing to a booth.

"You know I'll have to tell Sarah," she said. "Our safe server policy obliges us to report anyone over the legal limit." Mary Anne gave his stomach a poke.

"It'll be worth it," said Ben.

Ben took his seat and set the silver candy tin that had been clutched in his hand on the table. He eyed the front door expectantly.

A few moments later Mary Anne set a fresh cup of coffee in front of Ben. A cumbersome package followed. It was the copy of the police file on Simone's murder. He dug through the contents, sipped his coffee, and stopped at the page he was searching for—the description of items reportedly stolen from the victim. One of the items not recovered during the investigation was an eighteen-karat red gold necklace with a heart pendant. Ben opened the tin box. Inside was an assortment of junk jewellery, rings, necklaces, trinkets, coins, as well as a couple of cell phones. Among them was a gold necklace. It matched the one that had gone missing. He checked the report again. The missing necklace had been a gift from Simone's then-boyfriend, Jamie MacFarlane.

Ben's cup was empty when the waitress slipped a plate of waffles in front of him. Ben pushed the file and the tin to one side and dug into breakfast. He was famished. When he glanced up again, his coffee had been replenished, and Anne was standing alongside his table.

"You should be ashamed," she said, "and you know I'll have to..."

"I know, I know...you'll have to 'tell Sarah.' What is it with you women? Can't you leave a guy alone for one minute? Okay, so go ahead, tell her, but you'll have to wait in line. There's apparently a whole line of snitches ahead of you. Anyway, this stuff is delicious. It will be worth it. I suppose Mary Anne called you, did she?"

"Why didn't you call me?" Anne slid into the booth across from Ben.

"I figured you'd need a bit of time. I still think so. Go home, get some rest."

"I don't need rest. I need answers, and it looks like you're putting something together...with my file, by the way. Want to fill me in?"

"That's my question too, Ben," said Dit Malone.

Dit loomed over the table. Ben thought he looked taller than he remembered. His arrival took Anne by surprise. It was the first time they had been in each other's company since their falling-out at his place almost a week before. She glanced self-consciously at her hands. The gauze that covered her cuts and stitches had been replaced with several small bandages. She let her hands slip beneath the table and into her lap.

"Glad you could make it," said Ben. "I've got something I'd like you to take a look at. A cell phone…an old one…might be evidence in a crime. I need to know everything forensics can tell me about it, but I need to keep it hush-hush for the time being. What do you think? Possible?"

"If it hasn't been damaged, it shouldn't be a problem."

"What's the story?" asked Anne.

"It was hidden in MacFarlane's home…with this," he said, showing off the necklace. "I'm thinkin' it belonged to Simone Villier. That and her cell phone were never recovered."

"So MacFarlane killed his girlfriend?" said Dit.

Ben nodded.

"It's lookin' like it, but someone was trying to get their hands on MacFarlane's dirty laundry. I know who. I need to find out why. The cell phone might help."

"So Anne was on the right track all along," he added and nudged Anne with his elbow. Anne smiled sheepishly.

"I'll check it out." Dit slipped the cell phone into his pocket. "But now I've gotta run. Jet lag. A few more hours of sleep and a bit of time for the fog inside my head to lift, and then I'll tackle that cell phone," he said, getting up. "Oh, by the way, we're having a get-together at our house next Saturday night. Eight o'clock. Consider yourselves all personally invited."

"Sounds great," said Ben.

"I'll see," said Anne.

"Gwen specifically asked for you to come, and I insist," said Dit. "No excuses. She says to bring Jacqueline, too. It'll be fun. You'll see."

Anne's face flickered with a half-smile and then ebbed into an uncomfortable, noncommittal gaze that followed Dit as he shifted his crutches, walked to the door, and exited The Blue Peter.

"You've got your eye on somebody. Who is it?" Anne's tone had suddenly became resolute and businesslike.

"Peale. He admitted that MacFarlane was holding evidence related to some dodgy political shenanigans and using it as leverage against him. He was very, very anxious to get inside MacFarlane's house. He and a couple of cops from Stratford bullied their way past the RCMP constable guarding it. I had to get tough with them."

"How tough?"

"I locked them up. Temporarily, anyway."

"Peale?"

"Him, too."

"Holy shit! That's sticking your neck out. Do you think Peale had something to do with MacFarlane's death?"

"There's something there. I don't know what it is. But him killing MacFarlane? Can't see it. He doesn't have the know-how or the balls to pull it off. And there's nothing to indicate that it was anything but what it appears to be—a careless accident."

"Ben, I just can't get the idea out of my mind that it wasn't an accident."

"Who had motive?"

"First name that pops up in my head, though I hate to admit it," said Anne, "is Dawson. If anyone had a hate for the guy, it would have been him. He's younger than MacFarlane, clever, maybe just as strong, and in prison he would have picked up a trick or two. Then again, he didn't strike me as the killer type. And there was a possibility that he could get the conviction overturned. He was aware that my investigation was leading that way."

"If he's innocent. If not, all bets are off. And you should never underestimate the effect of a festering rage. Hatred confuses good judgment."

"There are other possibilities, too," said Anne. "Considering his criminal connection with Cutter, it could have been some crook he jammed up. Maybe the ex-wife he screwed out of property settlement, a bitter politician with an axe to grind, or some cop jealous of his fast track to the top. And I told you that MacFarlane got a cell call that took him away from the cabin. Connection or coincidence?"

"I recovered his cell phone, too. We'll check his calls and see where that leads. If it's a murder made to look like an accident, then it was organized and carried out by someone with a brain, but that's a big 'if.'"

Both Ben and Anne fell silent. Ben gazed numbly into his coffee cup. Anne stared into the ebbing sea of customers in the cafe. Both weighed the possibilities.

"Are you convinced that it's not Peale?" said Anne.

"Can't say that I am," said Ben.

"Does he have an alibi?"

"I don't know. Does Dawson?"

Anne shrugged her shoulders.

"What say we find out?"

76.

Anne felt the weight of the last two days bearing down on her. Coffee didn't lift her high enough, but it would have to do. She needed to push through another few hours. So much was happening so quickly. Everything seemed to be coming to a head. Even the weather. Wind had come up in the afternoon. A stiff northeasterly breeze. Air grew damp and cold. Sky darkened. Now light rain stung sharply with each lash of the wind.

The strongest coffee she could find was at Starbucks. She left the corner shop and ran to her car, her free hand guarding her eyes from the painful rain. She sipped and drove. The cogs in her brain picked up speed, but the blood in her veins moved like gelatine, and her stomach turned sour as stale buttermilk. She still felt like hell as she pulled into the driveway at Jacob Dawson's boarding house. A slit slowly parted in the curtains of a downstairs window. Anne rang the doorbell. It opened almost immediately.

"He's not here, if he's the one you're looking for."

Irene MacLeod stood in the doorway. One hand gripped the door; the other locked onto the frame. She shifted a restless arthritic leg. Her face was resolute, her stance feeble, and her demeanour unwelcoming. Anne danced uncomfortably in the chilled wet wind on the doorstep.

"Do you know where he is, Mrs. MacLeod?"

"He could be at the library again. Could be at an AA meeting. Or with that girl of his," she said. A sharper edge to her voice carved out her mention of the girl.

"Do you recall her name?"

"Another student. Sami Smith. Queer name for a girl if you ask me."

"And his meeting?"

"Sunday evenings at the community centre," she said, and stepped back with a hobble and a drag and fastened the door shut.

The neighbourhood community centre at one time had been an elementary school, decommissioned, sold off, hauled down the frozen North River by teams of horses in the 1930s, and relocated at the edge of Charlottetown. The wooden-frame building was partitioned into several smaller meeting rooms for public use. A few cars and a truck had parked on the street in front of it. Anne pulled up nearby and made her way inside. It was eight o'clock when she arrived. A few people passed her on their way out. They gripped their hats and dragged jacket collars tightly about their necks as they met the windy night.

The main room off the front door was high-ceilinged. Painted wainscoting skirted the wall. Above it and at the front of the room were several posters. One listed twelve steps to recovery. Two men and a woman were stacking chairs and straightening tables. The woman was first to take notice of Anne and approached her. Anne was staring at another poster:

God, grant me the serenity to accept the things I cannot change,
The courage to change the things I can,
And wisdom to know the difference.

"It's beautiful, isn't it?" said the woman.

Anne nodded slowly.

"Have you come for the meeting? I'm afraid it's just finished, but I could give you some information," she said, pointing toward a neat stack of brochures on a plywood table.

"Thank you, but I was just looking for someone. Jacob Dawson. I thought he might be here."

"He often is, but not tonight. Is there something I can do?"

Anne left the community centre with no more information. Her next stop—and hopefully her last, she thought—was the university library.

The library was busier than usual for a Sunday night. Students were on the verge of mid-term exams and the deadlines for papers and reports and group projects. Anne swept through the library one room at a time searching for Dawson. No sign of him on the ground floor. None on the second.

Anne returned to the foyer, took out her cell phone, and dialled.

"Edna? Anne Brown. I'm trying to locate a few students in regard to some work I'm doing. A Jacob Dawson and a Sami Smith. The Sami is probably short for Samantha."

"Jacob Dawson and Sami Smith," she said. She spoke the names slowly and thoughtfully. "Isn't Dawson the name of the one who killed that girl?"

"Yes."

"He's a student?"

"Yes."

"How extraordinary. But I'm afraid I can't be much help. I've never met either of those people…nor taught them. You might get their class schedules from the Registrar's Office tomorrow or you could check with Student Services."

Anne heard the signal for an incoming call on her phone, thanked Edna, and switched to the new caller. It was Ben.

"Any luck?"

"No. You?"

"Fenton's wife, Veronica, says he left on some business trip to Nova Scotia. Won't be back 'til tomorrow night. But she confirms that he was home before midnight last night. I didn't press her, but I think she was on the level. So I don't see how he could have done anything directly related to MacFarlane's death."

"Right. I'll track Dawson down tomorrow."

77.

A late-model white Honda Civic followed Fenton Peale's Lexus along the Trans-Canada Highway west from Charlottetown. The driver wore a blue rainproof coat. A hood covered the black ball cap on his head. Raindrops beaded the windshield, wind buffeted his car, and his hands clenched the wheel.

Peale had packed hurriedly and lightly. He had told Veronica that he would be returning tomorrow evening at the latest, but that was a lie. He had planned never to return—not to his family, not to Charlottetown, not to the Island or even Canada. He slipped Veronica's picture and a photo of the kids from the dresser and packed them in his valise next to his passport. He had already drawn out as much cash as he could from the bank without raising red flags, and he retrieved a stack of negotiable bonds from the wall safe in his bedroom. There was no more to do, nothing he could do. The curtain was closing on his deceits and crimes. The time had come. His flight from Halifax to Havana had been booked, and from there he would arrange passage to Caracas.

The driver of the Civic had been sitting in the car outside Peale's home for several hours. He had been waiting for his chance to kill Peale, but there had been no opportunity. He was ready to call it a night when the upstairs light clicked off. Moments later, the garage door raised. Peale slipped behind the wheel of his car, and he pulled away.

At seven o'clock, the evening was growing dark, and it was doing so more quickly than usual because of the thick, low clouds and rain. Both drove west for nearly an hour before Peale's objective became clear—boarding the ferry at Wood Islands and heading for Nova Scotia. Peale purchased a ticket for the passage and entered the embarkation compound. The Civic stopped short and pulled over onto the shoulder of the road. A transport truck and a pickup hauling a travel trailer entered the compound behind Peale. The Civic followed them.

A few minutes later, the vehicles in the compound crept forward in a queue toward the steep ramp and the open stern doors of the ferry. Deck hands waved the vehicles in alternating paths, port or starboard, toward the bow. The cars and trucks were packed tightly together.

A few inches separated bumper from bumper, and narrow corridors squeezed between each of the four rows on both sides of the ship.

A large superstructure divided the car deck and separated the two streams of traffic boarding the ferry. Several doors and companionways led to storage lockers, crew quarters, and maintenance rooms or to the engine room below; stairs and elevators led up to the lounge and restaurant on the passenger deck; further up was the wheelhouse.

A whistle sounded from the bridge. Massive steel doors clanged shut. The thump of the engine grew, dock hands cast off mooring lines, and crewmen manned the winches hauling them aboard. Within seconds, the vessel shuddered as a 3,600 horsepower engine lay into the propellers and broke the ship's inertia. The ship slid from its berth, slowly gained way, and glided through the breakwater.

By the time the breakwater light had slipped astern, nearly all the passengers had left their vehicles for the warmth and comfort of the upper decks. As the ship powered into the open waters of the Strait, it became apparent that the crossing would be uncomfortable. The hull quivered each time a wave struck. Even the crew of the vessel had traded duties on deck in the lash of rain and spray for less inclement duties below. Only the starboard watch faced the weather on the bridge, and only Fenton Peale and the sole occupant of the white Civic lingered unseen on the vehicle deck.

Peale was of no mind to go topside. As a politician he was sure to meet someone he knew in the lounge, and he had no desire to see anyone. His mind was running heavier than the seas around him. He wanted quiet. He wanted peace. He wanted to rewrite his last eleven years into a quieter script with a happier ending. He wanted a more hopeful future, but *want* had been his problem, he thought. *Want* had got him neck-deep into the mire he was trying to wade through now. *Want* was destroying him.

Peale's moist, damp breath slowly clouded the windshield of his car. At first it had made him feel alive and animate but, after it restricted all visibility beyond the cabin of his car, he felt as if he were suffocating, the same feeling he had experienced and suffered through while languishing for those few hours in the holding cell at the police lockup. Starting the car to clear his windshield was out of the question. Painted signs on the bulkheads cautioned against running engines, and to do so would attract attention, and he shunned unsolicited interest in his personal doings.

A fresh northeast wind was setting with the rising tide, and the ferry had made enough distance from Wood Islands to feel its discomforting effects. With the wind abaft the ship's beam, Peale could sense a small cant to starboard and, by the manner with which wind and sea struck the port side, one could feel an unpredictable short pitch and roll. Leaf springs and coil suspensions beneath the cars and trucks made them quiver and shake. The added movement made Peale grow ill at ease.

Jacob Dawson was not dismayed or even concerned by the erratic tremors and shakes he felt in the white Civic. Before his incarceration, he had spent a season as cork aboard an old lobster boat off Georgetown. The farmer who had been his foster parent sold Dawson's labour services to his wife's brother. Dawson didn't last the full season. It wasn't the hard work that drove him off. It was the inequity. Little cash for his work ever found its way into his own pocket. He stole some of it back before he left. Then he abandoned both farm and sea—and Kings County. He never returned to boat work, but he had learned never to fear that environment either. He remembered it as a cold job, a hard job, but he also recalled it as clean work, at least it seemed so, somehow, in his mind.

This, too, will be a cold, hard job, he thought. *Not so clean, maybe, but an obligation to be respected.*

His heart wasn't in it, as it ought to have been, but he had agreed to it. It was necessary, and he had every intention of carrying it out, come what may.

Dawson no longer had an elaborate and detailed plan to kill Peale. After MacFarlane's death, Peale's routine had fallen apart. Now it was more a matter of finding him alone. Peale was no match physically for him, and Dawson knew how to do it quickly. Renous and Dorchester—those prisons had been noteworthy institutions in which to learn the arcane skills he needed.

Dawson's vehicle was parked behind Peale's, the transport truck between them. Dawson couldn't see Peale's car, but he had a clear sightline of his left rear-view mirror, and his eyes fixed upon it as steadily as a fox upon a ground squirrel.

After half an hour, Peale's fear of suffocation and claustrophobia finally overcame him and, when he could take no more, he flung open the car door and headed for the lee rail. The storm front had deepened, or, at least, it appeared to have done so. The feel of fresh air and the vague hint of a horizon freed him for the moment, but the chill northeast wind, working around the open deck, was relentless. The weather side of the ship was dashed with a creamy froth, and the hull convulsed with the thrust of several quick-breaking waves.

Spume carried across the bow doors and showered the foredeck with a fine spray.

Peale stood at the rail. A bulkhead gave him some protection, but he still felt the spackling of cold drops and a mist of salty water. Peale wore a long camel hair overcoat. He gathered the collar tightly up around his neck and ears and held it there as if he were going to strangle himself with it. Then he forced down his too-loose cap until the headband ground against his skull, and he buried his free hand into a side pocket. He remained motionless, like a queer sad statue, shoulders unnaturally elevated, stooped over, as if waiting for a beacon of some sort. But there could be nothing of consequence this far off shore, nothing but endless water, broken lines of waves hurtling leeward, evening gloom, and an ill-defined grey horizon, signifying nothing at all.

"You murdered Carolyn Jollimore."

The words struck him with such horror that he was speechless. He whirled round and saw a man standing a few steps from him, a man he had never seen before. His hand held a tire iron. His jaw was set, his stance ready, and an expression almost mask-like and unreal plastered his face. It carried a grim vacant intensity and the twisted leer of a hunter having cornered some vile and worthless thing.

"You're mad," said Peale taking a step back. His face was deathly pale and his voice trembled. "You're mad," he said again.

"You're probably right," said Dawson. "Prison does that to a person. Being wronged does it even more quickly."

"I don't know what you're talking about. I don't know you. I don't know a Carolyn Jollimore."

"Chief MacFarlane might not agree with you."

At the sound of MacFarlane's name Peale felt a new chill creep through his bones. His left hand clenched his collar more tightly, his right hand clenched the bulky Webley revolver in his right-hand pocket.

A moment of hesitancy swept both men, the same misstep that kills green soldiers on a battlefield. Then Peale jerked the handle of the pistol, but the hammer caught on the seam of his coat. He fumbled to clear it. Dawson saw the dark glint of the pistol and doubted his ability to disarm Peale in time. He dropped the tire iron. It resounded with a painful clamour on the steel deck. He ran, vaulted the hood of the nearest car, and took cover amongst others. Peale wasted another split second drawing his weapon. When he looked up, Dawson had disappeared.

Now, it was his turn to hunt.

The pistol felt odd in Peale's hand. He was not a shooter or sports-man of any description. He had taken the gun with him as a deterrent, rather than a weapon. But now it had come to that. Point and shoot was all he knew of marksmanship, and that would have to do. It seemed obvious now that Dawson had killed MacFarlane, and that reasoning in itself would suffice to justify his killing Dawson, even more so knowing that Dawson intended for some reason to kill him.

Peale made a quick visual survey of the starboard vehicle deck before moving. He saw no passengers wandering about, nor a deck hand on a walk-through. So he edged his way aft along the starboard rail. Except for the trucks, it was unlikely that Dawson could conceal himself underneath a vehicle, and there was too little clearance be-tween bumpers to hide. Likely he was between rows.

Peale reached the end of the first row without sighting him. He felt too timid and inexperienced to walk up between the files of cars. He could be too easily surprised. Instead he traversed the ends of the remaining rows. Between the second and third he spotted something move about halfway up the queue, a leg perhaps. He rushed past the end of the final row, just in time to see the flash of blue, Dawson's rain jacket, disappear into an opening in the superstructure amidships. Dawson was heading up the stairs, Peale surmised, or maybe through a corridor to the port-side vehicles.

Peale's Webley preceded his cautious walk toward the portal where he had seen Dawson vanish. As he drew near, he heard the faint sound of a machine or motor, and, the closer he got, the more noticeable it grew. Caution slowed Peale even more as the edge of the portal drew near. Dawson could pop out of anywhere, he thought. Only a few feet more. He cocked the hammer, his back grazing the nearest car, and quickly sidestepped the opening. A short empty passageway faced him. Another hatch, inside and to the left, was open.

Peale moved gingerly toward it. He saw a ladder that led down into a vast, well-lit chamber. A draft of heat swept up from it. He caught the scent of oil. He poked his head into the opening. Suddenly, the full impact struck him as stunningly as if he had been electrocuted. Every nerve ending in his body quivered as if it had been assaulted. An unbearable noise had leapt from the mouth of the ship's engine room.

It was only a matter of a few steps forward or back between tolera-tion and painful noise, but in that brief venture, Peale had glimpsed Dawson huddled alongside a turbine just past the foot of the ladder. Dawson's eyes had a wild look to them; his hands clasped his ears.

The chief engineer sat at a small fixed desk out of sight in the control room, a narrow compartment just forward of the engine room. Industrial headphones covered the bald and deeply freckled crown of his head as he checked a panel lined with gauges and busily jotted entries into a log book.

Once more, Peale ventured forward, this time steeled against what he knew would be a necessary ordeal. He had a clear view of Dawson and, Dawson, quivering like a spooked dog in the nerve-jangling din, had not yet seen him. Peale leaned in, raised his pistol and fired. The bullet struck the steel bulkhead just to the left of Dawson. The sound of the gunshot was no more than a ripple amid the shriek and rumble from diesel pistons, whirling drive shafts, and throbbing manifolds. Dawson heard nothing of the shot, but he felt a spatter of lead fragments, flinched, looked up, and watched Peale level a revolver at him.

Although the engineer could hear very little in the control room, he sensed something. His fingers rose searchingly to his protective earphones. He turned in his chair, one eyebrow cocked attentively. Perhaps he caught only a single arrhythmic note in the clamorous ocean of noise that engulfed him. He gazed about, saw nothing. Then he stood, entered the engine room, and walked the metal grate of the cat-walk between two resonating ship's engines. He studied gauges, checked fuel lines, and, finding nothing amiss, wiped his hands on a cloth stuffed in a rear pocket of his overalls and disappeared into the aft heeling and trimming compartment.

Peale had held his second shot when he saw the engineer begin his rounds. Meantime, Dawson had shifted position. When Peale poked his head in again, Dawson was out of sight. So was the engineer. Another heavy sea struck. Peale tottered unsteadily with the impact. His gun hand, braced against the door frame, prevented a fall, but his torso swung forward with the momentum, and his left hand reached out instinctively for the rail of the platform just inside the engine room.

It could have been sharp peripheral vision. It could have been instinct. Or it could have been lingering agitation over the morning quarrel with his wife over his greasy boots dirtying her kitchen floor. But something drew the engineer to look up and, at the top of the ladder, he saw a man framed in the opening to the engine room.

The engine room was strictly off limits for passengers. Only an idiot could miss the bold warning at the entry. The engineer leapt forward, rushed toward the foot of the ladder, and wildly threw his arms about in order to signal his message to get the hell out of his station.

Peale's jaw fell open. His hands still desperately clutched the rail and door frame for balance. Surprise and horror coursed through his mind. He gawked stupidly at the engineer. Then Peale's eyes shifted toward the gun in his hand. Peale suddenly realized that the engineer couldn't see the Webley from where he stood. Relief and mortification supplanted Peale's fright, and a feigned composure, acquired through years of political fencing, quieted his surprise.

Peale backed up, made humble non-verbal *mea culpas* to the engineer, and withdrew from the threshold of the engine room. Once again the Webley found a temporary home in his coat pocket.

78.

Anne pulled into her driveway at eight-thirty. A dim light shone in the upstairs front bedroom, Jacqui's room. Another, a counter light, burned in the kitchen.

Anne was exhausted. She felt a weariness that seeped to the bone. God knows she needed a full night's sleep, a real night's sleep without interruption. And she hoped the coffee she had drunk earlier wouldn't keep that from happening.

Then her thoughts turned to Jacqui, whose world was upside down as well. But that was the fluky road of adolescent life, she thought, a reflection that gave neither succour for her daughter's pain nor relief from maternal anxiety. Teenage girls could cope with the occasional snap and snarl of adversity, learn from those experiences, and move on, but Jacqui had gotten both barrels of bad luck all at once, and she was bleeding. It didn't seem fair. It wasn't fair.

Anne locked the side entry door and stepped lightly up the stairs. A light had shone in Jacqui's room. Perhaps she had fallen asleep with her lamp still lit, she thought, and she made her way silently toward Jacqui's room. Her hand touched the doorknob, then stopped. Anne heard a faint something. She waited, listened. It was Jacqui. She was awake, and the sound was soft weeping on the other side of the door. Anne remained quietly where she stood and considered whether to intervene or let the passage of time heal her wounds.

Then she turned the handle and entered.

"Hi," said Anne. Her one word evoked delicacy and concern, as well as a tacit apology for the intrusion. Jacqui lay on the bed, her head cradled on one arm. She had buried the side of her face in a pillow. She stiffened a bit at her mother's entrance, and her whimpering subsided.

"Can I help?" said Anne.

Jacqui's head moved negatively back and forth. She sniffled twice, and the back of her hand swiped her nose.

Anne pulled a couple of tissues from a box on the side table and placed them next to Jacqui. She took one and blew her nose. She took the other and dabbed her eyes. She did it quickly, as if to conceal both tears and disappointment. Anne settled herself onto the edge of Jacqui's bed.

"I'm not going to school tomorrow," said Jacqui. An uncharacteristic finality coloured her declaration.

Anne responded by brushing a comforting hand gently up and down Jacqui's arm.

"I understand."

For a long while, Anne simply sat beside Jacqui, her hand touching Jacqui's shoulder or stroking her hair. Sometimes, simply being there is enough to relieve the ache of a loss, she thought, and, sometimes, saying nothing says everything.

A few minutes elapsed before Jacqui's tears dried and her breathing became regular and measured. Her eyes still reflected regret and sadness, but Anne also saw in them a lucidity and warmth that had not been there a short time before, and she felt confident that her daughter's old spiritedness lay not so far beneath the melancholy.

"I don't think I can face anybody ever again. My life…everything I've worked for…is falling apart. Everything is broken," she said. Anne watched a fresh gush of tears as she spoke, and Jacqui sank once again into a bleak silence.

"You know, I felt that way once…when I was young…a few times actually…and it hurts like hell. I have some idea what you're going through… I've been there, too."

As Anne spoke, she stared vaguely at the front window of Jacqui's bedroom. The houses across the street cut vague silhouettes against the dark, blustery night sky. Anne's eyes saw, but were oblivious. Her mind and memory had drifted to a place many years away.

Something circumspect in her mother's admission caught Jacqui's curiosity, and she looked at her for the first time since she'd come into her room.

Anne's reverie lasted only a few moments. Then it broke like a wave on a north shore beach, and Anne returned to the edge of the bed. She smiled a broken smile, bent down, and gave Jacqui a firm, tender hug. Anne's eyes clouded with a mysterious sadness.

"You want some hot chocolate?" asked Anne when she pulled away. Jacqui stared back, confused by the sudden disconnection and left wanting.

"What happened? What happened to you?" asked Jacqui.

Anne gave up a cheerless laugh and, with an ostentatious gesture, swept the question away.

"It was nothing…at least that's how I see it now…inconsequential…"

Jacqui braced herself up on one elbow, and her eyes probed for something more substantial than the trivial dismissal her mother had proffered.

"What's important, hon, is how I worked through it. Mind you, it wasn't a lightning bolt revelation, and, frankly, I didn't see it as any help at all, not at the time."

Anne shot a surreptitious look at Jacqui. She was still quiet, still attentive. So Anne went on: "When you share fears and worries with someone else, they lose their grip on you. That's what I learned."

"I don't get it. Why?"

"I don't really know. I suppose it's like turning the lights on while someone is telling a frightening story. The fear has nowhere to hide. Guilt can't fester."

Jacqui suddenly felt a rush of anger. It leapt from nowhere, and she couldn't contain it.

"But I'm going to be the laughingstock of the school tomorrow! Madame Desjardins will hate me, and Rada can never be my friend again! Nobody will want to speak to me. Don't you understand that?"

"That's quite a burden to carry. It is. And you think you're responsible...for all of it?"

"Yes...yes! Who else?"

"Why? Did you organize the party?"

"No."

"Did you invite those kids?"

"No."

"Did you do try to get them out? Did you try everything?"

"I guess."

"Was there *anything* else you could have done?"

"There must have been."

"If there must have been, then you would know what it was...and you would have done it. The Jacqueline Brown I know would have. And Madame Desjardins. What makes you think she hates you?"

"She hardly spoke to me when she found out."

"Did you tell her what happened?"

"Yes, of course."

"Did you apologize?"

Jacqui nodded.

"What did she say?"

"Nothing, really. Nothing at all."

"I'm sure she was quite upset, but that doesn't mean she was angry with *you*."

"Did you explain about Rada and Bobby?"

"I had told her that Rada might be coming over to help me and that Bobby was dropping by to get the birthday present I made for him.

That got broken, too, by the way," she said and sighed.

"And Rada's in trouble because she came over?"

Jacqui bobbed her head in two, quick, almost convulsive jerks.

"Had you encouraged her to sneak out of the house?"

"I didn't know she'd been grounded, but if I'd been a better friend I would have seen it coming."

"I don't recall reading minds as being a characteristic of the Browns...or the Darbys...on either side of the family...and frankly I don't see any suggestion that you should shoulder the blame...for any of it. However, you might eventually dig a few life lessons out of it for future reference."

After that, a bit of quiet time passed between the two of them. Jacqui propped herself up and leaned back against a pillowed headboard. Her knees cocked up, her hands folded in her lap, her eyes focused onto the corners of her semi-darkened room, her mind reflective.

"Feeling any better?" asked Anne.

"Not really."

"Hot chocolate?"

Jacqui gave up a small concessional smile, then added, "By the way, I'm thinking 'Jacqueline' is a bit too pretentious. What do you think?"

"Up to you, dear."

Anne put a kettle on in the kitchen. She took two heavy mugs from the cabinet and poured a tablespoon of cocoa into each. She returned fifteen minutes later with a tray of hot drinks and a small plate of sugar cookies, but Jacqui had already fallen sound asleep. A spare blanket lay at the foot of her bed. Anne spread it over her, turned out the lights, and returned to the kitchen.

Anne sipped her own mug of cocoa in the living room and paged through the phone directory. She looked anxiously toward a clock on the wall. It was nine-fifteen. Not too too late, she decided, and dialled a number.

"This is Anne Brown. I was hoping we could talk."

79.

Dawson emerged from the engine room as stunned as a prisoner stepping from stone dark solitary into an abhorrence of blinding light. He looked dishevelled; his ears rang; he felt disoriented; and he faltered like a drunk stumbling through a carnival fun house, where all is illusion and instincts are false.

Dawson had no idea where Peale was lurking, and, for his first few moments in the brisk salt air, he didn't care. He slunk down on the cold, wet vehicle deck, leaned up against the fuel tank of a refrigeration truck, and tried to make sense of himself and his situation.

Slowly the half-blindness of his mind began to clear and, in spite of the ringing in his ears, he felt stronger and more aware, and he stood up for a better look around. Priorities re-formed, and stopping Peale again became his foremost thought.

Dawson scarcely heard the blast of Peale's gun. To him it sounded like the pop of a child's toy cap pistol, but the bullet went high, struck the left side-mirror of the truck, and showered fragments of reflective glass on Dawson's head. He fell to his knees, crawled under the truck, and wriggled his way toward the next row of vehicles. As he did, he heard Peale cry out: "Dawson, go away. I don't want to kill you, but I will if I have to."

I need a weapon, thought Dawson. The tire iron he had used earlier came to mind, but it had disappeared. Then another idea struck him— the axe in the fire box on the bulkhead—but maybe not. Getting to it would leave him too exposed to another shot. Dawson had been lucky so far. Three shots taken and no hits. So now maybe it was Peale's turn to get lucky, he thought.

Then another idea, less risky, came to his mind. Dawson worked his way along another row and tried three other trucks before coming upon an unlocked cab. Once inside, he seized a portable fire extinguisher. Finding one turned out to be a blessing. Doubly so, in that it led to spotting Peale.

From the lofty cab of the truck Dawson observed Peale stalking him. Peale crouched low and moved cautiously, gun in hand, but his eyes never lifted above ground or car level. He never looked upward enough to see him, but Dawson was able to determine the search pattern he was following. It was a reversal of the pattern he had used to track him to the engine room, except that this time he had become bolder and more thorough—stalking him between the rows of vehicles, first from in-board rows and then moving toward the ones nearer the rail.

Dawson predicted where Peale would end up, and Dawson was determined to be there waiting for him. If he could surprise Peale—and there was no doubt in Dawson's mind that he could—he'd finish the job he'd started and be done with it or die trying.

Dawson left the truck, slunk away, and hid himself very near the same spot he had confronted Peale the first time. A steel partition by the winch gave him cover. The starboard rail stood behind him. He glanced back. The Caribou lighthouse blinked its cautionary signal into the night. At this point, the ferry was making its approaches. He had maybe ten minutes before docking in Nova Scotia and debarkation. This was his final chance to put an end to a long and complicated misery.

Dawson readied himself. He pulled the retaining pin from the trigger of the fire extinguisher, pressed his back against the cold steel frame, positioned the nozzle at the estimated height and direction at which Peale's face would appear, and listened to the agitated thumpa-da-thump of his heart and the tremulous wheezing of his own panting breath.

At the first glimpse of Peale's gun, Dawson thought his heart would stop. Peale edged within eight feet of Dawson's hiding place. It was farther away than Dawson had anticipated, but going back now was an impossibility. As Dawson stepped forward, Peale's face was averted, his concentration fixed on the last few cars in the line ahead of him.

Dawson squeezed the trigger on the extinguisher. Peale heard the scuff of Dawson's shoes and turned. The extinguisher failed to discharge. Peale stepped back reflexively, the gun wobbling in front of him. He stumbled, but his back steadied against the door of a car. Dawson squeezed the extinguisher's trigger again, and, when nothing happened, he hurled the heavy metal cylinder toward Peale's head and lunged forward.

As Peale emitted a small cry of fear and surprise, Dawson leapt ahead, his hands reaching out desperately for the gun, but the deck, wet from sea spray, was slippery, too slick for Dawson's shoes.

Dawson fell forward, flat, headlong on the deck, his arms outstretched, still three feet short of his mark, and, when he recovered and looked up, he faced the enormous blue-black barrel of Fenton Peale's Webley.

Peale's hands clasped his weapon firmly. His arms were locked. He waved the gun in a motion that Dawson understood to mean that he should move back toward the partition and the rail.

Peale's face was set, and his eyes were wide and fierce. A trickle of frothy spittle stained the corner of his mouth. Dawson saw desperation in Peale's look, and in that expression, Dawson read his own doom.

Dawson slowly rose and moved toward the starboard railing. He looked out. Almost nothing was visible but the Caribou lighthouse, now falling astern, and still blinking a silent admonition.

80.

After two large glasses of cold water, one fresh-brewed coffee, and an extra-strength Tylenol, Anne still felt like a sodden mat of leaves in a storm drain. Her sleep had been weird and dream-restless. Her bones ached, her muscles knotted, and, as she dressed, she felt a twinge in the ankle she'd twisted two nights before. All in all, not propitious omens for the work ahead. Anne muttered something sarcastic to herself, grabbed her purse, and rushed out the door to the car.

There would be no morning jog along the boardwalk today. It was alibi day, and, if it turned out as she hoped, it would be a day of reckoning for someone. She only wished she knew who it was. She was also confused that the likely suspects were disappearing like moths near a bat roost.

Anne pulled into a metered parking space at the entrance to the university campus. She weighed whether or not she could get her business done before some campus cop planted a ticket on her windshield, but she dug into a pocket, pulled out a coin, and dropped it into the slot. She had an hour.

The Registrar's Office was still closed. It was not yet nine o'clock. So she walked past that building and headed for the main door of the Vet College. A security guard at the desk gave directions for Edna Hibley's office and pointed her down a corridor to a linked building that housed offices for staff.

Edna's office was on the second floor. Anne strode along the rows of cubicles, each identical to the other and offering little privacy. Professors at work were in plain view to anyone who passed by. Every office had a glass front and a glass-panelled door. It reminded Anne of a zoo she once visited where animals had been exhibited behind a similar glass enclosure.

As she walked down the corridor, Anne mused whether Edna would have been labelled carnivore or herbivore, but, when she reached her office, she felt a wave of disappointment. Edna's cage was empty. Perhaps she was teaching class or supervising a lab or prepping for some lecture or other. Or perhaps she was still at home. Anne had had reservations about going straight to the Registrar's Office for information on Dawson. Likely they would balk at releasing info on student schedules without an official police request or a nod from someone like Edna who could grease the information slipway for her. Anne's disappointment changed to indecision, and she gazed blankly into the empty office.

Something about Edna's habitat held Anne's attention. Naturally, it revealed her public and professional face, but it also disclosed skills and accomplishments and even a few personal qualities, one of which was pristine orderliness. Anne prided herself on personal neatness and simplicity, clearing away distractions and clutter and all, but Edna had achieved a level of meticulousness that was quite superior. She preserved not only remarkable order, but applied an almost military precision to it. A notebook and a journal of some sort lay on her desk, one on top of the other, both squared and centred. A packet of new pencils stood erect as soldiers in a sparkling glass cylinder, their carbon cores sharpened to fine points. Stainless steel in/out trays fitted crisply at the outside corner of the desk, and it was quite evident that she had processed or disbursed the previous day's incoming mail and memos before she had left for the day. Even Edna's chair had been dutifully pushed in; cabinet drawers and cupboards were properly closed; and the lock on the filing cabinet had been engaged. Her books were regimented as well. The spine of each volume, binder, portfolio, and text had been marshalled exactly to the leading edge of every shelf.

Edna's precision impressed Anne but did not entirely surprise her. She had seen similar meticulousness in some teachers, scientists, and even a few cops she had known. A few uncommon criminals fit that profile as well.

Eventually, Anne's eyes drifted to the personal items in the office. One was a framed photograph of a young smiling Edna, an older woman, and her twin sister Carolyn. The girls looked to be about twenty. A second photograph with faded colour showed her mother and father together. Several large university degrees adorned the walls above the bookshelves. Simple black plastic borders framed them, but they stood in stark contrast to two other framed pieces, both showcased in warm wood frames. They were needlepoint pictures, handmade colourful representations of bluebells and peonies and roses and words of inspiration: "All power comes from Him" and "Reflect Repent Repair." They were expertly crafted, and Anne admitted an admiration for the dexterity that had crafted them. Several other small framed pieces acknowledged her work with UPEI Student Services, the Companion Animal Recovery Project, the John Howard Society, and Alzheimer's Society, and they filled the remaining wall space between cabinets.

Anne glanced at her watch anxiously. She was wasting time now and hurried off. The morning had brightened considerably since she had arrived. She headed toward the Registrar's Office but, on a whim, turned instead toward the library.

The librarian smiled. Anne had a feeling that the woman actually meant to be friendly, not an unusual expectation on PEI, but Anne, in the achy, sleep-deprived, frazzled state of her morning, found it too unlikely a prospect. Nevertheless Anne forced back the best pleasant expression she could muster.

"I'm looking for some information," said Anne.

"They say a library's the best place for that," she quipped.

"It's personal information."

"Try me."

"I need to locate two students, but I don't know their schedules."

"Names?"

"Jacob Dawson and Sami Smith."

The librarian's pleasant, staid expression sank beneath a choked smirk, only to return moments later. Then she said: "Room 206. A group study conference room. Up the stairs and turn right."

Anne suddenly felt like a rabbit caught with a mouth full of lettuce in her mother's garden. When she found words, she said, "So it's true what they say. Librarians are the gatekeepers to everything."

The librarian said nothing, but tossed back a cavalier look that exuded contentedness, omniscience, and a ripple of merriment.

On her way upstairs, Anne's cell phone beeped. She glanced at it. A text message from Ben read: "Meet me at Timothy's in an hour."

The conference room on the second floor had a fishbowl element as well. Behind the glass Anne saw Jacob, Sami, and three other students sitting around a table, notebooks out, papers shuffling, and students prepping for something. Anne knocked lightly. Jacob came to the door; a confused twist furrowed his brow. He shut the door behind him so no one could hear their conversation. He looked edgy.

"Jacob, you look almost as bad as I do this morning. Busy night?"

Dawson folded his arms in front of himself and glanced back uneasily toward the members of the study group who were watching, especially Sami, who gave Anne a look of either annoyance at the interruption or jealousy at the intrusion.

"Studying," said Dawson. A group project is due. A presentation."

"Where did you study?"

"I was at Sami's. Why are you asking?" Jacob's foot moved a guarded half-step back and his eyes darted elsewhere.

"Just curious. MacFarlane's dead."

"I know. I heard on the radio this morning. An accident or fire or something. Right? But what's that got to do with me?"

"So where were you Saturday night?" Anne's phrasing was blunt.

"I don't have to answer questions like that," he said. Jacob turned and his hand grasped the door to go back in. "Listen to me. MacFarlane's death is suspicious. You can answer my questions now, or the police will be tapping on your door later. Which will be less embarrassing?"

"All right, all right. I was at the library until closing. Then I had the study group," he said, pointing back to the others in the room. "We met at Sami's. I was there most of the night."

"Most of the night?"

"Okay. All night."

"Will anyone back you up on that?"

"They all will." Dawson's arm swung back toward the students behind the glass.

"Good. Thanks. Now you can go. Send her out," Anne said.

Sami put on a fresh scowl and resumed her insolent demeanour, all of which confirmed Anne's speculation that Sami was wrestling with jealousy. Anne also quickly deduced that Sami knew about Jacob's history and, like many girls her age, some compulsion drew her to pursue men on the fringe, men like Jacob, but, in spite of her capricious feelings and motivations, Sami produced a solid alibi for Jacob. She claimed that Saturday's study session began in her dorm room after the library closed at ten. Jacob grabbed a snack and arrived at her place shortly after eleven. Five of them were there until about two-thirty, and Jacob spent the rest of the night with her.

Sami wrote down the names and phone numbers of the others in her study group. She jabbed the list at Anne, shot her a final, scornful, menacing look, and returned to the study group.

81

Timothy's was a coffee shop in the heart of Charlottetown, two blocks from Anne's office if she cut through the flower beds and lawns of Province House. The shop had an old-time feel to it. It was long and narrow, like a dining car on the CNR. The floor was tile, the ceiling high and panelled in sheets of embossed tin, like ones still found in the kitchens of older rural homes.

Cabinets filled with pastries and sandwiches, cookies and breads, stretched along one wall of the shop. The service counter and food-prep station also shared that space. A string of eight or ten small tables lined the other wall and further along was a waist-high polished wood counter for a stand-up crowd on busy days.

It was not so busy when Anne arrived. The breakfast crowd had got their coffee and Danish and gone to work, and the mid-morning coffee break crowd had yet to descend. Ben sat at a table halfway down the aisle. One bright ray of sunlight illuminated the dust on his shoe. Three other customers sat at a window table. One bald-headed and two white-haired retirees chuckled amongst themselves, drank in the warm morning light, chewed the details out of city politics, and devoured old stories each had already heard but had forgotten since their first telling.

She sat down next to Ben with a creamy coffee and a large sugar cookie fresh from the counter. Her chair clanked and scraped on the tile floor; sweet granules on her cookie glittered in the reflected sunlight; and a wisp of steam rose from her cup, twisted, and curled in the air so beautifully that one would expect a genie to magically leap from the vapours. Anne's mood and temperament had risen since the library visit. She was feeling almost lively again.

"What's the news?" asked Anne. Ben hid behind his paper, absorbed with page two of the morning *Guardian*. Anne stared at him through the classifieds: "Dalmation, two years old, needs open spaces. Will sell or trade for house dog."

"Peale's dead," said Ben, without looking up from his newspaper.

Ben's two words squeezed the life out of any sparkle Anne had managed to resurrect that morning. The magic fled.

"How?"

"Went overboard on the ferry to Nova Scotia last night."

"That's tragic."

"So it is."

"And odd. Do we know what happened?"

"Nova Scotia police are guessing it was an accident. Sea was rough, weather nasty. They found his car abandoned on deck after the ferry docked. He was nowhere about. They drew conclusions, but they haven't recovered a body."

"Do you buy it?"

"It's hard to swallow. He had a pile of cash and bonds in his overnight bag. Investigators found it in his car. They also turned up his passport. He wouldn't need that for his supposed business trip to Cape Breton. Something else was afoot."

"So you think he killed MacFarlane and was making a run for it?"

Ben shook his head doubtfully.

"Veronica, his wife, swore that he was home before midnight on Saturday...and he didn't leave the house again until he got the call from Sergeant Schaeffer...and that couldn't have been until after two. The coroner puts time of MacFarlane's death between midnight and two o'clock and, putting that together with the Fire Marshal's guess-timate of the progress of that type of fire, MacFarlane didn't succumb until about one, one-thirty."

"So why was Peale running? It doesn't make sense."

"He was afraid."

Anne looked at him quizzically, and he explained: "Dit just phoned before you got here. He retrieved some text messages from Simone's old cell phone. It looks like, at the time, Peale and Simone were secretly carrying on...behind MacFarlane's back as well as Veronica's. MacFarlane finds out, kills Simone, frames Dawson, and blackmails Peale. The text messages didn't implicate Peale in Simone's death, but it would have been scandalous enough to hurt his business dealings, marriage, and political aspirations. And that's not all...," said Ben. He leaned back in his chair, folded his hands over his paunch, and wrapped a self-satisfied grin across his face.

"What?" said Anne curtly and gave his foot a sharp kick.

"There were several flirtatious interchanges between Simone and Wendell Carmody, too."

"That toad?"

Ben nodded. "Yep, I think she was bent on trading up and cast her net a bit wider than anyone had guessed."

"But we're still back to square one," said Anne. "MacFarlane killed Simone. We know that now. But the suspects in MacFarlane's death? Peale. He has an alibi from Veronica...and Dawson...he has an alibi for the time of death as well...his girlfriend and several other students. In the end, we've got nothin'. We're not even sure whether MacFarlane's death was an accident. Same with Peale's. Everyone's calling them accidents. Come to think of it...we haven't even reached square one. All we really have is a handful of suspicions and a funny feeling in our gut. Did the coroner's report come back?"

"The attending physician listed immediate cause of death as asphyxiation. Antecedent cause: smoke inhalation. He classified it as an accidental death."

"Another dead-end," said Anne glumly.

"I expected that. So I've asked the coroner to do a complete autopsy. See what, if anything, that brings to light."

Ben took a long final slurp of his cooling coffee and looked closely at Anne. His brows furrowed and he leaned back in his chair like a physician dictating a diagnosis to a nursing assistant.

"You look like hell," he said.

"I was feeling much better before I got your cheery news."

"Why don't you take a break, get some rest."

"Maybe...got to meet someone first."

82.

Jasmine's Tea House had been carved out of the lower floor of a once-stately smaller home in Charlottetown, not far from City Hall. Jasmine, whose real name was Bonnie Lee, was a second-generation Vietnamese who spoke English with a thick Tignish PEI accent. Jasmine bustled about as if preparing for a banquet, but, in all reality, the tea market was limited to a small coterie of regulars and passengers off Holland America cruise ships searching for a genuine Island experience before their twelve-hour shore leave expired, and they sailed to their next exotic port.

For Anne it seemed the perfect place to meet Mrs. Kikovic, Rada's mother. It would be a quiet and discreet setting, free from clashing cultural, religious, or political influences. Anne had no unrealistic expectations about the meeting. Her conversation with her the night before had been short and non-committal, but hopeful in that she had agreed to meet at all.

Anne played with her tea as she waited. She was tired and found it hard to concentrate. Anxiety about the meeting hadn't distracted her. It was something else, something she couldn't put her finger on. It was the same feeling she got when, sitting quietly, she hears a faint but odd speck of sound. Ears perk, the mind sharpens, and silence stretches out until a faint scratch in the wall tells a tale. In Anne's mind, though, the tale still hung there, its meaning not yet revealed.

A bell on the door of the tea house jingled merrily as it opened. The sound broke Anne's restless reverie, and her eyes followed the movement of the woman who entered. She was a tall, elegant woman, with a clear, smooth, unadorned complexion, and bright, intense eyes. Her hair and shoulders were covered by an orange and black print hijab. A black jilbab flowed to her shoes in a line broken only at the waist by a small loosely cinched belt. She carried a black leather bag over her shoulder. Their eyes briefly met.

Anne stood to greet her.

"Mrs. Kikovic, I'm Anne Brown. I'm so pleased to meet you."

"A'idah, and thank you."

They sat down together, but an awkward silence settled between them.

Finally, Anne spoke: "A'idah, over the last couple of months Jacqui and Rada have grown close and become good friends." A'idah nodded, and Anne continued: "Jacqui is brokenhearted about what happened, and I'm hoping to find some way for the girls to mend their relationship."

"Rada is unhappy too...very unhappy...but sadness and disappointment are part of growing up, are they not? They stimulate change... maturity. Your daughter and mine will grow from what they learn... as you undoubtedly did and I did, when we were children."

"But is losing a friendship necessary? Is that a good thing?"

"Perhaps not a good thing, but sometimes a necessary thing."

"In what way?"

"It is difficult for a Muslim child to live in a Western society. In a perfect world, she would grow up in a familiar country and thrive in traditions we value. But it is not a perfect world...and here we are... we must make do with what resources and resolve we have. Rada and I and Ahmed are not Western peoples. And Rada...she hears many voices now that are not ours...and too many of these voices teach self-interest, indulgence, disrespect, shamelessness..."

"Surely, Jacqui isn't one of those voices."

"I know Jacqui, and I like her, but Ahmed thinks, and I think so as well, that, although she may not speak those voices, she does not reject them either. Our religion, our traditions...we cannot ignore them or dismiss them."

"I understand, and I agree with you. Young people need good examples and guidance and limits. But does forbidding their friendship and association set a proper example? Can there not be a compromise of some sort?"

"Some things cannot be compromised."

"And some things can. Perhaps we can find a way to accommodate both. Perhaps we can set a good example by trying to find some ground on which we can all stand."

"The Qu'ran says, 'Whoever pardons and seeks reconciliation will be rewarded by God.' So I must accept that it is possible."

"What would you suggest then?" said Anne with a timid optimism.

"There may be a way," she said in a manner of reflection. Her bright eyes clouded with thought and reservation. "but my husband would have to agree. It would involve a mediator. An imam perhaps. Or some community leader whose opinion he respects."

83.

As Anne left Jasmine's Tea House, she felt a spring in her step that had failed to accompany her arrival there. She couldn't claim that a plan was afoot, but, at least, progress now seemed possible, even if it had not yet reached the doorsteps of probability.

As well, progress suddenly seemed moot as Anne realized that she was backtracking. Once again Timothy's Coffee Shop appeared ahead. The gardens of Province House lay just beyond it, and the Confederation Centre next to them. A young musician, guitar case open, sat on the concrete base of the war cenotaph and busked for money. On the memorial wall above him, a file of frozen bronze soldiers charged toward glory. The musician played Bob Dylan. His bilingual placard advertised "Tunes for Coins: No Tax." Anne dropped a dollar coin into his case and hurried through the shortcut to her office. On her way, she passed a yellow-fingered, haggard old woman searching the ground for discarded cigarette butts. Two pencil-thin men in rancid, ill-fitting clothes shared a paper bag on a bench, idly watched the old woman, and kept a keen bleary watch for roaming police cars.

Anne grabbed the mail from her office and headed home. Each step now seemed laborious and painful, but, within half an hour, she had locked herself behind the door of her house and fallen asleep.

Anne sank into a very deep but agitated sleep. She swam between one dead-end interview and another, then back, around, up and down, again and again, like a goldfish in a bowl, seeing everything with clarity and seeing nothing at all. Details flitted like fallen leaves tossed about in gusts of wind. Facts ground underfoot like unsettled gravel. She struggled forward. Momentum faltered; balance quavered; headway blocked. And there was no way out, no satisfying answer, no relief, no rest.

When she finally awoke three hours later, her mouth was parched; her throat was scratchy; and her head felt like it had been ransacked and scrubbed with sand. Barefoot, she stumbled to the bathroom and drank two large glasses of water, the second washing down an aspirin.

Though she wasn't hungry, the aroma of food drew her downstairs and into the kitchen where Jacqui was preparing supper. A kettle of pasta bubbled on the stovetop. Spaghetti sauce simmered in a pan, and a couple of dinner rolls heated in the oven. The table was set. Two tall candles burned between place settings, and icy water glimmered in a glass decanter.

"I didn't hear you when I came in," said Anne. Her voice sounded as if it came from someone else, someone feeble, old, and groggy.

"I wasn't home," said Jacqui.

"Oh?"

"I was at school."

"How did it go?" Anne fought off her feeble, groggy disposition and managed a semi-animate and attentive tone.

"It went well."

"And what changed your mind...about going?"

"You were right. I hadn't done anything wrong. Why should I hide like I had?"

"And there was no backlash," said Anne sensing a half-truth.

"A bit."

"How did you handle it?"

"I role-played. I imagined myself as Jeanne d'Arc. She too was blameless, yet persecuted, and still maintained dignity."

"And that worked?"

"It convinced me. 'All the world's a stage,'" she said with a dramatic flourish of her arm, "'and all men and women merely players.' And I think it convinced most of them," she added with boastful, delicious pleasure.

"Bravo."

Anne clapped joyfully and enthusiastically. Jacqui laughed at her own theatrics. Then they sat and ate and laughed some more.

"I have news, too," said Anne.

84.

It didn't have the grandeur of an epiphany, nor the wonder of a "eureka." It came to Anne more like an apparition exiting a fog and drawing near with a slowly resolving clarity until Anne believed she knew the answer to the question she had been asking. She chastised herself for not seeing it before, but it was the only possible explanation. The details had been there all along, but she had been slow to put them together, and just one phone call had confirmed her supposition. They had been clever murders, very clever indeed, and, though it was now clear to her who committed them, questions remained regarding how and why.

Anne pulled up in front of the house. The neighbourhood was dark and quiet. She knocked on the door. A dog barked two doors away. A curtain moved slightly, and after too long an interval, the door opened.

"What is it?"

"Edna, I've come to speak with you."

"This is not a good time, Anne. Try me at the office tomorrow."

"It's never a good time to talk about murder, is it, Edna?" Anne firmly pushed against the door and shouldered her way into the hallway.

"Are you mad, forcing your way into my home? Get out. You have no business here. You have no right to be here at all. Get out now. Get out before I call the police." Fear, anger, and desperation coloured her objections, and Edna bolted for the telephone extension in the parlour. Anne followed as Edna picked up the receiver and began dialling.

"I mean it," she said. "I'll call them."

"Thank you. That would be helpful, Edna. I'm eager to tell them about your connection with Jacob Dawson, someone you denied knowing."

"I don't know him. I've never met the man. I told you that." The telephone receiver slipped away from her ear.

"You're both recovering alcoholics. You're his AA sponsor, his advisor, his supporter. You know his problems, his weaknesses, his hatreds. You know what buttons to press, and you were eager to press them."

"That's preposterous," said Edna. She had gathered up a renewed confidence and coolness, a sneering haughtiness. She returned the telephone to its table-top cradle. Dead relatives stared back indifferently from photos on her mantel. Edna moved past the gleaming tea service on a mahogany side table. She stood beside a small antique desk and rested against it.

"I've checked. My contact with AA confirmed it," said Anne.

"What else do you *think* you know?"

"You're working together, you and Jacob. You killed MacFarlane for Dawson, and he killed Peale for you. A convenient arrangement, wasn't it? Neither of you were suspected because neither of you had an obvious motive for killing the person you did...and you both had alibis for the death of the person you had motive to kill."

"I admire your perseverance, Ms. Darby, and your vivid imagination, but you haven't demonstrated the skills to think through such a task. You attack a problem with the creativity of a dreamer rather than the logic of a philosopher. Everything you've offered is utter conjecture, and all you've succeed in doing so far is making a fool of yourself."

"You denied knowing Dawson. That's not conjecture."

"What happens at AA is confidential. I was only safeguarding his privacy and mine. What else have you got?"

"It's odd how, when a theory becomes evident, new ways of looking at a case come to light...like consideration of the car."

"What car?"

"The one that Dawson would have used to follow Peale to the ferry. He doesn't own one. My guess is that he used yours...that white Civic in the driveway."

"Guess?" Edna mocked. "Another conjecture! You're replete with them, and I've had enough. Go. Now!"

"One more guess, if you don't mind, Edna. It was the last ferry crossing of the night. Dawson would have to have had transportation back from Nova Scotia. A car was necessary, and his only route was across the Confederation Bridge, a two-and-a-half hour return drive to Charlottetown, and that triggers an unforeseen complication... bridge security. There's continual CCTV coverage of bridge traffic. If your Civic turns up on their tape, as I'm sure it will, then Dawson is through and so are you, Edna."

"You stupid girl...you stupid, stupid girl! You couldn't leave it alone, could you? You couldn't just take my cheque and be done with it, could you? I didn't want you on the case anymore. Why wasn't that enough?"

Surprise drew a wrinkled line across Anne's brow. Then it softened into forbearance.

"I wasn't doing it for you, Edna. I thought you knew that. I was doing it for your sister, Carolyn. I always was. It was her voice that cried out for justice, not your curiosity or craving for vengeance."

Edna's eyes flickered like a cornered squirrel. Then she whirled, drew a revolver from the top drawer of the desk, and swung it toward Anne. The inertia of the heavy pistol overshot the mark, but Edna corrected and steadied her aim at Anne.

The gun facing her was a Webley .455. Edna's hand looked too small for so large a gun, and Anne looked too small to survive a slug from so intimidating a muzzle. Edna's left hand clasped the hammer and levered it back with a solemn click. The barrel dipped momentarily. Edna struggled to hold the Webley. Her fingers nervously fidgeted in and out of the trigger guard, and her thumb struggled to find a comfortable position along the stock.

"Edna, why don't you put that gun down? There's no need in making things any worse than they are." Anne's voice had a calm and reassuring ring, but her jaw and tongue felt so taut she was amazed that any words had found the nerve to spill from her mouth.

Anne's other surprise leapt from a shape suddenly appearing in the doorway. It belonged to Jacob Dawson.

"She's right, Edna. Put the gun away."

"Don't interfere, Jacob...and don't come any closer," she said to him as he walked toward her. Her head jerked toward him, and the gun followed in the same direction. Jacob stopped, and Edna turned the gun back to its original target. "I know what I'm doing...what I have to do," she added.

"I hope that doesn't involve killing me," said Anne, "or Jacob. MacFarlane, I could understand. Peale even. They shared a lot of blame. Other than that...me, Jacob... I can't see you killing us."

Edna ignored her comment, but said and did nothing. She seemed bewildered, uncertain.

"I am curious, though," said Anne. "What led you to this?"

"At our meeting a week ago, you said that MacFarlane was likely the killer of both Carolyn and Simone. Then there was the explosion. You nearly died. It was too coincidental. Jacob and I talked. As you had said, there probably would never be enough evidence to convict him. So I vowed to make him pay for what he did to Carolyn...and me. He destroyed us both, you know. When he killed her, he killed me."

"How did you manage it on your own?"

"Oh, I wasn't alone. Jacob helped."

"But he had an alibi."

"For the time of death...yes. But I needed his assistance earlier in the evening. I had been watching MacFarlane for some time…waiting for the right moment. I saw Peale come…and I saw him go. I phoned Jacob, picked him up, and we drove back. Jacob knocked on MacFarlane's door and retreated. I waited in the shrubbery alongside. When MacFarlane stepped outside, I shot him with a tranquilizer pistol from the Vet College—we use it for anaesthetizing large animals. It took a few moments to put him out. I was lucky. The dart hit a blood vessel. He didn't realize what was happening until too late. I needed Jacob to drag him off the doorstep and back into the house."

"Then I had to leave," said Jacob. "I had my study group."

"Why didn't you just kill him on the doorstep?" asked Anne.

"I wanted the details of what he had done. Then I wanted to watch him suffer." The pitch of Edna's voice rose, and her words sputtered with venom as she went on: "I bound his wrists and ankles with tape and waited. As he began to rouse from the tranquilizer, I injected him with another drug. It paralyzed him but the right dose allowed him to remain conscious and speak."

"And he was able to tell you what happened?"

"With a little prodding…a carrot and stick approach," she said with a small guilty chuckle. "I told him I would let him live if he told me the truth. He admitted blackmailing Peale by convincing him that the only way to prevent his connection with Simone coming to light was to frighten Carolyn into silence."

"So *Peale* ran Carolyn off the road," said Anne with disbelief.

Edna nodded sadly. Her gaze lowered. Her right thumb tenderly caressed the wooden stock. Her left hand supported the black steel frame. Then she looked up suddenly and said, "I knew then that Peale had to die, too."

"And Jacob did that for you."

Edna nodded again.

"I never meant to kill anyone," said Jacob with a desperate urgency. "Not Peale, not even MacFarlane."

Then, fuelled by anger and frustration, he turned toward Edna. "You never told me that you planned to kill MacFarlane. You said it was an accidental overdose. You told me you just wanted to force a confession out of him. You wanted the truth, you said. That's all."

"I got the truth. Then I wanted revenge. If you have an infection, you purge it. If you have a boil, you lance it. If you have a cancer, you cut it out. MacFarlane…he was a plague on society. You should have seen his eyes when I put the oil and potatoes into the pan and lit the stove. He knew what was coming, but there was absolutely nothing he could do about it. How terrifying to know that you are about to die and can do absolutely nothing to prevent it. I relished every second I watched him. He had to be destroyed. And so did Peale."

"Jacob, maybe you should sit down," said Anne, looking apprehensively at the horror and incredulity spreading across his face. But Jacob ignored her, his attention riveted on Edna.

"You used me. You conned me into this mess, but I'm not going back to prison for murder again. No, not me. Not again. Not for you," he shouted and lunged toward Edna.

Edna's eyes had widened at Dawson's outburst but, when he sprang forward, fear charged through her. She swung toward him, her torso canted back defensively, her left hand stretched out to ward off an attack. Her right hand trembled and twitched, and the hammer fell. A flash of light and a terrific roar blazed from the Webley. A sudden enormous wave of sound engulfed the small sitting room and, just as suddenly, an ominous silence swept into its wake.

Dawson froze mid-stride; Anne's mind staggered to a halting immobility; and Edna struggled through a portentous astonishment.

Dawson grasped his stomach. Blood oozed through his shirt, filled the gaps between his fingers, and fell in a trickling, crimson stream onto his trousers. He looked down at the wound and, as if that slight movement unbalanced him, he fell forward, his head at Edna's feet.

Edna seemed too stunned to speak or move. The Webley dangled in her hand and fell to the floor next to Dawson's body. The stark sound of it striking the wood floor sparked a panicky thought, and Edna rushed for the door.

Anne didn't stop her. She ran instead to Dawson's side. He was conscious, troubled, and still breathing. She dialled 911 emergency services for help and tried to stave the flow of blood.

Outside, a car engine roared to life and sped away. Anne remained with Dawson, tried to comfort him and keep him still until paramedics arrived, but he insisted on uttering what he could. Several short verbal spasms, bursts of words and broken phrases, passed his lips. Then Dawson grew quiet.

Anne could make out the wailing siren of the ambulance not more than a few blocks away, and, somewhere nearby, another car passed Edna's house, its sound slowly fading toward stillness, just like the heartbeat of John Jacob Dawson.

Windshield wipers beat the light rain from side to side as Edna zigzagged across Charlottetown streets to Riverside Drive. Traffic was light on Monday evening, but she slowed to avoid notice by police patrol cars and made a left turn onto the Hillsborough Bridge.

Her hands trembled as she grasped the steering wheel. She eased into the left lane for a turn onto the Bunbury Road. The rain grew stronger on the bridge, gusts of wind as well. The windshield marbled with wet drops and streaks, and she increased the wiper speed, but that made no difference. The rain hadn't encumbered her vision. The tears running down her cheeks had. And knowing that truth, a more ardent flow ensued.

She drove past a string of homes along the Bunbury Road, but they were mere blips in her consciousness. Her mind was not elsewhere. It was nowhere. It dwelled in a vortex of images and a flood of emotions that plucked at her spirit and splintered her reasoning and left her like a dried-up leaf in a draft of wind, and, as such, she perceived herself alone, in an unfamiliar primal place, fleeing pain, seeking relief, searching for a glimmer of peace.

Peace. The word reverberated in her head.

Along the road, the houses and outbuildings of the town had disappeared entirely. Clusters of trees and low mounds of wild shrubbery and thick bush had gone, too. A vista opened in front of her. It looked so very big, unencumbered and free in the soft, emerging illumination of a full moon. She felt a weight lift from her shoulders. The rain had stopped, an expanse of water and green marshy fields filled her eyes with a satisfying loveliness, hope chimed softly in the warm glow of a pleasant October evening, and Edna depressed the accelerator with an intoxicating abandon. She felt a rush of elation, a delightful inebriation. A white wooden cross loomed from the shoulder of the road.

Serenity, she murmured to herself as the white Civic struck the steel culvert.

85.

Mr. Ahmadi opened the door to his office at Schnelling Engineering. He was a tall, slender man, stooped in posture, and casually dressed in a tweed coat and an open-collared blue dress shirt. Ahmed and A'idah Kikovic preceded him from the office, and, with no sidelong, telling glance or expression, both of them and their daughter Rada passed through the anteroom and headed for the building's main entrance.

Anne and Jacqui squirmed in the contoured metal chairs and followed the course of their exit. Only Rada had made eye contact. Her lips parted as if to speak, but she remained wordless and looked ill at ease.

"Mrs. Brown... Jacqueline...if you please," said Mr. Ahmadi with a gentle sweep of hand, and ushered them into his private office and toward even more comfortable chairs. Three of the seats faced a rather uninteresting windowless wall. The fourth, his chair, faced the others. Nothing stood between them.

"It must seem a bit odd to have me as a mediator," he said. He smiled disarmingly. Anne produced what she hoped would be a pleasant, open expression, though she wasn't sure she had successfully pulled it off. Jacqui had done the same but sensed that she had already revealed an aura of guilt. Accusations and recriminations hung like stale odours in the still air of the room, and she licked her lips anxiously.

"It sometimes seems like that to me, too. A civil engineer playing the role of mediator. Is that not so? Or a child playing policeman. Both seem absurd, but let me explain. Like the Kikovics, I, too, am a newcomer to Canada. I have been here fifteen years, they just four. Since I came, I have learned that I must change many things I had grown accustomed to." Ahmadi paused for a second in order to discern whether his words were penetrating their unresponsive eyes, and then he continued: "I also learned that many things need not change... nor should they change. But adjustment takes time and, when you know no one, and you understand little, you depend upon those who have gone before you. For me, it was Mohammed Attara. He was my guide to Western culture. For the Kikovics, it fell to me to acquaint them with local customs and guide them along a comfortable path in their new home. I look at this meeting as an extension of what the Kikovics and I have been working on. They trust me to listen to them and advise them."

"So you represent their side," said Anne. Anne's words were objective and unimpassioned but her eyes blinked concern. Jacqui swallowed and gazed at the closed door.

"I represent no one and no side. Today I listen to the Kikovics and I listen to the Browns. Tomorrow I explore what is custom and what is conviction, what is important and what is superficial, what is possible and what is not. In the end, there is no winner and no loser...just those who have found a path to move forward. Shall we begin?"

86.

It was nearing nine-thirty. The glow of evening had faded to a moon-less black, and a canopy of trees hid the stars as Anne and Jacqui drove along the road. *So close to the city and so little light*, she thought. How was it possible? Their car's headlights illuminated a small break in the tree line. A sign marking the driveway read "Malone." Anne turned. The driveway snaked through a grove of pines and, into the last half of the second curve, a blaze of light split the darkness.

It had been just a week, but it seemed like an eternity since Anne had last visited. Seeing it again brought back that old warm comfortable feeling, but it was fleeting. Tonight the structure was lit inside and out for Dit and Gwen's engagement party and get-together. A dozen cars lined the driveway. The flood of lights and the line-up of cars and the laughter from inside raised an inexplicable barrier in front of her. Anne felt a wave of dread. Her natural impulse was to circle and leave, but that would provoke the curiosity of Jacqui, and Anne couldn't conceive of an explanation or excuse that made sense enough to stand the scrutiny of her probing questions. So she parked, and mother and daughter made their way toward the front door.

Knocking had not been customary here but, as she reached for the knob, she froze. She felt a trembling inside of her. Perhaps the boisterous laughter on the other side of the door had stirred it up, but at that moment, cheer and joie de vivre struck her as offensive and unseemly, and she wanted to turn away lest it engulf her like a wave that topples and rolls and drags a person helplessly against a grinding sandy bottom.

"Mom, did you fall asleep or what? Open the door," said Jacqui, impatiently moving ahead, grasping the handle and pushing the door open.

Anne felt a touch of nausea and faintness at the sight of the crowd before her, but she managed to drive it down. *Jacqui isn't the only one who can act*, thought Anne, and she forced a smile and strode into the crowd of people.

"You keep this up and you'll get honourable mention in *The Guardian's* society column," said Mary Anne sidling up to her.

"They still have such things?"

"They're still popular on forties movies, but for the most part, they disappeared about the same time as gossip over a Monday morning clothesline. But you might generate a small trend on Twitter."

Anne laughed. The laugh surprised her.

"Thanks. I needed that," said Anne and took her first full breath since she'd entered the room.

"What?"

"Nothing," said Anne. "I could use one of those," she said pointing to Mary Anne's wine glass. Mary Anne walked her to a self-serve table of wines and whiskies. Anne filled her glass, drank half, topped it up, and surveyed the crowd.

"Who are all these people, anyway?"

"Kind of a *Who's Who on PEI*," said Mary Anne. "I don't know them all...but that guy, the one staring at Gwen's ass... Jeff Porter, Minister of Technology and Innovation. Over there's the Premier."

"Know him," said Anne. Mary Anne's discreet finger continued to point out other guests.

"John Dunne of Eckles, Dunne and Fry. That clique in the corner... some of Gwen's colleagues from Halifax...Dashiell, Dit's brother, Dottie, his sister, Connie, Dashiell's wife, and isn't that your buddy chattin' them up? Doctor who?"

"Dr. Little. I don't see Dit. Is he here?"

Mary Anne quickly checked the crowd. "Was here. Don't see him now."

"Anne," said a voice from behind her. "I'm so glad you and Jacqui could make it."

She turned quickly and saw Gwen Fowler. Gwen looked younger and even more beautiful than the last time they'd met. Gwen took Anne by her arm and began to lead her away.

"I've got to borrow Anne for a few minutes, Mary Anne. Promise to return her in mint condition." Gwen escorted Anne across the crowded room and down a short hallway. "Someone you have to see," she said to Anne.

Gwen escorted her about five steps down the corridor and into a room Dit used as his office. It was a quiet and cozy spot, dimly lit, the same room in which she and Dit had quarrelled about Gwen a week before.

Dit stood on his crutches at the far end of the room.

"Anne? What's going on, Gwen?" He had turned at the sound of someone entering. Even in the subdued lighting his surprise and confusion were evident.

"What's this about?" asked Anne, turning toward Gwen.

"Too much drama between you two. Sometimes I think I've wandered onto the set of a soap opera. I half-know what's going on…at least I think I do…but I can't resolve it. That's up to you two. Deal with it…tonight…now," she said with an uncompromising finality and, as she left, closing the door behind her, she added, "Text me when you've reached a resolution." Anne and Dit heard the turn of a key in the door.

"She locked us in," said Dit. There was some alarm in his voice.

"Where's Mom?" asked Jacqui.

"Gwen spirited her off somewhere mysterious," said Mary Anne. "And how are you doing? Your mom said that you had a rough time of it the other week. A babysitting gig that turned into party central… and about you losing your best bud."

"Yeah…not a good couple of weeks for me or Mom, but the last few days have gotten better. Mom's work is done, and Rada and I have begun to work things out."

"How did you manage that? I thought you were *persona non grata*."

"We've been seeing a mediator. Me, Mom, Rada, her parents, everyone."

"And?"

"She and her family are trying to adjust to a new culture. Rada wasn't quite fitting in socially at school. I thought I'd help, but I guess I blew it. Everything fell apart. Bottom line is I have to be more sensitive to what she wants to do…not what I think she should do."

"And Rada?"

"She has to have patience and show more respect for her parents. Her parents and Mr. Ahmadi talked a lot about how Muslim traditions vary from region to region, and he explained that some traditions go beyond what the Qu'ran says. I didn't understand a lot of that, though it seemed like they may have been stricter than they needed to be."

"I see," said Mary Anne, "and how's your mom doing?"

"Oh she's doing fine," said Jacqui. Mary Anne stared pointedly at her. Jacqui's eyes darted away and returned with embarrassment and guilt toward Mary Anne's. Jacqui had never been able to slip a half-truth by Mary Anne, and finally she gave up the truth. "She's not herself. She's quiet…kind of self-absorbed. A bit lost. Maybe a bit sad, too."

"She's been through a terrible ordeal. It'll take time to get normal again."

Anne had never seen Dit surprised and befuddled at the same time. He looked disarmingly boyish, guilty, and comical. An enormous quiet filled the room. Then Dit asked, "Brandy? I think I'll have one."

Anne set her wine glass down. "Seems appropriate, given the circumstances."

Dit puttered with the drinks, dropped an ice cube into Anne's glass, handed it to her, and sat down.

"I don't know what got into her. She's usually so self-assured and predictable."

Men are always last to know, thought Anne. She took a swallow of brandy, wrinkled her nose at the bite, and almost immediately felt a warm tingle steal through her limbs.

"She thinks I'm in love with you," said Anne. The words popped out of her mouth. She couldn't decide if they were deliberate or a spontaneous subtext to her thoughts and feelings and confusions. "At least she's not sure one way or the other," she added.

"That's ridiculous," said Dit. He moved to the front of his desk, leaned against it, and parked his crutches to one side. He stared at Anne incredulously. "Isn't it?"

A queer, crinkled smile hung onto his face, and faded into the long oncoming silence between them.

"How do you know all this?" he asked with a clouding seriousness.

"She asked me…in my office…a couple weeks ago."

"What did you tell her?"

"I told her the truth. I said I didn't know."

Dit grabbed his crutches and paced up the room as if he had lost a measure of clarity in some corner of it.

"I don't know what to say."

"Well, this is the time you could say, 'Anne, you're cute, but I'm in love with Gwen,' or 'Now that you've brought the subject up, why don't we run away together,' or even something lame like 'Those sports concussions in my youth have left me unable to focus.'"

Dit stared reflectively, this time directly into Anne's eyes. Anne felt a resurgence of embarrassment and humiliation.

"Why did you say 'you didn't know'?"

"Because I didn't know," said Anne defensively and with a bit more rancour than she had intended. She took another swallow of brandy, leaned back in her chair, and folded her arms across her chest.

"So what does Gwen want resolved here? I don't understand."

"Duh," she said mockingly. "On the verge of an imminent engagement announcement, she doesn't want to have to prepare for an end run around me or somebody like me. She wants a clear field. Get it?"

"So that's why we're here." Dit looked relieved but a trace of awkwardness remained. "Do you still have feelings for me?" It seemed almost an afterthought. Still the words struggled to voice themselves.

"Of course I do. And you?"

Dit nodded hesitantly.

"But it's not the same as with Gwen, is it?" said Anne. Dit slowly shook his head.

Now it seemed that it was Anne's turn to stand and pace through Dit's study. She took a few uncertain steps. Then she made for his desk, grabbed his brandy, and added a splash to her tumbler.

"We haven't had a real heart-to-heart since the last time we were here," she said.

"That was more tooth-and-fang, as I recall."

Anne grinned sheepishly.

"Yeah, tooth and fang," she said. "And I regretted that ever since. I was stressed out, impulsive. I shouldn't have said what I said. I'm sorry."

"Did you mean what you said then?"

"At the time I did. Later...later I got to know Gwen. I came to realize that I was wrong. She loves you, and she has your best interests at heart. I know that now. I have a lot of respect for her, but I was afraid that I was going to lose you...that you would slip out of my life. We've been through so much together the last few years. You're my friend. You're my best friend, and I didn't want that to disappear, but that's all I could see ahead of me. And I'm sorry... I really am."

Anne's lip quivered as she spoke. Tears welled in her eyes. Her voice rose little above a hush as she stood in front of him.

Dit looked down at her, reached out, pulled her toward him. They held each other for a long time. Anne felt the warmth of his chest soothe her like a tonic. Tears streamed down her face. A few quiet, convulsive sobs shook her body.

"We'll always be best friends, Anne. I know that, you know that... and Gwen knows that, too. That's why she locked us up in here."

Anne looked up, smiled, forced back a sniffle, reached around to his desk, and pulled a tissue from a carton.

"Is it time to text the warden?" she asked.

Dit grinned mischievously and pulled out his cell phone.

87.

Ben had circled the crowd several times but failed to find Anne. The party room had grown warm. Ben, having worn a suit, was warmer than the other more casually dressed guests. Perspiration clung to the shirt under his jacket, and sweat beaded his forehead. So he grabbed a fresh bottle of beer from a pail of ice, opened the patio door a crack, and slipped into the refreshing October air.

Ben's eyes adjusted to the darkness enough so that he could make out the swimming pool in front of him and the chairs and recliners encircling the perimeter. He took a seat on a chair that faced the Charlottetown skyline. The twin spires of St. Dunstan's Basilica rose majestic and dark out of the bath of city lights. The edge of the city faded into the black watery sheet of West River to his left and narrowed into the glimmering necklace of Hillsborough Bridge on his right.

"Gorgeous, isn't it?"

Ben jumped at the words from an unseen figure sunk into a plush recliner so close by. He lurched forward in his chair, the up-tipped bottle dribbling onto his only clean tie.

"Jeez!" he said, sputtering and frantically brushing away the sudsy spill.

"You should try yoga or tai chi or something to settle your nerves, Ben." Anne sat up. Her face caught the light from the terrace door. She looked greatly amused.

"I've got my medicine, right here," he said lifting his bottle.

"Yeah...and how's that working for ya?"

"It takes the edge off."

"I can see that."

Ben grunted something indecipherable in reply.

"You going to the funeral?" Anne asked.

"MacFarlane's? There will be a police presence there...out of duty... professional courtesy...even though a smell of corruption hangs over him. Me... I plan to have food poisoning that day."

"Any talk of exposing his crimes?"

"Not much in the way of proof exists anymore. No witnesses alive. No admissible evidence. And no political will to tar and feather a dead man. Especially since he gave a helping hand to so many politicians over the years...the good ones and the bad. In the end everyone gets smeared with the same brush. On the other hand, pundits may stir the waters as time goes on, and political memory is pretty short."

"And Peale's?"

"I believe I can drag myself to that one...if they ever recover the body, but the Northumberland Strait can hide a lot of secrets for a long time." Ben cocked his head toward Anne and looked expectantly. "Anything you want to share?"

"Dawson spoke to me before he died. I think he wanted to clear his conscience."

They stared across the water and the glittering skyline. The light illuminated a plume of smoke from a stack at an industrial site. The billows swelled and thinned, twisted and undulated in the light sea breeze.

"He said Peale could have killed him but, at the last moment, Peale raised the gun to his own head...to kill himself. Jacob wrestled the gun from him, but Peale pulled away and vaulted over the rail."

"Did he say anything?"

"'I'm sorry.' That's all."

"So Dawson never killed him...never killed anybody?"

Anne shook her head in the twilight of the empty terrace. Ben leaned back again and took another swig of beer.

"How did you put it together? One minute you're dead in the water, the next your fire's stoked, and you're up to your eyeballs in trouble."

"It came in a flash...kind of out of the blue...when a number of little things began to make sense. The missing puzzle piece was a connection between Jacob and Edna, but there was none...nothing obvious, just bits and pieces...like Edna's needlepoint at home and on her wall at work. Eventually I realized that they contained key words or phrases from Alcoholics Anonymous...the twelve steps or the serenity prayer. That was a thread that connected them, and a contact of mine with AA confirmed it. Edna was Jacob's sponsor. She supported his drug rehab, but she also fanned his hatred of MacFarlane and stirred his drive for revenge, and that led to MacFarlane's murder. Neither Edna nor Dawson had known about Peale's role before that. So Edna convinced Dawson to kill Peale. After all, she had done him the same favour for him. He owed her...not that we can prove much of that now."

"But we can prove MacFarlane was murdered," said Ben.

"What? How?"

"None of the usual toxins were found in his system, nor anything obvious to suggest foul play but, thanks to Edna's admissions to you, I asked the coroner to look more closely. He found a small puncture mark on MacFarlane's arm. I did another search of the grounds around his house and found a dart. After it struck him, MacFarlane must have brushed it off. It disappeared into a hedge alongside the door step and got hung up on the thick foliage. It showed traces of a sedative used by vets for quickly immobilizing animals."

"So that's what killed him?"

"No, the amount injected was only enough to put him out for a few minutes."

"According to Edna there was a second drug, something she administered to paralyze him, keep him conscious and force a confession."

"Does the coroner have any ideas what she might have used?"

"Based on Edna's experience as a vet and an emergency room nurse, he thinks she might have used something called succinylcholine."

"Succ...suc," Anne stammered. She sounded as if she were choking.

"Nurses call it 'sux,' for short. It paralyzes the spinal column but the patient is conscious. It's used for special operations. It's been replaced by a newer drug in most hospitals. So probably no one would miss a vial or two of sux gone missing."

"Can the coroner confirm that?"

"Apparently, it breaks down quickly into naturally occurring elements. It's very difficult to identify unless you're testing for that specific chemical...and he's doing just that now."

"That means that MacFarlane would have been conscious when Edna started the kitchen fire, and he must have known he was going to die. What terror he must have felt!"

"Especially seeing Edna grinning over the top of him...him helpless and all. It was almost a perfect crime," said Ben.

"...except for Peale's panicky attempt to salvage his reputation," said Anne.

"...and the persistence of a pint-sized pit bull of a PI I know."

"You forgot. I'm not a private investigator anymore."

"Meaning to talk to you about that. This passed by my desk yesterday afternoon," he said and handed Anne a card, her investigator's license. "It's all good now."

Anne looked at it sadly and said, "I'm not so sure that's what I want to do anymore, Ben. I seemed to muck things up pretty badly on this case. So many people dead...and who won? Nobody. It would have been better if I'd never become involved with it."

"None of the fallout's on you."

"You would say that. You're a friend."

"I'm not the only one who's vouching for you."

"What do you mean?"

"The feds are about to ante up. You've been granted your security clearance to conduct background checks on federal employees through Darby Investigations. It's their part of the bargain that was struck on that international case we handled last year. The one that got me this job."

"Do they know that I lost my license?"

"Yeah, and they know why, too. You don't let anything stand between you and doing the right thing. They call it reliability. It means a pretty nice pile of cash to support you and Jacqui. No more digging for scraps."

"What the hell took them so long? I had no clue."

"The security check takes forever anyway. Then there's paperwork, government bureaucracy, yada yada yada...congrats."

They heard the rollers on the sliding patio door followed by "Mom! Are you out there?"

"Over here," said Jacqui raising her arm over the back of the recliner.

"Mom... Oh, hi, Ben... Dashiell is about to make the toast. I've been looking all over for you. Quick."

Ben and Anne got up and moved toward the entrance and the now-quiet crowd standing with drinks poised and facing a beaming couple. Dashiell, more sober than not, self-confident and proud, had already begun his tribute toast. Anne and Ben and Jacqui stood at the back of the gathering.

"...and I remember once when Dit said to me that he could outrun or outskate or outswim any girl who had the fancy to corral him into a permanent relationship." A titter of laughter rolled through the guests. "Apparently, he's slowed down a bit since those freewheeling, fanciful days. Gwen has caught him for sure, and says she plans to keep him. In spite of such steely, Irish determination on her part, I never heard my brother utter a peep...not a howling lamentation, not a grumble, not a whimpering complaint at the state in which he so recently has found himself. In fact he seems now more nimble of foot, and glib of tongue, and settled in mind than I can ever recall him being as a wild youth. And with that observation, I feel completely confident that happiness will follow the pair of them through all the years that God has set aside for them. So I raise my glass, and invite you to raise yours, in wishing Diarmud and Gwendolyn all the happiness and joy that we can heap upon them. To Dit and Gwen..."

Ben raised his bottle of beer. Jacqui gave an excited little jump that nearly spilled her glass of cola over Mary Anne. She grabbed her mother's arm enthusiastically. Anne smiled broadly at Jacqui's youthful enthusiasm and raised her half-empty glass of brandy to join the toast. Through a thin spot in the crowd she saw Dit and Gwen. They kissed. Gwen beamed joyously. Dit grinned like a naïve little boy. He looked embarrassed and happy. Anne sipped her brandy. The ice had melted. It tasted watery, bland, and a touch bitter.

Acknowledgements

Most artistic endeavors are solitary undertakings, but few take as long to complete as the writing of a novel. I penned the last words to this book about a year and a half after I had begun it. Along the way I gleaned technical information and advice from experts in various fields, all of which helped add realism to the plot and provide enjoyment for mystery readers.

Among those who generously offered advice were Fazal Malik of the Ahmadiyya Muslim Community, PEI; Dr. Sandra McConkey; second mate Murray MacLeod and the crew of MV Holiday Island; Dr. Marvin Tesch; Dr. Lamont Sweet; several anonymous legal minds; and law enforcement personnel at local and federal levels. Their advice and experience has been invaluable in enabling me to hammer together complex technical details in *The Dead Letter*.

In spite of excellent expert advice, however, keen readers may uncover a half-truth here and there. Believe me, these are not the result of any faulty guidance that was given me. They are simply the product of my effort to tweak and twist the truth enough so that it conveniently fits within the confines of a believable story and an exciting plot line.

But that is not the end of it. I must also thank the first readers of the manuscript, my wife, Brenda, and family members, for their discerning takes on character and plot. Their observations have always been my first line of defense against the recklessness of my imagination and the uncontrollable dancing of my pen.

Also, a very special thanks to my editor, Jane Ledwell. Jane is a detective in her own right. She hunts down inaccuracies, time glitches, misplaced phrases, and wordiness with the dedication of a bloodhound tracking a convict through a dismal swamp, and she does so with a sprinkle of good humor as well.

Finally, thanks to Laurie Brinklow who ran a final fine-tooth comb through the novel and uncovered flaws which had slipped into the text in spite of everyone else's valiant efforts.